The
Capstone Decision

A Novel

Isabelle Morton

Atlantic Freelance Publishing
Manchester, Connecticut

The Capstone Decision

Copy editing: Heather Seferovich
Cover design: Ryan L. Morton
Back cover photo: AriaRay Brown
Cover hand model: Kellan Navarre

ISBN-10: 0615271561
ISBN-13: 9780615271569

Published by
Atlantic Freelance
P.O. Box 4065
Manchester, CT 06045

Visit our website at
www.isabellemorton.com
where you can download a digital version of this book.

First printing July, 2009

Printed and bound in the United States of America

For my Dad
With love

Contents

Part One – The Key

Egypt, Connecticut

August, 25 years ago

1.

Late August, twenty-five years ago.

The trench was long, narrow, and deep. It looked as though a gash had been cut into the earth between the Great Pyramid of Giza and the leonine Great Sphinx. Local Egyptians referred to the trench as a wound in the sacred hillside, and a few academics pronounced it the grave in which Dr. Ian McHenry's career would be forever buried. Ian hoped it would be a window to the truth—the real truth—about Egypt's ancient past.

A professor of archeology at Yale University, Ian was responsible for the trench that his students and a small army of workers had been digging all summer long. Ian's goal was to find a tunnel that connected the Great Pyramid with the Sphinx. Such a discovery could lead to evidence of the pyramid's true age and purpose. Long-forgotten secrets would be revealed.

In particular, Ian yearned to prove that the pyramids were more than elaborate tombs built by egocentric pharaohs. He had not seen any definitive data to support the tomb theory, despite how many people believed it. On the contrary, evidence against the tomb theory seemed obvious to him. Real tombs were either filled with a Pharaoh's possessions or looted, and their walls covered with scenes of daily living. The Great Pyramid was completely empty when it was opened for the first time in 820 A.D. and its walls were bare. Ian had no idea why Egyptologists insisted on the theory. More pressing: What was the real purpose of the pyramids?

Ian wanted answers. Alternative researchers speculated the Great Pyramid was everything from a place of spiritual initiation, to an astronomical observatory, to a transport station. Yet these theories, too, were based on loosely woven facts — or none at all.

On this last day of the dig, without a trace of the tunnel found, Ian dropped his supervisory role in frustration and picked up a shovel himself. He climbed down to the bottom of the furrow where dozens of Egyptian workmen dug, shoulder to shoulder. Everyone wore the traditional lebda on their head and loose-fitting pants and long-sleeved gray gallabiya that fluttered at their ankles. The tall blond Ian looked typically American in his straw hat, khaki shorts, and polo shirt.

It was hard work in the summer heat, and even harder to ward off the encroaching specter of failure. At this depth, Ian thought, they should reach at any moment the stonework that he believed comprised the tunnel's ceiling. But he had been telling himself that for days. A knot of self-doubt tightened Ian's stomach. He stopped to wipe the sweat and dust from his face.

Ian reminded himself that other pyramid complexes around the world incorporated systems of tunnels, the most famous of which was the Pyramid of the Sun in the Mayan city of Teotihuacan. Ian believed this pyramid was the sister of Giza's Great Pyramid. In addition, the central pyramid of the ancient Toltec city of Aguateca stood atop so many caverns, it had collapsed into itself because of them. It was no great leap of logic to assume the greatest pyramids of the world, those at Giza, would also harbor an underground labyrinth.

Ian's suspicions got scientific support when a team from Stanford Research Institute investigated the geography surrounding the Sphinx. They found an anomaly that they surmised was a tunnel, and it headed toward the Great Pyramid. Finally satisfied to have tangible evidence for the tunnel, the Egyptian Bureau of Antiquities, which was in charge of the Giza monuments, granted Ian permission to dig.

"Hey, Professor." The eager voice of one of Ian's students interrupted his thoughts. "Look what I found." The young woman presented him with a tray of bone fragments. Her eyes gleamed with hope.

Ian looked at her and thought of the running joke about digging in Egypt—all you had to do was poke your shovel in the ground and you'd uncover something from the past. Since the dig began, they'd found plenty of animal bones and broken pottery. Then, in the past week, they started uncovering pieces of weaponry and then evidence of a massive fire, but no trace of a tunnel and nothing significant enough to get the go-ahead to extend the dig.

Ian examined the pieces of bone. They were canine. "They're not human. Sorry."

The girl shrugged and turned to leave.

"Have you seen my daughter?" Ian called out to her.

"She's near the Sphinx riding horses with the kids," the student called back.

Ian was raising his eleven-year-old daughter, Daria, by himself. Since his wife had died when Daria was two, Daria accompanied him on all his expeditions, and Ian had home-schooled her when necessary. A precocious child, Daria was fascinated by ancient cultures and gifted with an ability to learn foreign language. She could hold a conversation in most European languages and since they'd been in Egypt she'd become fluent in Arabic. Daria had an outgoing personality and had made friends with the local children their first day in Giza.

Ian didn't look forward to telling her that his dig had been a failure. Just that morning Daria reminded him that he had made his greatest archeological finds only in the final days of previous expeditions.

"History holds its secrets from all but those who persevere," he had told her. And those who were gifted with a bit of luck, he now realized. If only he could be lucky one more time. Ian worked harder and faster, and sweat poured in rivulets down his face.

Suddenly his sharp eye caught something shiny near the toe of his boot. He pulled a brush from his back pocket to dust the sand away from a strange silver item, and recorded its position in his notebook. Then he picked it up.

The item was essentially flat, about three inches long and half as wide. Its design was centered on a thin, one-inch long rod that terminated in three disks of increasing size. At its other end was a spiral of wire that held four more disks, also of increasing size. A circle at the center of the spiral was large enough to hold a marble, and two disks inside the circle were bent in such a way as to suggest that they could indeed hold a marble in place.

Ian wiped his face and neck again, and then gave the item a second look. Admittedly, the object's design wasn't Egyptian. In fact, it appeared brand new, yet he'd never seen anything like it before. Feeling perplexed, Ian left the trench to show the item to his long-time friend and colleague Albert Winslow. Ian found Winslow under the canvas awning that provided shade for the dig supervisors.

Best of friends, Ian and Winslow were often referred to as the 'odd couple.' Winslow was of medium height and stocky, with straight jet black hair that he let grow to his shoulders. Ian was tall, lean, and blessed with thick blond curls that he kept reasonably short. Winslow livened up a party, while Ian would wander to the quiet corner at gatherings. Winslow was less gutsy than Ian, but smarter and more knowledgeable. Everyone respected Winslow and his opinions were considered gospel.

"We need to focus all our efforts in the mid-section of the trench," Winslow said as he studied a map of the dig site.

Ian sighed in agreement. He suspected the tunnel might have curved off the course suggested by the Stanford researchers. But he admitted Winslow's plan was the way to go.

Winslow handed Ian a bottle of water and noticed him toying with something shiny. "A gift for Daria?" he asked. Her twelfth birthday was the following week.

Ian handed the item to his friend.

"I found it in the trench."

Winslow furrowed his brows. He flipped the item over a few times, and looked at it closely. "Looks like metal, but it feels like plastic," he observed. "And it's remarkably strong considering how thin it is," he said as he tapped it and carefully tried to see if it would bend. "Its design reminds me of those faux-Celtic trinkets I've seen lately. No doubt dropped by one of the workers," he concluded, and handed it back.

Ian groaned. It was no use arguing. The item he found couldn't possibly be a true artifact. It looked too new. Its design wasn't Egyptian, and it wasn't like anything that anyone had ever found before. Yet Ian knew how deeply the item had been buried. He could only imagine how Virginia Steen-McIntyre must have felt when she found sophisticated bifacial spearheads embedded in a Mexican rock formation over 250,000 years old. Current dogma insisted humans didn't even exist in South America until 15,000 years ago. If Ian insisted his find was genuine, all the experts would inevitably try to explain it away as a hoax or criticize him for contaminating the dig. Or, like Steen-McIntyre, he could lose his job.

Winslow caught Ian looking at the item.

"It isn't Egyptian, Ian," Winslow insisted. "Give it to Daria for her birthday. C'mon we've got work to do."

Ian put it back in his pocket.

Finally, their ten-hour workday was over and no tunnel had been found. The workers received their paychecks and went home. Ian declined an invitation from Winslow and their students to grab a beer with them, as he had to pick up Daria.

Ian took one last look at the Great Pyramid of Khufu and the equally impressive Pyramids of Khafra and Menkaure that stood picture perfect against a clear blue sky. Although beaten by time and weather, the pyramids were icons of mystery. No records had ever been found that suggested when or why these pyramids were built, or named their purpose. Ian believed that if Khufu actually did build the Great Pyramid attributed to him, there'd be volumes of references to such a great pharaoh. But only one small statue of him existed, and of the few records that mentioned him, one suggested the pyramid was already built during his reign.

And why was the Great Pyramid built with such precision? It covered over thirteen acres and was level to within less than an inch. Its four sides were almost equal in length, varying within a mere 1.75 inches. The pyramid consisted of over two million blocks of granite and limestone weighing from 2.5 to 70 tons apiece, each so perfectly shaped and squared that the mortar-filled joints between them measured one-fiftieth of an inch. They bore no tool marks and their corners were not even slightly chipped.

Sir Flanders Petrie, an Englishman who made the first precision measurements of the Great Pyramid in the late 1800's called it 'the finest optician's work on a scale of acres.' Surely the deliberate accuracy of the pyramid's measurements gave it a purpose far more meaningful than simply entombing a pharaoh.

Ian lamented the fact that the truth would remain hidden, despite his effort. He was so certain, so sure, that he would find the tunnel—and some answers—that he felt dazed by his failure.

Suddenly Ian felt a burning sensation on his thigh and he yanked the thing he'd unearthed out of his pocket. For a moment it was too hot to hold, but it quickly cooled. Ian stared at it, wondering at its supernatural power and whether or not it would again grow hot. Suddenly, a rush of blood filled Ian's veins and left him feeling flushed. It finally occurred to him what the thing might be. He closed his eyes to try to quell his growing excitement. Why hadn't he recognized it sooner? If he was correct, then it was more ancient than anything he had ever touched, witnessed, or seen in photographs. He hadn't found a window to the past, but a key. And although he hadn't found a tunnel, the dig might have been successful beyond his wildest dreams.

2.

D aria McHenry stood outside the Giza stables oblivious to the voices of passers-by and the cacophony of carts, cars, pack animals, and bicycles — rarely with just one rider — that crowded the street. She looked down at her high-top sneakers and let strands of her long brown hair fall in front of her face, creating a barrier between herself and the world, which made her feel invisible. Only minutes ago she shared last good-byes with her friends at the stable. Tomorrow she and her father would be leaving Egypt.

She didn't want to go. Daria'd had the time of her life this past summer and she'd almost had her first kiss.

Finally, her father arrived.

"Hello, Honeycakes," Ian said with a bright smile.

For a moment Daria thought he'd found his tunnel. His eyes told her otherwise, but for now she was consumed by her own problems.

"Hi," she sighed. She reached for the pendants she wore around her neck and held them for comfort. One was a gold cross that had belonged to her mother, another was a locket with family photos, and the third was a leather pouch that a Hopi Indian woman had given her while her dad was digging in Arizona.

"We'll be back again next year, won't we?" Daria asked.

Ian patted his daughter's leg, "Sure, why not."

Daria let go her pendants and held his hand. Saying goodbye was easier when you had something to look forward to.

Ian and Daria walked back to their hotel and returned to their room. It was decorated with red jacquard drapes and matching bedspreads on the two twin beds. A wooden fan hung from the ceiling and sketches of the pyramids of Giza adorned papered walls. Ian dropped his knapsack on the floor and picked up the phone.

Daria watched her father order room service and tried to read his body language. She admired her dad for fighting so hard to win permission from the Egyptian Bureau of Antiquities to try to find his tunnel. He'd faced mountains of paperwork and endured scorn from his peers who believed he was risking his well-earned academic reputation on a ridiculous pursuit. No one could argue with her dad when his gut told him something. He had sensed the fabled Isthmani Temple and the Golden Statue of Tapajos existed — and he'd found them both. Daria had been with him each time. She looked at him more closely.

Her father didn't look defeated, yet he hadn't mentioned success. Daria knew that if he'd found the tunnel, he'd tell her. But if he didn't say anything by bedtime, Daria decided, she'd ask him about it. Tomorrow, she knew, government trucks would plow the earth back into the trench. Soon there'd be no trace it ever existed.

Ian and Daria took turns showering and then dinner arrived.

Daria opened the window to let in the cool evening breeze and the sounds of rustling palm leaves. When she turned back toward the room, she saw her father quickly stuff something into the pocket of his pajamas.

"Come. Eat your dinner," he said. "Before it gets cold."

"What's in your pocket?"

"Nothing."

"Don't believe you."

Ian sighed. He pulled out the item he'd found, but hid it between his hands. "I'll show it to you, if you keep an open mind."

"Promise." She held up her pinky finger and curled it — an act meant to seal her word.

He handed it to her. "I found it today."

"At the dig?"

"Yes."

Daria humphed. "It doesn't look Egyptian."

"Look again."

"Its shape looks Celtic, but it has a flavor of high tech. Probably dropped by a tourist or one of the workers."

"You sound like Winslow."

"Do not."

"If you can't keep an open mind, look at it again with an open heart," Ian said.

Obligingly, Daria looked at the item again. Her father always reminded her to observe things subjectively, with feeling, instead of relying on what she could see.

"I like how smooth it feels and how perfectly its circles are arranged." She held the item on each wrist and then below her neck. "It could be a pendant. Yet its shape is too perfect," she paused. "It must have another function."

"It was deeply buried under thousands of year's worth of sand."

Ian watched his daughter's expression change from one of curiosity to introspection. Her large brown eyes reminded him of her mother, Clara, and he watched them focus blankly on the wall. Was it possible that she, too, recognized the object he had found?

3.

Daria thought the object that her father had unearthed looked familiar, which was strange because she'd never seen anything like it before. Or had she? Her mind wandered and she thought about her father's stories. Ever since she could remember, he recounted legends about ancient Egypt and long-lost civilizations, which he had learned from an old Bedouin mystic.

Every night before bed, back home in Connecticut, Daria snuggled up with her father on his leather wingback chair before the fireplace in his cherry-paneled home office. As she grew older she began sitting on the identical chair beside his. While he spoke, she closed her eyes and vividly imagined the stories' details. One of those details had been a key, a certain extraordinary key, which could supposedly unlock the powers of the pyramids.

Daria wasn't sure the pyramids ever had any powers. They were simply monuments, which may have had various purposes. But powers? She found that part hard to believe. Yet she loved her father's stories, which seemed as real as memories.

After dinner, Daria climbed into bed while still holding the item her father had found. She looked at him. "Tell me the Last Tale of Atlantis."

"I thought you said you'd outgrown bedtime stories," Ian teased. His mother had warned him that girls in their tweens could act like a grownup one minute and a child the next. Daria hadn't asked for a story since they'd arrived in Egypt four months ago.

"Please?" As Daria held the object she felt a warm sensation emanate from it and spread throughout her body. It helped her body relax and suddenly her muscles didn't feel so sore. She felt better too about leaving her friends. Somehow her heart didn't hurt as much; the pain was replaced by a sense of peace.

Ian turned off their bedside lamp. Now their room was bathed in a soft glow from the lights outside. He slid into his own bed and faced his daughter who was now hugging her pillow.

Ian recounted the story just as it had been told to him. "In the twilight of the Age of Atlantis," Ian began, "the evil ones forced the Emperor and his wife to flee the continent while their family and followers hid in the secret subterranean city beneath the Atlanteans' own great pyramid. Meanwhile, the world was being swept with another cycle of devastating earthquakes and hurricanes. Worse, the evil ones were getting close to finding the pyramid's hidden entrance. If they should find it, they could also find the subterranean city as well as the pyramid's control room and power center. Then the full powers of Atlantis would fall into their hands and all hope for restoring the royal family's rule would be lost.

"Sileen, the Empress-elect, was their only hope.

"Sileen's ancestors had built a second pyramid identical to the Atlantean one—just in case some catastrophe occurred and they needed to begin a new, free Atlantis elsewhere. This second pyramid became the Great Pyramid of Giza. To keep the power center safe, Sileen had no choice but to relocate it there."

Ian looked over at his daughter, whose eyes were now closed. "Honeycakes, are you awake?"

"Of course I am."

Ian continued, "Anyone might guess that Atlantis's power center was located somewhere inside its pyramid. Sileen knew it was housed in the pyramidion, the ten- to fifteen-foot tall uppermost portion of the pyramid."

Ian paused a moment. "We believe the power center was a large sphere, about three feet in diameter.

"The greatest secret of all was how to work the power center. For that, Sileen needed a special key that she wore as a pendant." He stopped again. At this point in the story, he always described the key just as it had been described to him: silver, flat, about three inches long, consisting of disks of increasing size and a circle of wire that could fit a sphere the size of a marble. This time, he omitted the description.

"First, Sileen had to reach the one-inch capstone that topped the pyramidion. To get there, she entered the pyramid through secret passageways that lit up as she passed. They led to a chamber where she could consult with the artificial intelligence that ran the pyramid. This intelligence could interpret data, analyze it, draw conclusions from it, as well as communicate with people. Before the evil ones came, the pyramid had acted like an oracle, speaking directly to individuals. The Atlanteans had even named their pyramid *Pharaoh*, which meant 'the great house of knowledge.'

"Sileen needed Pharaoh's help to remove the pyramidion and

its power center from the pyramid and transport them to Giza. The Giza pyramid had been specially built without a top, in case this pyramidion was ever moved there.

"In case Sileen should fail," he continued, "Pharaoh devised a backup plan. At some point in the future, if the power center was lost or dormant, it would awaken. Pharaoh would become whole once again and the civilization of Atlantis would be given another chance to be reborn."

"Do you have any idea when the power center will wake up?" Daria asked. She immediately regretted her question. It only proved that once again, she'd gotten suckered into believing the story was true.

"No, I don't," Ian said, but he wondered if the time would be soon, since the Key to the Capstone of the Great Pyramid of Atlantis, and of Giza, might have been unearthed that day.

Daria had been toying with the object, and stuck her finger through the circle of wire upon which its design was based. It felt oddly empty, like an unfinished sentence. Something belonged there, Daria wondered, but what? Obviously something round, like a marble. The two slanted disks inside the inner circle seemed as though they could hold one. Daria imagined what it would look like with a marble in place and felt waves of healing warmth pass through her body. She closed her eyes to enjoy the feeling.

Ian looked tenderly at his daughter who held the shiny key gently between her fingers. She had grown a lot that summer. Her face and arms were darkly tanned and she had put on a few extra pounds — but so had her mother when she was in her early teens, and Clara had grown into a slender and athletic adult. Ian predicted the same for their daughter.

Daria's breathing grew deeper.

"Daria?"

Ian got no reply.

He carefully removed the key from his sleeping daughter's fingers, turned on the lamp on his nightstand, and studied the object once again. It was in perfect condition. A clairvoyant would have described the key's aura as a palpable shield of white light. Ian was only sensitive enough to know the object carried a presence that made it seem much larger than its physical size.

Suddenly Ian felt flushed with embarrassment. What were the odds of finding *the* Key to the Capstone—if such a thing actually existed at all?

The more Ian thought about the improbability of finding the key, the more doubt overcame him. After all, there was a single source of information about the key and that was Mikta, an eccentric old Bedouin.

Ian had met Mikta during a symposium on Egyptology when Ian was an undergraduate at Yale. The gentleman with an English accent and three-piece suit began a conversation with the shorts- and t-shirt-clad youth. Mikta engaged Ian in tales of ancient Egypt and a lasting friendship grew. Whenever Ian visited Egypt, which was almost every year after he graduated, the two would meet and the stories continued. From the start, Ian knew Mikta was an Egyptian physician who had gotten his medical degree at Oxford. But when he visited Mikta, he learned Mikta was also in fact the leader of a nomadic tribe who roamed the desert offering medical and spiritual help to anyone they met. Ian often traveled with them.

Mikta filled Ian's imagination with visions of the pyramids in their golden glory. He described the ceremonies that took place along the mysteriously illuminated, underground hallways that linked each pyramid, as well as the Great Pyramid with the Sphinx. He told Ian about the Great Pyramid's missing pyramidion and the small capstone that once pointed its apex. Mikta had also told Ian about a key that had been used to activate the power center hidden inside the pyramidion. This power center could manipulate the earth's gravity and magnetism, produce and direct lasers, enable transportation and communication long distances, and more. At first, Ian thought Mikta was recounting science fiction. Over the years, Ian saw how seriously Mikta told these legends. He seemed to want Ian to memorize every detail. Yet Mikta had never told him where the legends had come from.

Weren't they just stories?

It was originally Mikta's idea that a tunnel linked the Great Pyramid and the Sphinx—and as hard as Ian had tried, he and his team had failed to find it. He started to doubt Mikta's story of the key and its capstone. Yet, hadn't he unearthed that very same key?

Uncertainty gripped him. To believe in legends was one thing, but to hold something in your hands that could prove they were real, was quite another. Beliefs gave you room to be cocky, out-spoken, even arrogant. Evidence—if you chose to acknowledge it—moved you closer to the truth. Proof set you face to face with it. No wonder so many of Ian's peers refused to concede the possibility that evidence existed for theories other than their own. It was easy to settle into one's own beliefs—and uncomfortable to change them.

Ian battled his self-esteem. The key had been lost for millennia. What were the chances of anyone finding it? He had made significant archeological discoveries during his career, but nothing came close to this. If this was really The Key, finding it had been a miracle.

Ian realized his next logical step. He had to verify the key was real. Only two people could do that. One was Mikta, and Ian had only a phone number for a man who only sometimes knew where Mikta could be found. In the past, Mikta had always contacted Ian to arrange their meetings.

The other person was Faoud Fayed, a renowned dealer in Egyptian art. Ian and Fayed had known each other for years— ever since Ian's first visit to Egypt. Fayed had quickly demonstrated himself to be generous for a price, and a friend for a favor. He could be trusted as long as he was making a handsome profit. He was also the most knowledgeable man in the Middle East when it came to Egyptian antiquities. If the key were real or if it had any historical value at all, textbook or not, Fayed would know. Ian decided he would visit Fayed tomorrow.

4.

In the morning, Ian and Daria packed their bags, had a quick breakfast at the hotel's Pyramid Café, and took a taxi to the Cairo museum, where they were to meet Ian's parents, Sarah and David McHenry. They had flown in the day before, rented a yacht, and planned to take Ian and Daria for a vacation on the Nile before Ian had to be return to Yale.

On the busy streets of Cairo, the taxi driver competed with cars and donkey carts to advance inch-by-inch. Traffic officers in white uniforms with black adornments stood in the center of each intersection—in lieu of traffic lights—trying to make order of the mayhem.

Daria was unusually silent during the long cab ride.

"Did you remember your dreams?" Ian asked her. The question and the discussion that followed was a morning ritual they both enjoyed.

Daria reached for her pendants and held them.

"I dreamt about the capstone," she replied. She held out her other hand with her palm up, as though the capstone rested upon it. Daria was usually good at remembering her dreams, but struggled with this one. "In the dream, the Giza pyramids were burning," she said. To her frustration, these details had also evaporated. "How could pyramids catch fire if they're made of stone?"

"Sometimes a dream ends with something scary to catch your attention so you'll remember the dream," Ian explained.

"Why would I want to remember such a stupid dream," Daria whined. "Pyramids can't burn. The capstone probably isn't real, either." She knew the statement would irk her father. Yet she was beginning to realize that denial was like aspirin. It took away the pain of the unexplainable.

Ian wanted to argue but held his tongue. He felt proud his daughter had made a link between the item he'd found and the capstone of Mikta's stories. He wanted to believe that her intuition about the key's identity was another proof of its authenticity.

When they arrived at the plaza in front of the Cairo Museum, Sarah and David were waiting for them. It was easy to spot Sarah in her bright paisley sport jacket. Her platinum blonde hair was well styled and heavily sprayed—the do was as unmoving as she herself could be once she set her mind to something. Her face was expertly made up without looking overdone, and her skin was youthful and glowing. Sarah was an intelligent and creative woman who had built a lucrative business designing and selling three-dimensional puzzles. They were combinations of wood, rope, and metal that appeared impossible to take apart—or put together again.

David was a professor of history and dressed conservatively in navy blue pants and a gray sport shirt that matched his hair. An avid sportsman, David was well muscled for his age. Now retired, he preferred the outdoors over museums. Nobody was surprised when he made an excuse not to join them. David explained that he needed to get the boat ready before their trip. He gave Ian directions for finding the marina and their yacht, and then took Ian and Daria's luggage, so they wouldn't have to store it at the museum's coat room.

Ian turned to his mother, "How about if it's just the two of you? I have some business to do."

"That's fine," Daria said. It would be more fun without her dad—this way she could be in charge of showing her grandmother around the museum. Everything about ancient Egypt fascinated Daria. She had visited the Cairo Museum as many times as she could convince her father to take her there. Now her enthusiasm grew as she began to plan exactly what she would show her grandmother.

"I'll be back around noon," Ian promised.

"Be careful," his mother said. The comment was habitual.

They said brief good-byes. Daria took her grandmother's hand and led her to the museum. Ian walked to the curb, got his bearings, and proceeded down one of the narrow streets of Cairo. A few blocks later, the high-curbed thoroughfares turned into cobbled streets. The modern edifices became old buildings no more than two and three stories high, whose aged mud-brick walls were riddled with cracks. It was like walking back in time. Even the smell of engine exhaust was replaced with a curious mixture of ageless scents including that of frying food, scented oils, and animal dung. The streets were crowded and lined with vendors hawking everything from pots to pita bread.

Ian located a curtained doorway between two storefronts and slipped inside.

5.

Ian entered the old building and climbed a dark staircase to a narrow landing. He knocked on the first door to his left and waited. Clouds of dust hung in the rays of sunlight that streamed through a small window at the end of the hallway. The air was stale and hot. Ian again wiped his brow and replaced his hat. Moments later the door opened.

"Ian McHenry here to see Mr. Faoud Fayed," he told the fez-topped servant who answered the door. Ian's eyes watered from the cigar smoke that billowed out the door.

The servant bowed slightly and let him enter. The waiting room was lined with shelves cluttered with pieces of tile and pottery, assorted beads, and small statues—all thick with dust. Fayed had spent years building his business and was considered an expert in Egyptian art and antiquities, which he appraised for museums and private collectors. Daringly, he also bought and sold objects openly, but nearly every policeman and politician in the city was in his pocket and so he got away with it.

"Tell Mr. Fayed I have something he might be interested in," Ian told the servant who again bowed, then disappeared behind a curtain. A few minutes later the servant returned and invited Ian into the next room. Fayed's office was as cluttered as his anteroom.

"Ah, Ian McHenry, my friend, come in, come in," said Fayed. He motioned for Ian to enter his office. "A thousand welcomes." Fayed was a handsome Egyptian man in his early forties and regularly wore a white linen suit. He stood to shake Ian's hand and then sat down behind his desk.

"Please, sit down, sit down," Fayed repeated, puffing on his cigar. His voice was raspy from chain smoking and rang with an accent. Throughout his youth, Egypt had been a British protectorate, and Fayed had been educated at the British University in Cairo.

"Thank you," Ian replied, but he remained standing. He placed the key on Fayed's desk and watched the man's eyes carefully for any sign that might betray his thoughts.

There! A split second of recognition was quickly concealed by Fayed's infamous poker face. In that second, Ian had obtained all the information he needed. His key was genuine.

Fayed then said something to his servant in a dialect Ian didn't understand. "Something to drink. I have asked my servant to get us something cold," Fayed lied.

Fayed turned the item in his fingers. "It isn't real silver. But you know that," he said. "And it isn't Egyptian. I'll give you five American dollars for it."

Ian reached for the piece.

Fayed wouldn't let it go. "Twenty," he offered. "It would make a nice pendant … for one of my daughters," he said.

Ian took the key with a sure motion that Fayed could not politely resist. Direct confrontation wasn't Fayed's style. He had other ways of getting what he wanted and they always worked.

"If this had any historical value, you would be the one to

know." Ian used flattery to smooth an exit. "Since it does not, I won't take any more of your time."

Fayed shrugged, hoping to convey nonchalance. "Maybe next time, my friend. Ensh Allah."

"Ensh Allah," Ian replied. This was an expression that ended most conversations in Egypt. It meant, "By the will of God."

The moment Ian left Fayed barked some orders to his servant and then quickly made a series of phone calls. Years ago, Fayed had gone into the arts and antiquities business in hope of finding the very item that had just walked into his office—and then walked out. No matter. Ian McHenry could easily be trailed.

Outside, Ian was accosted by Fayed's servant, who had taken a back stairway to overtake him.

"Wait," the servant said with a thick accent. "I give one hundred American dollars for da piece."

"It's worthless," Ian told him in order to brush him off. "Fayed said so. Don't waste your money."

The servant stepped in front of him, blocking his way. "Then you don't need it. But it special to me. Five hundred. Last offer."

Ian perceived a pressure against his back. Someone was behind him and Ian sensed danger. But as he turned to see who it was, his knees buckled in response to an innate sense of self preservation. Ian collapsed, just in time to avoid a flying knife. The servant also fell—the knife planted firmly in his chest. Ian turned to face the man who had thrown the knife.

"Give me that," the attacker said gruffly.

Strength returned to Ian's knees and he stood up. So, Ian concluded, if Fayed couldn't buy the key and was willing to have someone kill him for it, obviously Fayed thought it was genuine. Ian was now ready to protect the key with his life.

The man drew a second knife from the folds of his old gray gallabiya.

Ian turned and ran.

The man was joined by a handful of others who all ran after Ian.

To slow his pursuers Ian knocked down some vendors' tables

behind him. His mind raced to recall possible escape routes, and he scanned his memory banks for every alley in the neighborhood. Where could he run or hide? Even in the most public places the police could conveniently turn their backs on any crime committed by someone known to give generous baksheesh, and Fayed was famous for it. Ian had seen it happen too often. What had happened to the great civilization of ancient Egypt?

Ian rounded a corner and hid in the eaves of a doorway. He closed his eyes and took long controlled inhales and exhales to calm his breathing and his racing pulse.

"Think with your heart," Ian repeated silently. Mikta had suggested he use this phrase like a mantra when he found himself in need of help or faced with an important decision.

Then a wave of horror swept over Ian, as he realized that the knife meant for him had struck Fayed's servant. What if the servant died? The thought made Ian feel deeply remorseful. It wasn't his fault; Ian tried to reason with himself. If his knees hadn't instinctively buckled, he might be dead himself. Then who knows what might have become of the key.

At least Ian knew the key was a genuine artifact, at least a desirable one. Now he needed to discover if the stories about it were true. Mikta had said whoever bore the key had a special destiny. The key would lead its bearer to the capstone of the Great Pyramids of Egypt and Atlantis. With capstone and key in hand, the key-bearer could return the powers to the pyramid.

Ian didn't care so much about the pyramid's powers. After all, the Great Pyramid of Giza was in ruins; it was unlikely to be a source of power anymore. But finding the capstone would fulfill Ian's greatest hopes and dreams. With it, he could prove that advanced ancient civilizations truly existed. Then, he believed, people would look to the past to find out why those great civilizations had disappeared. This information might ensure the survival of humanity in case history repeated itself, which it usually did.

Foremost, Ian's deepest questions about the pyramid would finally be answered. He could barely imagine what wondrous secrets might be revealed.

Just then, two thugs ran past him. Ian's thoughts jumped back to his present situation. He looked to see if anybody was behind the men. Nobody was. Ian decided to double back. Since he knew he couldn't blend in with the crowd — his fair skin and blond curls stood a head above the sea of black veils and lebdas — he had to get off the streets.

Then another knife whizzed by, finding a home in a vendor's pile of grapefruit. Ian ducked down an alley and into another neighborhood. For a few minutes, it seemed he had once again escaped his pursuers. Ian slowed to a walk to catch his breath. Then he saw them. About ten young men were crowded together only thirty feet down the road. They began taunting him, trying to lure him into their trap. Ian turned. Another group of youths gathered behind him sneering. They knew they had him now.

The fear of capture sent a fresh surge of adrenaline through Ian's veins. There was nowhere to run or hide.

This time there was no escape.

6.

A car's persistent honking grew louder. The ruffians who were about to determine Ian's fate opened their ranks to let the car pass. Once clear of the human barricade, the car sped up and headed toward Ian, who stood his ground in front of the oncoming vehicle. He locked eyes with the driver — a tourist wearing a cowboy hat — who slammed his foot on the brakes. Ian ran for the back door, opened it, and jumped in.

"Get me out of here. Please!" Ian said.

The driver looked in his rear-view mirror at Ian and then at the knife-wielding Egyptians both behind and ahead of him.

"Quicker 'n a hiccup," the driver replied undaunted, and he floored the gas pedal. The thugs in front hurled themselves aside to avoid being hit, and those behind vainly tried to pursue.

The well-dressed woman in the passenger seat turned and quickly sized up their unexpected passenger. She too had taken the excitement in stride.

Ian became self-conscious of the sweat pouring down his face and wiped it off with his sleeve.

"What kinda trouble are y'all in?" the woman asked.

"Martha," the man whispered to his wife, though he was glad she'd asked because he too was curious.

"They tried to rob me," Ian said, catching his breath.

"Glad to he'p," the man said, tipping his hat. What a story he'd have to tell his buddies back home.

"Where ya'll headin'?" the woman asked.

"My father is waiting for me at our boat." Ian directed them to a road that ran parallel to the Nile, and soon they reached the marina.

Suddenly they heard the sound of screeching tires behind them. Ian looked out the back window and saw a car speeding toward them.

"Better git goin'!" the driver called, as Ian scrambled out of the car. He raced down the dock looking for the number of his father's mooring. No sooner did he find it when he also saw his father on board.

"What's the hurry?" David asked.

He was answered by gunfire.

Ian untied the boat from its mooring while David revved the engine.

"Keep your head down!" Ian shouted.

David sped away from the marina, as two motorboats began chasing them.

"Can't you go any faster?" Ian shouted. But speed wasn't the issue. David's yacht had an engine that could out-race almost anything that floated. He was dodging, as best he could, the motley array of fishing boats, Egyptian felucca, sailboats, barges, and other craft that cluttered the river.

Minutes later it seemed they had outrun their pursuers.

Ian sat down on the cushioned seats at the stern, his body rocking to the rhythm of the yacht as it bounced through the water. His thoughts turned to Fayed's servant. Ian's regret weighed against his sense of victory for having escaped with the key. Many had wanted it, but he still had it. He had won. For a moment he let himself revel in his triumph. Standing up, he faced the direction his pursuers had come and raised his prize high.

Suddenly, a speedboat appeared from behind a large sailboat and headed recklessly toward them. David spun the wheel to avoid it, but the captain of the oncoming craft wrongly turned in the same direction.

"Ian jump!" David screamed, and the two boats collided and exploded into flames.

7.

The noon hour came and went. Sarah and Daria were tired from walking around the Cairo Museum and too hungry to wait there any longer for Ian to return. So they went to the restaurant across the street and chose a table on the patio, where they had full view of the museum entrance. When Ian showed up, they would see him.

Sarah was prone to worry, but today she was especially concerned.

Daria tried to convince her that her father often got delayed, but he always left her in good hands, and he always came back.

They ate lunch and waited. Still Ian didn't return. Sarah decided to hire a boy to wait by the museum entrance for either Ian or her husband. She gave him their descriptions and a message for them to call her at her hotel.

Back at Sarah's room, Daria turned on the television to practice her Arabic. Sarah played with a Rubik's Cube, solved it, and tossed it on the bed.

"It should be 'Sarah's Cube,'" Sarah complained, wishing it had been her own invention. Then she tried reading a magazine, but it didn't help. Her thoughts kept wandering to Ian and what might have happened to him to make him so late.

Sarah got up and began pacing the floor.

"Grandma, what's bothering you?"

Sarah looked at her granddaughter carefully then sat down on the bed beside her. For a few long minutes she stared blankly before speaking.

"I had a dream last night," she finally said.

"What about?"

"Your father." Sarah's eyes moistened and immediately she regretted saying anything. Sarah didn't think it was right for an adult to cry in front of a child. Yet she had become so wrapped in worry that her guard had dropped.

Daria got up and returned with a tissue, which she gave to her grandmother.

"Was it scary?"

Sarah nodded and blew her nose.

Daria tried to console her grandmother. "Sometimes a dream gives you a frightening symbol to catch your attention, so you'll remember it. At least, that's what Dad says."

"That's what I told your father when he was a boy."

"You did? I didn't know you believed in dreams."

"Your father is doing a good job teaching you about them."

Daria nodded. Her father had taught her that dreams were real experiences, and if they were riddled with symbols, the truth they masked must be especially important. He believed they were a type of inner guidance—of the most personal kind. Daria used to believe him wholeheartedly. Now she wasn't sure.

"I've been having strange dreams lately," Daria said.

"Oh?" Sarah took the opportunity to turn the topic off herself. Yet she was glad to have opened a conversation with her granddaughter that she'd never had before.

"I've had nightmares about things that don't make any sense," Daria said.

"Often a puzzle doesn't make sense until you find one critical piece."

"Well, none of the pieces make sense, either."

"You're wondering if dreams have anything to do with real life," her grandmother suggested. She knew that Daria was entering the age where she would begin questioning everything, including her own beliefs and especially those her father held so dearly.

"Maybe," Daria replied, feeling relieved that her grandmother understood.

Then the phone rang.

Sarah jumped to answer it.

"Ian?"

"Dad and I are okay," Ian said quickly. He knew what his mom needed to hear first.

He and his father had leapt from the yacht just before the collision. Ian could hardly believe their good fortune.

"Where are you?" Sarah demanded.

"We have a change in plans. Take Daria to the Ramses Station and book a compartment for Daria and me on the sleeper train to Aswan for tonight. It leaves at 7:30 P.M., so we have time. I'll meet you at the station. Also, we lost our luggage. Would you mind buying Daria some clothes?"

"What's going on?" Sarah asked. Aswan was the southernmost city in Egypt, over 450 miles south of Cairo. Sarah couldn't imagine why Ian and Daria would be going there. And what about their boating vacation on the Nile?

"I'll explain later," Ian said.

Ian had already made another call, one to a phone number

that Mikta had given him in case Ian ever needed to reach him. The contact who answered Ian's call told him that Mikta was in Edfu, a town just north of Aswan. The man couldn't make any promises, but if possible, Mikta might be able to meet Ian there the following morning. He hoped Mikta would get his message.

After Ian had made his phone calls, he again thanked the fisherman who had so graciously plucked him and his father from the Nile. The man had also taken Ian and David to his riverside home, where his wife and daughters served them a modest but filling meal of fish cakes, chickpeas, and pita bread. It was then that the fisherman had let Ian use his telephone.

When Ian and David finally said good-bye to the fisherman and his family, Ian reached for his wallet to give him some monetary compensation. The fisherman refused. It was his duty to God to help those in need, he explained.

Ian and David walked up the streets toward the nearest main thoroughfare. On the way, Ian told his father about what he had found, his meeting with Faoud Fayed, and what had happened afterward.

"I don't understand how Fayed could have mobilized so many against you so quickly," David said.

"He's a powerful man with many connections."

"He told you the item was worthless. Why would he then try to steal it from you?"

"Maybe there's something about it that we don't know," Ian said. His father would have scoffed at Mikta's legends. No point telling him about them now.

Then they considered the possibility that someone might have seen them escape the explosion. Yet nobody had bothered them at the fisherman's home, and they'd watched other motorboats circling the debris, poking at it with long poles, even while David and Ian had climbed aboard the fisherman's felucca and even as they sailed out of sight.

"I'm leaving with Daria tonight on the Aswan sleeper," Ian said.

"You plan on going home through the Aswan International

Airport?"

"Yes. If Fayed has scouts looking for me, the chances are greater they'll be watching the airports in Cairo or Alexandria. I think we'll be safer in Aswan."

His father agreed. "Daria might be better off with Mom and me," David added. He said he planned to head back to the States as soon as possible. Daria was welcome to come with them.

"You were seen with me," Ian said. "You're also in danger."

"I'll be careful," David assured him. "You're the one who has what they want."

They reached a main street and flagged a cab.

"Ramses Station," Ian told the driver.

8.

The Ramses Station, located in downtown Cairo, was the hub of all rail traffic in Egypt. Trains regularly headed in all directions: north toward the cities of Alexandria and Damietta on the Mediterranean coast, east toward the Suez Canal, southwest toward the Al-Bahriya Oasis, and south to Aswan. The station itself was of quasi-Moorish design and cavernous inside. It was named after King Ramses II, one of the greatest pharaohs of Egypt.

Ian and David waited for Sarah and Daria in the shadow of one of the decorative statues. The girls arrived about half an hour later with the train tickets and a new duffle bag filled with clothes for Daria.

"I'm so glad you're okay!" Sarah said as soon as she saw them. She was about to embrace her husband and son when she changed her mind, and exchanged only a quick kiss on each cheek. The men's clothes stank of engine oil.

Daria also refused a hug, squeezing her nose in explanation.

David spotted a nearby vendor and went to buy himself and his son a pair of pants and a gallabiya—traditional Egyptian menswear. Meanwhile, Ian gave his mother an edited version of their mishap, saying that another boat had accidentally crashed into theirs, damaging their yacht beyond repair. To avoid worrying his mother, Ian implied they had gotten wet trying unsuccessfully to retrieve their belongings.

After a barrage of questions, Sarah accepted the fact that her son and husband were okay, the yacht was irretrievable, and their vacation together as a family would have to be postponed.

"Today and forever," Sarah said to Daria as they hugged good-bye. The phrase was a farewell the McHenry family had shared for generations.

Ian and Daria boarded the train.

Their compartment, one of thirteen, was small but efficiently furnished. On the far wall, in the center of the room, was a small washbasin. To the right was a pair of bunk beds neatly covered with a cotton blanket with colorful intersecting stripes, and to the left was a row of seats that faced the beds. The toilets were down the hall.

"Give me a minute," Ian said. He needed to wash up and change.

Daria set her duffle bag on the seat and went into the hallway to give her dad some privacy.

Ian washed up and put on the pants his father had bought. They fit snugly and the gallabiya reached just to his knees. Carefully he removed the key from his Nile-beaten khakis. He was about to examine it once again when he heard a knock at the door. Quickly he stuffed the key into the pocket of his new pants.

It was Daria at the door followed by the ticket taker, who punched their tickets and welcomed them aboard.

The train left on time. The McHenrys went to the diner car and sat down for an Egyptian meal. After a selection of mezzes, or appetizers, Ian ordered a stew of lamb, okra, tomatoes, and rice. Daria ordered lamb kabobs with pasta.

"Why are we going to Aswan?" Daria asked.

"Do you remember Mikta?"

Daria nodded.

"I'd like to see him before we go back home. I heard he was in Edfu."

"That's where the Temple of Horus is located," Daria exclaimed.

Ian smiled broadly. He loved how enthusiastic Daria was about Egypt and its history. "We'll arrive about eight o'clock tomorrow morning," he said.

During their meal, Daria chatted away as usual. Tonight, she couldn't stop talking about the Temple of Horus. Every so often her father would correct her facts or add to her knowledge. Ian was impressed by what she already knew. She told him how the temple was built during the Greek era, when Egypt's kings were no longer called pharaohs, but rather *ptolemies*.

"Ptolemy III began construction in 237 B.C.," she said, "but the temple was completed about 200 years later by Ptolemy XIII," who, Daria happened to know, was Queen Cleopatra's father. "The Temple of Horus is supposed to be the best preserved ancient temple in Egypt and one of the largest," she continued. "It was built in the style of Old Kingdom architecture and situated upon the ruins of another ancient temple. Some say the temple wasn't just built, it was brought back to life."

"You sound like a tour guide," Ian said.

"Do not."

Daria then told him how much she looked forward to seeing for herself the hieroglyphs and bas-relief carvings that covered the temple's every wall. It was her interest in this ancient Egyptian writing and artwork that had prompted her to study the Temple of Horus and all its details in the first place.

After dinner they prepared for bed. Ian took the top bunk.

"Dad."

"Yes."

"Tell me how Atlantis's power center got lost."

"You fell asleep on me last night," Ian teased.

"Did not."

Daria snuggled under the covers and hugged her pillow as she waited for her father's story to begin. The vibrations of the train and its rhythmic clickety-clack were loud, yet comforting.

"Once upon a time," Ian began, "a woman named Sileen wore an ancient key around her neck. She was next in line to be ruler of Atlantis, and so it was her responsibility to guard this key." Ian stopped. Was it coincidence that Daria wanted to hear the old stories again now that he had found the key?

"Go on," Daria said.

"It was the eve of the autumn equinox," Ian continued. "While everyone was enjoying the festivities, Sileen went inside the pyramid and consulted with Pharaoh, the pyramid's artificial intelligence. He confirmed that it was indeed time to transfer the power center. That would give Atlantis a chance to be reborn again in the future. And, as I said last night, in case she failed in her mission, they made an alternate plan.

"Sileen then climbed barefoot through a secret door to the outside of the pyramid. The night was black. She looked back on the twinkling lights of her city but had no time for a sentimental good-bye. Anyone could spot her because the pyramid was illuminated with floodlights.

"Quickly she ascended the pyramid's side to its apex. Her opal-powered headband provided just enough light to see. An inch below the pyramid's perfect tip she found a small rectangular slit between tiny silver blocks. Sileen reached for the key, inserted it into the slit, and turned. The capstone fell easily into her hands, and she placed it carefully inside a pouch she wore around her neck.

"With capstone removed, the top of the pyramidion was shaped like a flat one-inch square. Sileen found a small slit in the center of the square, put in her key, and turned it. The pyramidion began to vibrate. Sileen felt a pulsing sensation beat through her body.

"Suddenly the pyramidion lifted off of the great pyramid and surged upward. Turning the key had started the pyramidion's anti-gravity propulsion system—the same system that fueled the other flying vehicles the Atlanteans enjoyed. The system was based on magnetism, and a magnetic field now surrounded the hovering pyramidion. So even if Sileen had let go she would have remained attached to its side. Still she clung to the pyramidion with all her might.

"The pyramidion flew beyond the hundreds of small islands that dotted the shoreline of Atlantis. For hours they flew over the sea under expansive starry skies. Just before dawn, Sileen saw a ship and shifting her weight, steered the pyramidion toward it. Exhausted from the journey and drained by the electromagnetic currents that made the journey possible, Sileen fell to the deck of the ship moments before the pyramidion landed. She lay there unconscious.

"Meanwhile, Captain Rohn had been deeply asleep, sprawled in a hammock in his small cabin. But the sound of a thud instantly awoke him, and he ran outside. He spied the shape of a human being lying on the deck and ran to it."

Ian paused. "Honeycakes, are you still awake?"

"Don't stop, Dad, this is my favorite part."

Ian embellished the tale with details Daria liked to hear. "Captain Rohn's heart leapt when he saw there was a woman on his deck. Rohn had prayed daily for a wife and companion, but the women he had met over the years had not been interested in seamen who were never home. Rohn's mind worked overtime. How had the woman gotten here? Where did she come from? He looked to every horizon. His ship was alone on the vast sea.

"The woman's long brown hair graced the deck. Her slender arms stretched elegantly beside her. She wore the amber tunic of the royal family and looked like the Empress-elect. But it couldn't possibly be her. Who was she? He knelt down to stroke away the few strands of hair that covered her face. Her eyes were gently shut, indicating a woman unafraid of sleep or the dreams that accompanied it. She looked healthy, strong, and beautiful, and the aura about her was soft and kind—everything he had ever dreamed to find in a woman. He knew then, in that moment, that he would love her until the end of time.

"Wait, he cautioned himself. Was this a dream?

"'Eh, Cap'n,' came the salty voice of his first mate.

"Rohn didn't answer. If this was a dream, he didn't want to wake up.

"'Eh, Cap'n,' the voice repeated. 'We have a pyramid on our ship.'

"By now the pyramidion was quiet, a hunk of silver, perfectly shaped except for its missing capstone.

"At first, Rohn didn't see the pyramidion through the bulk of lowered sails. Besides, his entire focus had been on the woman. Now he saw it and realized this was no dream. Miracles—good ones—happened in the presence of a pyramid, and he was witnessing one.

"Rohn decided the pyramid could wait, no matter its importance or the appropriateness of paying it respect. The girl mattered more. He considerately inspected her body for wounds and found none, so he lifted her up and brought her to his cabin. How deeply she slept, he thought as he placed her inside his hammock. Her journey must have been long and grueling, he decided. Only when he was certain she was comfortable and warm did he leave her to see the object that had landed with her.

"He approached it slowly, knelt beside it, and then caressed its smooth sides. It reminded him of the great pyramid of his homeland. Atlantis was beautiful with its snowy mountains and vast meadows, neatly manicured farms, and bays that surrounded the city in a series of concentric circles. To reach the capital by sea, one had to navigate through hundreds of islands, and then, upon entering the bay, scores of rock pillars that jutted from the ocean like sentinels. Every Atlantean sailor knew his way through them by heart—Rohn included. The Atlantean pyramid was located miles inland but could be seen clearly from the shore.

"Rohn surmised that what had landed on his ship was either the pyramid's top—which was hardly likely for that would imply the end of his civilization—or else a copy of it. Either way, it could fly. And it had brought him a woman!

"In gratitude, Rohn pledged to serve the pyramid. Its cold metallic sides grew warm beneath Rohn's touch, as if it were responding to him. Indeed, Rohn also would devote his life to the woman, and if she didn't recognize him as her mate or love him as such, he would serve her still. These were his promises — ones that a man of Rohn's integrity would keep forever.

"Meanwhile, the evil ones who had taken control of the Atlanteans' capital city discovered their pyramid's missing pyramidion. They located it with their crystal imaging systems and found Sileen had stolen it. They swore revenge: the Empress-elect would pay with her life. Psychically they located her position and sent beams of energy into the sky and sea around her.

"Drops of cold rain awoke Rohn from his contemplation with the pyramidion. Billowing clouds erased the dawning sun. Rohn called orders to his crew, but the sails were still lowered from the night before. Only a few things needed tending to brace the ship for the storm.

"The seas began to pitch and roll. Thunder rumbled across the waves, and the ship trembled with hits of lightning. Rohn went back indoors to check on the woman. Her hammock swung wildly back and forth, so Rohn secured it with ropes that he tied to his cabin walls to make her sleep more peaceful. Yet he hoped the thunder would wake her, as he eagerly wanted to meet her.

"The storm's intensity increased quickly. Rohn took one last look at his sleeping beloved, imprinted her face upon his memory, and then ran to the helm. Neither Rohn nor any of his men had ever witnessed a storm such as this. Rohn held the wheel with all his might, leaning into the wind as the rain beat him to the bone. He would survive, he promised himself. He would save his woman and his crew. Yet the boat tossed about like driftwood, scaling one-hundred foot waves, first up — nearly straight up. Then down.

"Up. Then down.

"Up. And then down.

"And then sideways.

"A bolt of lightning hit the pyramidion as it slid into the ocean, breaking apart its silvery casing and casting its spherical power center to the ocean floor. Still gripping the wheel, Rohn screamed to his men to save themselves. Then the ocean consumed them.

"Rohn's final thoughts were of the woman he loved but had never met."

9.

The Cairo-to-Aswan sleeper train chugged south at a hypnotic pace. The following morning its brakes began screeching as it approached the Edfu Station.

Ian checked the pocket of his pants, as he had done many times during the night, to make sure he still had the key that he had found and so many had wanted.

"Let's see if Mikta's waiting for us," Ian said to Daria, who was dressed and fed and ready for the day. They left their compartment and headed toward the exit. Ian opened the door and while holding a handle bar leaned out of the train to scan the small crowd at the station. Almost all were men in gallabiyas and older children in loose-fitting gray trousers and shirts. They were there to assist the tourists who were about to swarm off the train. Egyptians were friendly that way, though custom required they receive a tip, or baksheesh, in return. If you gave enough, you were warmly welcomed into the land of Egypt and the hearts of her people.

Ian knew that Mikta would blend perfectly into the crowd and hoped his friend would see him first. Ian jumped off the train just as it rolled to a halt and made sure Daria got off safely.

"Ian McHenry!"

Ian turned at the sound of his name and saw the outstretched arms of an old Egyptian dressed in a gallabiya, just like all the rest.

"Mikta!" Ian stooped to embrace a man much shorter than he.

Daria stepped beside her father.

"Ah, my dear Da-ya," Mikta said and bowed to her. "It very good see you."

Ian almost laughed. Mikta was speaking broken English like every other tour guide there. He had taken his role to perfection.

"I'm sorry, I don't remember," Daria said politely.

"It okay. Now, let's go to hotel."

He then headed toward the crowd of tourists, who competed for taxicabs. Drivers accepted those with the most aggressive tour guides first—or the one who secretly indicated their tourist had already given them generous baksheesh. Yet the tour guides stepped aside as Mikta passed and their faces brightened. Mikta nodded to them, and then as if nobody else was there, he walked up to the first taxi in line and opened the back door. Daria and Ian slid inside while Mikta sat up front.

"Hesham, how are you my old friend?" Mikta said to the driver in fast Arabic.

"Mikta! It is a gift of Allah that you have chosen my cab," Hesham replied equally fast. "Where can I take you today?"

"The Edfu Hotel," Mikta paused only a moment. "And how are your wife, Nora, and your children, Mohammed, Saman, and Nassar, if I remember correctly. All sons. You must be a proud man."

The driver groaned. "Business has been good. I made some wise investments and was able to afford a second wife. Now Nora won't sleep with me. She says times have changed, and that men don't have more than one wife anymore. I tell her she should be glad to have a second wife to do the chores. But now Nefiri is jealous, too, and she won't let me into her bed either."

Daria understood what they were saying and covered her mouth to hide a giggle.

The train station was located on the east bank of the Nile, and they were presently driving west over the bridge to Edfu. To their left, the Temple of Horus towered over the town. Daria tapped her father's leg and pointed out the two enormous walls, or pylons, that formed the temple's east entrance.

"My problem is big," the driver lamented.

"It is easily solved."

Hesham laughed. "If you can tell me how, I will owe my life to you."

"Be careful what you promise," Mikta replied. "You have two wives when a man of today should have but one. Therefore treat them as one. Begin with a gift—rather two gifts. Jewelry would be a nice choice to begin with, but each piece must be exactly the same. Then call each wife to your side. Take one gift from your left pocket and give it to the wife standing to your left. Now, this is very important, at the same time, take the gift from your right pocket and give it to the wife standing to your right. Do this every day.

"Give to one as you give to the other at the same place, at the same time, and with the same affection. When you want to kiss one, call the other to you and kiss both. Say to one everything that you say to the other, even if you find yourself tediously repeating things. Soon, you will have no trouble sleeping and may need a medicine. My people are camped to the west of the temple, just beyond the hills. Go there and ask for blue lotus."

"Blue lotus," the driver repeated.

"It is an aphrodisiac."

The driver grinned.

Minutes later they arrived at the Hotel Edfu. Mikta offered to pay the driver who absolutely refused to accept the fare. Wisely, Ian handed him generous baksheesh, which Hesham accepted gratefully. Ian knew the driver would never say a word to anyone about Mikta's guests.

The small hotel lobby was undecorated except for a rug on the floor in front of the aged counter.

"*Anah ahwiz ohdah, minfahdluk* [I want a room, please]," Ian said in Arabic, and the manager smiled.

"I will show you the room myself."

The stairs creaked as they climbed to the second floor. The room had a ceiling fan, two narrow beds, and a chest of drawers.

Mikta went over to the window and opened it for some fresh air.

"Look Daria," he said. The window offered a spectacular view of the Temple of Horus.

"Dad, can I go? Please?"

"We'll be right behind you," Ian said.

Daria flew out of the room.

The manager turned on the fan and the light to assure his guests that they worked.

"*Shokran* [thank you]," Ian said and gave the man baksheesh.

"Ensh Allah," he replied, and left.

Ian shut off the light, and he and Mikta followed Daria downstairs and outside.

The Edfu Hotel was located on the same wide dirt road that led to the northern entrance of the Horus Temple. The street was lined with vendors selling locally made souvenirs. It was a long uphill walk, and many tourists chose instead to reach the temple via horse-drawn carriage. A small cafeteria was located across from the temple's northern entrance. Tourists were gulping bottles of water and soda, and the already hot temperature would still rise at least another fifteen degrees before the day was over. August was as grueling a time to tour Egypt as it was to do archeology.

They saw Daria among the trail of tourists that were turning left toward the temple. She waved to them. Ian waved back, and Daria took the gesture to mean that she was free to explore the temple on her own. Ian knew she'd be safe. He and Mikta continued to walk past the temple entrance, so they could be alone.

Mikta could tell something weighed on his friend's mind and waited until Ian was ready to talk.

"Are the stories true?" Ian finally asked.

Mikta didn't reply.

"The ones you've been telling me ever since we first met," Ian prodded.

Mikta looked deeply into Ian's eyes. "What does your heart tell you?" Now he was speaking perfect English and continued to do so.

Ian wished Mikta would just give him a direct answer. Ian closed his eyes and settled his attention into a blue field of light in the center of himself as Mikta had taught him. Mikta said this was the most direct way to know things. Soon Ian felt clearer, the clouds of doubt and fear, as well as those of desire and hope, evaporated to reveal the truth, which came simply as knowing. Of course, this was much easier to do in Mikta's presence, and the answers Ian got were always more obvious.

"The stories are true," Ian said opening his eyes.

Mikta nodded.

"All of them?"

"Every one of them."

They walked a few more paces in silence.

"Have you passed them on to your daughter?" Mikta asked.

"Yes"

"All of them?"

"Every one," Ian replied. He casually looked around to make sure they were alone on the road. "If the stories are true," Ian said, pulling the key from his pocket, "then this must be the Key to the Capstone of the Great Pyramid of Egypt, and of Atlantis." He handed it to Mikta.

For a second, Mikta looked surprised. Then he put the ancient item between his palms and pressed them together. He rested his chin on his fingertips and took a deep breath. His eyes closed.

Ian tried to keep his thoughts calm as he awaited Mikta's response.

"I didn't think the world was ready," Mikta finally said.

"For the key?"

"No, for the capstone," Mikta replied, looking at Ian. "Whoever bears the key shall find the capstone, and then the capstone will lead the key-bearer to its original home. It is destiny. There can be no other outcome."

Ian couldn't hide his excitement. Finding an intact capstone, not to mention an Atlantean pyramid, would validate all his work and fulfill his dreams.

"Where do I start looking?" Ian asked eagerly.

Mikta gave the key back to Ian. "You are the finder of the key."

"Yes."

"Not its bearer."

"But, I do bear the key," Ian insisted. "It's in my hands. A great destiny lies before me."

"You are the finder of the key, not its bearer," Mikta repeated.

"But ... ." There was no arguing with Mikta. Ian felt crushed. First he had failed to find a tunnel at Giza. Now he was being denied the opportunity of a lifetime?

Mikta gave Ian some time to come to terms with his emotions. Then he asked, "Has anyone else seen the key?"

Ian told Mikta what had happened with Faoud Fayed and the hoards who had wanted to kill him.

The news was out.

"Your destiny to find the key is fulfilled. Now you must give it to its rightful bearer," Mikta said quietly.

"Yeah," Ian sighed, resigning himself to fate. "I just dig for a living."

Mikta smiled and the two friends laughed. The laughter eased Ian's disappointment, and he felt better afterward. After all, he had a full life ahead of him. Plenty of time to unearth something else that could prove the existence of ancient advanced civilizations.

Then Mikta said, "This key is tied to a destiny that can only be fulfilled by the true key-bearer. You must find its rightful bearer and pass it along. The key-bearer must receive the key as a gift. The legends have told you that."

"So anyone who steals it from me won't be able to find the capstone anyway," Ian thought aloud.

It was a consolation and a comforting thought amidst the more pressing one: To whom should Ian give his key?

10.

The northern entrance to the Temple of Horus was wide enough for one person to enter at a time. Ian and Mikta passed through it into a large open-air courtyard, which was lined on three sides by a total of thirty-two massive columns. The fourth side to their left and to the east consisted of the one-hundred-foot tall walls that Daria had seen from the Nile Bridge. Every stone surface throughout the temple was covered with hieroglyphic writing and bas-relief art carvings.

Ian scanned the courtyard for Daria but didn't see her.

They made a right turn, toward the west, and entered the first hypostyle hall—a room filled with columns. It contained two rows of six evenly spaced columns that were about seven feet wide at the base. The columns reached upward over thirty-five feet to an arched ceiling. Even the columns had hieroglyphs on them.

Ian watched Mikta gently touch one of the engravings on a column and wondered how he could engage his friend in a conversation about the temple. Mikta needed no prompting. He soon began to speak, although at first he seemed to be talking to the engravings themselves.

"People today wait hungrily for someone to unearth texts that would validate a high civilization in pre-dynastic Egypt," Mikta said. "But many such texts have already been found—

centuries ago.

"Take Imhotep, for example." Mikta turned his attention to Ian and spoke with animation. "Imhotep was born a commoner. As a youth, he worked as a land surveyor's assistant. One day while on the job, he unburied ancient texts. It took him years to learn to read these texts, but after applying what he learned he rose to the rank of high priest of Heliopolis, chief astronomer, and vizier for the Pharaoh Djoser in the Third Dynasty. Imhotep is attributed with inventing the science of medicine as well as stone masonry, which he then applied to building what Egyptologists claim is the "the first pyramid," or the Step Pyramid. All this knowledge Imhotep learned from the texts he had found. Imhotep's students continued to decipher more and more of the texts and, after Imhotep's death, led Egypt in a flurry of pyramid building."

"No wonder the technology for building pyramids evolved so rapidly it seems to have come from nowhere," Ian said.

"Egyptian pharaohs were motivated to build pyramids," Mikta explained, "because the texts Imhotep discovered told of the extraordinary powers of the Great Pyramid of Giza and its two consorts, the pyramids of Khafra and Menkaure, which were also already long-standing monuments during the Old Kingdom. Yet the phase of pyramid-building that Imhotep initiated ended in the Sixth Dynasty, only a few hundred years after it began.

"I should mention that another series of pyramids were again attempted a few hundred years later, during the Twelfth Dynasty, but these were made of mud brick and little remains of them today.

"My point is that nobody wanted to build pyramids anymore when they realized that nothing they could build evidenced the powers attributed to the Great Pyramid, which had been their blueprint and model for success. This was, of course, because the capstone that had given the Great Pyramid of Giza its powers had long been lost."

Mikta paused momentarily as though to catch his breath. He continued, "Ancient texts were again discovered during the reign of Ptolemy III, when Greek archeologists found a cache of documents right here in Edfu. To give you a sense of time, this was roughly fifteen hundred years after the Twelfth Dynasty ended. The documents were brought to the Ptolemy's attention. When his priests translated them, they found they were an encyclopedia of ancient knowledge. Ptolemy III was wise enough to realize that this information could again be lost, so he commissioned the construction of the Temple of Horus on the site of the older temple where the documents were found.

"This temple represents the information they discovered. The mathematics, harmonic proportions, geometry, symbolism, and history are contained in the temple's architecture and artwork."

Ian scanned the temple walls as if seeing them newly.

Mikta continued, "In the Old Kingdom and before, the arts and sciences, particularly mathematics and astronomy, were inextricable. Not because artists tried to incorporate science into their work, or because scientists were artistically or architecturally inclined. Their way of looking at life and expressing themselves naturally combined both. It was their mindset."

"Perhaps," Ian suggested, "they had less separation between their right brain, which is responsible for creative thinking, and their left brain, which is associated with analytical thought."

"It was the Greeks who began seeing art and science as separate," Mikta continued, "although, ironically, their greatest art and architecture do incorporate scientific principles."

Just then Daria whizzed past them.

11.

"I want to scout the entire temple before I stop to study it," Daria announced to her father and Mikta as she scurried through the first hypostyle hall of the Temple of Horus.

"Looking for something in particular?" Mikta asked her.

Daria stopped and wondered briefly at his question, then shrugged her shoulders and ran into the adjacent room. This was the Temple of Horus's second hypostyle hall—another room filled only with tall columns. The adults followed Daria and saw her heading toward the entrance to the long passageway that wound around the perimeter of the temple's many inner rooms. When Ian and Mikta finally entered the passageway themselves, they saw Daria standing quietly listening to two boys about eight and ten years old. They were both thin and blond and dressed identically. The eldest was reading aloud from a German guidebook.

Daria knew German and could understand him.

"The writing on this wall tells the legend of Osiris and Isis," the boy read and then paraphrased. "It's one of the most important myths of ancient Egypt. It's the Egyptian version of the Resurrection, and local communities have been reenacting the story during the Festival of Osiris every year for centuries."

"What's it about?" the younger boy asked.

Daria knew the story well. But the elder brother shared only certain parts he thought would taunt his younger brother. "It says that the god Set chopped up his brother Osiris into pieces. Osiris's wife, the goddess Isis, found all the pieces except for his member and with magic put Osiris back together."

"His member?"

"His penis," the older boy whispered. "Says here it was lost in the Nile and eaten by a fish. Osiris and Isis later had a son named Horus, who killed Set and became the first great leader of Egypt."

"Did he get his penis back?" the little boy asked.

"It doesn't say," his brother said, and they walked away giggling and clobbering each other as though chopping each other into pieces.

Daria went over to the writing the boys had been referring to. She touched the wall gently. Suddenly, it felt as though her head was expanding into another dimension. She focused on the hieroglyphs to keep herself grounded in reality. By now her body felt so large that the entire Horus Temple was contained within her. All its knowledge was available to her. Anything she wanted to know was hers. But the writing had caught her attention. Right now, more than anything, Daria wanted to know what these hieroglyphs really said.

Ian watched her take a few steps back from the wall. It looked as though she'd entered a trance because she was so absorbed in the symbols before her.

"The myth of Set and Osiris can be interpreted quite differently," Daria said quietly, knowing her father and Mikta could hear her.

Daria explained, "Osiris's loss was obviously symbolic since he later fathered a son. But people take it literally and then assume the entire story is myth, so they fail to look deeper into the history the story portrays."

"What do you mean, Daria?" Ian asked.

"This is indeed a story of resurrection—but not of a man, of an empire. It tells how an ancient kingdom evolved into the Kingdom of Egypt. The ancient kingdom is personified by Osiris, who was actually a leader of this original empire."

"Go on," her father insisted. He wasn't sure how or when Daria had learned to read hieroglyphs, but knew she was capable.

Daria continued, "The guidebook will tell you that Osiris was at war with another kingdom called Lebanon. Osiris's younger brother, Set, was jealous of him and devised a devious trap. Set made a large box inlaid with precious minerals and jewels, trapped Osiris inside, and sent it to the King of Lebanon.

"Yet the word "trap" can be translated "ship," and "Lebanon" can refer to the Eastern Mediterranean area in general. A truer translation is that Set lured Osiris into a ship bound for Lebanon.

"According to the popular story, Isis made a bargain with the King of Lebanon and brought Osiris back to Egypt. Then Set found him and chopped him up.

"But here, it says that while Osiris was in Lebanon, Set tried not to "chop" him but to "divide" him—and not his physical body, but the states of his worldwide empire. Set had convinced the lords of these states to call for independence. But Isis reached them before civil war began. She convinced the lords to meet in a secret council located here in Egypt, where they would consult the most ancient and revered oracle they knew, the Great Sphinx. In the end, they agreed to peace. That's the "magic" Isis used to reunite Osiris's body, or more correctly, his empire.

"Horus was born after Isis reunited the lords of Osiris's kingdom. Horus was the first Egyptian-born ruler and became one of the most powerful gods."

Daria ran her fingers over another section of text, "While the lords met in Egypt, a great flood prevented them from returning home and working together to rebuild a peaceful empire." Daria explained, "Over time, the local peoples interpreted the great flood as the Nile's annual deluge and the Nile as the resting place of Osiris's missing piece.

"Osiris's missing piece," Daria repeated and rubbed her chin as she recalled her father's stories. "If Osiris symbolizes Atlantis, then his missing piece was a piece of Atlantis that got lost in the flood. It was the piece that prevented the powerful worldwide Atlantean civilization from reproducing itself in Egypt." She was out of her trance now. Her mind no longer felt expanded, but she remembered what she'd read and came to a startling conclusion.

Daria's face grew pale. "Dad, the Legend of Isis and Osiris is really about the missing pyramidion and its power center!"

Ian understood her expression immediately as he'd felt the same way just the night before. It was one thing to believe in a legend that said the ancient Egyptian civilization was founded by people from Atlantis, another to find connections that proved it true. Still, he was at a loss for words.

"It says all that, Honeycakes?"

Daria pointed to the wall and Ian and Mikta stepped forward to look.

"It is here," Mikta said.

Ian closely inspected the hieroglyphs.

"I wasn't reading it word for word," Daria said. "Somehow I just knew what it said and tried to explain it to you."

"You did well," Mikta said. Then he spoke a few words to her in a strange tongue punctuated with consonants.

Daria knit her brows.

Mikta tried again, this time using a different language and he got the same response.

"*Fehem teenee,*" Mikta said in Arabic, asking Daria if she had understood him.

"*La.*" No, she had not. "*Esmahlee,*" she added, asking to be excused, and ran off. She didn't go far. Unsettled by the strange experience she'd just had, she decided to stay close to the adults.

Mikta explained, "Daria translated the hieroglyphs that are here for all to see—but from a fresh and unfettered mindset."

"I don't understand," Ian said.

"We interpret what we see and read based on our experiences, culture, and upbringing," Mikta replied. "It is hard to be fully neutral and almost impossible to see things as they truly are. For example, Europeans who visited the Great Sphinx in the 1500s and 1600s returned with drawings of it that depicted European facial features and curly hairdos, which was a popular European style at the time."

"So, what we see isn't always what's really there," Ian summarized.

"What we see is a combination of what we want to see, what we expect to see, and what our experiences and beliefs tell us should be there," Mikta added.

"I must give another example," Mikta said. "Egyptian myth says that creation began in a chaos they describe as primordial wateriness. Out of this emerged a mound and on it a solar deity. Egyptologists are convinced the chaos reflects the Nile's annual flooding, the mound is the silt left behind each year, and the solar deity is the need for sunlight to grow crops out of the silt.

"We who see a greater truth consider the primordial wateriness the Great Flood that prompted huge migrations of people into the Mediterranean basin, where life for them essentially began anew. The mound was the ancient temple upon which the Atlanteans built the Great Pyramid of Giza, and the solar deity referred to the round power center inside the pyramidion that was meant to be placed at its top. Instead, only the capstone arrived, but it sufficed."

"I thought the great sphere was contained in the pyramidion, which was lost at sea," Ian said.

"The capstone also contains a sphere," Mikta reminded him. "It was about the size of your thumbnail. It was called the Eye of Ra by its makers, who lived long before the Age of Atlantis. Ra was a sun god and imparted certain powers into the little sphere. When the capstone reached Egypt, Osiris gave it to his son Horus. The sphere then became known as the Eye of Horus.

"It is said that: to whoever holds the Eye of Horus, the invisible can become visible. The Eye of Horus is a window to other worlds, other lands, and other times. It grants freedom from want and sickness, and it will allow itself to be possessed only by those truly worthy of it."

"So he who finds the capstone finds the Eye of Horus," Ian said.

Mikta nodded.

Ian digested the news as they walked the length of the surrounding corridor and ended up back in the second hypostyle hall.

"By the way, what did you say to my daughter?" Ian asked.

"I spoke to her in the language she had just read. She did not understand me. I tried a later version of ancient Egyptian, and she still did not understand. Yet she can read, or rather perceive, the meaning of the written language. Furthermore, she read it purely, and without the bias of modern translations."

"Daria has a talent for learning foreign languages," Ian said, feeling pride for his daughter's abilities. "So this doesn't surprise me."

"It should," Mikta said. "To read and accurately interpret an archaic script without prior training is miraculous."

Ian beamed.

Mikta frowned. His friend didn't comprehend the gravity of what was unfolding. "It is the capstone," he said. "It is beginning to awaken the key-bearer."

"Daria?" Ian exclaimed. "That's impossible!"

"The key will guide her," Mikta assured him. "It will lead her through the experiences she needs to develop the physical, emotional, mental, and spiritual strength to take responsibility for the capstone—and finally, to know what to do with it once she finds it."

"She's too young," Ian stated firmly. "And it's too dangerous," he added, recalling the persistence of those who believed he carried the key.

"The key-bearer shall find the capstone," Mikta repeated. "The earth is in the process of changing once again. The powers of the capstone, used rightly, may be able to avert another worldwide disaster."

Ian had no doubt the capstone was powerful enough to impact the planet. But Daria was only eleven, soon to be twelve. Maybe he would hold onto the key until she was eighteen, or maybe twenty-something. Then, when the time came for her to find the capstone, Ian promised himself he would be at her side, protecting her, every step of the way.

"One more thing," Mikta said. "You must tell Daria to keep her talent for reading ancient script a secret. She may use her ability, but she must never reveal it to anyone."

"I'll be sure to tell her," Ian promised.

12.

A few days after a long journey back to the States, Daria celebrated her twelfth birthday. That morning, her father invited her into his office at their home in Hamden, Connecticut. She passed through French doors into a room with floor-to-ceiling bookcases, a wood parquet floor, a large desk that partially hid a picture window, and two brown leather wing-backed chairs that stood before a stone fireplace. Ian was sitting in one of the chairs, holding a box dressed with shiny aluminum foil and sapphire blue ribbon.

"I want to tell you a story of an Egyptian pharaoh and his daughter," Ian said.

"Oh, Dad, *puh-leeease.*" He had announced every birthday gift he'd ever given her with a story. At age twelve, she felt old enough to forego the ritual.

Ian continued as though she'd said nothing. The prompting he'd received in a dream the night before to give his daughter the key today was undeniable. Daria would have to listen.

"On his beloved daughter's twelfth birthday," Ian said, "the pharaoh presented her with a box inlaid with lapis and silver. The daughter smiled wide-eyed with anticipation and opened the gift carefully. As she lifted the lid, a ray of sunlight reflected off a sparkling silver pendant. It had the general shape of a key, with a spiraling handle that swirled into a half-inch circle. The shaft of the key was decorated and ended in a series of disks."

In a flash, Daria knew what her gift was, and in the same instant she realized her suspicions about the key's identity were true.

"Holy Sh … ," she began.

"Daria," her father warned in a low voice.

"I mean Holy Shepseskaf, son of Menkaure," Daria exclaimed. "You found Sileen's Key!"

Daria leapt to her father and hugged him. "I always knew if anyone could find it, it would be you."

"It was miracle," Ian replied, as he accepted his daughter's embrace.

Moments later, Daria abruptly let go the hug and returned to her chair. She couldn't believe she had just allowed herself to once again get caught up in Mikta's silly legends. After all, they were only stories and nothing in them could be scientifically verified. Still, she was grateful for the upcoming gift, no matter what her father thought it might be.

"Those who wore the key knew all the secrets of the Great Pyramid and could control its powers," Ian said. "At age twelve, the Princess was now old enough to learn not only the skills of leadership but how to use the pendant to keep her people healthy and happy."

Daria started to fidget.

"And now my gift to you," Ian said, "is that very same pendant." He handed her the silver and blue box.

Daria opened it. She admitted to herself that it was more fun to know what she was about to unwrap than if her father had presented the gift without the elaborate introduction. After all she had already seen the key — the very day her father found it, and although she had suspected its identity when she first saw it, she had dismissed the thought.

The key was strung on a silver chain. Daria fastened it around her neck, adding it to the collection of necklaces already there. She thanked her father and went to hug him. Then the telephone rang. Ian kissed his daughter on the forehead and got up to answer the phone.

It was his mother, Sarah, and she was insisting that she speak with him.

"This will take a few minutes, Honeycakes," her father said while cupping the receiver.

"Dad," Daria whispered forcefully. "Don't call me Honeycakes anymore. I'm too old for that."

Ian nodded and suggested that she go down to the creek in back of their home. After his phone call he would meet her there and take a walk with her in the woods. "There's a lot more about that key that I need to share with you … now that you're twelve," he added and winked.

Daria went outside.

Their large back yard sloped gently downhill for about a hundred yards to a creek with an arched wooden bridge. The bridge led to a meadow and then a few wooded acres where her grandfather had blazed trails, shown her how to make shelters from fallen tree branches, and imparted other scouting skills. The blanket of late summer wildflowers had turned the meadow into a fairyland, and Daria intended to pick a huge bouquet for the dinner table.

Soon she heard the dogs barking their usual greeting to visitors. Daria wondered who it might be, but she didn't particularly care to stop playing to find out. Her grandparents weren't scheduled to arrive until later that afternoon.

The dogs barked for what seemed an unusually long time. Then the barking turned to shrieks and abruptly fell silent. Alarmed, Daria ran toward the house. Halfway up the back yard she heard shouting from the open windows.

"No. I don't know anything about a key!" her father was saying loudly. Was he intending for her to hear him, she wondered? "No, I don't have this object you speak of. I lost everything when I fell into the Nile." More shouting. But the other voices were muffled. "Give me your phone number; I'll contact you if I hear anything about it," Ian said.

Terrified, Daria leaned against the trunk of the oak tree that shaded their yard and supported her rope swing. For comfort, she clenched the key her father had just given her.

Soon she could no longer hear her father's voice, only the

sound of furniture being thrown, bookcases falling, and glass shattering. She yearned to run inside the house, but her legs felt frozen in place.

What seemed like hours finally passed. Daria heard a car screech as it sped away down the driveway and skid as it turned onto the street.

Daria emptied her stomach by the tree. Too shocked to cry and her throat too tight to call out, she inched her way toward the house. None of their dogs came to greet her. Inside, the silence hung in air too thick to breathe. Daria crept slowly, step after labored step, into her father's office. Her heart pounded so loudly that she could hear nothing else. Instinctively, she knew what had happened but fought her knowing with every piece of logic she could conjure in hopes of creating any other reality than the one she knew had unfolded.

When she stood at the office doorway she saw her father sprawled on the floor.

Dazed, she knelt beside him and touched his hair.

"Dad?" she said quietly. "Hey, Dad?"

She nudged his shoulder. "Daddy, wake up. It's me, Daria. You said we'd go for a walk."

Ian didn't answer.

Daria stroked his cheek. "Daddy?" His skin had lost its warmth. Daria shuddered. She felt lost being unable to wake him. An emptiness overcame her stronger than the sum of a thousand good-byes. Her entire body seemed hollow, as though her guts had been carved out. Her heart ached with uncommon pain.

She and her father had often talked about the possibility of a heaven and of life after death. But Daria doubted it because nothing had happened despite all her attempts to dream of her mother or inwardly communicate with her. It was as though her mother never existed. Now her father must be equally gone. He was simply, immediately, and completely evaporated from her life, and so was his love. Never again would he cheer her up or talk to her about her dreams. Never again would she bask in his embrace.

The murderers had overturned every piece of furniture, smashed every lamp, tore down every picture, and spilled the contents of every drawer across the room. Every book was thrown onto the floor and every pillow had been slashed. Not to mention what they had done to her father. The police never found out who did it or why. There had been no suspects and no motives. The assailants left not a single fingerprint and no clues as to why they'd been there or what they were looking for.

Later Daria would brutalize herself with questions such as, "How could anyone do such a thing?" "Why single out my father?" And "Why me?" Now Daria desperately tried to sort through the experience. She touched the key her father had just given her. It symbolized everything about him — his lifelong goals and dreams as well as his love. Now that he was gone, none of these things existed anymore and she didn't want to be reminded of them. She carefully righted the waste basket by her father's desk, and put the key inside it.

Then she sat down on the edge of a wingback chair, stared into nothing, and let her mind go numb. Time passed. The only movement in the room was a trickle of her father's blood that slowly inched toward her.

When her grandparents finally arrived for her birthday dinner, they knew immediately something terrible had happened. Desperately they ran through the house, calling for Daria and Ian without getting an answer. Then they entered Ian's office and stopped at the horrific scene before them.

Sarah ran to her son and grasped his face between her hands. He was gone. She closed his eyelids. Then she scanned the room to surmise what might have happened.

Meanwhile, David scooped Daria into his arms. He sat on the wingback chair, held her tightly on his lap, and stroked her head. Daria was still in shock and remained silent.

"It will be alright," David kept saying as he rocked her back and forth.

Sarah repeated something different. "Daria, where's the key?"

Daria couldn't – or wouldn't – answer.

Sarah noticed the waste basket in place among the mess and retrieved the object that Ian had told her about that very morning. Sarah had called to tell him about her premonitions, but Ian had wanted to talk instead and dutifully Sarah listened to her son. Ian shared with her a dream in which he stood atop a large pyramid. In the dream, it was essential to help Daria climb up the pyramid to stand beside him as soon as possible. This meant giving her the key, which he did, and then he fell off the pyramid. More correctly, he began to simply hover beside it. Ian felt it meant he should give the Key to the Capstone to Daria for her birthday the next day or else something terrible would happen. Of course, by sharing the dream with his mother, he also had to tell her about the key and what it might mean for Daria. He wasn't surprised that she took the information in stride. After all, she had supported him emotionally and financially in his quest to dig for fabled tunnels at Giza. She, more than anyone, understood him as well as his ambition and his need to fulfill it.

Now Sarah stood amidst the chaos in her son's office, thinking about a nearly identical dream she'd had her first night in Cairo. In her dream, Ian had fallen off a mountaintop. She had interpreted this as a portent of his possible death. To her horror, her dream had come true.

Sarah decided to hide the key and give it back to Daria later, when Daria had put enough of the trauma behind her. It was what her son would have wanted. One day, she knew Daria would want it as a keepsake.

Sarah called 911 for the police. She gave Daria a hug, and took a seat in the chair next to the one now occupied by David and Daria. Then she buried her face in her hands and wept.

Finally, in the comfort of her grandfather's arms, Daria also started to cry. Uncontrollable sobs, too big for her young body, wrenched themselves out. They were sobs that emerged from the deepest part of her and shook her every limb. They were sobs that lasted for hours and could have continued but for the temporary peace bestowed by one of Sarah's valium.

Part Two – The Capstone

Andrews Air Force Base,
Connecticut, Egypt, Antarctica

January 22,
September 6th – 14th

13.

Twenty-five years later. Wednesday, January 22nd.

It was a frosty morning when Tomas Sebastian Seymour drove his Chevrolet Blazer from his hotel through a foot of snow to Andrews Air Force Base, located in Maryland, twelve miles east of Washington D.C. They'd never had snow like this before. As a native of Maine and a resident of Boston, Massachusetts, Tom was accustomed to driving in foul weather but was thankful to be alone on the roads.

When he finally reached the gate of the base, he told the guard about his appointment with General Robert P. Taylor, USAF. The guard, who seemed naturally suspicious, asked Tom for his driver's license. Then he disappeared inside the gatehouse to make a phone call to verify Tom's claim.

A minute later the guard returned with a more welcoming demeanor. "The general is waiting for you," he said. He gave Tom his license back, plus a visitor's pass and directions to the 89th Airlift Wing, where Taylor had his office. "Have a good day, Sir," the soldier said, and Tom forged ahead.

He parked in front of a large red brick building. Two rows of flag poles extended from the building entrance to the main road. One flag for each State, Tom figured, though no flags were flying that day. He trudged through the snow and entered the building.

An officer approached him. "Mr. Tomas Seymour?"

"Yes."

"This way, please."

The officer took Tom's coat, and handed it off to someone else. Then he escorted Tom through practically empty hallways to the general's office. The snow had kept almost everyone home. Nobody was sitting behind the secretary's desk. The officer knocked on the general's door, waited for a reply, and then entered.

"Tomas Seymour to see you, Sir," he said.

"Have him come in," Tom overheard the general say.

"Be brief," the officer advised Tom.

Tom walked into the spacious, wood paneled office, as the officer closed the door. General Taylor was sitting behind his desk.

"Thank you for taking the time to see me," Tom said.

Taylor looked up and did a double-take. Tom looked almost identical to his father, Carlos Seymour, who had been Taylor's closest friend. Carlos' father had been British, his mother and his wife both from Columbia. Tom's Latino heritage dominated his features. But the shape of Tom's lean frame, his strong, square chin, and that soft expression in his brown eyes that couldn't hide an inquisitive nature—these traits especially reminded Taylor of the man who had died to save his life while on a mission in Indonesia. When Taylor had received Tom's phone call, he was overcome with memories and gratitude. The least he could do was to meet his buddy's son and hear what Tom had to say.

Taylor stood and shook Tom's hand heartily. "It is a pleasure," he said. "Your father was a good friend." His voice was loud and bold, his handshake confident and strong.

"Yes, Sir," Tom replied. He remembered little of his father, as Carlos had died when Tom was just a boy.

"What can I do for you, young man?"

"I'd like to show you something, Sir, if I may."

He handed the general an 8" x 10" photograph of a ten-foot square hole in a patch of snow. A depth-pole inserted in the shaft measured fifteen feet deep.

"I call it *ice-melt technology*," Tom said. "The photo shows a test I did near Moosehead Lake in Maine." Then Tom put a thick file of his research on Taylor's desk. It included sketches, schematics, and mathematical formulas.

Taylor flipped through the pages before him. Meanwhile,

Tom tried to sell his idea.

"Sir, ice-melt technology will give the U.S. military an enormous power over nature. It can be used to build and maintain clear runways in arctic regions, keep airports open in winter, melt rivers, and unblock frozen shipping lanes. We would be able to develop oil and mineral reserves presently out of reach beneath glacial terrain. And if comets are really made of ice, we might even be able to modify the technology to neutralize ones that threaten earth."

Taylor kept on reading.

Tom continued, "I think you might be particularly interested in the fact that ice-melt technology can be used to create missile shafts. Imagine being able to hide missiles inside glaciers in the strategic Caucasus Mountains north of Iraq, or in the Hindu Kush Mountains in northern Afghanistan, or even in the Himalayas of northern India. In one night, we could secretly melt a shaft inside a glacier without the hassle of carving out rock. A helicopter could bring in the missiles, and a small group of special ops could install them. The shaft's icy walls would hold the missile's supports just as well as rock ..."

Tom stopped speaking as Taylor closed the file. "Now why would the U.S. military want to hide missiles?" Taylor asked.

"It's just a thought."

Taylor leaned back in his chair. "I'm impressed with your research."

"Thank you, Sir."

"Tell me, Mr. Seymour, what do you have in mind?"

"I'm offering you the technology, if I can test it here." He placed a three-by-five card on Taylor's desk, upon which he had written: 81°52'05" S.; 111°18'10" W.

Taylor read the card. "Eighty-one degrees, 52 minutes, 5 seconds, South; 111 degrees, 18 minutes, 10 seconds, West. These are southern coordinates."

"In Lesser Antarctica, Sir." Tom pulled out a map of Antarctica with a red dot on the proposed melt site. "On land between the Ross and Ronne Ice Shelves."

"Why here?"

"Begging your pardon, Sir, I'd rather not say." He doubted Taylor would believe him anyway.

"I'd rather you would."

Tom hesitated. One hard lesson he had learned was to keep quiet about his unusual experiences. Yet Tom had to take the risk. General Taylor was the only person he knew with the authority to help him.

"It was a repetitive dream-like vision," Tom explained. "The numbers and letters came over and over again in a sequence: 81, 52, 5, S, 111, 18, 10, W, starting when I was a kid. I had episodes at least once a month where they continually flashed onto the screen of my mind until one day, about twenty-five years ago; I realized they were geographical coordinates. Then the experiences stopped."

"And you want to melt ice there."

"I believe we might find something extremely valuable at those coordinates."

"Like?"

Tom hesitated again. "They say that if you read about a topic before you go to bed and ask to know more about it just before you fall asleep, then you'll get a higher or clearer understanding of it in the dream state."

"And …"

"Well, Sir, before bed one night I had been reading a book about …" Tom cleared his throat, "a lost civilization."

Taylor's expression didn't change.

"I wanted to learn the truth."

"Did you?"

"I dreamed I was pouring white-hot light onto an ice field. The ice began to melt. Then something important was unburied, but I don't remember what. When I woke up, I knew what the hot light was and how to make it. It's as if the technology was downloaded into my brain, though it has taken me years to perfect it."

"You think melting on these coordinates will reveal some ancient civilization."

"Yes, Sir."

"Sounds improbable."

Tom noted how Taylor's tone of voice had remained un-changed the entire conversation. Taylor sounded neither sarcastic nor doubtful. They could have been talking about the weather.

"Are you aware of the Treaty of Antarctica?" Taylor asked. "Wouldn't melting a hole on your coordinates be a violation?"

"I'm aware of the Treaty," Tom replied. "A scientific experi-ment would not be a violation. We won't disrupt the ecology, pollute the air, or leave anything behind. However, the treaty re-quires experiments and test results to be shared with the other thirty-nine nations who have signed it. In fact, they have the right to inspect our experiment at any time. So, if you want to keep this secret, well, we can be in and out in a matter of days. When the melt is complete, a small blast of dynamite will collapse the shaft. A few windy days later, the drifting snow will cover our tracks and nobody will ever know we were there."

"You've thought through all the details." Taylor tapped Tom's file of papers.

"I've done my best, Sir."

They shared a few comments about the snow, and then their meeting ended. Tom thanked the general for his time, doubting they would ever see each other again.

Meanwhile, General Taylor made sure the U.S. Military gave Tom's project top priority. They had been secretly working on ice-melt technology for years without success. Taylor wasn't about to discount potentially viable information—no matter if the source was dreams or hobgoblins.

14.

Later that year on Saturday, September 6, just past midnight.

Daria McHenry slept alone in her apartment. She occupied the third floor of a large, well-kept Victorian home in New Haven, Connecticut, near Yale University, where she worked. Her sleep was fitful, and for the first time in years, she began to dream. It was a dream so vivid that its details impressed themselves upon her mind's eye as though she were watching a movie.

In the dream, a man named Commander Evans entered the control room of a U.S. naval submarine and climbed into his seat. They'd been cruising the mid-Atlantic when Evans received orders to investigate a nearby anomaly. A satellite had picked up odd signals coming from the ocean floor near the Cape Verde Islands, off the west coast of Africa. Evans was ordered to identify the source of those signals.

Fast, quiet, and efficient, the submarine was now crisscrossing the area that corresponded to the quadrangle of coordinates the commander had been given.

"Maier," Evans said, addressing his sonar man. "Report."

"There are no ships or submarines in our vicinity, Sir." Had they been there, the sub's complement of advanced sensors and passive sonar could give their precise locations. "We're alone, Sir."

Minutes passed.

"Sir," Maier called out. "I'm picking up a large congregation of biologicals 150 feet ahead."

Evans stroked the stubble that was adding texture to his face. Biologicals could be anything from whales to schools of shrimp.

They usually fled from submarines, yet something was attracting them. Maybe it was the source of the signals? Weren't marine life attracted to certain frequencies? Since the fish weren't fleeing his boat, whatever had caught their attention must certainly be compelling.

Evans decided to enable the Low Frequency Active (LFA) sonar. LFA sonar would return as echoes, which would create an accurate picture of whatever was attracting the fish. However, LFA would emit sound comparable to a twin engine fighter jet at takeoff—loud enough to kill any fish that didn't move out of the way.

Daria, still deeply asleep, began to toss and turn. "Don't turn on the sonar," she wanted to warn the commander.

"Maier," Evans said, "we need to get a picture of this thing. Enable LFA."

"No." Daria said aloud in her sleep.

"Enable LFA, aye-aye, Sir," Maier replied.

Suddenly, the submarine shook violently.

Evans signaled red alert. All sailors on board raced to their battle stations.

"Shut down the LFA!" Evans shouted.

"LFA shut down, aye."

Then, all was quiet. Officers from every quarter relayed damage reports. Repairs would be complete within the hour.

"Mr. Daniels," Evans addressed his officer of the deck. "What hit us?"

"Unconfirmed, Sir. But it wasn't a torpedo."

"Maier?"

"I'm picking up a spherical shape, Sir, approximately three feet in diameter, thirty feet ahead."

"Quartermaster, give me a visual," Evans said.

"Aye, Sir."

Evans turned to a screen that lowered from the ceiling in front of them. Their sub was equipped with direct-feed video. When combined with high-intensity blue-green floodlights, they could see the ocean floor in all directions. Conditions today were clear. To the left and right of the sub, nothing but silt and a few scattered rocks carpeted the ocean floor.

"Give me the forward camera."

"Forward camera, aye, Sir."

The quartermaster repeatedly pushed the button that should have turned on the forward camera. To his frustration, it had been damaged. They were unable to see what lay directly in front of them.

"Forward camera not functioning, Sir."

"Re-enable the sonar."

"No! Don't!" the sleeping Daria called out. "The sonar will wake up the power center!"

"Enable LFA, aye, Sir."

The sub shook once again. This time, more intensely.

"LFA off!" Evans ordered.

"LFA off, aye."

Again the sub quieted.

"Maier, find out what's hitting us and where it is. Daniels, give me a course to pass the sphere, so we can pick it up on the starboard camera."

"Aye, Sir," Daniels replied. "Recommend 045 to port, Sir."

"Make it so."

"Helmsman, come left to 045," said Daniels.

"Left 045, aye."

The sub shifted its course. Evans kept his eyes on the starboard camera, and soon the sphere came into view.

"What the hell is that?"

The men on his bridge looked up at the screen in disbelief. It looked like a ball of pulsing light now ten feet in diameter. Fish carcasses were scattered around it.

"Maier?"

"It is a sphere, Sir," he confirmed, viewing the graphic that the echo portrayed on his monitor. "It's grown since we first spotted it. I think it's responding to the sonar."

"Full stop," Evans ordered.

"Full stop, aye."

Over the next few minutes the orb quieted and so appeared less bright and much smaller. It now looked like a translucent, highly lustrous pearl — three feet in diameter once again.

Evans wanted to be sure the sphere was in fact responding to the sonar and was indeed the source of the blasts that were shaking them. "Reactivate LFA for one second."

"One second, aye."

Evans watched the sphere brighten and finally decided they should leave it alone. They had its precise coordinates as well as a visual. What it was and who put it there could be worked out later.

But instead of calming as it had done before, this time the sphere continued to grow.

The sub trembled.

"Sonar off!" Evans ordered.

"It is off, Sir."

"Get us out of here. Now!" Evans shouted.

The sub's engines revved.

The commander watched the sphere grow brighter still. The submarine shook until its hull could no longer handle the growing vibrations. Finally, it broke.

The sphere shot out beams of light in many directions and also sent a pulse of energy that broke through the surface of the ocean and continued upward. It lowered local atmospheric pressure, and a hurricane was born.

15.

I n a dream that seemed profoundly real, Daria desperately tried to warn her dream characters of their impending doom. Her covers, soaked with sweat, were twisted around her strong and slender limbs. Her shoulder-length brown hair was a tangled mess upon her pillow.

Don't activate the sonar!

Then, in a blast of light, the dream was over.

Daria sprang out of bed and turned on the lamp. Her heart pounded against her chest, and for comfort, she grasped the pendants hanging around her neck. In addition to the ones she'd worn as a child, her collection now included an amethyst crystal that her best girlfriend, Carol, had given her; a purple velvet pouch that contained a small vial of bergamot oil to inhale when she got stressed out; and a wooden leaf that had been a gift from an old boyfriend—Daria wasn't sure why she'd kept it, other than she really liked the exquisite carving. Finally, Daria also wore a silver pendant that her father had given her on her twelfth birthday. The pendant was a beautiful arrangement of disks and curved metal wire. It was Daria's most precious possession.

"It was just a dream," she repeated to herself. "Just a stupid dream."

Daria sat down on the edge of her bed and wrapped herself with her blanket. She was still shaking. In an attempt to replace the haunting underwater images with those of the real world, she looked around her wallpapered bedroom. The blue easy-chair in the corner was buried under clothing. Her bookcases were stacked with books, and her glass shelves lined with rollerblading trophies. Two pairs of rollerblades hung beside them. A large poster of the Pyramids of Giza dominated the wall between two lace-curtained windows. Her desk was covered in multiple piles of paperwork. The wall above her desk held her framed diplomas, a bachelor's degree in linguistics from the University of Connecticut, a master's in Egyptian studies and a doctorate in foreign language, both from Yale University. She was one of the youngest full professors at Yale, and her reputation for deciphering ancient languages was growing worldwide. A recent article about her in *Archeology Today* magazine, a copy of which was mounted in another frame, pictured her inside the Pyramid of Unas, in Saqqara, Egypt, standing in front of hieroglyphs called the *Pyramid Texts*. She had made groundbreaking progress finding new meaning in them.

By now her heart was beating normally. She checked the clock. It was 4:30 A.M. on Saturday. If she got up now she could get a head start on her day. She'd spend the morning in her Yale office reading the field study protocol she'd asked her graduate students to write before their upcoming trip to Saqqara, Egypt. Then she'd take an hour to practice rollerblading and finish grading their papers either that night or Sunday. Sometime that weekend she also had to pack and take care of last minute details, as she was leaving on Monday for Cairo and would meet her grad students at Saqqara on Wednesday.

Her pendants were the last thing she removed before bathing and the first thing she put back on afterward. She donned a terrycloth bathrobe and went to make some coffee. While it was brewing, she fit a few pieces into a 3,000-piece jigsaw puzzle that covered her dining table. Her grandparents, who had raised her through her teen years, had taught her to find joy and relaxation in jigsaw puzzles. While studying the pieces, Daria could let her mind wander to the problems that faced her without her emotions clouding her judgment. This time, the nightmare was on her mind. She hadn't remembered a dream since she was a kid.

"What do you think it means, Honeycakes?" She could almost hear her father's voice. "Dreams can be a source of truth," he would insist.

The memory was bittersweet. Even though Daria wore the

pendant he'd given her, she coped with losing her father by doing her best to forget him and anything that reminded her of him, such as the habit of remembering dreams. Now that a dream had crept in, she could feel the pain, sadness, and separation of unresolved grief encroaching upon her.

"No," Daria admonished herself. Her father was gone. It would do no good to start thinking about him and grieving all over again.

Yet the image of the luminous sphere nagged at her.

What would Sigmund Freud, the father of psychoanalysis, have said about it? Daria thought he'd be far more interested in the broken submarine. He would have called it a phallic symbol and told her it represented repressed sexual desires. Daria hadn't dated since her divorce two years ago, but was too engrossed in her work to care. On the other hand, Freud's student, Carl Jung, didn't believe dreams were attempts to conceal one's feelings, but windows to them. He'd probably tell her that something suppressed and hidden—like the submarine—was about to be broken open. A new light would shine in her life.

Bunk. Bunk to them both.

Daria was convinced that dreams were simply the result of nervous system chemicals activating the brain. Dream images were the mind's response to those chemicals as it processed a storehouse of the previous day's activities and experiences.

Daria forced her mind to forget the dream and think instead about her upcoming day.

She stepped onto her roof-top porch to check the weather and decide what to wear. The air felt warm, moist, and soft. Then she went back inside, poured herself some coffee, and turned on the Weather Channel. The news confirmed it: the weather would be hot and humid again today. The Eastern seaboard was clear and the Atlantic was generally quiet—except for a tropical depression west of the Cape Verde Islands that had in the past hour been upgraded to a tropical storm and officially named Ingrid.

16.

Later that day …

Tomas Seymour had been elated when he heard that General Taylor approved his request to conduct his ice-melt experiment in Antarctica at the coordinates Tom had specified. Today, he was about to meet Taylor again at Andrews Air Force Base for a debriefing before his long journey to Antarctica to enable the experiment.

General Taylor was looking forward to seeing Tom again. He had some questions to ask him.

The two men shook hands and sat down.

"We've built your equipment per your specifications," Taylor said. "Your diagrams and formulas were quite clear."

"Thank you, Sir." Tom knew everything would be state of the art. A far cry from the homemade contraptions he'd made previously with materials begged for and borrowed. He couldn't wait to see what the military's scientists had put together.

"You withheld one or two minor procedures," Taylor continued.

"I didn't want anyone to see the ice disappear without me."

"But you have them."

"Yes, Sir."

Taylor's men were close to figuring them out anyway, but he didn't want them to spend the time, or effort, in duplicating what Tom could provide. Plus, he had other reasons for ensuring Tom's presence on the mission.

"Since our last visit I have looked into the writings of Plato," Taylor announced.

"Plato?" Tom tried to sound naïve.

"Plato. The famous Greek philosopher, who gave us the only written records of a lost ancient civilization — and it wasn't even a firsthand account. The Greek statesman, Solon, supposedly learned about Atlantis on a visit to Egypt, and then wrote about it in an epic poem, *Atlantikos*. He died before finishing it."

Inwardly, Tom sighed with relief. The skeptic-alarming word *Atlantis* had finally been uttered, and it hadn't been by him. He dropped his guard.

Taylor again referred to his notes. "About 150 years later, around 360 B.C., Solon's manuscript was given to Plato, who rewrote it into two dialogues, the *Timaeus* and *Critias*. These were also unfinished. I find it curious that people don't seem to want to accept the story as fiction."

"With all due respect, Sir, I've read that in 260 B.C., a follower of Plato, called Krantor, wanted to validate the legend of Atlantis. He went to the Temple of Neith at Sais, Egypt, where Solon had learned about it. Krantor found the original tablets, which confirmed Plato's account in every detail."

"Still," Taylor said, "after more than 2000 years, why do you think people are still fascinated by Atlantis when it's a very unlikely probability it ever existed."

"Actually, Sir, the interest has never waned. Plato's *Timaeus* was translated by the Roman Cicero, who was born about a hundred years B.C. Then, around 360 A.D. a Christian by the name of Calcidius translated it again into Latin. What's interesting about this translation is that it was one of only a few works on classical philosophy and the only work of Plato available to Latin readers of the middle ages. These translations, among others, were published and republished in the 1500's and 1600's.

"There was also a renewed interest when America was discovered," Tom said. "In the *Timaeus*, Plato seems to suggest that Atlantis is an 'opposite continent.' A sixteenth-century explorer and cartographer, Francisco Lopez de Gomara, believed that America was this opposite continent. As a European, of course, he assumed the lost continent would be opposite of Europe."

"Has any serious research been done?" Taylor asked.

"The first relatively recent scholar to investigate Atlantis was Athanasius Kircher, a German who was born in the early 1600's. He was a polymath who was, by the way, among the first to study Egyptian hieroglyphs. His interest in Atlantis may have been inspired by a novel written by Francis Bacon in 1629 called, *The New Atlantis*.

"Anyway, Kircher was initially skeptical until he began collecting mythic traditions of a great flood from cultures around the world. His search led him to the Vatican Library where he found a well-preserved map – apparently of Atlantis. It exists to this day because Kircher copied it into his book, *The Subterranean World*."

"A map."

"Yes, Sir."

"The next significant work on Atlantis was done by the American, Ignatius Donnelly. He wrote *Atlantis: The Antediluvian World* in 1882. It was an instant hit both here and overseas. Donnelly's book set the compass for real and serious research. He compiled a huge amount of well-observed similarities of language, culture, architecture, religion, customs, symbols, and legends among people in Europe and the Americas. His conclusion was that these similarities could only be possible by the existence of a common background.

"And today, many authors and scientists are piecing together even more evidence of an ancient high civilization."

"Tell me about Solon," Taylor said.

"In his time," Tom replied, "Solon was considered one of the seven wisest of all men. According to his biographer, the Roman historian, Plutarch, Solon visited Egypt and spent time studying and discussing philosophy with two of Egypt's highest priests."

Taylor leafed through some papers on his desk. "In the *Timaeus*, one of the Egyptian priests says that Solon's city was founded a thousand years before his own. And that his city's constitution was eight thousand years old. Moreover," Taylor began to read aloud, and Tom recognized immediately it was an excerpt from the *Timaeus*. "Thereupon one of the priests, who was of a very great age, said: O Solon, Solon, you Hellenes are never anything but children, and there is not an old man among you. Solon in return asked him what he meant. I mean to say, he replied, that in mind you are all young; there is no old opinion handed down among you by ancient tradition, nor any science which is hoary with age."

"It suggests a high civilization existed long before the Greek's," Tom said, speaking boldly.

Taylor was silent for a moment.

"Plato also seems to describe a precise location for Atlantis." Taylor read aloud again from the *Timaeus*. "There was an island situated in front of the straits which are by you called the Pillars of Heracles; the island was larger than Libya and Asia put together, and was the way to other islands, and from these you might pass to the whole of the opposite continent which surrounded the true ocean, for this sea which is within the Straits of Heracles is only a harbor, having a narrow entrance, but that other is a real sea, and the surrounding land may be most truly called a boundless continent."

"To the Greeks, Libya and Asia referred to North Africa and the Middle East," Tom said.

"That would curtail its size," Taylor said. "The 'Pillars of Heracles' clearly refer to the 'narrow entrance' at the straits of Gibraltar, and the Mediterranean Sea is clearly a harbor compared to the Atlantic Ocean. The islands mentioned could be the Canaries, the Azores, or even the Bahamas."

Tom interjected, "To the ancient Greeks, the Pillars of Heracles had another meaning besides its geographical one. It also referred to a psychological barrier between the known world and the unknown."

Taylor continued, "The 'opposite continent' is clearly the Americas. But here Plato's description fails and becomes confusing. The Americas do not surround 'the true ocean.' If anything, the Atlantic and Pacific surround the Americas. Furthermore, it's obvious Atlantis was located somewhere in the Atlantic, but geologic maps of the ocean floor prove that's impossible."

Tom wanted to give Taylor another viewpoint of Plato's

geographic location for Atlantis, but Taylor changed the subject.

"By the way, Tom, have you ever read *Nature* magazine?"

"No, Sir, why do you ask?"

"I've done some research on your coordinates. They were mentioned in the February 1993 issue of *Nature* magazine." Taylor pulled a copy of the article from a folder on his desk. "The authors of the article say they found at those exact coordinates, and I quote, 'strikingly circular features' around what they believed to be a volcano with a unique magnetic signature."

Tom shifted uncomfortably in his chair. How could he explain the capital city of Atlantis had supposedly been encircled by metal walls, which might account for the unique magnetism that the authors had found?

"We've employed ICESat to map your coordinates," the general said.

"ICESat?"

"It's a satellite that works like radar but uses laser technology to measure ice sheet thickness. We've used its data to get a good picture of the land at your melt site. Seems you've pinpointed what appears to be a mountaintop."

"Appears to be?"

"It has a unique magnetic signature and is surrounded by strikingly circular features," Taylor said. Then he looked Tom in the eye and added, "When you return, I want you to tell me exactly, in detail, everything you find when you reach the surface. I want a personal report."

"Yes, Sir."

Taylor removed a thick blue file from his desk, and handed it to Tom. It was stamped *Top Secret*.

Taylor explained, "Inside you'll find the mission itinerary, information about Antarctica and extreme cold weather survival, camp rules and regulations, plus a list of what we expect of you and your ice-melt technology. Do you have any questions?"

"No, Sir."

"If any come up, they're probably answered in that file," Taylor said.

"Thank you, Sir."

"Colonel Bretton Greer will be your commanding officer at the Antarctic station. No one, including Greer, expects you'll find anything beneath the ice but bare earth. But I've given him explicit orders to obtain a sample of whatever you uncover."

"I understand."

"Someone is waiting outside my office right now who will escort you to the terminal where you will board your first flight."

Taylor stood. Tom did too, and the two men shook hands once again.

"Good luck," Taylor added.

17.

Sunday, September 7th.

Omar Fayed entered his father's penthouse, which overlooked the Nile River and the city of Cairo. Faoud Fayed's apartment was richly and colorfully decorated with Bedouin rugs and tapestries, Egyptian statues and objects d'art on lighted pedestals, plus palm trees and potted flowering hibiscus. Instead of furniture, the spacious living area had oversized pillows neatly arranged in a square on the central carpet.

"Son?" Faoud Fayed called.

"Yes, Father," answered Omar. He was a good-looking thirty-something, with dark eyes and an easy smile that was topped with a neatly trimmed mustache. Today, he was wearing khaki pants and a fine silk orange shirt that revealed his well-defined chest and shoulders. Omar entered the dining room, which, unlike the living room, was distinctly European. A long mahogany table surrounded by a dozen matching chairs dominated the room. A large crystal chandelier hung from the frescoed ceiling and a red and gold silk Afghani rug covered the wood floor. To his left, a large, elaborately carved breakfront held Waterford glassware, Swarovski crystal, and sets of English china.

Faoud Fayed sat at the head of the table facing the entrance to the living room. His thick white hair matched the white linen suit he wore daily like a uniform. A cigar hung from the side of his mouth, and he puffed on it with every other breath.

Omar went over to his father and received a brief but warm embrace. Omar was Fayed's only son, and Fayed had high expectations for him, which Omar routinely fulfilled. Fayed was driven by ambition, yet unlike most other men he knew, he spent quality time with his son and seven daughters. They were most important in his life—except for one thing.

"Sit down, my son," Fayed said. "We have matters to discuss."

"Yes, Father."

"I have told you about the Navubala." Fayed spoke with authority.

"Yes, Sir," Omar replied. "It is the key to the Great Pyramid and has been lost for millennia."

"No longer," Fayed announced. "Many years ago an archeologist named Ian McHenry brought me an item that shone like polished silver. Yet, it was too thin, lustrous, and rigid to be silver. It was about three inches long and made of curved wire and disks arranged in a precise geometry."

Omar pretended this was news, yet he probably knew more about the ancient Key to the Capstone than his father did. An old Bedouin sage named Mikta had befriended Omar years ago. Mikta had caught the boy's attention with tales of ancient Egypt. Omar had proved worthy of keeping secrets, so Mikta had spoken freely of his country's mysterious past.

"And you knew this to be the Navubala?" Omar asked, feigning awe and curiosity.

"Have you ever held a battery in your hand and felt its

energy?" Fayed said. His fingers gripped the air as he remembered the moment when Ian had brought the key to his office and Fayed had held it in his own hands. "The energy of the Navubala was even more palpable. It exhilarates and enlightens, and I wanted it."

Fayed sat back and waved his cigar. "McHenry refused to sell it. Of course I saw that as no obstacle. When he left my office, I had my men follow him. Unfortunately, they became aggressive when McHenry continued to evade them on their own back streets. Others joined the chase and almost cornered him," Fayed puffed hard and blew a giant smoke circle.

"Then he jumped into the backseat of a tourist's motorcar. We thought we'd lost him," he continued. "Until we spotted him trying to get away on a small yacht. It was mayhem. Boats began chasing boats, and most of the pursuers joined the melee for the fun of it with no knowledge of the objective. Not surprisingly, McHenry's boat crashed and erupted into flames."

He paused. "Only a few Egyptian pounds bought information that a fisherman had pulled two Americans from the Nile that very day."

"McHenry survived." Omar said.

"Not for long." Fayed puffed hard.

"I heard he died at home of sudden heart failure," Omar said quietly, suddenly realizing that wasn't what had happened.

"McHenry led us to believe the key was lost when he leapt into the Nile," Fayed said. "Of course, we didn't believe him. But we could find no trace of it."

He tossed a copy of *Archeology Today* across the table toward Omar. "This appeared not long ago."

Omar opened the magazine to a bookmarked page, where he found an article written by Dr. Daria McHenry, including a photograph of her wearing what appeared to be the Navubala around her neck. It was partially hidden by other pendants she wore, so it was hard to positively identify. Fayed also provided a close-up of the printed photograph, which zeroed in on the woman's pendants. The close-up showed the key more clearly.

"McHenry gave the Navubala to his daughter," Fayed said. "She wasn't there when we visited him. Otherwise ..."

Omar fought with his self-control. "Otherwise, what?" he wanted to say. But he kept his cool. It would do no good to reveal his differences with his father now. Omar remained calm and scanned the article. "It says she is coming soon to Egypt with a group of students," he said.

"They are scheduled to arrive in Cairo this Wednesday," Fayed said. "I will have men at the airport. They are instructed to follow her to her hotel, and then call you with her room number. I want you to obtain the key with minimal trouble. The police are demanding higher and higher prices for their cooperation," he complained. "I want it quiet."

"Pardon me, Sir?"

Fayed leaned over the table. "I want you to respectfully relieve the McHenry daughter of her burden. Do it in a way that she will not regret, and if necessary, not remember."

"Father, what can the Navubala give you that you don't already have?"

Fayed laughed.

"It is the destiny of the key-bearer to find the capstone," Fayed explained. "When I find the capstone, I will be able to awaken the powers of the pyramids and know their secrets. Can you imagine that, my boy?"

No, Omar could not. Some secrets were best kept hidden, especially from men like his father. Over the centuries, thousands had died in search of the key. Omar didn't want an innocent woman to be one of them.

"I understand," Omar said.

"Good." Fayed replied. "Ensh Allah."

"Ensh Allah," Omar said. He thought it ironic that his father would so often and casually use a phrase meant to evoke God's will, when Fayed seemed to enjoy deciding what that will was.

Omar stayed to enjoy a meal with his father, mother, and his younger sister. Not another word was spoken about the key. Thanks to Mikta, Fayed's news about Daria and the key was old news. Mikta had also alerted Omar to the photograph in the magazine, and Omar had already sent a man to New Haven, Connecticut, where Daria lived and worked. After losing track of her all day Saturday, he found her again on Sunday morning and learned she would arrive in Egypt a day sooner than Fayed expected.

Now Omar could reach her first.

18.

Monday, September 8th.

Daria packed the last of her clothes and her cosmetic case into her duffle bag. Then she stuffed a paperback in a pocket of her loose-fitting jacket. Her wallet, passport, travel visa, e-ticket receipt, credit cards, and driver's license were tucked into a travel pouch that she wore around her waist beneath her clothing. Her sole carry-on item — only one was allowed for international travel — was a pair of rollerblades.

It was 4:00 P.M., and time to leave for the Tweed New Haven airport, where she would take a puddle jumper to Kennedy Airport in New York. At 11:00 P.M., she would board Egyptair flight 984, nonstop to Cairo.

While waiting at the airport lounge to board her plane, Daria listened to the news broadcast aired on the terminal's television monitors. An update on political tension in the Middle East was followed by the weather report. "In the past forty-eight hours, Hurricane Ingrid's wind speeds have increased remarkably, from 50 m.p.h. to 135 m.p.h.," the newscaster said. "At 10:00 P.M., less than an hour ago, it became a Category 4 hurricane. It is headed directly for the East Coast."

Daria worried that if the hurricane hit New England, her grandparents' seaside home in Stony Creek, Connecticut, would be at risk. This was the house that Daria grew up in after her father had died. A few years ago, Grandpa David had rebuilt the home to look like a miniature mansion with tall white columns on the front porch and a circular driveway. Daria's favorite addition to the home was the living room he designed with a cathedral ceiling and wall-to-wall windows that overlooked the Long Island Sound. Daria decided that if necessary, she would cut short her trip and return to help secure the house.

The flight attendant called for boarding. Daria had a window seat and shared the row with another person who took the aisle seat. She moved her wristwatch ahead to Cairo time. The flight would last over ten hours, and because she would gain time flying east through time zones, she would land at about 4:30 P.M. Tuesday.

Soon after takeoff, Daria rested her head on a pillow and leaned against the airplane window. Feeling relaxed, her mind wandered to her dream of the large, underwater sphere. She could still see the sphere with the broken submarine beside it. Oddly the picture wasn't static, as a photo in an album or like a dream memory. The sphere was pulsing with light. Without the submarine's sonar prompting it, the sphere was growing again — this time on its own.

19.

Tom arrived in Antarctica to find the military had already set up a temporary station at the coordinates he had requested. The station consisted of heavy canvas Jamesway tents, which were leftovers from the Korean War and salvaged by the National Science Foundation for temporary housing for its United States Antarctic Program (USAP) scientists and support personnel. Jamesways were made of a series of arched wood supports covered in canvas and then with a layer of Nanoprotect, a hi-tech insulating fabric. They were shaped like the inside of a railway tunnel.

Four adjoining Jamesways, attached to form the shape of an "x," housed the officers, and consisted of a computer room, kitchen, and meeting room. Another Jamesway provided dorms for Tom plus the two dozen or so soldiers who were privy to this top-secret operation. Life there was little better than an ice-fisherman's camp, but Tom didn't mind. His entire attention was on finding whatever it was that had been calling to him from beneath this ice.

Tom left the Jamesway dorm and braced himself against the Antarctic cold. Although the first day of spring was about two weeks away, the temperature could still dip to minus thirty degrees Fahrenheit. The sun was above the horizon for about eight hours a day, and daylight was increasing an impressive twenty-two minutes every twenty-four hours. Soon the sun would bless Antarctica with unending daylight.

A hundred feet from the station, Tom reached his collection of ice-melting devices. The Ice Sensitive Laser Producers, or IS-

LAPS, looked like black metallic lighthouses that stood five feet high and were anchored deeply into the snow. Each marked a corner of a one-quarter acre square. Smaller instruments, called modifiers, also black, were positioned between the ISLAPS, three to a side. Polypropylene bags that contained a dry chemical heat source had been wrapped carefully around the more sensitive components to protect them from the extreme cold. These bags had to be replaced every six to eight hours to combat the subzero winter temperatures.

Tom removed gloved hands from his fur mittens and began adjusting the primary ISLAP. Every movement of his fingers took conscious effort. He was anxious to get his experiment going before he had to go inside again to warm up.

The frigid Antarctic breeze chilled Tom despite the layers of extreme-cold-weather clothing he wore. His red Gore-tex pants and a hooded, down-filled parka covered two layers of fleece inner garments and polypropylene long johns. He wore three pairs of socks inside "bunny boots" which were large, heavy white boots lined with wool. He was glad to be growing a beard as it helped keep his face warm. It was coming in thick and black, like the hair on his head. He also wore a face mask, two fleece caps, and the hood of his parka wrapped closely around his face. The parka was bright red, so it could be seen more easily in a white out—when blowing snow reduced visibility to zero.

The mission was sanctioned by the U.S. Air Force in cooperation with the USAP. If anyone asked, they were studying the effects on the atmosphere of recent bombing in the Middle East. To avoid notice they had chosen to do the ice-melt experiment in winter, which was, because of the cold, an admittedly insane and foolish time to do field research.

Tom's job was to melt a square shaft of ice as far down as it would go. He guessed the military wanted ice-melt technology to hide missiles. Melting a shaft one-hundred feet wide was much larger than any hole they'd need for a missile silo. Tom had convinced them that these dimensions would test the limits of his technology. In reality, the hole had to be small enough that his instruments would still work, yet wide enough to uncover something significant, for he was certain they would unbury *something*. His dreams had assured him of that.

Seismic readings plus soundings from ice radar had revealed glacier depth at the test site to be about 4,593 feet, almost seven-eighths of a mile deep. Geologists had surmised this might be a volcanic peak, as it reached 2,133 feet above the surrounding land. Obviously, if the military wanted to test the full potential of Tom's work, they would have moved the experiment off the mountaintop to a place where the ice was deeper. Tom had insisted on these coordinates and miraculously General Taylor had agreed to use them.

Tom checked each of the ISLAPS one more time. He made sure they were securely anchored to the ground and aligned perfectly. He then lowered a rod from the center of each device into the snow. It would sample the ice and analyze its unique molecular makeup. Although ice is essentially frozen hydrogen and oxygen atoms, a myriad of other elements get locked within the ice's molecular structure. This makes every patch of ice distinct.

Each ISLAP would retrieve this unique molecular information from the underlying snow and then relay it to the other IS-LAPS. Working together, the ISLAPS would use this information to customize a laser. Each ISLAP would send this special laser to each of the other three ISLAPS. This would produce a phase conjugate mirror of ricocheting light, which grew in strength until a critical moment. Then, the modifiers between the ISLAPS would tag the light beams with inaudible sound waves. The modifiers would broadcast the modified beams over the entire melt field. As the ice molecules received these beams, they would respond by turning in such a way that the bonds between their atoms would break, sending hydrogen, oxygen, and whatever other elements they held directly into the atmosphere. The sublimation would be invisible. Since no heat was involved, there wouldn't even be steam.

Tom tried to imagine what would then occur. Because hydrogen and oxygen gas occupies much more space than they do when locked in ice and snow, Tom expected a strong updraft of these gases as the hole formed. This updraft might be so compelling that it could leave behind a weak vacuum that would then suck regular air back down into the shaft. The speed of these up and down drafts depended on how quickly sublimation occurred. Tom expected strong howling winds that lasted about a minute. He smiled to himself as he thought how unusual this would be.

Finally, Tom coaxed his gloved fingers, stiff with cold, to make the final alignment of the fourth ISLAP. Then he turned on the switch.

Nothing happened.

Patiently, Tom once again trudged across the snow to examine each ISLAP. "Three feet per second," he repeated to himself. This was the melt rate his calculations had predicted. He knew a logical reason could explain the ISLAPS' failure and wracked his brain trying to find it. The ISLAPS had worked perfectly when he had tested them in Maine. But the conditions there were mild compared to here and the snow a fraction as deep — although snow depth shouldn't matter, he thought. Maybe the problem lay in the relatively large size of the melt area. Tom had calibrated the ISLAPS to account for the distance between them. He decided to go inside to warm up and re-check his math. He desperately needed to thaw his fingers and face. His lips had cracked in the dry air and were bleeding, and he had lost contact with his feet.

"Seymour!" barked Colonel Greer, the commanding officer.

He couldn't have picked a worse moment, Tom thought.

Greer was a big, imposing man, who was tough and liked to prove it. He covered his gray crew-cut with only an officer's field cap beneath his parka's fur-lined hood. Only someone who truly didn't mind the cold could be comfortable like that in the subzero weather. Tom also found the colonel to be well organized, focused, and determined. He held high standards for his men and they seemed eager to comply. Greer was also a man who enjoyed his privacy and spent his free time tucked away in his office. The only personal thing about him that anyone knew about was that he was a Yankees baseball fan; the colonel kept everything else to himself.

"What the hell is holding this damn thing up?" Greer barked.

He was accompanied by his executive officer, Major Davison. Everyone at the camp liked Davison. He was a rusty-haired, freckle-faced Virginian whose good humor and light-hearted demeanor was a well appreciated contrast to Greer's sandpaper personality.

"I have to start the ISLAPS manually," Tom explained, as he started fiddling again with one of the instruments. "The remote control doesn't like the cold."

"Who does," Greer mumbled to himself. He resented this assignment in the middle of nowhere, where your coffee got cold before it filled the cup and your pee froze before it hit the latrine. Every minute without success compounded the risk of being there, Greer worried. If the international community discovered the camp, somebody would have to do some fast talking and it probably would be him. Greer had devoted his life to the U.S. Air Force, and his promotion to brigadier general would be ready for review in the next few months. Getting caught in Antarctica would not look good on his Promotion Recommendation Form. The thought increased his blood pressure, making the veins on the side of his neck bulge. He was so engrossed in his concerns that he didn't notice a perfect, one-hundred-foot square depression suddenly appear within the test area.

"Colonel, look!" Tom exclaimed.

Only a few inches of ice had disappeared.

"Three feet per second," Greer reminded him.

Tom was nevertheless elated. He also felt sorry that Greer was oblivious to how significant even a small amount of sublimation was. It meant the ISLAPS worked.

They just weren't working fast enough.

20.

D aria's first stop in the Cairo airport terminal was the currency exchange. She needed some large Egyptian pound bills plus a wad of one-pound and fifty-piastre notes and some smaller coins for baksheesh.

Daria proceeded to the baggage claim area, where she waited for her luggage. She kept her eyes down, trying to deter the many tour operators who tried to nab tourists and sell them Nile cruises or guided tours of the pyramids, the shopping district, or anywhere else the tourist wished to go — or the guides wished to take them.

One daring one accosted her anyway. "Ma'am, you want to see the Great Pyramid?" The man's eyes lowered, and she caught him staring at her chest. Men could be such jerks, she thought. Didn't they know a woman could tell? It never occurred to her that he wasn't interested in her breasts, but what lay between them. The man was transfixed by her necklaces. He then looked up with a completely different expression. Suddenly he turned and ran swiftly out of the terminal.

"That was odd," Daria said to herself, but she soon became too busy retrieving her luggage to give it a second thought. Daria then passed through customs. The officials smiled at the woman traveling alone and let her duffle bag pass with only a perfunctory palpation. Now it was time to swim through the sea of boys who fought for the opportunity to carry her duffle bag to a taxicab. Five of them managed to find some part of the bag to hold. Each of them received baksheesh.

She got in the cab and asked the driver to take her to Giza, a growing city west of Cairo where the Great Pyramid was located. Neither she nor the cab driver noticed that someone was following them. In Cairo's bumper-to-bumper traffic, it was a fact any-body could have missed.

Daria stayed at the Mena House Oberoi, where she and her father had stayed when they visited Egypt. She took a modest room that had a view of the town. Daria ate dinner at the restaurant across the street, which was always crowded with locals and offered good Egyptian food. The restaurant hadn't changed much since she'd been there last. Her memories only gingerly touched that last summer that she and her father had shared. It was too risky to look back for too long and possibly bring up unwanted pain.

Around 9:30 P.M., Daria returned to her room, oblivious to the fact that she was being followed. Jet-lagged and exhausted, she quickly bathed and went to bed.

21.

Wednesday, September 10th.

Daria awoke at dawn, got up, and dressed. She donned a pair of shorts, a dark blue t-shirt, sneakers, and a black sweater. It was a chilly sixty degrees outside, though the desert sun promised to raise the temperature significantly by mid-morning. She had an early breakfast at the hotel's famous Pyramid Café, where enormous picture windows offered diners spectacular views of the pyramids. Without realizing it, she chose a table where she and her father usually sat.

After breakfast, she walked by the hotel's newspaper stand to scan the front pages of the many international papers. Since she could read every one of them, she found it interesting to study the varying viewpoints different countries had on world events.

Hurricane Ingrid was in the news. It remained a Category 4 storm, and was still several days from landfall. One paper gave it a particularly somber spin, predicting devastating damage all along the East Coast. Daria worried about her grandparents' waterfront home, but at this point there was nothing she could do.

Daria returned to her room to freshen up and get her rollerblades. Then she went outside, sat on the hotel's front steps, and put on the skates. She surfed the hotel's long curved sidewalk, before turning right and heading toward the pyramid complex.

Although it was still early, the streets of Giza were already crowded. Daria's smooth, easy ride on her rollerblades caught attention. Not only was she an attractive woman, but the locals eyed her as though they had never seen anything like her before. The closer she got to the pyramids, the more tourists filled the crowd. Among them were people who didn't give a second thought to skaters, so Daria felt more comfortable.

Looming over the town of Giza, the monumental pyramids of Khufu, Khafra, and Menkaure sat atop a barren hill of sandy yellow desert. A well-paved road led up the hill between the pyramids to a parking lot, where the first tour buses of the day had already congregated.

It would be fun to skate the road downhill, Daria thought, and wondered how much baksheesh it might cost for the privilege. But first, she wanted to visit the Great Sphinx, which was located a short distance southeast of the pyramid of Khufu, also known as the Great Pyramid, and further down the hill.

For the best overview of the Sphinx and pyramids, Daria went to the pavilion across from the Sphinx. The pavilion served drinks and snacks and hosted the nightly *Light and Sound Show*. Daria remembered it to be an extravaganza of flashing colored floodlights and melodramatic music that served as a background, while the legend of the pyramids as the tombs of three pharaohs was told over a loudspeaker.

Despite her wheeled shoes, Daria adeptly climbed the steps to the pavilion rooftop, where a crowd of tourists were gawking at the Giza monuments and snapping pictures. Daria waited, knowing the busload of tourists would soon be off to another venue. Finally she was alone except for a handful of onlookers. It was her turn to lean against the railing, gaze at the Sphinx, and get lost in contemplation.

Something about the Sphinx seemed timeless to her. It had been carved into the bedrock and stood about seventy-two feet high; the length of its leonine body was more than twice that. Its human face had always looked so familiar—as if she had known the man whose image had been carved into that great stone. Aside from his marred face and missing nose, he could have been quite handsome. He appeared godlike, a noble protector, invincible except by time and the vandals who had scarred him—including Napoleon's army who had used the Sphinx for target practice. It certainly looked as though the Sphinx was guarding the pyramids, and that they were not randomly placed. No wonder her father had wanted to find a tangible link between them.

Daria's thoughts were interrupted by the voices of local boys swarming a fat sunburned tourist in white shorts and a flower-print shirt. They were trying to sell him postcards. The man had his hands up and was retreating backward, as though the boys were holding him at gunpoint.

"You buy. You buy," they insisted.

The poor tourist hesitated when the first boy had accosted him. Without giving the urchin a clear, "No thank you," he became instant bait.

Daria looked at the tourist. He caught her eye, and his expression begged for help.

"*Emshee! Sibooni fehali!*" Daria scolded the boys in perfect Arabic. "Go away! Leave him alone," she repeated in English.

The boys looked at her with surprise and scurried away. The man sighed with relief.

"They can be persistent," Daria explained. "Say 'No' firmly, if you don't want what they're selling. Then they'll leave you alone."

Still flustered, the man uttered a quick "thank you" and hurried away.

While Daria's attention had been on the tourist, someone leaning on the railing had been carefully eyeing her and her pendants.

"You handled that well," he said.

Daria turned to the man with the rich baritone voice. He was a tall, good-looking man, of Middle-eastern descent, in his thirties, and nicely dressed in khakis and a short-sleeved polo shirt. His oversized straw hat and the binoculars slung around his neck pegged him as a tourist.

"You speak Arabic like a Cairene," he said. The man's bright eyes looked kindly at her.

"I teach languages back in the States."

"Ah, you're American. I'm Omar Fayed, and pleased to meet you." He bowed slightly.

"Daria McHenry. Nice to meet you too."

Daria was much more attractive in person than in her photograph, Omar thought. He would look forward to getting to know her better. "Where do you teach?" he asked.

"Yale University."

"That's in New Haven, Connecticut, if my memory serves me."

Daria saw a glint of interest in his eye and turned back to the Sphinx. "That's correct," she said, wishing a cold shoulder would make him go away. Daria was okay with men as long as they were just friends—or if she pursued them. The moment she felt their interest, she would balk, or she would no longer find them attractive.

She'd had one serious romance with someone she had met in graduate school. It had lasted several years because they had been introduced by friends and remained friends even as the relationship grew. Once he proposed marriage, however, Daria ended it abruptly. Then she fell in love with a Venezuelan doctorate student and proposed to him. He said yes, and then divorced her a year later. Ever since, her focus remained, by choice, on her work. Although she attracted suitors, any who were lucky enough to obtain her phone number never got beyond her answering machine. Daria convinced herself she was far too busy to feel lonely and didn't miss being in a relationship. She decided she would look at the Sphinx until she was finished and not say another word to Omar Fayed.

Omar sensed Daria's uneasiness and nonchalantly moved away from her. His servant, Akbar, had reported her arrival at the airport and then followed her to the hotel. Omar's presence at the pavilion had been no accident, nor was his touristy attire. He wanted to befriend Daria and if necessary, protect her from his father.

As he expected, Daria was wearing what looked like the ancient Key to the Capstone. The pendant was the right shape, size, and color. Of course, he couldn't be absolutely sure because nobody, well almost nobody, knew exactly what the key looked like. Somehow, he had to find a way to show the pendant to Mikta. Only then could he be absolutely certain it was genuine.

Omar wondered what Ian had told his daughter about it. Probably nothing since she openly wore the thing around her neck — and in Egypt of all places! She probably had no clue what she bore. No idea of the millions who had benefited and prospered from its gifts in ancient times, and more recently, the thousands who had died trying to possess it and the power it promised.

"The Sphinx is remarkable, isn't it?" Omar commented.

Daria rolled her eyes. "They call it *Abu 'l-Hol*, or the Father of Terror," she said.

"Do you know why?"

Daria sighed. The teacher in her couldn't ignore him. "They say the Pharaoh Khafra built it around 2,500 B.C. to guard his pyramid — that one," she pointed to the second largest pyramid, the one in the middle of the three.

"Some people say the Sphinx is much older."

"I don't think any evidence exists to confirm when the Sphinx was built," Daria said.

"Look at the walls of bedrock that surround it."

"What about them?"

"Water erosion." Omar removed the binoculars from his neck and handed them to her.

Daria held the glasses to her eyes.

Omar explained, "See the vertical fissures where rivulets poured into the Sphinx's enclosure? That's clearly water erosion. And the upper strata recede, suggesting more erosion there than in the lower layers. This is inconsistent with wind erosion. The sides of the Sphinx looked exactly that way too, before they were plastered and restored."

Daria didn't have to know much about geology to agree that the vertical fissures were obviously made by running water. But how long ago did water run freely in Giza? At least 7,000 B.C.? Then add a few thousand years for the civilization that built the Sphinx to flourish before dying out and letting the great statue go to ruin in the rain.

Daria was intrigued, "If it's that obvious, why don't the scholars see it?"

"They do. Geologists unanimously agree. But Egyptologists refuse to reconsider their theories. Dating the Sphinx's origin at 12,000 or even 10,000 B.C., when the Giza plateau was lush and green, poses too many unanswerable questions. People back then were supposedly too primitive to build such a thing."

Daria thought of the well-ordered progress of history that she learned in school. According to the textbooks, civilization began from primitive origins about ten thousand years ago in the Indus Valley and grew and evolved to its present, all-time height in the twenty-first century. Believing this version of history gave her a sense of safety and security. It wasn't easy to accept that an advanced civilization existed any earlier because that meant it had been completely wiped out—lost even to history. It also meant that people today, too, were somehow vulnerable.

There were those, her father among them, who believed that many people ten thousand years ago were primitive because their technology had been destroyed in a devastating global flood. Daria wanted to mention that idea to Omar but hesitated. She avoided revisiting thoughts that reminded her of her father.

"Scientifically determining the age of the Sphinx doesn't prove the age of the pyramids," she said instead. "I find it interesting that the Sphinx appears to protect Khafra's pyramid and is linked to it by a causeway. Actually, I think Khafra's pyramid is the most important one, as it's located in the middle of the other two and was built on a hill that makes it appear tallest. Yet Khufu's Great Pyramid gets all the attention."

"It's the most often and the most accurately measured structure on earth," Omar said.

"People are fascinated by it," Daria agreed.

"Some of its measurements give exact figures for the earth's dimensions including its circumference," Omar said, testing to see how much she knew. "And for the length of time it takes the earth to travel around the sun."

Daria looked at him in disbelief.

"I'm not kidding," Omar insisted. "A unit of measurement used by the pyramid builders is called a *sacred cubit*. A sacred cubit measures one ten-millionth of the earth's polar radius."

"One *ten-millionth*?" Daria tried not to sound sarcastic. What could be the significance of such a small number?

"The perimeter of the pyramid's base measured at its sockets is 365.242 sacred cubits. This is exactly the number of days in the mean solar tropical year. The tropical year is the time required for the earth to make one complete revolution around the sun, measured from one vernal equinox to the next."

"That number could be easily fudged."

"It could," Omar admitted. "Measure the pyramid's base perimeter incorporating the indentation found on all four sides and you get 365.256 sacred cubits. This is the number of days in the sidereal year—the time required for one complete revolution of the earth around the sun, relative to the stars. Measure the base from the corner sockets to the midpoints of each side and you get the length of the anomalistic year. This is the time taken for the Earth to complete a revolution from one perihelion, or closest point to the sun, to the next."

"So?" Daria felt overwhelmed by the details.

"So ..." Omar persisted. "The Great Pyramid's size was intentional. Professional surveyors' calculations reveal that the pyramid's measurements reflect a plethora of geologic and astronomic information. For example, the length of a minute of latitude as measured at the earth's equator, the sun's radius, the mean distance from earth to the sun and moon, the earth's volume, mass, and speed around the sun, and more. In the pyramid's measurements you can find the golden ratio, or phi, and, if you divide the pyramid's perimeter by twice its height, you get the mathematical constant, pi."

Daria didn't understand the significance of Omar's statement.

"The number attributed to pi is intimately associated with circles," Omar explained. "Most Egyptologists agree that wheels were not available to the pyramid builders. Yet pi is demonstrated in the most obvious, eye-catching aspect of the Great Pyramid—it's actual size."

"I still think a lot of this could be coincidence."

"Yet the more facts I give you, the less likely they are coincidence," Omar said.

"Surely these measurements could be tweaked to give any outcome you want," Daria argued.

Omar didn't want to insult her by reminding her that the same technologies used to measure the pyramid also helped get a man to the moon and back.

He continued, "The Great Pyramid is extraordinary in other ways too. Its inside temperature is the average temperature of the planet's surface. Even its location seems planned. The height of the Giza Plateau above sea level is the average height of all land above sea level—something only measurable by satellites and computers. Look at a globe and you'll find the pyramid is located at the exact center of the earth's land mass. In other words, the lines of latitude and longitude that intersect the pyramid also pass through the most land possible around the entire planet.

"Also, the Great Pyramid points to true north. True north, as opposed to magnetic north, corresponds to the earth's polar axis. The pyramid deviates from true north by less than three minutes of one degree. This is extremely accurate. The Paris Observatory, also designed to point to true north, is off by six minutes of one degree. Today the pole star, Polaris, marks true north. But the ancient Egyptians had no such marker because the position of the stars was different back then. So they must have been extremely clever to have figured out how to align the pyramid so perfectly."

"Or lucky." Daria immediately regretted the comment. Omar was being serious and she didn't mean to insult him. It was just that his evidence was piling up, and it felt unsettling to have her basic ideas challenged. The pyramids were tombs. They had been built by tens of thousands of slaves dragging each multi-ton block long distances and heaving them into place. Granted, they hoisted them up impossible heights without chipping any edge or corner, and put them precisely into place.

"There's something special about the pyramid that these measurements are trying to tell us," Omar said. "Here's one more. Not many people know that all four sides of the Great Pyramid are very slightly and evenly bowed in, or concave. The fact was discovered around 1940 by a pilot taking aerial photos. Today's laser instruments have proved this indentation duplicates exactly the curvature of the earth."

Daria looked at him blankly as she evaluated the possibility that what he said, or at least some of it, might actually be true. She wanted to hear in his words the dissonance of two untuned bells sounding at the same time. But all she heard was harmony, and it was stretching her mind. Was it really possible for the Egyptians to have had access to such knowledge in 2,500 B.C.? The curvature of the earth and the measurement for its orbit were determined only in the twentieth century by the world's top astronomers.

What made the least sense was why the pyramid builders would have gone to such trouble to impart these measurements into their work. If to catalog and keep track of them, then why not simply write them down? If a civilization had command of this math, certainly they wrote down their calculations somewhere. Yet no records of this sort had ever been found – at least not yet, she thought. Maybe the pyramids were a legacy for future generations? No, that was not likely either. It wasn't human nature to care about the welfare of future generations. After all, she figured, despite the efforts of thousands of people, her own generation wasn't stopping pollution, deforestation, or global warming that could catastrophically change the planet for our children and grandchildren.

"Even if all you say is true," Daria said, "What difference does it make to incorporate geologic and astronomic data into the pyramid? It doesn't give the pyramid any special powers over the earth or solar system." This time she couldn't help sounding sarcastic. The pyramids were tombs. To claim them as anything else took a lot of imagination.

Omar's next statement made her feel better for its sheer absurdity. "What's more, I doubt the Great Pyramid ever had a real top—just a fake one that made the pyramid only visually complete."

Daria laughed. "Now how can you prove that one? In the Cairo museum I've seen pyramidions of several pyramids. Surely the Great Pyramid's top must have fallen off at some point. Probably during the earthquake of 1301 when most of the pyramids' casing also came loose. I imagine it broke into a hundred pieces."

"It's easy to be convinced of that," Omar said. Obviously she knew nothing of the Great Pyramid's fake pyramidion, built simply to hold its small capstone in the proper place.

Omar looked down and saw Akbar entering the pavilion. "Mind if I buy you a Coke?" he asked.

"Sure," she replied. Omar hadn't flirted with her a bit during their conversation, and his warm and engaging personality had made Daria feel comfortable, despite his far-fetched ideas. Besides, she wanted to hear his explanation for the pyramid's missing top.

"I'll be back in a minute." Then he took the stairs to the bar, which was located on the first floor.

There he met Akbar, a short, skinny, Egyptian man who wore a gray gallabiya. His head was covered with a darker gray lebda.

"Is it the key?" Akbar asked eagerly. His eyes were hopeful.

"I was unable to get a close enough look."

Akbar grinned, "Ah, but you will, eh?" His teeth were brown from never having seen a toothbrush.

Just then, Omar saw Daria hurry down the stairs and skate determinedly away. Two men appeared to be chasing her. "Akbar! I didn't tell you to have her followed."

"Those aren't our guys."

Omar swore and ran to his car. On his order, several more men appeared from the shadows and began running after her too.

22.

When Omar went to get the Coke, Daria watched him walk to the staircase and descend. Her eyes lingered on his broad shoulders, and she liked what she saw. Then she noticed two men who stood out among the crowd of tourists. Both were heavy set and one was a few inches taller than the other. They both wore mustaches, black lebdas, and sport coats. Inadvertently they caught her eye and quickly looked away.

Daria sensed they were more interested in her than in the Sphinx. It was something about the way they looked at her and the odd feeling she was left with.

She needed to leave.

The men lingered in front of the staircase. There was no other way down.

Daria pretended she didn't notice them and turned again to look at the view, but her senses were on full alert. Maybe they had seen her skating, she thought. She didn't blend in with the crowd. Blending in was the first rule of safe tourism. But Daria loved rollerblading, and she could take care of herself.

When the men's attention didn't sway and she felt them inching closer, she casually moved near a small group of tourists who stood between her and the stairs. By circling them, she eased toward escape. When she was close enough, she pushed hard against her wheels to reach the steps quickly. Then turning her feet sideways, she held the railing while she vaulted down several steps at a time. Once on the ground floor she sped to the main avenue.

Daria soon found herself pursued by men not only on foot but also in cars. The two Egyptians must have company, she thought. Yet the chase didn't make sense. Who would take such pains to accost a tourist, she wondered? She had nothing of value on her. Even her thin waist-wallet was hidden. The locals never harassed tourists like this. Surely, she thought, they mistook her for someone else, and no doubt would soon let her alone.

Luckily, she knew Giza. Though the city had expanded since she'd been there last, the rest of it hadn't changed at all, and it was hard to get lost. All you had to do was look up, find the pyramids, and you'd know relatively where you were. Wearing rollerblades also gave her an advantage. She could blade where cars couldn't go and speed along faster than anyone could run. Daria reveled in her athletic ability and expertly used skating tricks to maneuver over obstacles in her path. She needed to find a large group of tourists for safe haven—as soon as possible.

Then someone grabbed the back of her sweater. Daria swung around and landed her fist against his face. Her sweater nearly slid off her arm, but the assailant let go when he toppled backward.

"Yes!" Daria exclaimed. She sped off while managing to re-secure a few buttons of her sweater on the way. Thankfully, her legs were strong and would support her for miles more, so would her well-trained lungs.

Now she could hear the sound of a motorcycle in pursuit. She could out-skate a running man but was helpless before a motorbike. What she couldn't outrun, she had to outsmart. First she had to disappear and chose a populated side street to do that.

Then they cornered her. Ahead of her and behind her, they closed in on her. Daria looked quickly left and right. Stone walls. Closed doors. No way out.

Then she spied a doorway covered only by cloth. Daria slipped inside. The house was empty except for a few rugs and a small table with very short legs. Daria skated over the concrete floor through the living room and kitchen, past a very surprised cook, to an uncovered back door. It led her to a small backyard and an unknown alley. She stopped to scan her surroundings; she saw the pyramids and got her bearings. The sound of shouting voices set her off again.

The voices got closer.

"Over there!" she heard someone call from an adjacent alley-way.

Finally, inevitably, a pair of strong hands grabbed her. One hand caught her arm, the other wrapped around her mouth to prevent her from screaming. Daria struggled fiercely, but fear quickly overcame her and she fainted.

23.

At the bottom of the world Tom lay on his cot, his hands behind his head, supporting his neck. He was staring at the curved canvas ceiling of his Jamesway tent. The metal heating ducts snaked its length, and the electrical wires draped from one support pole to the next much like Christmas decorations. The ISLAPS had been unable to melt any more ice and Tom wondered how much longer he had before Greer ordered them to pack up and leave.

In his imagination, Tom rebuilt every component of the IS-

LAPS, trying to figure out what was wrong. Failure never entered his mind. It wasn't because he was so sure of himself. Rather, he was certain of the intuitions and other guidance that had led him to this point and the fact that life had given him one opportunity after another to keep following it. Still he knew that success depended on giving everything he had. He was willing to do that.

So why hadn't the ISLAPS begun the chain reaction that would disrupt the ice molecules enough to break their chemical bonds, he asked himself? The instruments had worked before. What was in their way now? Maybe they needed to build a head of steam? He smiled to himself at the unintended pun. Maybe the laser beams needed to reach a certain saturation point. That had not occurred in the experimental fields in Maine, however. What was different about this ice?

Tom had questions but no answers. Frustrated and unable to sleep, he decided to gear up again, go outside, and readjust the ISLAPS one more time.

24.

After being chased through Giza and finally captured, Daria awoke on a pile of Egyptian rugs, her body covered by a thin cotton blanket. The room was bare except for a single dresser and yellow linen curtains that ruffled gently in the soft breeze. The sand-colored plaster walls and ceiling were chipping, but the cement floor was well swept. From the sounds that drifted in from the window, she knew she was on the second floor.

Then she remembered she'd been caught and that she fainted, and a flood of anxiety rushed through her veins. She scanned her body. She was still clothed, her pendants were around her neck, her waist wallet was intact, but her skates were not on her feet.

She held an urge to flee. It would be wiser to lie still, she thought, and find out as much as she could about where she was and who had abducted her. She strained to listen to the sounds inside the house. Some women were chattering, but their voices were too muffled to understand. A few minutes later Daria heard them leave.

The house was silent.

Then she heard footsteps.

Daria froze. Her heart pounded. Should she pretend to sleep?

"Hello?" someone whispered at the doorway.

It was Omar.

"You?" Daria exclaimed and sat up, relieved. At some unknown moment during their conversation at the Sphinx café Omar had crossed the unwritten line between potential suitor and friend. Daria felt she could trust him.

"Are you okay?" he asked. Omar had hoped she would still be unconscious so that he could examine her pendants—and then leave before the women of the house returned. They would not let him near her after he'd brought her in.

He felt badly that he had to swipe her off the streets so abruptly. But he had no choice. He assumed his father had people following him, and when they had found Daria with him, they chose to go after her themselves and retrieve the key that she was wearing.

"I'm fine," she said, still feeling dazed. "What happened?"

"You fainted." Omar handed her a tall glass of bright red liquid. "I brought you something to drink," he said. "It's *karkade*, a local favorite."

Daria was familiar with it. The beverage was sweet, perfumed, and tasted like hibiscus. Daria drank a few sips and felt some energy return. Suddenly she realized that Omar may have saved her life. How do you thank someone for doing something like that?

"How long have I been out?" she asked, not knowing what

else to say.

"Not long," Omar replied. "It's about 10:00 A.M."

Daria took a deep breath and tried to reorient herself to the lost hour.

"Where are my skates?"

Omar nodded to the wall behind her. The skates were leaning against it.

"I'm sorry, if I hurt you," Omar said.

"You didn't."

"I had to bring you inside before they caught you."

"I know." Then she added. "Who was chasing me?"

"I'll explain later. First, we need to get you out of here."

"I'm meeting my students tomorrow and heading for Saqqara," Daria said.

Omar shook his head. If Daria knew nothing about the Key to the Capstone, it would waste precious time to explain it now.

"In case you didn't notice," Omar said, "someone is trying to kidnap you." Or kill her if necessary, but he didn't want to frighten her.

Omar insisted that Daria leave the country, and Daria argued against it. The opportunity to show her students the Pyramid Texts in the Saqqara pyramids was too compelling to abandon. She explained how these pyramids were the only ones ever to have been found with hieroglyphs inside. The Pyramid Texts were among the most ancient writings in the world, far older than the Dead Sea Scrolls or the Egyptian Books of the Dead. Though they had been translated a few times, she wanted to show her students how to find fresh metaphors in the hieroglyphs. Ones they could apply in their own lives.

Besides, she was sure she had been mistaken for someone else and Omar's concern about the kidnapping was just a big misunderstanding.

Finally, Omar convinced her that until this misunderstanding was cleared up, her life was at stake. He suggested the safest exit was the port at Mersa Matruh, a city on the Mediterranean coast, west of Alexandria. From there she could take a ferry to Greece, and then fly back to the States. He told her it was too dangerous to return to her hotel, and the Cairo airport was out of the question. Too many people might recognize her—or the key, but he didn't mention that.

Adding to her aggravation, Daria was unable to get a telephone call through to the U.S. and Omar didn't want to risk taking her to an Internet café. Daria wasn't sure who would be more worried about her: her grandparents, her students, or her boss, Albert Winslow, who had known her father and remained a family friend long after his death.

Daria and Omar ate a quick lunch of pita bread and hummus, and Omar went out and bought her a pair of scandals. Once again she tried, unsuccessfully, to make a phone call to the U.S.

Then Akbar picked them up in a Land Rover. Daria didn't recognize him as the airport tour operator, who had run away from her so rudely. Omar sat in front and Daria in the back.

Akbar took the back roads along the Nile instead of heading straight for the highway. Omar said it was because he had to stop at the home of a friend, who could help them and make arrangements for her in Mersa Matruh.

On the way, Daria looked out the window. They passed groves of date palms; stands of sycamores, poplars and acacias; groups of hardworking children carrying palm leaves and water jugs; and one small farm after another. Despite the modern world encroaching upon them, these farmers still tended their land with the help of donkeys and water buffalo. Their homes were made of river sediment packed over a structure of date palm lumber. Tapestry covered the front doors. Many homes had ladders that leaned against the outside wall. The flat rooftops were used for storage or for sleeping in hot weather.

In this moment, Daria envied them. They appeared to live a peaceful life and never before had Daria's life felt so unsettled. Who had been following her? And why? A petty thief would never pursue a tourist that way, and a terrorist would have had a kidnapping well planned and aborted the mission if not immediately successful.

Now they were on their way to Mersa Matruh, where she was about to leave the country. Misunderstanding or not, she would soon be home. Daria resigned herself to her fate. At least she'd be home to help her grandparents in case the hurricane hit.

"So, what's your theory about the Great Pyramid's non-existent pyramidion?" she asked.

Omar turned to look at her. She was sitting with one leg tucked beneath her and her elbow was resting on the car door. The wind danced in her brown hair, strands of which floated in front of her face. Casually, she kept brushing them away. She was lovelier each time he looked at her, he thought.

Omar explained, "Egyptologists in the seventeenth and eighteenth centuries, who studied the Great Pyramid noticed that its top consisted of a heap of limestone blocks. These blocks had not been cemented like the pyramid's other blocks. They were much smaller and not as well made. The scientists surmised the pyramid was never finished, and its top put in place at a much later date to satisfy some pharaoh who wanted to make the pyramid appear complete.

"However, back in the first century A.D., the Greek historian Diodorus noted that the summit of the Great Pyramid was flat. He states that the pyramid was otherwise in perfect condition including its smooth unblemished casing. How could the casing be unblemished if a pyramidion, which would have weighed over one thousand tons, was removed or had fallen off? In either scenario, the casing would have been damaged."

"The other two pyramids of Giza, the pyramids of Khafra and Menkaure, had pyramidions," Daria said knowingly.

"Yes. And they survived at least two major earthquakes," Omar said. "They disappeared only after the locals started quarrying the earthquake-dislodged casing stones."

"If the pyramid builders were so precise in their measurements," Daria said, recalling their earlier conversation, "it makes no sense they would leave the Great Pyramid incomplete."

"They didn't."

"You think the pyramid's top was supposed to be flat?"

"No," Omar said. "It was supposed to have a top, a very special top that contained a power center. At its apex was a tiny capstone. This capstone, which held a much smaller source of power, arrived safely in Egypt, but for some reason the main power center didn't. The uncemented limestone blocks were put there instead to support the capstone at its proper height and position. These blocks must have also contained a corridor so that the capstone could be accessed when needed. With the capstone at its apex, the Great Pyramid could still be used for its intended purposes. But it was never as powerful as it was meant to be."

For some reason Daria could not explain, she felt uneasy about what Omar was saying. His words sounded uncomfortably familiar.

Omar continued, "Over time, the capstone was lost, but there are those who believe it will soon be found."

"What happened to the power center?" she prodded.

"Nobody knows." Then he said, "By the way, that's quite a collection of necklaces you're wearing."

Daria smiled. Her necklaces meant a lot to her, and she also appreciated what she thought was a change of subject. She told him a little about each one and finally introduced the silvery pendant, saying nothing more than it had been a birthday gift from her father.

"It's very unusual," Omar said, "do you know where he got it?" He already knew, but he wanted Daria to make the connection herself.

"He found it near the Giza pyramids."

"I've heard a legend that says the Great Pyramid's capstone has a key," he told her.

Daria stared at him. To avoid the pain of grief, she had purposefully and carefully purged from her memory any thoughts of her father—including the stories he had once told her. The gift he had given her was simply a pendant. She hadn't thought about it as the Key to the Capstone in over twenty-five years. Even now, she failed to recall her pendant's identity.

"The key-bearer is destined to find the lost capstone," Omar said.

"I've heard that before," Daria said quietly. The memories were encroaching and couldn't be stopped. "What happens when the key-bearer finds the capstone?" she asked.

"The capstone will lead the key-bearer to its original home. There, the key-bearer will learn the secrets of the Great Pyramid and restore its powers."

Daria laughed. "The Great Pyramid is in ruins. How could its powers — if indeed it ever had any — possibly be restored?"

"We believe the pyramid has undiscovered chambers and passageways that are still intact, and that the lost capstone has remained unharmed. It will be found in its original condition."

"Why are you telling me this?" As soon as she voiced the question, the answer hit her.

Omar watched the blood drain from her face, and he knew that she knew.

Daria felt faint. She reached for her pendants and singled out the one her father had given her. Holding it tightly, she leaned against the car door. She recalled one of her father's stories in which he'd said, "The one who wore the pendant could know all the secrets of the Great Pyramid and control its powers."

"This is the Key to the Capstone, isn't it," Daria said, remembering the day her father had found it, and then the day he had given it to her.

Omar nodded.

"It's the reason those guys were chasing me."

Omar nodded once again.

25.

A kbar stopped the Land Rover in front of the large mud-brick home of Omar's friend.

"I'll just be a minute," Omar said. He handed Daria a few packages of small, triangle-shaped prepared cheese and a round of pita bread. Daria gave him a faint smile. While she waited for him to return, she nibbled the food and washed it down with some water. Meanwhile, Akbar got out and put his prayer rug under a nearby tree and recited one of his five daily prayers to Allah. Daria rested her head against the car door. She had a lot to think about.

She remembered that her father had found the Key to the Capstone twenty-five years ago on the last day of his dig at Giza. The next day, they had taken an unexpected visit to Edfu, where they spent some time with her dad's friend Mikta. A few days later her father gave the key to her on her birthday—the same day their house was ransacked and he had been murdered.

His murderers must have been after the key, Daria realized. Were they the same people who were after her too? If so, why had they let her alone for so many years? Didn't they know she'd had it all along?

Omar finally returned with some handwritten maps. Then they proceeded down the road and got on the highway going north. They took an exit that lead to the Wadi-en-Natrun Valley. The land was a mix of geography. They passed marshes, random tracts of cultivated land, palm groves, small villages, dried salt lakes, and chemical plants. Akbar chatted about how the ancient Egyptians had once mined the salt lakes for sodium carbonate to make natron, an important ingredient in their mummification process. Now the compound was used industrially, hence the factories. When they reached the cliffs that bordered the desolate Western Desert, Akbar told her they were riddled with caves. Thousands of Christians had once hid there. Seeking freedom from Roman persecution, they'd also built over sixty monasteries, though now only a few remained. Daria bit her tongue as she suppressed a desire to add to the conversation. She wanted to mention how these monasteries had no doors. People and supplies had to be hauled up by rope. But she thought it more polite to keep silent and let Akbar be the authority. After all, Egypt was *his* country.

Omar consulted his maps and directed Akbar to a nearly hidden road that zigzagged up through the cliffs. Soon they were on a dirt piste that led into a great expanse of emptiness that reached interminably westward.

"Where are we going?" Daria asked. They easily could have reached Mersa Matruh by taking the highway through Alexandria. Now they were heading into no-man's land.

"We need to show your pendant to someone," Omar replied.

"What for?"

"To see if it's real."

"And if it's fake?"

"Either way, Sidi Mikta will tell us what to do."

Daria knew *Sidi* was an honorary prefix for a holy man. She wondered if he was the same Mikta who had been friends with her father.

"Sidi Mikta is a Bedouin Saint," Akbar said. "They call him a "Khawi," a healer and the leader of his tribe. They say he has supernatural powers."

"He knows more about the Key to the Capstone than anyone," Omar said.

"Sidi Mikta lives out *here*?"

"He's a Bedouin," Omar said. "His tribe is one of the few remaining nomadic ones and is smaller than most. They roam the desert helping anyone they meet."

"Well, they mustn't do much business," Daria said, awed by the barrenness of the rocky desert, which reached beyond the horizon and displayed more shades of brown and tan than she'd ever seen. What a contrast to the rich, green landscape of the Nile delta only a few miles behind them.

"A Khawi like Mikta reads the desert and navigates by the stars," Akbar said. "He listens to the sand, and it tells him of footsteps hundreds of miles away – and even of hidden water."

"Where are we planning to meet him?" she asked. Then she realized there was no way Omar could have made an appointment with Mikta. Bedouin nomads didn't have telephones, cell phones, or Internet access.

Omar was silent.

Akbar finally replied, "Ma'am, he will find us."

A wave of anxiety passed through Daria's body as she considered the uncertainty of finding anybody in the vast desert.

"Do you expect us to drive out into the middle of nowhere and sooner or later cross paths with him?"

"It is the way of the desert," Omar replied calmly.

"You really have no idea where to meet him?" she finally asked.

"Don't worry," Omar assured her. "The Key to the Capstone is too important. Mikta will find us."

Daria reached for her bottle of bergamot oil that she kept in one of her pouches around her neck and inhaled its essence. Despite its relaxing aroma, Daria was unnerved by having no control over her situation or her future. Her stomach knotted and the bread and cheese she had eaten felt like lead.

26.

Faoud Fayed flipped open his cell phone at the sound of its ring.

"Mr. Fayed?"

"Yes."

"Omar is with Daria McHenry. They're headed west into the desert."

Fayed mumbled a profanity. They're probably trying to find Mikta, he thought. What idiots. The desert was a vast and dangerous place for many reasons besides lack of water. Landmines had claimed the lives of thousands not to mention the bandits, snakes, scorpions, and the lack of service stations. It was unthinkable to order his men to follow Omar and the woman, he decided.

"Alert our contacts in the Western Desert from here to Libya," he said. "Let me know the moment anyone locates Sidi Mikta, my son, or Professor McHenry."

"Yes, Sir. Ensh Allah."

"Ensh Allah."

Fayed hung up the phone then touched the intercom button on his desk set to reach his secretary.

"Get me a line to the United States; I want to speak with Mrs. Sarah McHenry."

"Yes, Mr. Fayed," a male voice replied.

A few minutes later, Fayed was on the phone with Sarah.

"Mrs. McHenry?"

"Yes?" Her voice sounded groggy. Obviously Fayed had awakened her. Then he remembered the seven-hour time difference between Cairo and Connecticut, but continued as though that fact was of no consequence.

"My name is Mr. Faoud Fayed, and I am associated with the police here in Cairo," he said, stretching the truth. Fayed's voice grew soft, and he tried to sound sincere. "I regret to inform you, Madam," Fayed continued. "We have reason to believe that your granddaughter has been kidnapped."

"Daria?" Sarah gasped in disbelief. She now was sitting up in bed and wide awake.

"Yes, Madam. Your granddaughter is Professor Daria McHenry?"

"Yes. She is my granddaughter." Sarah doubted what she'd heard and asked Fayed to repeat himself. When he did, the reality sunk in, her throat tightened, and her mouth dried.

"Are you in charge of the investigation?" She could barely speak.

"Yes," Fayed replied. "I assure you, I will do all in my power to see that she is found as soon as possible and returned safely to you. We already have a suspect and are following his trail."

Sarah pressed her hand against her chest to comfort the growing tightness there. "You've got to find her," she pleaded.

"Madam, keep calm and try not to worry."

Sarah struggled to control herself. Fayed didn't know how emotionally distraught she already was. Her husband, David, had been called to England to care for his sickly brother — their only living relative other than Daria. Plus there was a major hurricane approaching. Now Daria had been abducted.

"Have you received a call for ransom?" Sarah asked. "I'll pay anything they ask."

"I understand," Fayed said, taking note of her desperation. He then left his phone number in case Sarah received a call from Daria or the kidnappers. Sarah promised she would contact him the moment she heard anything.

Fayed ended the conversation satisfied that he would hear from Sarah soon enough.

27.

When Akbar stopped the car somewhere in the Western Desert, everyone piled out to stretch. The endless sand was punctuated by the occasional rock formation. A mountain range shaped the northwest horizon, and dunes sculpted the view to the south. The ground beneath them consisted of random clumps of grasses and a few hardy bushes. Except for the dust kicked up by their Land Rover, the air was exceptionally clear, though hot and dry, and carried its own unique desert scent.

Once again, Akbar unrolled his prayer rug. This was his fourth spiritual salute that day. He knelt on the rug, prostrated himself facing Mecca, and sang his love to God. Daria listened to him and admired his religious commitment. Daria's grandparents were Catholic. They'd never forced her to attend church, although Daria accompanied them on occasion when she was living with them. Now she practiced no religion in particular because none provided answers that satisfied her. Besides, she wasn't sure what she believed. Was there a God? If so, then there must be a heaven. If there was a heaven, then her mother and father still lived. If they still lived, then why did she never dream of them, or feel their presence, or intuit messages from them? She'd heard of other people with departed loved ones who had experienced such things. Why not her?

Akbar finished his prayers, got a gas can from the back of the Land Rover, and started filling the tank.

"Do we have enough gas," Daria asked worriedly?

"*Maalesh, maalesh,*" Akbar replied. This was an all-soothing phrase that Daria knew loosely translated as "never mind," or "it doesn't matter."

"I'd prefer a simple *iwah* or *la* [yes or no]," Daria said.

"*Maalesh, maalesh,*" Akbar repeated.

Omar asked them to get back into the car and they drove on. The position of the sun told Daria they were still heading west. Soon it would be evening, and the desert would get cold.

"Where are we going to spend the night?" Daria asked.

"A little ways from here," Omar replied.

A *little ways*? Daria thought. She was again feeling anxious. She had some idea of the few towns sprinkled across the Western Desert. Eventually, they might reach the Siwa Oasis, where a sacred oracle was once located. Alexander the Great had consulted this oracle and soon afterward an army of fifty thousand Persians, enemies of Egypt, set out to destroy it and were lost in the desert. How could fifty thousand men get lost? It would take at least another day of driving to reach Siwa. What if they too were doomed?

Akbar continued to follow the dirt path westward over gravelly ground that Daria hoped wouldn't turn into soft sand and trap them. Most of the time, the piste was hardly a road at all. She held her pendants for comfort. Her thoughts turned again to her father's murderers as well as her own pursuers.

"Omar, do you know who was chasing me?"

Omar turned in his seat to face her. "Have you heard of the *Shemsu Hor*?"

"*Shemsu,*" Daria said, "is a word derived from *shemesu* and means followers or companions. *Hor* refers to Horus, an important Egyptian god who was the son of Isis and Osiris."

"Yes, that's right. Shemsu Hor means the followers of Horus. Horus, Isis, and Osiris, plus a dozen or so others, were the original rulers of Egypt. They called themselves and their companions the *Zep Tepi*, or the first ones. It's said that each of the Zep Tepi originated from a different land. For some reason, they were unable to return home and so stayed in Egypt. Each brought a unique art, technology, or knowledge to aid the local people, who were indeed primitive. The Egyptian culture grew and quickly became prosperous. The people naturally respected their leaders as gods."

Daria knew exactly what he was talking about. The Zep Tepi were originally the lords of the Atlantean kingdoms, gathered together by Isis to consult the oracle of the Great Sphinx before partaking in civil war. They decided to reunite instead, but were unable to return home because of the great flood. So they became the Zep Tepi and helped Horus build their civilization anew in Egypt.

How did she know this?

The answer made her stomach knot. She'd read it herself on the walls of the Temple of Horus, years ago, with Mikta and her father.

To her relief, Omar continued talking. "The Zep Tepi were mortal but very smart," Omar said. "To preserve political stability, each chose a special emblem that would identify him or her for eternity. These emblems were masks or headdresses and they can be seen today in the paintings of the Egyptian gods. This clever idea allowed them to personally select their successors, who would then wear the mask generation after generation and essentially immortalize the original wearer."

"Horus chose the mask of a falcon," Daria said.

"Yes. And the eye of the falcon, the Eye of Horus, could see and know all things, including the ancient truths and mysteries." Omar continued.

"The Eye of Horus is a religious icon," Daria said.

"Actually, it was a real thing with exceptional powers," Omar explained. "As the first King of Egypt, it was Horus's duty to ensure that future kings would fully earn not only the mask of the falcon, but honorably wield the powers of the eye. So Horus and his most trusted priests founded the Shemsu Hor as a mystery school to train future kings, who were eventually called pharaohs. Membership was originally open to anyone who was willing to study their dreams."

Omar didn't wait for Daria to object. He spoke quickly to elucidate his claim. "The ancient Egyptians believed in dreams. Even the Pharaoh Tuthmosis IV recorded a dream in which the Great

Sphinx appeared to him. Even today, details of the dream exist, recorded in hieroglyphs on a fifteen-ton stone stela that Tuthmosis set between the Sphinx's paws."

Before Omar could continue, Daria quickly replied, "What you claim about dreams is well supported by evidence." This time, she simply couldn't keep quiet. The topic was too compelling.

Omar was startled. This was the first time Daria seemed to be agreeing with him.

"It wasn't uncommon for the ancient Egyptians to dream of their gods," Daria said. "In fact, the study of dreams and their meanings was an ordinary aspect of the ancient Egyptian lifestyle. Egyptians even kept dream dictionaries. They'd list dream scenarios in one column and their interpretation in another.

"A book of dreams was once owned by a scribe called Qenherkhepshef. It's known as the Papyrus Chester Beatty III and is presently housed in the British Museum in London. Although it dates to the period of Ramses, in the New Kingdom, scholars have noticed its language is older—very Middle Kingdom. We think it's a copy of a text originally compiled even earlier than that."

"So you believe in dreams," Omar said.

"Don't be silly!"

Omar was again surprised by her. Here was a woman who could talk freely about the validity of other people's dream experiences, yet she had no faith in her own. He decided to return to his previous discussion.

"According to Horus, those who listened to their dreams would remain free," Omar quoted what he had learned from Mikta. "Horus maintained and promoted a society of free individuals. He also believed truth should be available to all—since only those with open eyes and understanding hearts can see it. Those who listened would stand out above the crowd and emerge as true leaders. Thus, Horus found those worthy to assume his identity.

"This worked for a few thousand years. By the time Dynastic

Egypt began in the Old Kingdom, it was common knowledge that each new pharaoh simply donned the mask of Horus. It was about this time, too, that the pharaoh could assume the mask only, as the Eye of Horus had been lost. But I'm getting ahead of myself."

Daria made a mental note to ask about the eye later and listened. This was a part of Egypt's history she'd never heard before and was keenly interested, though she kept a sharp ear for anything that sounded wrong or felt untrue.

"During the Old Kingdom of Egypt," Omar said, "the purpose of the Shemsu Hor changed. Members became devoted to preserving knowledge that even then was considered ancient. Several times since, the Shemsu Hor were forced into hiding. Sometimes, to preserve the ancient knowledge, they put some of it into the hands of other secret societies."

"Like the Freemasons?" It was the only other secret society Daria knew of.

"Some say the founders of the Freemasons were descendents of the Shemsu Hor," Omar said. "The Freemasons were originally stone masons."

"The pyramids are made of stone," Daria commented.

Omar continued, "An example of a time the Shemsu Hor taught openly was during the height of the Greek empire. Egypt was well known then as a mecca for scientists and philosophers. Among the better known truth seekers who made the long journey to Egypt were Solon, Pythagorus, Phidias, Plato, and Aristotle. Centuries later Copernicus, Da Vinci, Galileo, Kepler, and Newton also made the journey. All came home with a new way of thinking and with knowledge that influenced science and made a difference in people's lives. Even Jesus is believed to have visited Egypt as a young man. Some also believe the sacred word *amen* originates in Egypt."

"It does," Daria said. "It is referred to many times in the Pyramid Texts, where it means what is hidden, what is not seen, or what cannot be seen. These phrases describe the characteristics of the Egyptian god whose name was Amen."

"I didn't know that," Omar said smiling. "It's the way of Horus brothers to share knowledge with each other, so that eventually all the pieces can come together and the puzzle of history can be solved."

Daria wondered what would happen if the general public became aware that such mysteries even existed. "Are you a member?" she asked.

"Yes."

Daria wondered if her father also belonged to the Shemsu Hor.

Omar continued, "Since the advent of the Internet and a renewed interest in secret societies and ancient prophecies, people around the world have stumbled upon the Shemsu Hor, and the brotherhood is growing. We want to see the ancient truths help people find spiritual understanding. It's also the job of every Horus brother to keep the secrets of earth's history alive, gently stoking the flames of interest among our peers. One day, hopefully soon, scientists will find definitive evidence of ancient advanced civilizations. Once the fact is generally accepted, we can then do serious research into the secrets of ancient astronomy, mathematics, and architecture which still elude scientists today. We might even learn why the ancients incorporated so much astronomy and mathematics into their pyramids."

Daria was fascinated, but she hadn't lost sight of her original question. She wanted to know who'd been chasing her. "What does this have to do with me?"

"Centuries ago, a group separated from the brotherhood. They call themselves the Renegades. Their sole intent is to find the *djed*, the sacred object."

"You mean the capstone?"

"Yes, I believe the djed is either the capstone or what may be contained inside it. The Renegades want its power. At the same time, they want to prevent the public from discovering the truth about ancient history. Such knowledge would decentralize power and put it back in the hands of the individual."

"How can anyone hide truth," Daria asked, "when there are

so many ways to share it with whoever is looking for it?"

"Some do so without realizing it," Omar explained. "For example, they humiliate those who propose logical yet alternative theories. They make it harder for researchers to access ancient monuments, and they even prevent certain work from being published at all."

"So people can be Renegades and not even know it," Daria said.

"And many support truth and individual freedom without calling themselves Shemsu Hor."

"Tell her about the Navubala's rightful bearer," Akbar whispered to Omar.

"The word *Navubala* is another name for the Key to the Capstone," Omar explained. "The prophecy states that only the true key-bearer, one who has received the key as a gift, can find the capstone. Anyone else who tries is doomed. So another difference between the Shemsu Hor and the Renegades is that the Shemsu Hor believe that when the time is right, the key-bearer will naturally emerge and find the capstone. The Renegades believe that anyone who has the key can find the capstone."

"Can they?"

"As a Horus brother I say no, they cannot."

"So, the Renegades want my pendant."

"Yes."

"They think I'm the key-bearer."

"And it's my duty to protect you and ensure that nothing interferes with your destiny," Omar said.

"My *what*?"

Daria thought she knew what her life mission was, and she enjoyed every minute of it. As far as she was concerned, her destiny was to excite modern youth with the desire to read ancient languages, particularly Egyptian, so they might learn from the past to lead better lives today. This was why she was so disappointed about not being able to meet her students at Saqqara.

Besides, if the Renegades wanted her pendant, why didn't they just ask her for it? Then again, maybe that was what those two men at the Sphinx pavilion were planning to do. After all, it was she who had run away. They, naturally, had pursued. Yet where had all the others come from? She clearly remembered at least six different people chasing her.

Daria thought about the men who visited her father before they killed him. How did they know he had found the key? As far as she knew, Mikta was the only one he'd told. Then she remembered that when she and Grandma Sarah had visited the Cairo museum, her father left for the entire day. When they finally met up with him that night, his clothes were soiled and he had some goofy story about Grandpa David's damaged boat. Had the Renegades chased her father, as they'd chased her?

Well, she thought, whether or not her father was a member of the Shemsu Hor, he had known the truth about her pendant. Vaguely she remembered something he'd said about how to use the pendant as a key. She now wished she hadn't forgotten his stories. It had been so long since she'd thought of them.

She also wondered why he had given her the key—especially if he knew what it was and how many people wanted it. Did he really think the safest place for it was around her neck? Yet he was the one killed and not her.

He had died because of the key.

Somehow, finally understanding the reason for his death gave her a sense of resolution, and she felt stronger because of it. Every truth you face gives you strength to face more, she realized with satisfaction.

At least the murderers had left empty-handed.

28.

The afternoon sun was sinking and Akbar drove faster over the parched earth. He sped the Land Rover at about forty miles per hour, recklessly hitting rocks and making the ride uncomfortably bumpy.

"What else do you know about the Eye of Horus?" Daria asked.

Omar faced her. "What do you know of it?"

"It's a symbol that appears throughout ancient Egyptian art and hieroglyphs as a human eye embellished with dark eyeliner," Daria said. "It's commonly known to represent healing, wholeness, strength, and perfection."

"That's a relatively recent description," Omar said. "Farther back in history, the Eye of Horus was a symbol for the sun, particularly as it appeared during a total eclipse—the only time when the sun's mysterious corona becomes visible."

"So the Eye of Horus is related to the sun?"

"We believe its powers may be associated with solar activity. Anyway, the highest initiation available in the original Shemsu Hor was given when an individual discovered, through his or her dream state, the true nature and purpose of the Eye of Horus. This discovery was so secret and so important, that it made one worthy to succeed as pharaoh.

"I never thought of the Eye of Horus as being an actual object," Daria said. "Come to think of it, though, the Pyramid Texts often refer to the time when Horus restored his father Osiris's life by giving him his eye. Those references make more sense now."

"Restoring life, healing ills, wielding supernatural powers," Omar mused. "We don't know the full extent of the eye's potential. However, we do suspect the eye was kept inside the pyramid's capstone. That's why the quest for the capstone is so important. That's why the discovery of your key is so ominous." And, Omar thought, that's why his father, Faoud Fayed, wanted the key so badly. It was the Eye of Horus that he was really after. Eternal youth and unlimited power—his father would do anything for these.

They rounded a hill and stopped.

"Now what?" Daria asked.

"Now we wait," Omar replied.

Daria gave him an exasperated look. "I'm going to take a walk."

"Watch out for landmines," he said.

She thought he was kidding.

"There're over fifteen million of them here leftover from World War II." Omar rolled out the warning his father had so often given him as a boy.

Daria headed up the hill anyway. Right now, she didn't care. She needed to find a creative solution to what she felt was a grave predicament and hoped that from atop the hill she might get an idea, or better yet, see a nearby settlement. Her footsteps crunched through a thin crust of earth that covered the softer sand beneath. Other than that, the silence of the desert filled her ears with its hum.

When she reached the top of the hill she was surprised to see a huge expanse of water, miles long, surrounded by sand dunes. Could this be a mirage? No, she thought, mirages occur when you look into hot sand at a sharp angle with the sun overhead. Now she was looking down the hill into the setting sun. Besides, this lake was irregularly shaped and clearly reflected the pink and gold clouds on the horizon.

This must be the Qattara Depression, Daria realized. It was a series of salt lakes, two hundred miles long, which filled a hollow of land that was, at its deepest point, about 440 feet below sea level. It was all that remained of an ancient sea that had once filled the Sahara Desert. What struck her as most odd was that nothing at all grew around the lake. It was far too salty to support life. Yet her brain expected to see greenery, and Daria scratched her head at the inconsistency. It was beautiful though, in its barren way.

She looked around. In every other direction loomed the unwelcoming desert filled with sand, rocks, and dried up weeds. But from the southwest, a small train of camels was heading toward them.

"Someone's coming!" she shouted down to Omar. He couldn't hear her. Daria counted seven camels packed with gear, plus seven herders leading them on foot. Daria could hardly believe it. She raced down the hill with the news.

"They're over there," she said excitedly, and within fifteen minutes the camel train had reached them. The herders, babbling in Bedouin, quickly introduced themselves. Daria hoped Mikta was among them, but he was not.

The herders hurried Omar, Akbar, and Daria to the camels, which had been coaxed to lie down so they could be mounted. Daria had ridden camels before. After you climbed into the saddle you had to lean way back to keep from falling off while the camel straightened its hind legs. Then you had to lean forward, as the camel lifted the front of its body to stand.

Daria sat on a colorful wool blanket that provided inadequate cushioning for the hard wooden saddle. The herder held the reins, so Daria rested her hands on her thighs. She looked over at Omar who looked as uncomfortable as she was. Akbar, on the other hand, was sitting with one leg draped over the front of the saddle as though he'd ridden camels all his life. He chatted and laughed with the herders.

It took awhile, but once Daria grew accustomed to the rhythm of the camel's walk, she grew sleepy and found herself dozing. Admittedly, she'd been through a lot that day.

The band headed southwest. The sky grew dark quickly in this latitude, and the thickening clouds blocked the moonlight. Undaunted, the herders used flashlights to find their way. They'd turn them on for a few seconds, examine the terrain ahead and then turn them off, sometimes for minutes at a time. Daria was amazed they could keep going in the darkness. It was getting chilly, and the herder who was leading her camel offered her a blanket to keep warm. She accepted it gratefully and wrapped it around her shoulders.

At about 10:00 P.M., they stopped and set up camp. One herder made a fire and began cooking a vegetable-lamb stew. Others hobbled the camels and set up a one-person goat-skin tent apart from the camp. Daria suspected this was where she would sleep. The men would probably bed down around the campfire. Although Daria would have preferred that herself, she knew she needed to respect their hospitality.

At dinner everyone sat around the campfire and received a large round of pita bread. Daria watched the men take turns dunking pieces of the bread into the stew pot, which was hung over the fire. Daria followed their example.

While they ate, the Bedouin camel herders spoke in classical Arabic, so that Daria could understand them. The Cairo dialect that she spoke and which she taught at Yale used consonants that sounded harder and more abrupt, like 's' instead of 'th,' and 'd' instead of 'z.' Their version was softer and more melodic. When the men began boasting of trading camels and finding hidden sources of water, the conversation no longer interested her. She looked over at Omar and Akbar, who had moved outside the circle and were chatting together. Omar looked up and caught her eye, and then returned to his conversation.

Throughout the evening, Daria sensed that Omar might be flirting with her, although in a subdued way that went unnoticed by the conservative Bedouin. Daria ignored him and wished he'd stop wasting his time.

She felt turned off by men who pursued her. Even when she initiated a date, the men would sooner or later remind her of her father. She would begin to miss him terribly, unresolved grief would emerge, and the relationship would fizzle. Daria tried to convince herself it was okay to be by herself, and to not need a relationship. Now alone with her thoughts in the middle of the desert she realized how lonely she really did feel. It wasn't about a lack of company, for she was with students and faculty all day long. She wondered if the emptiness came from the absence of someone to love, and who would love her in return. The voice of her unresolved trauma tried to convince her it was the loss of her father that caused the pain. Now she wondered if that pain wasn't partially self-inflicted by her refusal to allow anyone else but her father to love her. She grasped her father's pendant and realized how much her heart still needed to heal.

She looked up into the blanketing expanse of the star-filled sky and became aware of a profound sense of oneness with the earth and all life. It lulled her into a deeper sense of peace with herself. She felt at home in the universe and inextricably part of it, as though every action she took contributed to its encompassing rhythm, and every thought and emotion added to its substance and energy. It no longer mattered if she was alone or not, or if the ancient key might bring changes to her life. She was suddenly okay with whatever destiny life had to offer.

She also decided it was time to stop ignoring Omar. It was time to give him a chance.

29.

At the Antarctic station, Tom was back in his room toiling with calculator, pencil, and pages of paper, recalculating the equations required to make the ISLAPS work. Suddenly the green canvas door of his room flung open.

"Tom! We have melt!"

Tom jumped to his feet.

"The hole is as empty as a bucket after feedin' time," Major Davison said in his Virginian drawl.

"I'll be right there," Tom said and began piling on his layers of cold-weather gear as fast as he could. If the ISLAPS reached their melt potential of three feet per second, ice would seem to disappear before their eyes. The urgency and disbelief in Davison's voice made Tom's mind race. What if they had over-melt? A chain reaction where ice began melting laterally, outside the perimeter of his instruments? Tom felt angry at himself for never having considered that possibility before. He always had assumed the melt would be restricted to ice inside the ISLAPS' perimeter. Didn't physical laws insist on it? If lateral melt did happen, how could he stop it? On the other hand, if things went according to plan—and previous experience—the melt would cease as soon as it met the earth's surface.

By the time Tom reached the ice-melt area, everyone was lined up along the ropes that outlined the perimeter, gawking at the empty hole before them.

"I'll be damned," said Colonel Greer.

It was as close to a compliment as Greer could give, and Tom took it as such. "Thank you, Sir."

Then Greer ordered Davison to organize the men to begin assembling the elevator that would eventually take them to the Antarctic floor.

"When did the melt kick in?" Seymour asked.

"Who was on watch?" Greer asked.

"I was, Sir," said a boy-faced soldier who had been eagerly awaiting his turn to speak. "Nothin' was happening. Nothin' at all. Then, suddenly, at 17:12 hundred there was a hole!" The soldier was unable to hide his excitement. They had witnessed a miracle. Nobody had thought it would work—but it had.

The updraft of oxygen and hydrogen gases escaping from the shaft was occurring, but not in the form of a strong wind as Tom predicted. Still, it would be wise to wait until it, and the anticipated downdraft of air to compete their cycle before they went inside the shaft. Tom checked his watch. Melt had started about ten minutes ago. At a rate of three feet per second, it should take twenty-five minutes to sublimate about 4,593 feet of ice.

Fifteen minutes later, Tom approached Greer and straightened his posture. "Sir," Tom said. He knew the colonel appreciated the decorum. "May I have permission to examine the hole by helicopter."

"Do it."

"Yes, Sir!"

Over the Atlantic Ocean, the winds of Hurricane Ingrid, after holding a steady 135 m.p.h. the past thirty-six hours, suddenly picked up speed. It rose to a Category 5 storm, with sustained wind speeds at 160 m.p.h. and gusts even faster.

30.

After dinner, the Bedouin herders made a strong brew of mint tea, to which they added many spoonfuls of sugar. When Daria received her cup, she got up and went to sit beside Omar, who'd earlier moved outside the circle with Akbar.

When Omar saw her coming, he politely got up, took the camel blanket she was carrying, shook it out, and laid it newly folded on the sand beside his. He wondered what was on her mind, as she seemed to have been ignoring him all evening.

Daria wasn't sure how to start the conversation. This was out of character for her, so she took a deep breath, relaxed, and said the first thing that came to mind.

"So, of all the things you've told me about the Great Pyramid, what fascinates you the most?" she asked.

Omar raised his brows. "If you had trouble swallowing what I've already told you, you might get indigestion if I told you what truly inspires me."

"I'll be open," she said, and suddenly hoped her comment didn't sound like a double-entendre.

"You are aware of the precession of the stars?"

"It has something to do with the wobble of the earth's axis, doesn't it?"

"That's what they say," Omar replied. "For whatever reason, the path that a star follows across the sky changes in its relative position to the earth. It takes a star just about 26,000 years to return to a previous position. Take the star *Al Nitak*, for example, which is the lowest of the three stars that form the belt of the constellation Orion, the hunter. In 10,500 B.C. Al Nitak was at the lowest point of its precession. In about 2500 A.D. — thirteen thousand years later or half the precessional cycle — the star will be at its highest point."

"That will be in about 500 years."

"Yes. Precession applies to the Milky Way too. Its relative position also changes."

"Okay."

"And you are aware that every 2100 years or so, the sun enters a new 'age' as it rises in a different astrological constellation during the spring equinox?"

"Yes," Daria said. "I think we're supposed to be entering the Age of Aquarius sometime soon, if not already."

"That's right. Now, imagine you are standing on the Giza plateau just before dawn on the spring equinox that marked the beginning of the Age of Leo. It's about 10,500 B.C. The stars shine so brightly that the Milky Way stands out as though it had been spray painted."

Daria looked at the sky above them. It too would have been sprinkled with stars, but for the clouds that covered them. She closed her eyes and easily slipped into visualizing Omar's descriptions.

"Pretend you are looking east, over the Nile river. Just as the sun begins to dawn you notice that it is rising into the constellation of the lion, or Leo. The sun will be one of four heavenly bodies that form a nearly straight line on this morning. To the right of the sun, just above the horizon, is a bright star, which is actually Jupiter. It looks much larger than usual because of refraction — the same phenomenon that makes a rising moon look much bigger than it actually is. To the right of Jupiter and slighter higher is the star Regulus. Many cultures give this star names associated with kingship and greatness. Just to the right of this appears another bright star, which is actually Venus. The planets' proximity to each other produces a gentle aura comprised of the generosity of Jupiter and the goodwill of Venus.

"Now, look to your right, which is to the south. The Milky Way touches the horizon almost perpendicularly. Where it meets the earth, it also meets the Nile river. So close is their connection that it appears as though the river of stars pours into the Nile.

"To the right, the constellation Orion stands upright. The hunter's arms stretch outward toward the Milky Way, as though guiding it into the Nile. The atmosphere holds a magic, and it portends the dawn of a great age."

He continued. "The lowest star in Orion's belt, the star Al Nitak, is at its precessional nadir. Not for another 26,000 years will it be closer to the horizon than this. The ancients call this the First Time, and I think for good reason."

Daria noted his comment, but didn't want to interrupt the vivid yet peaceful experience that had descended upon her.

Omar looked over at Daria whose skin reflected the dancing light of the campfire. Her face was soft and her eyelids flickered. He wondered how deeply into a trance-like state she had relaxed into.

"Can you envision it?" he asked.

"Yes."

"And where do you stand as you watch the sky?"

"Upon an outcrop of limestone."

"Now look behind you, to the north and west. What do you see?"

Daria replied, "Two mounds of earth with stone temples upon them. I also envision a gathering of scholars. They hold various instruments and seem to be trying to find the exact position of a third temple."

"They are planning the precise location for the foundation of Giza's third pyramid, the Pyramid of Menkaure."

Omar was afraid this would rouse Daria, and it did. She looked at him in amazement.

He said, "The orientation of the three stars of Orion's belt, as they were positioned in 10,500 B.C., perfectly matches the alignment of the three Giza pyramids."

"Exactly?"

"It's been confirmed with archeo-astronomical software."

"Wait. Hold on," Daria said as she realized how real her glimpse into the past seemed to be. It felt like a memory. "What just happened?"

"Some places on earth are windows to the past," Omar said.

Daria tried to shake the dazed feeling that had come over her. It reminded her of a similar experience she'd had as a child reading hieroglyphs at the Temple of Horus.

"Geologists," Omar said, "have confirmed that the two largest pyramids of Giza are built on mounds. Likely the remains of earlier structures, as your vision suggested."

"My vision?"

"It's okay, Daria," Omar tried to reassure her. "Many people who can vividly recall the skies on that particular morning also remember other details, and they are similar to yours. What you experienced wasn't uncommon."

Daria had a distaste for the uncommon. She much preferred the comfort of the ordinary.

"I get it that the astronomical alignments are special," she said. "Is that what fascinates you?"

"It fascinates me," Omar admitted. "But what knocks my socks off is where my imagination goes when I wonder why anyone would want to map this particular configuration of astronomical events. For some reason, they are literally reflected in stone. What incredible thing happened at this time that it needs to be recorded in a way that would last millennia?"

"Any ideas?"

Omar studied her expression and found no sarcasm, only sincere curiosity. It gave him the courage to voice his belief. "Did you know that precession occurs between the earth and the stars, but not between earth and objects within our solar system? This has been proved by studies of Venus and the Perseid meteor shower."

"You're implying the earth's wobble has nothing to do with precession," Daria said. "Otherwise our planet would precess against objects both inside and outside the solar system."

Omar nodded. "The simplest explanation is that the solar system is itself rotating around something, on a journey that lasts just about 26,000 years. The Egyptians knew this. To identify that which our solar system revolves around they needed to triangulate it in time/space. This moment in 10,500 B.C. was one point they needed. The other must be some other extraordinary alignment between the pyramids and the stars. The one that comes to mind is the alignment that occurred around the year 2,450 B.C. when two stars shone into the shafts of the King's Chamber in the Great Pyramid. I believe that these two stars, at about this date in time, was the second triangulation point. But it stretches my mind to the breaking point trying to figure out how to use these data points to find the third point, which would reveal the object our solar system revolves around."

These thoughts were stretching Daria's mind too. She picked up another thread of their conversation that dropped when the subject had changed. "Why did you think the ancients called 10,500 B.C. the First Time?"

"I may be alone in my theories," he said. "But I believe this date coincides with an earthquake that released a natural dam upstream, causing a devastating flood in the Nile valley—the very first of the annual floods. It was the 'first time' the floods occurred. Although massively destructive, it left a layer of silt that made agriculture possible. Ever since, the annual flooding of the Nile has replenished the silt. It made the Nile valley one of the most fertile in the world."

"But it would take years for the valley to become so fertile," Daria said. "How did the Egyptians know this astronomical configuration would coincide with an annual flood that would ultimately bring agricultural prosperity?"

"Now you know another reason why thinking about this blows my mind," Omar said.

31.

Daria and Omar had been discussing the unique configuration of the Giza pyramids that Omar felt intentionally mapped a certain arrangement of stars back in 10,500 B.C. She was hoping Omar might make a pass at her again, and this time, she would respond to him. But he didn't and she wondered why.

"I think some things will forever remain a mystery," she said, intending a double-entendre. It was better they were just friends. It would be too difficult to maintain a relationship with someone living on another continent.

She finished drinking her tea and stood up.

"Ready to turn in?" Omar asked.

"Yes." It was getting late.

He handed her a flashlight. "Sleep well," he added. "We have a long journey ahead of us. If you need anything, let me know." His eyes were hopeful.

"Thank you." She met his gaze. Now he was interested in her again? It caught her off guard, but she forced herself to continue to watch his face. She saw so many things in his eyes, as if he wanted her for many reasons. She could decipher one of them, but the others would take all her skills as a language translator.

"*Tesbahee ahlah khayr* [good night]," Akbar said, not realizing he had interrupted their silent conversation.

"*Wentah minahl el khayr* [good night]," Daria replied. It would be a graceful exit. She turned and headed to her tent.

Clouds had recently blackened the sky, so the flashlight

proved essential. She used it to find a spot behind a dune on the far side of her tent to relieve her bladder, and then she crept into her tent. Inside, Daria found several camel blankets, a bottle of water, plus a bag of pita bread, a few hunks of packaged cheese, and a hair comb. She appreciated the Bedouins' thoughtfulness.

It seemed a long time since Daria had combed her hair, and she began immediately with the task. She kept the flashlight off so that nobody could watch her shadow through the tent walls. Then she arranged her bed. It was pitch black inside the tent, but it was small enough that she could feel her way around. She folded one blanket into a pillow, and then tucked the others around herself.

Tired as she was, her body wouldn't settle down. She tried to relax by listening to the herders' conversation. The growing wind snatched away more and more of their words, which eventually became impossible to hear. For a while, she imagined what might happen if Omar slipped into her tent. They would talk, and they would touch, for the first time, as more than friends.

But her fantasy didn't help her sleep. Still she tossed and turned, looking for a comfortable position. The blankets provided some cushion, but the ground beneath was too rocky. With a groan, she got up, folded her blankets aside, and started to clear the ground.

She piled the loose rocks and stones along the edge of her tent. One of the rocks had a sharp point that scratched her finger when she pulled it up. She sucked on the wound and continued her task. Finally, the sand was smooth and she lay back down.

Still it wasn't right.

Damn that lump behind the small of her back!

It was probably a large rock, she thought, and lucky her, it was right in the middle of the narrow tent. There was no room to lie elsewhere. So Daria moved her blankets to the side once again and continued digging. She used a flat rock, which she had unearthed earlier, to help her.

After removing an inch or two of sand, Daria still had not uncovered the rock. Why had that area been so uncomfortable? She was determined to find and move the annoying thing. She pushed the blankets farther to the edge of her tent and dug another few inches before she found the culprit. She moved the sand from around the rock to free its sides, intending to lift it from beneath.

In the darkness her fingers identified the shape of the rock she had unburied. She couldn't believe what they were telling her.

Daria crouched over the hole she had dug and turned on her flashlight. Something with four glassy sides reflected the light back to her. Quickly she shut off the flashlight. This was unbelievable, she told herself. It must be a fluke of nature ... unless her destiny had already started to unfold. The thought made her shudder. How could the Bedouin have known where exactly to put her tent? The coincidence was impossible.

Daria continued to dig around the rock, hoping to find its bottom edge. The more sand she cleared from it, the more clearly her hands and fingers confirmed what she had seen. She had unburied the uppermost two feet of an object whose four smooth sides ended in a perfect apex that pointed directly upward, and whose bottom was an unknown distance under the sand.

The discomfort she'd felt wasn't from a rock, but from the energy emanating from the tip of a forgotten, fully intact pyramid.

"When the time is right, the key-bearer will find the capstone," she remembered her father saying. "There can be no other outcome."

32.

Helicopter pilot Captain Patrick Flint had been briefed on the possibility that his services would be needed when melt occurred and he was already preparing his bird for takeoff. Flint was operating a Sikorsky Blackhawk UH-60L, a twin-turbine helicopter capable of flying over 1100 nautical miles without refueling. A smaller chopper would have given them more room to maneuver inside an ice shaft, but the UH-60L was more reliable and stable—a good thing if they were negotiating a 4,593 foot hole. Plus, the heli could lift an awesome 9,000 lb external payload, just in case they uncovered something worth extracting. Flint had orders to be prepared for anything.

"Ready, Sir?" Flint asked, as Tom ran past him.

"Be right there," Tom called back, as he headed to the Jamesway dormitory. He scooped up his knapsack, binoculars, camera, videocam, and a sonar device to measure snow depth just in case the melt wasn't complete. And in that event, he also grabbed a remote control and monitor for the ISLAPS if he needed to restart the melt while they hovered above the hole.

Tom ran back to the chopper and belted himself into a back seat.

Greer was already on board beside the pilot.

Flint took off, giving Tom an aerial view of the melt site. Every available man was scurrying about preparing to install the elevator that would reach the bottom of the shaft. Tom admired how well Greer could get people moving.

The captain carefully positioned the helicopter over the hole. The UH-60L had a sixty-five foot rotor span. Though they had plenty of room on either side for their descent, a special computer program had been installed that would monitor the heli's distance from the shaft's four walls and keep it centered between them. Still, it would take the captain's full attention to make sure the program operated properly to keep them from crashing.

Meanwhile, Tom fastened the videocam to the outside of the helicopter door. He also adjusted the sonar device and turned it on.

His heart leapt. The cavity beneath them was exactly 4,590 feet deep. "We reached ground!" he yelled over the roaring motor.

"Take her down!" Greer shouted to Flint, pointing downward with his thumb to pantomime his order.

Inside the hole, the noise of the chopper was deafening as it reverberated off the shaft's walls. After descending a few hundred feet, the daylight dimmed and the ice turned from white to pale blue and then, further down, indigo.

Tom reached out the door and looked up at the square of light that was the hole they had entered. It seemed miles away.

Flint turned on the floodlights. They illuminated the cliff walls and reached into the void below. Tom got out his binoculars. He had no idea what to expect. They were uncovering land that had not seen daylight for thousands of years. He leaned out the door once again and this time looked down into the darkness. He could see nothing. The hole swallowed the floodlight like a hungry animal. Tom put away the binoculars but kept looking down.

Soon he began to see a faint light from within the void. It seemed to grow larger as they approached. Was it his imagination? Tom studied it carefully through the binoculars, and sure enough, it looked like a light.

"Colonel Greer," Tom shouted. "Do you see that?"

"Flint, turn off the floods," Greer ordered in response.

The pilot complied.

The light at the bottom of the hole went away.

"Now turn 'em back on."

The light returned.

"Colonel, it must be a reflection," Tom said.

Of what?

The reflection intensified as the helicopter approached. Then its source finally came into view.

Awestruck, the men remained speechless.

"Good God!" Greer exclaimed, finally breaking their silence.

33.

The howling desert wind tugged at the stakes of Daria's tent as she worked to unbury more of the pyramid. It wasn't easy to dig with one hand, for the other was still bleeding from the cut on her finger. Periodically, she sucked the wound to remove the sand that kept bothering it.

After Daria had dug a hole large enough to sit in, she realized she might never reach the pyramid's base. She sat in the hole and leaned against the pyramid to rest. Its energy was palpable, and somehow it felt comforting and friendly.

Daria couldn't wait to tell the others about the pyramid and get an archeological study of it started as soon as possible. But first, she wanted to study it more closely by herself. To hide the light of her flashlight and the shadow it would produce through the tent's walls, she draped a blanket over her head. She chuckled to herself when she realized it was like playing under the bed-covers at night with a childhood friend.

"Okay, you," she whispered to the pyramid as she started to examine it. "Tell me about yourself."

The pyramid was smooth and shiny. Its interlocking bricks separated by a hairline. Its silvery surface was the exact color and had the same shine as her pendant. She examined the pyramid's apex. It was pale yellow and reminded her of the alloy called electrum, a mixture of gold and silver that was often used on the tips of ancient Egyptian obelisks and pyramidions.

Then she noticed something that looked like a defect in the pyramid's otherwise flawless construction. On one side, about an inch from the top, there was a rectangular crack between the capstone and the miniature bricks below it. Was it too perfect to be a flaw?

Without thinking, Daria reached for her pendant. She removed it from around her neck and slipped the end of it into the opening. It fit perfectly. Awestruck and intensely curious, she turned the key and the uppermost one-inch portion of the pyramid lifted up. She caught the capstone in one hand and removed the key with the other. The capstone was lighter in weight than she had expected.

A chill spread through her.

Daria immediately noticed the writing on the square top of the pyramid where the capstone once sat. It clearly wasn't Egyptian. She turned the capstone upside down to look for more writing and instead, in the center of its underside, she found yet another slit. It was the same size as the previous one. For the heck of it Daria tried the key again. It fit. She turned the key.

The capstone fell to pieces!

Daria's reflexes reacted in full speed to catch them all, and in doing so she dropped the flashlight. At the same time, a light briefly burst inside her tent, momentarily blinding her. Daria thought it was the falling flashlight shining into her eyes. She picked up the flashlight and used it to collect the angular pieces of capstone that had fallen into her lap.

She also found a sphere, the size of a marble, which brightly reflected the flashlight's beam. Apparently the sphere had been housed inside the capstone. Daria picked it up and cradled it in her palm along with the other pieces of capstone. The sphere was translucent, opalescent, and highly reflective.

Her main concern was the capstone. Had she broken it? Did she have all the pieces? She looked around. A minute later she was sure she had them—nine in all. Daria repositioned herself beside the pyramid, smoothed a patch of sand, and put the pieces down. Over and over again she tried fitting them back together but without success. She wished Grandma Sarah were there. Sarah was a puzzle expert who surely would have been able to put the capstone back together.

After many minutes of struggle, Daria's despair brought her to tears. No way could she fix or replace the capstone. She leaned against the pyramid wondering what to do next. She put her cut finger back into her mouth.

"That's funny," she said aloud as she examined her fingertip. The cut was gone. Maybe it wasn't so bad after all.

Suddenly a gust of wind, stronger than any before, threatened to upend her tent. Daria put the key back around her neck. She placed the pieces of capstone inside her leather pouch and put the sphere inside the velvet one—she didn't want to risk the capstone pieces possibly scratching the sphere. Then she moved all her necklaces inside her sweater.

The wind now pounded against her tent in waves. Its howl was deafening. This wasn't the season for a *khamseen*, Daria protested. Sandstorms usually occurred in April and May. Nevertheless, fine sand was now blowing inside the tent from underneath making it hard to breathe, coating Daria's eyelashes, and darkening the flashlight's now faint glimmer. Daria rolled herself tightly in the blankets, wrapping them also around her head. Then she huddled against the pyramid using the hole she had dug for what scant shelter it provided.

The next angry gust of wind strained the tent's stakes one last time. In the next moment the wind carried away the tent, leaving Daria at the mercy of the stinging sand. She screamed for help, but the wind stole every sound she made. It also filled her mouth with grit. The night was black and though she tried to open her eyes to look for the others, the fiercely blowing sand stung too badly.

The wind was as strong as it was unusual, and sand soon filled the hole she'd dug and then piled up against her. She'd heard horror stories of people who had attempted to wait out such storms lying down and were buried alive. Desperate, she stood up, clutching the blanket for dear life. She fought to remain upright, as the wind forced her to wander, blindly, into the night.

34.

Thursday, September 11th.

The sandstorm eventually ceased, and Daria fell to the ground exhausted. The night was still pitch black, and sleep came easily.

Daria dreamed she was riding a flying pyramidion, gripping its sides so she wouldn't fall off. With equal tenacity she clutched the blanket in which she was still wrapped. It had protected her from the stinging sand, and her life had depended on it. As the sun rose, its heat began to beat down on her, and in her dream, the pyramidion took her closer and closer to the sun until she became terrified of burning in its heat. For a few moments the surreal experiences of the dream bled into the blatant reality of her outer predicament. Where did one end and the other begin? Soon she realized that her body really was baking inside her woolly cocoon. A wave of terror produced a shot of adrenaline that made her wrestle with the blankets, panic-driven, until she was free.

"Oh God I hate nightmares," Daria said aloud, spitting sand from her mouth, shaking it out of her clothes, and brushing it away from her eyes. When she opened them she found herself, to her horror, alone in a valley of towering sand dunes.

Without a moment's hesitation, she trudged up the dune, with blanket in hand. When she reached the top she saw that her predicament was far more frightening than any nightmare.

The sand dunes reached to every horizon. There were no

rocky outcroppings to provide shade, no towns, no tents, no people, and no camel trains. Not even the waters of the Qattara Depression, which would have given her some sense of where she was. Worse, the wind had erased her footprints. She had no idea which direction she had come from, or where Omar and the Bedouin herders might be.

Surely Omar would send someone to find her … or her key, she thought. Wouldn't he be surprised to learn the Horus prophecy had already come true and that she'd found the capstone? Or, at least *a* capstone—how could she know if this was the right one? If it was, Omar would no longer need to protect her on her journey to find it. What would be his role in her destiny now? Could he put the capstone back together? Or would he be angry that she'd broken it? Maybe the capstone was now worthless. She also lamented the fact that the wind had moved her away from the pyramid, which surely was buried again. She wished she had told the others about it instead of hoarding the discovery. In that case, maybe someone could have stayed with it, or somehow marked its location, despite what happened to her.

Daria stopped herself. This was no time to think about such things. She was in a desperate situation and needed to focus all her attention on what she could do to survive.

The sun was hot and the sky perfectly blue. In September the average temperature in Cairo was seventy-nine degrees Fahrenheit. The desert could be over twenty degrees higher, and the sand like a hot frying pan.

Sealing her fate was the fact that she had no water, and her tongue already felt like sandpaper. Daria was doomed if she expended any energy looking for help—and doomed if she didn't. The most she could do was protect herself from sunburn, so she draped the blanket over her head for shade. She kicked away a layer of sand from the top of the dune, digging until she found some cooler sand beneath, and then curled up inside the hole she'd made. The blanket made her sweat, but at least it protected her from the sun, which would otherwise roast her alive.

She asked for a miracle.

When none came by mid-afternoon she was sure she was going to die. How she yearned for water! She considered biting herself and drinking her own blood she was so thirsty. Soon she stopped sweating. Finally, she lost consciousness.

That evening, noises in the desert roused Daria from her oblivion. But she couldn't awaken. She could only look down at herself, like a pair of eyes hovering about thirty feet above the ground. From that viewpoint she saw a handful of Bedouin men clamber up her sand dune. They were laughing and singing, and the pots that hung from their camels' saddles made quite a racket. Daria was strangely distanced from the events happening before her. She had no emotions to feel hope, no voice to yell out, no thought to feel gratitude for her rescue or fear for what it might entail, and no energy to wake up. Once again she felt a profound peace, and whether or not they revived her didn't matter.

She watched one of the men blot her face and lips with a wet cloth and then wrap the cloth around her head. He picked up her body, rolled it loosely in linen, and gently laid it over a camel's back. Then they headed west, in the direction from which they had come.

35.

It had been over twenty-four hours since Sarah McHenry received the phone call from Faoud Fayed announcing Daria's abduction. Her husband, David, promised to leave England and fly back home immediately, but Sarah convinced him there was nothing he could do in Connecticut. David was better off helping his brother, who health was failing and who desperately needed him.

Sarah distracted herself by trying to solve Rubik's cubes in less and less time. The world record was just over twelve seconds, with the solution found in twenty moves or less. Her personal best was still about thirty seconds. The sport of speed-cubing required memorizing countless algorithms, which kept her mind alert, although it also strained her wrists and forearms. Today the pain helped to keep her from worrying.

When her aching arms let her play the puzzle no more, she wept.

Part of her despair stemmed from the deep remorse she still felt for not having acted upon the dream premonitions she'd had about her son's death twenty-five years ago. Although she'd come to understand that the dream ultimately had prepared her for losing Ian, so his death hadn't been the paralyzing shock it could have been, she felt guilty for not having listened and done something to save him.

When it occurred to her that she might have had dreams about Daria's abduction, she got up and scoured her dream journals for clues. She found nothing that seemed to have anything to do with her granddaughter.

Sarah also asked, rather begged, for a dream that would tell her what she could do to get her granddaughter back alive. Previously whenever she'd asked for dream guidance, it was an admittedly half-baked request that she simply sent off into the universe. More often than not, it resulted in a dream that made some sense and gave her insight. This time the stakes were too high to be so casual. She needed answers—clear ones—and she wanted them now. The dilemma had made her ponder how she should make her request and to whom. The one thing she was certain about was that her requests had been answered before. So somebody 'up there' was indeed listening.

Sarah sat back down in her easy chair, closed her eyes, and let herself imagine who that person might be and what he might look like. In her mind's eye she conjured the image of a clean-shaven man with tanned skin and long blond hair, clothed in a white robe. At first she thought she'd envisioned Jesus, but then remembered he had brown hair and a beard in all the pictures she had seen of him. No matter, the exercise was making her feel more peaceful.

She rested her head against the back of the chair and let herself relax into her imagination. The man in her vision held up a small stack of letters. Sarah recognized her stationary. They were the letters she had written earlier that day to God, to Jesus, to several Catholic Saints, as well as to Moses, to Buddha, and even one to Ramtha. Of course, she didn't have addresses for any of them, but she pretended to mail them by putting them under her pillow. She rationalized these silly actions as those of a desperate old woman, and besides, nobody would ever find out. Except somehow, this beautiful being had.

Suddenly Sarah realized she hadn't imagined the being showing her the letters. The vision had happened spontaneously, as though it had been a real dream. The thought that one could dream while still awake startled Sarah, so she got up, headed to the kitchen to make herself some tea, and tried to forget it had happened at all.

While the tea was brewing, she noticed Mr. Fayed's phone number on a piece of paper she had taped to the kitchen counter and suddenly had an idea. It was around noon in Connecticut. Cairo was seven hours ahead, so it was evening there. She phoned anyway and reached a man who identified himself as Fayed's secretary. She cleared her throat and, tired as she was, did her best to sound businesslike and authoritative.

"Good evening," Sarah said, "I'm from the Hartford Courant, a major newspaper in Connecticut, on the East Coast of the United States. I understand a woman from Connecticut, a renowned Yale University Professor, has been kidnapped and I was wondering if Mr. Faoud Fayed could give me a statement."

"Kidnapped?"

"Yes. Soon after she arrived in Cairo," Sarah said.

"I have not heard of this. We at Fayed Enterprises are dealers and appraisers of Egyptian art and antiquities," the poor man said defensively. "I think you have the wrong number," he added.

Egyptian antiquities?

In a split second Sarah remembered the Key to the Capstone that Daria wore. She recalled everything Ian had told her about it, including the responsibilities and destiny of the key-bearer. No doubt Daria's destiny was unfolding on her very first return to Egypt since she'd received the key. Daria was involved in power-ful forces that would also protect her. Sarah's despair evaporated, and she knew immediately that whatever happened, Daria would be okay.

"Forgive me," Sarah said over the phone. "You're right. I must have dialed the wrong number. Please do not tell anyone I made this error."

The man understood completely.

36.

Friday, September 12th.

Daria awoke alone in a large rectangular tent made of strips of brown cloth woven from camel and goat hair. A line of palm-wood poles supported the center of the tent. Between these poles hung a colorful curtain, which Daria recog-nized as a *ma'nad*. It divided the men's side of the tent from the women's. A large loom dominated the woman's side where Daria lay. The loom held a rug—a work in progress—made of beige, brown, and black wool. Baskets of the yarn were arranged neatly on the floor beside the loom.

Poles of palm wood also supported the sides of the tent. Nails had been driven into these poles and upon them were hung vari-ous items for daily living including colorful fabric; a *jubbe*, or woolen overcoat; nets containing dates and apricots; pots and cooking utensils; a lantern; a *shabbaba*, which was a long flute-like pipe; a *rababa* or one-string violin; plus sacks of unknown contents.

Daria was feeling much better. Her tongue was tolerably dry, and the cracks that had formed around her once dehydrated lips were covered in a ghastly tasting balm. She closed her eyes and took an inventory of her body and immediate surroundings. Hadn't she been in a similar predicament only a few days before?

She was resting on rugs once again, but this time she was covered with a warm camel hair blanket. Her clothes and waist-wallet were gone, but her necklaces had been untouched. Heavy, damp poultices had been placed behind her neck and around her shoulders, elbows, and wrists, as well as her hips, knees, and ankles.

Daria listened intently. She could hear enough sounds to surmise she was in a village—a nomadic one, based on the kind of tent she was in. Chickens clucked, goats brayed, and a breeze rustled the fronds of palm trees. There were voices too. Unfortunately, she couldn't understand the Bedouin language, though occasionally someone would say something in Arabic. However, the giggles and shrieks of children playing happily were the same in any language. A man's deep voice gave orders to someone. It turned out to be a woman, based on the sound of the voice that replied.

Someone entered the tent.

"*Sahbah el khayr* [good morning]," said a woman speaking Arabic. "I see you are awake, though trying not to show it. Don't worry, you are safe here."

Daria opened her eyes. The woman wore a loose-fitting, floor-length, long-sleeved dress of a colorful floral print. Silver bracelets adorned her wrists and ankles. Two heavy, silver rings found a home on each hand. A black silk georgette hajib framed her wrinkled brown face and covered her head, throat, and shoulders. A string of silver disks encircled her head, denoting the woman's relatively high rank in the tribe. She also wore a necklace of large gold and silver disks.

The woman smiled and put a damp cloth over Daria's fore-head and then used it to wipe her face. "We expected you would wake up today," she said.

Daria wondered how long she'd been unconscious. She was too tired to speak or think clearly.

The woman brought her a bowl of something that looked like porridge and fed it to Daria. It was salty, tasted like mashed nuts, and would have been nourishing if she could get past the texture of moistened sawdust. Daria tried to swallow it.

"Too dry yet," the woman said before pouring some water into the porridge. Daria wished that the woman would just let her drink the water. Instead, she encouraged Daria to drink the porridge from the bowl.

"It is healing," the woman said. "Drink it all."

Daria did so, and then felt light-headed and lay back down.

"Yes, you rest," the woman said.

Daria's eyelids grew heavy and closed.

37.

Colonel Greer and Major Davison checked the construction of the elevator that would eventually take them down the ice shaft to the Antarctic floor. Despite their good progress, Greer's elevated blood pressure was making his neck veins bulge. He was also hoarse from shouting orders.

When they returned to the Jamesway station, Lieutenant Manning greeted him with a salute and an urgent message.

"Colonel Greer, Sir, General Taylor wants to speak with you immediately, Sir," he said.

Greer cleared his throat. "Open a line."

"Yes, Sir." An oncoming storm made it difficult to obtain a

secure line of communication, but finally Manning was able to patch Greer through to Andrews Air Force Base.

"Greer?"

"Yes, Sir."

"What's going on down there?"

"Sir? I sent word, we had melt. The technology works."

"Are you sure there's nothing unusual going on?"

"The elevator is under construction ..."

"Colonel Greer," General Taylor interrupted, "there's an unidentified power source on the floor of the mid-Atlantic. We've been studying it for months and have been unable to identify where it came from or who put it there. Six days ago, its emissions suddenly intensified, and we believe they are responsible for the Category 5 hurricane that's threatening the Eastern Seaboard. Shipping is paralyzed and civilians are panicking."

"I'm unaware of that, Sir," Greer said.

Taylor wasn't finished. "Furthermore, at 17:37 hundred hours yesterday new, unidentified beams began shooting from the power source, headed in your direction. In fact, they stop at your precise coordinates. When other governments notice these waves, track them and find you, they're going to want to know what's going on. Hell, *I'd* like to know. We're going to violate the Antarctic Treaty if we don't let reps from other countries visit the mission. You reported melt. I want to know what in damn hell you found."

Greer swallowed hard. He'd never heard Taylor raise his voice before. Telling the truth about what they uncovered could risk his career. Nobody would believe him. He'd be labeled a lunatic.

"Sir," he said, trying to sound matter-of-fact. "At what time did you say this anomaly began?"

"17:37 hundred."

That was exactly twenty-five minutes after the melt had begun. It was also about the time when the melt should have ended.

"I have nothing additional to report at this time, Sir. Greer out."

Taylor could sense Greer was hiding something. But what? Could it really be so extraordinary that a United States Air Force colonel would lie about it?

Taylor hoped so. On the other hand, Greer's lack of cooperation was intolerable but right now there was nothing he could do about it.

38.

Saturday, September 13th.

Tom, Colonel Greer, and Major Davison stepped inside the elevator that would take them down to the bottom of the ice shaft. They wanted to confirm what they had seen from the helicopter and what the soldiers who built the elevator had reported.

The elevator door, as well as its left and right sides, were made of sheet metal and had metal railings to hold onto. The side opposite the door consisted of a waist-high gate of vertical, cage like bars. This gave them an unobstructed view of the far wall of the ice shaft and what lay below. A light bulb was fastened to the elevator ceiling and floodlights beneath the elevator pointed downward. The elevator also carried an extension ladder plus tools and testing equipment.

When Davison moved the start lever, the elevator lurched into a freefall.

Tom grabbed a railing for support and clenched his teeth. When the elevator's gears regained control and began to lower the cage more evenly, Tom maintained his white-knuckled grip on the railing.

Davison laughed.

Tom groaned.

"I'll have the boys tweak the system and make sure the initial drop isn't so bad next time," Davison assured him.

Tom nodded. "How long until we reach bottom?"

"About thirteen minutes," Davison replied. "This baby drops 350 feet per minute. That's a quarter as fast as the high-speed elevators in the Empire State Building." Davison paused, as if preparing to deliver a punch line. "Bet you didn't know that," he finally said, hoping his love of trivia would cheer up Tom, or at least take his attention off his queasiness.

Tom tried looking outside the elevator, but its movement in relation to the ice shaft caused too much vertigo. Thankfully, the feeling went away when Tom turned and focused on the elevator's solid walls.

Feeling better, Tom let his mind wander. He worried what he would do now that he had fulfilled his dream of making ice-melt technology work. He had achieved his life-long goal with so many years yet ahead of him. What was next?

Then he noticed how quiet it was in the shaft without the blaring noise of the helicopter's blades. The silence was invaded only by the elevator's rhythmic clanking, and that was easy to shut out. Tom felt a kind of sacredness in the moment. According to conventional theory, they were going where nobody had been for 122,000 years. Although other scientists claimed the ice sheet was anywhere from 400,000 to 3,000,000 years old. Geologists couldn't agree on exactly how old the ice sheet really was. Maybe ice-core dating techniques were completely misleading, Tom wondered. After all, 11,000-year-old frozen mammoths had been found in northeastern Siberia—directly opposite Lesser Antarctica on the globe. Shouldn't two opposing geographic locations share the same weather? They did now, why not also 11,000 years ago? If this was true, then Lesser Antarctica could have supported wildlife back then too. It would have been ice free.

Tom wondered what Davison and Greer were thinking. Did anyone share his awe?

Greer had only one thing in mind: complete the mission and

go home. He couldn't stop thinking of the far more important work that he *should* be doing at the Pentagon. His department recently had uncovered some new data on nuclear weapons in the Middle East. Greer wanted to be at the forefront of the military's plans to deal with them. He cursed the assignment that had taken him away from what he felt was the real action.

Luckily, the melt had been a success. Now Greer's orders were to take a sample of whatever they found down there, inspect the stability of the shaft's walls, and assess the feasibility of using similar shafts for military purposes. After compiling his report, he would radio General Taylor to inform him they were ready to dynamite the hole and cover their tracks. Greer would be back in Washington in less than a week. The only problem was the unusual *thing* they'd unburied. What would he tell Taylor? And when? Maybe it was nothing — just a natural mountaintop.

Nearly 4,590 feet down, the elevator stopped. It was dark inside the hole, and Davison turned on the extra floodlights.

The monument before them could not be mistaken.

Between the slick walls of the ice shaft emerged a pyramid whose shiny surface brightly reflected the elevator's lamps. The perfect pyramid filled the hole and likely extended for countless feet further down. Oddly, its top was missing so its apex looked like a square instead of a point. Tom suggested it had been broken off by the weight of the ice that had buried it.

The ice shaft wasn't centered precisely over the pyramid. Its top was about ten feet away from one of the shaft's walls. Greer noted the pyramid's off-centeredness when they first had seen it from the helicopter. Wisely, he ordered the elevator be built close to the apex, where a sample could be taken more easily.

Tom was anxious to climb down to the pyramid, but had to wait for Davison to set up and check the radioactivity monitor and air quality analyzer. Meanwhile, Tom noticed that at this depth, the shaft's frozen walls were devoid of layers, like one would expect from years of falling snow. He quelled an urge to point it out to Greer and Davison. Was this area once deeply flooded and then frozen? If only he could find a fish or some seaweed embedded in the walls, his idea would be vindicated. But to whom? Showing the evidence to the scientific community would mean revealing this technology to the world. Tom doubted the U.S. military would allow that. Not after the contracts of secrecy he had been obliged to sign before departing on this mission. For the rest of his life, Tom had agreed to tell no one that ice-melt technology even existed and to never redevelop the technology later.

Although Tom continued to study the ice, to his dismay, he found not a piece of evidence to support his frozen flood theory.

Davison reported no radioactivity and air quality was acceptable. They were free to proceed to the pyramid.

Tom opened the elevator's gate, and took a short jump down to a platform of scaffolding the soldiers had also built. He then helped Davison with the extension ladder.

Greer remained in the elevator to make his own visual inspection of the shaft to include in his report. The light from the elevator's floodlights and from the lamps on their helmets cast eerie shadows on the ice walls. The ice looked bluish and smooth. In some places it was mirror like. Yet it also was rock solid and would surely make a secure missile silo, he decided.

Tom descended the extension ladder and stepped carefully into the slippery and sharply angled crevice between the ice wall and the pyramid. He found his balance and then removed his gloves to stroke the pyramid's shiny unblemished surface. He traced the hairline edges between the blocks that comprised the pyramid.

"Is it a precious metal?" Greer called down.

"I don't think so, Sir," Tom replied. "It's silvery but I don't think it's actual silver."

"Humph," Greer replied. "Davison, start the saw. I want a chunk of this thing."

Tom's stomach knotted. This was by far the most significant ancient monument ever unearthed, and Greer wanted to damage it?

"But Sir!" Tom protested.

Greer ignored him.

Davison gave Tom a look of understanding and shrugged his shoulders. He had to follow orders. The roar of the gas-powered saw ricocheted off the icy walls.

Defiantly, Tom moved the extension ladder so it rested against the pyramid's side. He climbed the ladder onto the pyramid's flat top, which was about ten feet wide. There he discovered that the pyramidion wasn't broken off. The pyramid's flat top was the same color and material as its sides, and was also polished. The top either had been removed, or it never existed.

Meanwhile, Greer's impatience grew as Davison's saw was obviously making no progress. The hammer and chisel Davison then tried didn't make a dent either. Damn this bad luck, Greer thought. The pyramid filled the entire hole as his men had reported, so they could not take the surface samples that General Taylor had specifically asked for. They needed to do another melt. Unless the storm died down soon, it could take days before Seymour could set up his equipment again. Greer needed to be back at the Pentagon and the entire mission needed to be out of there before other governments found them and started asking questions. Where did these melt coordinates come from anyway, he wanted to know? Of all the places they could have melted, why did they have to do it here and uncover something so strange? A pyramid for god sakes. What a headache!

"Colonel Greer," Tom called. "You should see this. There's a three-foot circle engraved on the top of the pyramid, filled with symbols. A small circle in the center looks like it might contain a map." He pulled the camera from his knapsack and began taking pictures.

"I don't give a damn about the pyramid," Greer hollered. His booming voice filled the hole and echoed off its walls. "My orders are to obtain a sample of this continent's surface, and I want you to melt another hole as soon as possible!"

"Yes, Sir," Tom replied. Then he tested Greer's blood pressure by quickly taking a few more photos of the pyramid's engraved top. "Coming, Sir," he said as he repacked his camera and scrambled back to the elevator.

On the ride up, Tom could hardly contain his excitement. Minutes ago he had feared the end of a life-long dream. Now he realized that one dream leads to another, but you can't see what's next until you achieve the first. He had melted over 4500 feet of ice in about twenty-five minutes. And there, beneath the ice, Tom had found kindling for a new dream. This pyramid had called to him since childhood. First by giving him its coordinates. Then by giving him the technology to unbury it. Now he found ancient writing and a map. Where did it lead?

As they neared the surface, the howling winds of a storm grew louder. Clouds of falling snow drifted into the shaft, swirling into whirlpools on the confined air currents. They collected on the icy walls, frosting them with sparkling fluff.

"Damn the storm," Greer muttered. In Antarctica, winds of hurricane magnitude could appear out of nowhere. Visibility could become instantly zero, and the cold reliably ridiculous. It was impossible to set up the ISLAPS for further melting at this time. They would have to wait until the winds died down.

"Sir," Tom said. "Can I have permission to study the pyramid? It may be my only chance. Archeologically, this is ..."

"Just be ready to do another melt again on my command," Greer interrupted.

"Yes, Sir," Tom replied.

"Oh," Greer added, "and see if you can find out if that thing was once a radio receiver of some sort." Maybe Tom could find an answer to the signals being sent to their coordinates by General Taylor's anomalous underwater power source.

39.

Tom clenched the handle bars of the elevator as it again dropped in a freefall before the cables grabbed control of its descent down the ice shaft. This time, Tom didn't mind the nausea. He couldn't wait to get back to the pyramid. He knew Greer would eventually confiscate his film and any notes he took, but he was eager to copy the symbols he'd found on the pyramid's top anyway. By doing so, he hoped to memorize some of them and research them when he returned to the States. He also wanted to look for other writing on the pyramid's sides.

Tom lamented the fact that his ice-melt experiment had to be clandestine. They should bring in an army of archeologists, he thought. The pyramid's very presence demanded a new look at human history. Now Greer wanted to melt another shaft. What would they find on the ground? The pyramid looked intact; other artifacts were likely as well preserved. Tom would look again for seaweed and other flood evidence, which would be more likely located on or near the ground.

What a miracle it had been that General Taylor agreed to use his coordinates. Maybe Taylor knew more than he let on. After all, it was the general who had broached the subject of Atlantis. Maybe the military had the technology to see through the ice and knew of the pyramid already? Then, Tom's proposal to melt ice on these precise coordinates was an opportunity the military couldn't pass up.

The elevator reached its end and stopped. Tom made his way to the pyramid and climbed to its top. He adjusted the lamp on his helmet, got out his notebook, and began to draw. A minute later he realized his efforts were fruitless. He simply couldn't accurately copy such unusual writing. What if he missed an important detail? To get an accurate replica he had to try something else.

Tom tore out a page from his notebook and placed it against the writing. Using a pencil, he scratched back and forth over the entire paper to capture the indentations in the stone. It would be too laborious to make a rubbing of everything, so he focused on the map and symbols in the center. It was tedious work and required several pencils and pieces of paper. When Tom was finished, he filed the papers in his backpack.

Then he stood up and stretched. Immediately, he felt lightheaded. He was at the top of an ancient world – and at the bottom of a hole in a modern one. Both worlds seemed equally far away. The solitude was tangible. Tom closed his eyes to let his imagination wander. This pyramid once overlooked an entire city, he thought. At its base, he envisioned beautiful homes, shopping centers, schools, recreation facilities, and government buildings. He saw trees, lakes, fountains, and waterfalls.

His reverie was interrupted when, without warning, a tremor shook the ground. Chunks of ice hurled down from above. Startled, and immediately defensive, Tom covered his head with his arms to protect himself. Dodging a particularly large piece, he lost his balance, slipped on the surface of the pyramid's top, and tumbled over its far side into the darkness below.

The side of the pyramid was steep and sheer and although Tom groped for a handhold, there was nothing to cling to. Dislodged snow and chunks of ice accompanied him down the pyramid's slippery side.

Then his helmet fell off and his lamp went out. At any moment he would meet the crevice where ice wall and pyramid met. Desperately, he tried to maneuver himself so his feet would hit first, but his body was moving too fast. He braced himself for impact.

When Tom's body hit the wall, he let out a grunt.

He rested motionless while he inventoried himself for injuries and let his heart rate come back to normal. Thankfully, his thick pants and fleecy thermal underwear had provided essential padding. Tom's body felt like one big bruise, but nothing was broken.

He feared another tremor. Earthquakes were not uncommon in Antarctica, but the seismic recorder had shown the area had been quiet for months. But if another quake came — and if it was any stronger than this last one — he risked being buried alive from falling snow and ice. Or worse, the elevator might break. Then he'd really be stuck. He had to get back to the surface as soon as possible.

He waited until the last of the snow and ice finally stopped sliding down the pyramid's side. He was encased in darkness except for the outline of the pyramid's flat top, back-lit by the elevator's floodlights. The opening of the ice shaft was somewhere in the distance, too far away to see.

Feeling his way, Tom clambered over the chunks of ice that cluttered the crevice. It was a difficult task. Both the pyramid's side and the ice shaft's wall were slick and offered no hand-holds. He kept slipping and straining his ankles and knees, which soon began to throb. He wished he were in better shape and promised himself he'd start jogging if he lived through this.

Then he tripped and twisted his knee. He rubbed it hard, trying to brush off the pain. To his fortune he had tripped over his own helmet and the headlamp hadn't broken, it had just shut off. He turned it back on, put the hat back on his head, and continued his journey. The light was a welcome relief as it allowed him to pick his way more carefully.

Soon he reached the corner of the shaft where the edge of the pyramid turned upward at a sharp angle. He stopped and leaned against the pyramid to rest. His knee hurt and he was exhausted.

Then he remembered how, as a child, he used to climb to the top of the playground sliding board not by the ladder but up the board itself. The trick was to have really good sneakers or else go barefoot. He removed his boots, tied the laces together, and hung the boots around his neck. Then he took off his socks and stuffed them in his boots. He stepped onto the pyramid's side and as he had guessed, his bare feet clung to the cold surface. All he needed to do was lean forward as though walking up a steep hill.

This was his opportunity to examine the pyramid's sides and he meandered sideways. Now that the earth had stopped shaking, he felt comfortable enough to take his time. He would make his ascent gradually. On his way up, Tom searched for symbols or ornament but found none. Each block that comprised the pyramid was smooth, about the same size as the ones that formed Egypt's Great Pyramid, and placed perfectly against the ones beside it. Then Tom found a block that was considerably smaller. It was no more than a foot wide and six inches tall. Curious, he stopped to study it and casually outlined it with his fingers. On impulse, he pressed it.

Suddenly, a large block to Tom's left slid inward.

Tom stepped back.

"Dios mío," he whispered.

There before him was an opening the size of a doorway. Tom had stumbled upon an entrance to the pyramid!

40.

Daria slept almost twenty-four hours and awoke to the rhythmic tapping of wood against wood. The woman who had taken care of her was sitting at the loom working. She smiled at Daria, then got up and offered her water. Daria was so thirsty that she took the cup greedily. She had much more energy now.

"*Shokran* [thank you]," she said when she was finished drinking.

"*Alafu* [you're welcome]," the woman replied smiling again.

Daria smiled back.

"*Ana ismee Gateefa* [name is Gateefa]," the woman said. "*Entee ismik ay* [what is your name]?"

"Daria. My name is Daria," she replied.

"Dree ar aya," Gateefa said slowly, trying to pronounce "Daria" correctly.

"*La la* [no no]," Daria said, and repeated her name.

"Ah, Dah-ya," the woman said, knowing she had said it almost right that time.

Daria nodded.

Gateefa nodded in return. Then she took the cup and left the tent without saying where she was going or when she would come back.

Daria looked around for something to wear so she could peak outside but found nothing suitable. Where were her clothes? And what about her waist wallet? At least she still wore her necklaces.

Just then Gateefa returned with a meal. Although Daria had the strength to feed herself, she politely allowed the woman to feed her the meal of flat bread and eggs that were one-third the size of a chicken's egg. To wash it down, Gateefa gave her a cup of goat's milk.

"Are we near the Siwa Oasis?" Daria asked in Arabic.

"Yes."

"How far is it?"

"No place is too far away when you are meant to be there," Gateefa said.

Gateefa asked Daria to stand up so she could dress her. Daria received a floor-length dress, similar in style to the woman's, though Daria's was blue and embroidered with red, black, and gold. On her legs she was given a pair of loose-fitting pants. Finally, Gateefa draped a black hajib over Daria's head, neck, and shoulders. Gateefa filled Daria's wrists with bracelets and put two rings on each of her hands.

"Shokran," Daria said. She wasn't giving thanks just for the adornments, which she knew were only borrowed, but for everything Gateefa had done for her.

"*El ahfoo* [don't mention it]," Gateefa replied. "Now, come with me."

Daria guessed she would now be taken to the tribe's leader, its sheik. She decided she would politely request an escort to the nearest town, where she might then find her way back to a city on her own.

Daria followed the woman out of the tent and finally saw the community her ears had tried to paint. Gateefa's tent was one of many located in a large grove of palm trees that stood beside a pool of fresh blue water. Goats and sheep grazed in the tall green grasses that grew by the water's edge. A few of the older children were tending the animals, while younger children played freely everywhere else. It was an idyllic scene, Daria thought, exactly the way she had pictured an oasis to be.

Daria and Gateefa passed small groups of Bedouin women sitting in front of their tents doing daily tasks such as grinding flour, mending baskets, and embroidering cloth. Most of the men Daria saw were standing around talking.

As Daria passed by, everyone stopped what they were doing and looked at her. Not just a brief gaze, but a long, intent stare. It was one of the most uncomfortable experiences she'd ever had.

"Pay them no mind," said Gateefa. She explained that staring was their way of protecting themselves from what they called the evil eye — basically anything unfamiliar to them.

Gateefa led Daria to the center of their community where one especially long tent stood. The longer a Bedouin's tent, the more prestige and wealth he had. Daria surmised this central tent belonged to the sheik. Every Bedouin tribe was ruled by one. The sheik was a patriarchal figure who inherited the position from his father. His political clout depended upon his wealth, the strength of his personality, and the size of his camel herd. Daria estimated there were over a hundred camels grazing beyond the perimeter of the tents. They were corralled simply by tying one of their legs into a bent position so they could not wander far.

When they reached the doorway of the sheik's tent, Gateefa urged her inside. Daria entered a small vestibule that was empty but for colorful rugs piled on the floor three deep. A tapestry separated the vestibule from the main tent. She peaked through it.

Her presence was noticed.

"*Etfah dulee, etfah dulee* [come in, come in]," said a richly dressed man who must have been the sheik. Daria noted mentally that he used the formal version of welcome.

The sheik sat cross-legged on a heavily carpeted floor. He wore a red gallabiya that was embroidered with gold and black thread. His face sported a long, thick black beard, streaked with gray. His head was covered with a kufiyya cloth that was secured around his head with an agal rope. A large embroidered carpet hung from the ceiling behind him and separated this section of the tent from the rest of it.

The sheik smiled at Daria.

Daria slowly stepped toward him. The isolation that the desert nomads endured plus the harsh dry climate and need to keep moving in search of grazing land, gave the Bedouins a reputation for having both resilience as well as hospitality.

She addressed him in Arabic, "Thank you for your kindness. You saved my life, and I am eternally grateful to you." She bowed respectfully.

The sheik smiled. "It is an honor to care for one as important as you are," he replied.

Daria looked bewildered. It was unlikely he would flatter her. What did he mean?

The sheik saw her expression but chose not to mention the good fortune Daria had given his people. Word of her presence had brought the Khawi Mikta to their tribe. According to legend, Mikta was over a thousand years old, as wise as the sky, and as knowledgeable as any ancestor. For some reason unknown to the sheik, Mikta had come to see this woman and while he was there, he would give spiritual and medical help to the sheik's people. Mikta's visit alone would make the sheik's tribe noteworthy. From then on, others would consider their carpets more comfortable, their camels more healthy, and their tapestries more valuable.

The sheik said, "You are fortunate to have survived the desert. Allah must look kindly upon you. Now, please, have a seat." He waved his hand toward a large pillow across from him on the rug. "You are safe here. The sun cannot hurt you, nor the wind and sand. My people are your friends."

"And I am yours," Daria said.

A servant brought them a silver tray with a matching teapot and two teacups, a bowl of sugar, a plate of biscuits, a bowl of goat-milk yogurt, and a basket of dates. He poured a dark liquid into each cup. Both Daria and the sheik sipped the drink. It was coffee, not tea, and it had been heavily spiced. Daria recognized the aroma of cardamom.

"Delicious," she said.

"Shokran," the sheik replied. He respected his guest; it was his honor and duty. Yet he couldn't help wondering about her. What had given this American woman the responsibility, the right, and the honor to wear the Navubala openly around her neck and draw the graces of Mikta?

"Have you ever wanted to visit the Library of Alexandria?" the sheik began.

Daria lit up. "The one rebuilt in 2003 or the ancient one?"

"The ancient one."

"It would be my greatest joy," she said. The Library of Alexandria, Egypt, was built around the third century B.C. by Ptolemy II. Charged with the task of gathering all of the world's knowledge, it was supposedly the greatest collection of ancient papyrus and parchment scrolls, containing some 400,000 to 700,000 documents. It was also a center for learning. Recent excavations had uncovered thirteen large lecture halls with a podium in the center of each. Together, they were able to seat as many as 5,000 students. Archeologists found one hall whose walls were once mounted with shelves for the collections of scrolls. Carved into one wall was the inscription: *The place of the cure of the soul.* The library had been burned to the ground sometime before 20 B.C. Nobody knew exactly when, nor who was actually responsible for the destruction.

To Daria, visiting the library would have been akin to being in heaven. All the knowledge in the world would be at her fingertips, and she had the unique ability to read and understand it. Answers to the ancient mysteries would be hers to discover. It would be a delight her heart could only yearn for.

"Excellent," the sheik replied, pulling Daria from her thoughts. He had just asked her the secret question Horus brothers used to identify each other, and Daria, unknowingly, had answered using the correct wording. "I invite you to tell me something I may not know."

"Pardon me?"

"You are a follower of Horus, are you not?"

Daria thought of the capstone and the sphere. Had the sheik inspected her pouches while she slept? Did he know what she had found?

"You are intensely curious about the ancient past, and you want to excite this same interest in others," he prompted.

Was he giving her the parameters of membership or describing her innermost being?

"Then I suppose I am," she replied.

"Then tell me something I may not know."

"I'm sorry, I don't understand."

"Each of us contributes a thread to the tapestry of truth by sharing our knowledge and understanding. When our threads interweave, we gain a greater view of the whole."

"How do I know what you might not know?" Daria asked.

"It is enough to share what you are most curious about."

"Won't you be skeptical?"

He laughed. "I must not be. To refuse or deny your thread would leave an unfilled hole in my own tapestry. I must keep my mind open to receive your thread, acknowledge its place in the universal tapestry, and allow it to weave itself wherever it must go—even if that means into my own. If I can do this, I can return the favor with a thread of truth for you. Then you will have the task of acknowledging and accepting my thread in the universal tapestry. The Shemsu Hor have practiced this art from the beginning."

Daria wondered what she could share with the sheik without

revealing the capstone or its key. Minutes passed in silence. The sheik was a patient man. Daria fought her own skepticism, as she realized it was closing her mind. She also was concerned it would be disrespectful to say something the sheik might not agree with.

"Voice what you know," the sheik finally said.

She knew about Egyptian writing. "The pyramid builders didn't leave any writing in the Giza Pyramids," she said. She was about to mention the writing in the pyramids of Saqqara when the sheik, who was accustomed to this exercise in which you combined inspiration with pieces of information you already knew, quickly expanded on what she said.

"Yet knowledge is available for all to see," the sheik replied.

That was a tenet of ancient Egyptian philosophy that Omar had mentioned too.

"For all who are able see," Daria said, "because they had enough light to see with," she added. Her comment was her best attempt. Daria wasn't sure how to weave an informational, ideological tapestry.

"Or the proper light."

Daria thought about infrared light used in forensics and cryptology, and she wondered why she had never tried using these tools before. "Certain light can reveal words invisible in sunlight," she began to explain.

"Such as firelight?"

"There is no evidence of soot in freshly opened tombs, even in the darkest ones where hieroglyphs were found," Daria said.

"Then light such as from the moon and stars."

Daria again recalled her conversation with Omar. "They say each of the two shafts in the King's Chamber in the Great Pyramid of Giza was once aligned with a star."

The sheik nodded. He knew this fact. "Yes, for about one hundred years, one shaft pointed to the star Al Nitak, the lowest star in Orion's belt. The other was aligned with the star Alpha Draconis."

Daria was impressed the sheik knew this. Then again, he was a Horus member, and probably learned it from other members.

He continued, "But did you know that the shafts are not straight, but bend back and forth at precise angles before exiting the pyramid in the same direction from which they started?"

Daria shook her head. She had imagined the shafts like telescopes, pointing directly to their respective stars.

"It's a recent discovery," the sheik said. "Measured by something called a robot."

Daria wondered if the sheik had any idea what a robot was. "If the shafts were meant to point to these stars, shouldn't they be straight?" she asked.

"Maybe they did point to the stars."

"And the stars moved as the pyramid was built?"

"If this were true, the shafts have recorded a time in stellar history that is highly significant."

And improbable, Daria thought. But she remembered the rules of this dialogue. She wasn't to deny or refute anything the sheik said. She tried to change the subject. So she mused, "I wonder what it looked like inside the King's Chamber when these stars were aligned with the shafts?"

"Ahh," the sheik replied, as though realizing something, "they lit up the chamber so the writing on the walls could be seen."

Daria again she felt both struck and puzzled by what the sheik said. He had turned the subject of their conversation back to where she had started it. She thought carefully of a reply. "Why would the pyramid builders include writing that could be seen only by starlight during a span of a hundred years?"

"To make it more noteworthy," the sheik suggested. "Around 2,450 B.C., when the stars were aligned with the shafts, someone must have found the King's Chamber and saw what was written there. Or if they already were regularly visiting the King's Chamber, the information must have appeared from out of nowhere, as though sent by the stars."

"And when the stars moved out of alignment about a hundred years later?"

"That would have been around 2,350 B.C.," the sheik said.

Daria gasped with a sudden realization. "That date, 2,350 B.C., is well within the reign of the Pharaoh Unas. What if the writing in the King's Chamber began to fade when the stars started to move out of alignment, and Unas had the foresight to copy the writing into the pyramid he built at Saqqara? If so, it exists as the Pyramid Texts, which can be found in the Pyramid of Unas and read today by anyone."

"The knowledge is available for all to see," the sheik repeated.

The flow of their dialogue ebbed.

"We have added to the universal tapestry," the sheik announced. "It is stronger now for all. Can you feel it lifting you?"

Daria wasn't sure, but nodded anyway.

They finished their coffee in silence. The sheik offered her the biscuits and Daria took a few. They tasted of goat's milk. A servant soon appeared and silently stood off to the side of the tent waiting for the sheik to acknowledge his presence. When the sheik finally addressed him, they spoke briefly in Bedouin.

"Very well," the sheik said to Daria, returning to Arabic. "Sidi Mikta is ready to see you."

"Mikta?" Daria exclaimed. How did he know she was there?

"Please, my servant will take you to him," the sheik said.

Daria stood up, bowed to the sheik and said, "A thousand thank yous. I will speak with Sidi Mikta." She walked backward, out of respect for the sheik, then turned and followed the servant out the door.

41.

After finding an entrance to the pyramid, Tom stepped inside it without a second thought or regard to safety or consequence. It was an opportunity he could not pass up.

Before him was a dark, empty hallway. He could see no more than ten feet ahead of him and proceeded cautiously. This was a chance of a lifetime, he thought. An experience that exceeded anything he had ever dreamed. He sighed with delightful anticipation.

To his surprise, the hallway lit up. The walls, which were the same silver color and material as the pyramid's surface shone brilliantly. "Holy shit!" he exclaimed.

The lights went out.

Tom froze with fear. "Who's there?" he choked hoarsely. His imagination filled with stalking mummies, half decayed. He retreated backward toward the door, accidentally bumping into the wall when he reached it. The door closed, fueling his terror.

Tom's shaking legs gave way and he slid to the floor. His heart beat so fast his chest hurt. He felt completely defeated, at the mercy of powers and beings far beyond his control. Thankfully the light of his helmet still worked, but for how long? It was slim comfort. He focused on his breathing and recalled the counselor who had successfully helped him deal with a gripping fear of heights. Tom decided to try the mantra she had given him, but his throat was so tight he could barely speak.

"HU." He finally forced a whisper.

The lights came back on.

Was someone playing tricks on him? He didn't appreciate the humor. He removed his helmet and strained to hear footsteps, voices, or breathing other than his own.

"HUUU," he sang again, this time with more confidence. He repeated the mantra until his voice stopped quivering. The sound calmed him, connected him to his heart, and gave him strength and inner fortitude. Whoever was watching him was leaving him alone. He might have time to escape.

Tom got up to examine the closed door. Its seal was as perfect as the hairline spaces between the outside blocks. There were no door handles or latches. Tom studied the walls on either side, looking for a button, lever, symbol, or anything that might open the door. Then to the right of the door, he saw a small block similar to the one he had pushed on the outside of the pyramid. It was perfectly flush with the side of the wall. Tom pushed it. The door opened. He pushed it again. The door closed. Once again, and it opened. Tom reasoned that the door had closed when, in his panic, he had backed into the wall and accidentally touched the block.

Knowing how to work the door gave Tom a sense of confidence. He turned toward the hallway.

"Anybody there?" he called out.

No reply.

Tom couldn't figure out where the light was coming from. There were no fixtures or recessed lighting. The walls themselves appeared to glow.

At the end of the hallway he found a set of spiral steps and beyond them a short corridor that ended in a wall. Tom inspected the wall, found a small rectangular block, pressed it, and a door opened. He entered a room filled with bookshelves stuffed with tubes. Each tube had a symbol on its end, probably to denote what was inside, Tom thought.

Tom dared to remove a tube. After all these years there wasn't a speck of dust on it. The cap came off easily and inside he found a large scroll.

"Ancient texts," Tom said aloud, scratching his chin. "I'll be damned!"

Suddenly the lights turned off.

"Geez," he said aloud. "Now what?" This time he didn't feel

fearful. He knew he wasn't going to meet the living dead. He could find his way back with his headlamp, and he knew how to operate the doors.

"HUUU," he said to clear his mind.

The lights turned back on.

That was curious, Tom thought. He decided to experiment. "Damn," he said.

The lights turned off.

"HUUU."

The lights came back on. So the lighting system wasn't broken, Tom realized. It was only sensitive to vibration. Swearing emanated a coarse vibration that turned off the lights. Singing HU, which was a relaxing, peaceful, spiritually uplifting word, had a high vibration. It turned the lights back on. Tom didn't want to risk testing his theory with too many different words or sounds. He didn't want to over work the ancient system. Besides, he was more curious about what was stored inside those tubes.

Tom turned off his headlamp to conserve the batteries.

He placed the scroll on the table that was located in the center of the room. As soon as he unrolled the scroll, the table magnetically latched onto the paper and made it perfectly flat. The paper felt like parchment and looked blank. Maybe the writing had faded over time. Tom leaned on the table for a closer look. Once both his palms were against the table, it automatically lit up. The paper then revealed its contents. It was indeed a map that denoted landmasses, rivers, even towns, and certain important buildings.

He stood back to look at it. When he removed his hands from the table, the map rolled itself back up. Nanotechnology, Tom thought. The paper is atomically designed to behave a certain way under certain circumstances. Amazing!

He returned the map to its tube and replaced it in its spot on the shelf. He could always come back to study the documents later. He was eager to discover what was up the stairs and climbed them. On the next floor he found a shorter corridor. Although the stairs continued up, Tom decided to see what kind of room might lie at the end of the corridor. He found the door, opened it, and stepped into the room. It was completely empty. Nothing of interest here, Tom thought, so he climbed to the next and last floor. Here the stairs lead into a room whose ceiling slanted inward on all four sides. He had reached the top of the inside of the pyramid.

To his right, a console decorated with various geometric shapes spanned the short length of the room. The wall over the console consisted of a wall-sized screen. It was producing a residual blue glow, like that emitted by a television that had just been turned off in a dark room. Two square maroon-colored chairs with flat backs and seats awaited occupants.

This must be a control room, Tom thought.

He took a seat in one of the chairs, which instantly molded to conform to the shape of his backside. It was surprisingly comfortable and had wheeled feet that were very slippery. He would have to be careful how he sat.

Tom studied the console. It was made of a clear glass or plastic, which appeared to protect the geometric shapes beneath. At the back of the console, and spanning its length, were lines of much smaller symbols that Tom thought might be instructions of some sort.

Because he was accustomed to using a mouse at his computer, Tom placed his hand on the console. Instantly, colors on the screen came to life, revealing a picture of the earth, with Antarctica in the center, as though taken by satellite. Antarctica was mostly ice free, and the coasts of Africa and the Americas didn't appear as he remembered them.

Then, as if the pyramid realized the view on its imaging system was severely outdated, it fast-forwarded the images through time, stopping only when it revealed the geography of present-day earth.

Tom was eager to learn more about the console and the viewscreen, but wondered how much time he'd have before he should check the weather and report back to Greer. The scene on the viewscreen shifted. It now showed an image of the Jamesway camp, looking down from above. The storm continued to white-out the camp with blinding snow. Nobody was outside.

Was the viewscreen thought-driven? To test his theory, Tom thought of one of his favorite places on earth — the north shore of the Hawaiian island of Kauai. To his amazement, the viewscreen showed an accordion of vertical green canyons, lush with vege-tation and the waterfalls they harbored, which cascaded into the sea.

Then his mind wandered to his hometown team. "How are the Red Sox doing?" he asked with his thoughts.

The viewscreen displayed a scorecard, not unlike those found in the newspaper. That very day, Boston had lost to the White Sox — the score was three runs to one. The night before, Boston had won, seven to four.

Will Boston make the playoffs? Tom asked. In reply, the viewscreen displayed a picture of itself, unburied and with cap-stone intact, its silver surface shining in the sunlight. Apparently, the pyramid knew about the past and present, but it couldn't predict the future.

Suddenly, another tremor shook the pyramid. This one was stronger than the last. Was the pyramid somehow causing them, Tom wondered? Suddenly the lights went out and Tom's chair rolled across the floor. He hit his head on the slanted ceiling and fell to the floor unconscious.

42.

The sheik's servant led Daria to a small tent located away from the others and beneath a crowded stand of palm trees. Four Bedouin guards stood at the corners of the tent. The servant walked up to the door, which was a heavy cloth made of woven camel and goat hair, and spoke to someone inside. He then opened the door and motioned for Daria to enter.

The only occupant inside the carpeted tent was a man sitting on pillows. Beside him waited a silver tray with two teacups and a silver teapot supported over a burning candle to keep it warm. The man wore a dark brown jubbe over a light brown gallabiya and loose-fitting beige pants. A woolen lebda capped his head and his chin sported a thin, gray beard. His deep brown eyes greeted Daria before his words did.

"Welcome, my dear," Mikta said. "Make yourself comfortable. I know these nomadic furnishings can be hard on a body accustomed to tables and chairs, so arrange the pillows to suit you."

"Thank you," she said, feeling instantly at ease. This was indeed the same Mikta she'd met years before.

Mikta's tent looked much the same as Gateefa's, but smaller, and all his articles were concealed in goatskin bags that hung from the tent's supports. He also had pillows that were made of the same fabric as the rugs. Likely they were a luxury much appreciated by an old man — and Mikta looked old. His thin frame and deeply wrinkled skin belied his youthful attitude and quick mind.

Mikta's kind smile and cheerful eyes seemed so sincere. She wondered if he remembered her.

"Are you being treated well?" he asked.

"Yes."

He poured them each a cup of cardamom coffee from the teapot. He regretted not contacting her after her father's death. Ian was a close friend, but Mikta had no choice. If they followed Mikta to Connecticut to see Daria, she too might be dead, and the Key to the Capstone would have fallen into the wrong hands.

"Anything we can do for you?"

"You can help me get out of here."

"So you would like to go back to the desert?" he teased.

She grinned. "I am grateful for your hospitality. But I'm ready to go home."

"And where is that?"

"New Haven, Connecticut." Then added, "it's north of New York City." She always said that to foreigners, who usually had a sense of where the city was but knew nothing of Connecticut.

"You are far from home indeed," he said. "Why are you here?" He asked this question from the deepest part of himself, so it begged from her a truth from the deepest part of hers.

"I originally came to help my students read the Pyramid Texts," Daria answered.

But Mikta had spoken so calmly, so evenly, and had looked so carefully into her that Daria sensed his question had a deeper meaning. What *had* brought her so far? Unexpectedly a deeper truth did emerge, but it was too big for words to lasso. She was about to let it go when Mikta asked again, "Why are you here?"

"To finish what my father started," she tried.

"And what was that?" Mikta asked. His eyes didn't move from hers.

Daria hesitated. The words were just out of reach. Yet she wanted to find an answer. Something about Mikta's presence made her feel she could access a deeper truth. She wanted that.

"His gift," she finally stammered.

"What did he give you?"

Daria wanted to tell him about the key her father had given her for her birthday. But it was more than that. Her father had bestowed upon her a responsibility that seemed far beyond her ability and means.

"Something I'm not sure I'm ready for," Daria admitted.

Mikta eased the conversation by changing the subject. "I liked your father," Mikta said. He sipped his cardamom coffee. "We met in the Yale University auditorium while attending a seminar on Egyptology and became good friends." Mikta took a moment to reminisce. "We spent a lot of time together before you were born. Here in the desert, in Cairo, at Yale, and also in London. In fact, I first met you in Giza when you were just learning to walk."

"I remember meeting you at Edfu," Daria said. "When I was eleven."

Mikta smiled broadly.

"You were a precocious child," he said. "And gifted."

Mikta continued to reminisce, but he did so with a purpose. He knew Daria still wore the key, and to fulfill her destiny, she had to learn to hear what most people could not—the promptings of universal wisdom, which often spoke through the heart. The fate of the earth depended on her making the right choice, at the right time. Before she could do that, she had some healing to do.

"Your father loved to talk about the ancient worlds," Mikta said. "He was always asking me questions and pressing me to tell stories. I enjoyed his light-hearted good humor."

Daria hesitated to remember; although she knew what Mikta said was true.

"No matter how bad things got," Mikta said, "Ian always had a way of tuning in. Such admirable trust he had in his heart!"

"His heart told him to dig for a tunnel at Giza and he failed," Daria said, surprised by the bitter tone in her voice. "It didn't stop him from getting killed either." Ian had always told her to look to her heart for answers, truth, and rightness and to follow its guidance no matter what. But his heart's stupid guidance had let him down. He had died anyway. She hated the thought of it.

Daria's face reddened with anger and she bowed her head, leaned her forehead on her palms and tried to regain her composure. She couldn't believe she'd lost control of her emotions. She never did that, not even when she was alone. The suppressed pain now gushing forward was uncontainable.

Mikta could sense what she was feeling. He imagined a blue stream of water running beside her. Of course, she was unaware of it, but her subconscious could sense it. Daria was free to dump into that stream whatever feelings she was ready to let go. It was a technique that Mikta always found effective.

"What do you grieve?" Mikta asked. His gentle voice diffused her tension.

Daria wasn't ready to surrender it completely. "I stopped grieving years ago," she said, more sharply than she expected to.

"Grief has a mind of its own," Mikta said as calmly as though she hadn't raised her voice. "It doesn't leave until it has smoothed every jagged thread of emotion. Sometimes that can take awhile."

"It's been twenty-five years," Daria said. "Isn't that long enough?"

"What do you grieve?" he calmly asked again.

Daria sighed. It was so unnerving to talk to this man! She just couldn't stay angry or sad, or retain any stress in his presence. Most aggravating, she couldn't hide. She couldn't turn the conversation to the weather or other chit chat. Mikta was forcing her to look inward.

"Well, I don't miss my dad anymore, if that's what you mean," she said, and as soon as she said it, the tears erupted as she realized how much—how very much—she really did miss him.

Mikta handed her a handkerchief and gave her time to cry.

"What else do you grieve?" he asked gently.

This sudden emotional vulnerability allowed her to be more honest with herself about this topic than she'd ever been. She admitted to herself that she missed other things about her father too. How, for example, in the morning she'd come bounding down the stairs into the kitchen to tell him her dreams. Ian would always look up from his newspaper to listen to her so carefully. Inevitably he would say, "What do you think it means, Honey-cakes?" And in the evening Ian would tell her stories and their conversations would wander from subject to subject. Sometimes they'd look up facts in Ian's extensive library, or else they'd stay cuddled before the warm fire and share conjectures.

Daria remembered her father's favorite sayings. She missed the excitement in the house when he'd exclaim, "I *knew* it!" and the calm acceptance of change when he'd quietly say, "Now how is life going to solve this one?" Another of his favorites was, "Think with your heart." Daria remembered her father trying to explain to her that true intelligence had nothing to do with the brain. Even the ancient Egyptians, he'd said, believed the heart was the seat of wisdom. They had no regard for the brain; and after it was removed during the mummification process they simply discarded it while the heart was replaced safely in the body. He told her they believed the departed Soul needed its heart in the afterlife. In order for the Soul to be judged, its heart was weighed on a scale against the feather of Maat, the god of truth.

Just then, as though a curtain opened within her, Daria understood her turmoil. She had been blaming her father's death on his inner guidance. No wonder she'd chosen not to remember her dreams anymore. It was also the reason she stopped looking into her heart for answers. Now, she needed these precious resources to figure out what to do with the gift her father had given her.

She wished he were still alive. Surely he could help her. Her father knew about so many things and carried such wisdom. Was he wise because he considered his inner guidance as inseparable from himself? True guidance came from a place only the heart could access—that was what he had told her. Her father trusted himself because he knew himself well enough to be able to discern the true voice from its many imposters. Could Daria ever know herself that well? Did a person need to keep listening to her heart to stay in touch with who she really was? Could she regain what she had lost?

More of her memories surfaced. Her dad once told her life was like an ocean wave. If you listened to your heart, you could learn to ride the wave. You may not know where the wave was headed, but you could enjoy the comfort of knowing you were going in the right direction. If you didn't listen, you'd bump along beneath the wave, moving into your future blind and unaware.

Daria felt as though she had just spent the last three days being bumped along by life. And now she had a capstone to deal with—at least a broken one.

Didn't Omar say Mikta could identify the key? Would he also know about the capstone? Daria removed the leather pouch from around her neck, opened it, and spilled its contents onto her palm. The pieces of capstone were intermingled with flakes of dried lavender. She poured them into Mikta's hand. In doing so, she had followed her heart, but had this fact been pointed out to her she would have denied it. Showing him the pieces was simply the next logical thing to do.

Mikta reverently examined each piece and then deftly put the capstone together as though he'd played this puzzle thousands of times before.

Daria was amazed.

"It won't stay together," he said. To demonstrate, he let go the capstone and it fell apart in his hands. "That's because the sphere is missing."

How did he know? She reached for her other pouch and produced the sphere. It was colorless, flawless, and mirror-like.

She handed it to him.

"The Eye of Horus," he announced and looked at the sphere for just a moment. Then he rebuilt the capstone with the sphere inside. This time it held together. He handed it to Daria. She tried to loosen the capstone but couldn't. Nothing about it suggested it could ever be taken apart. Its small blocks looked and felt glued together.

"So the Eye of Horus was kept inside the capstone," Daria said, recalling what Omar had told her. "And it looks as though the capstone itself is nothing without it."

"Both sphere and capstone are more than they appear to be," Mikta replied.

Meanwhile the air outside rumbled with distant thunder. Mikta looked up and listened, but Daria didn't notice.

Daria examined each side of the capstone. Its upper sides were smooth. Its base was engraved with a circle with writing inside of it. Funny, she thought, it looked like Aymaran. But an old Chilean language in Egypt? It couldn't be.

The thunder rolled again, and this time they heard the excited voices of the villagers. Mikta knew the intact capstone could disrupt the environment. It could also disrupt a mind that was untrained to obey the heart. Such a mind could turn easily to greed and a lust for power. To ward off these temptations the capstone bearer had to be well aware of her heart and how to think with it, listen to it, and follow it.

Mikta knew the capstone's secrets. They had been given to him by his father who had learned them from his father, and so on for countless generations. Mikta's ancestral line could be traced to the high priests of ancient Egypt, the Guardians of the Sacred Knowledge of the Shemsu Hor. Further back in time, they were the Zep Tepi, the First Ones of Egypt.

Another thunderclap, closer this time, made Daria jump. Instinctively, she reached for the key that hung around her neck.

"They call it the Navubala," Mikta said. "The Key to the Capstone. Look, this is its symbol." Mikta gently turned the capstone upside-down. He pointed to a symbol within the writing that looked like one curve of the pendant's side. "And here," pointing to a symbol beside it, "is the glyph for woman."

Was Mikta now suggesting the makers of the capstone somehow knew the key-bearer thousands of years into the future would be a woman? Impossible!

"Maybe the key-bearers were always women," Daria suggested.

"Men might have had the opportunity too, now and then," Mikta said and smiled. Then he continued, "The Zep Tepi, the First Ones of ancient times, knew how to see the future. They recorded their visions in places where only certain people of the future could find them." He paused. "So they left what I call, 'confirmations of destiny,'"

"I'm not sure what my destiny is anymore," Daria admitted.

"That is precisely why the Zep Tepi left such confirmations. They knew that conditions of the future cycle—meaning now in this century—would constantly test one's ability to tune into the heart. So they left clues that would verify the destinies of those who were listening to their inner guidance."

"I don't believe in inner guidance," Daria said, stubbornly clinging to what she had convinced herself was true.

"The beliefs we hold most tenaciously are those we are most ready to let go," Mikta said.

"Well, I'm quite certain about what I believe and what I don't," Daria replied. Again she was feeling angry.

"A true belief lives quietly and contentedly in one's heart," Mikta said. "One does not need to defend it or convince others to believe it, but gives it room to grow."

"Well," Daria said, "I simply don't care about inner guidance and I don't give two hoots about my destiny." Yet the sound of her voice didn't ring true. She knit her brows in confusion. The words conflicted with what she knew deep in her heart.

In her heart? The realization made her light-headed. The idea of listening to one's heart sounded like such a cliché. Maybe it was more correct to say that her heart reflected what she, herself, truly wanted and believed.

"The capstone's inscriptions are not like modern writing," Mikta said. He knew Daria loved ancient languages, and that what you love opens your heart. Once that happens, its connection with universal wisdom, which is perceived as inner guidance, becomes clearer.

"The ancients didn't use writing like we do to convey neatly packaged thoughts and ideas," Mikta said. "Rather, they used symbols to lift the reader to a higher understanding. Then the reader could know far more about a topic than even the writer."

"Symbols are a springboard," Daria said, agreeing with him.

"Exactly," Mikta replied.

More thunder rumbled, followed by a downpour. It was more rain than the villagers had seen in years. By their joyous shrieks and chatter, it sounded as though everyone was outside celebrating.

"Tell me," Mikta said, corralling Daria's attention, "what do you know about interpreting ancient symbols?"

Daria lit up. "Symbols can speak to each person individually," she said. "Though you and I may see the same symbols in these inscriptions, the understanding they leave us with can be unique. In other words, what these symbols tell me may be different from what they tell you, because my challenges and experiences are different than yours." She paused. "Therefore, what I need to understand from this capstone will be uniquely for me. Of course, it is possible to read a message to learn the author's original intent. But that is an intellectual exercise. If you perceive the symbols with a certain feeling, their message can be profoundly personal."

"You mean you read them with your heart?" Mikta said.

Daria was struck by his words. She didn't think that's what she'd been doing. But the possibility took a moment to process.

Mikta didn't give her time to begin arguing with herself. He asked, "What do these inscriptions say to you now?"

Daria looked closely at the capstone's base. She used her mind not to read but to perceive. Instead of interpreting each symbol like reading a modern language, she embraced all the symbols as one whole, complete message. She kept her mind as relaxed as possible and tried to fall into the familiar trance that would allow her to read any writing she wanted. Then she would know what the capstone was telling her.

But her attention began to wander. Omar had told her that according to the prophecy, the key-bearer would find the capstone—and she had. What were the odds of that happening? Maybe she did have a destiny that was tied to the capstone. Where would the capstone lead her? As her thoughts rolled along, she was indeed learning from the inscriptions. Something inside her softened, and she gained a greater acceptance of herself and of her destiny. Furthermore, her heart was becoming her ally.

Still she didn't think anything had happened.

Mikta pointed to the capstone. "This symbol refers to the key, and this one means woman. Now hold the capstone so its edges are oriented with the points of the compass. The slit that is the keyhole points north."

"This circle is earth?"

"Yes."

"Then the key and the woman are located in the center," Daria replied. "Somewhere on the equator?"

"You are too accustomed to seeing the earth from only one viewpoint," Mikta replied. "When you get home, go look at a globe."

"And how am I to get home?"

"That is being taken care of. The sheikh's men will take you by camel to Bi'r Fu'ad, a small town west of here. There you will meet a man named Muhammad, who will take you to the coastal town of Mersa Matruh. Then, you will catch a ferry to Piraeus, Greece, and a cab to your hotel near the Athens airport."

Torrents of rain were now falling and a small stream of water snaked into Mikta's tent.

"It's time we take apart the capstone," Mikta said.

Daria did so using the key and put the pieces back into her pouches.

The rain stopped.

Mikta pulled out Daria's waist wallet.

"I kept this for you," he said. "It has been unopened. You will also need these." He handed her a pile of papers bound with twine made from a dried palm leaf. The papers included a travel visa, a plane ticket, and directions to a hotel. "There are enough Greek drachmas here to cover your travel expenses and to buy some clothes. Your flight leaves out of Athens in two days."

"Where did you get this?" Daria asked about the money.

"There are many who support you and your mission, Daria," Mikta said softly.

"What mission?"

"Just keep listening to your heart and follow it, no matter what."

This was the last thing Daria wanted to hear. She had no clue how to listen to her heart. She'd forgotten how. Yet his words left a warm feeling within her and she felt calm, centered, and hopeful.

43.

Tom awoke lying on the floor in the pyramid's control room. The lights were off, and the room was illuminated only by the blue glow of the viewscreen. Tom didn't know how long he'd been out, but his body felt stiff.

"HUUU," he sang quietly. Thankfully, the lights came back on. A lump had grown on the back of his head, which hurt. Otherwise he wasn't injured. He stood up, stretched, then picked up the fallen chair and sat down again.

What's with the earthquakes, he wondered.

Within seconds, the pyramid's viewscreen lit up. It showed an aerial view of the Atlantic Ocean, then telescoped onto the waves and then beneath them. Tom was amazed at the pyramid's capabilities. Where was it obtaining such images? Was it connected to a satellite of some kind? The zoom-in stopped at a scene of a sandy ocean floor, barren except for a large submarine broken in two, a clutter of dead fish, and a strange sphere, swollen with pulsing light.

The viewscreen used graphics to show how the sphere's pulses were comprised of two kinds. The first emanated from the sphere in ever-widening concentric circles. The second was a simple beam. To illustrate their effects, the viewscreen panned out. A map of the Cape Verde Islands and the west coast of Africa was now on the right side of the screen, the Atlantic Ocean in the middle of it, and the East Coast of the Americas on the left. Filling the Atlantic was an enormous hurricane whose eye was clear and defined. Tom had never seen a hurricane so big. The pulses that emanated as concentric circles were feeding the hurricane.

Then the screen showed the sphere's second type of pulse. It was an energetic beam that was being sent to various points on the globe at uneven intervals—sometimes hours and sometimes only minutes apart. The viewscreen conjured images of the beams' destinations. All were pyramids, but they were either buried by time or standing in ruins, like those of Egypt, Mexico, and China. The strongest beam was being sent to Antarctica—to the very pyramid that Tom's ice-melting technology had revealed. Seconds after a beam hit the pyramid, Tom felt a slight tremor. So that was his answer: the earthquakes were caused by beams emanating from the sphere on the ocean floor.

"Amazing," Tom thought. Was this what Greer had meant by the pyramid possibly being a receiver? "I wonder what the beams are for?" He voiced his question aloud, although he didn't have to.

As if it were alive and intelligently communicating with him, the viewscreen showed a moving picture of what would happen if a signal was returned from any of these pyramids. The sphere would stop pulsing. The storms would cease. The floods upon the shorelines would recede.

"And if we don't return a signal?"

The screen then showed him a series of images that made him wish he hadn't asked. The earthquakes would grow stronger and the hurricanes more intense and more frequent, not only in the Atlantic but in the Pacific too. Eventually coastal cities would be swallowed by waves and rising water levels. Coastlines would be rearranged.

Tom had seen enough. Obviously, the only operational pyramid left on earth was this one. Was it still capable of returning a signal? What buttons to push? What kind of signal to send? What were the exact coordinates of the pulsing sphere? He had to take action. But what? Tom hadn't yet learned how important it was to control one's thoughts in the presence of a thought-driven computer. His flood of questions seemed to confuse the viewscreen, which began spattering colors randomly.

"Sorry about that," Tom said aloud, realizing the problem. "One question at a time. How do we return the signal?"

The screen gave him an image of the pyramid as it once stood in all its glory—with capstone and pyramidion intact. From the capstone came a beam of light that flew over the ocean, through the water, and directly to the sphere. Immediately, the sphere shut down.

"Great," said Tom sarcastically. "In case you haven't noticed, your capstone is missing."

Undaunted, the screen zoomed in on the pyramid's flat top and focused on the writing engraved there.

Did the symbols lead to the capstone?

The screen responded affirmatively to Tom's telepathic question by repeating the image of the intact pyramid.

Tom knew what he had to do. He had to find out what the writing meant, locate the capstone, and shut down the trouble-causing sphere.

But first, he had to explain all this to Greer.

44.

After her meeting with Mikta, Daria went to bed that night with a lot on her mind. She watched the lantern light flicker on the camel skin ceiling as Gateefa came into the tent and got ready for bed. Daria could feel Gateefa's gaze upon her and knew the woman was wondering about Daria's meeting with Sidi Mikta. At the same time, Daria needed someone to talk to. Would Gateefa understand?

"Do you know anything about the heart?" Daria asked.

Gateefa pressed her hand against her chest. "My eyes and ears," she said.

Daria wondered what she meant.

"Your heart has its feelings and emotions," Gateefa said, "but if you listen to it, it can also tell you the truth about your surroundings, about the people around you, and also about your-self."

"What if you can't hear your heart?" she asked.

"When a child loves her parents," Gateefa said, "she listens to them and they teach her how to live a good life. When she grows up and falls in love with her husband, she listens to him, and he shares his world. When a Bedouin loves the desert, she listens to it, and it shares its secrets. When you love your heart, you listen to it, and it leads you to what is true."

"What if your heart tells you the wrong thing?"

"The heart never lies," Gateefa said assuredly. "Never be afraid of it. That would be like being afraid of your own self. And that is such a silly thing."

Had Daria cut herself off from her heart all these years? It was a humbling thought. "How do you listen to your heart?" she asked.

Gateefa laughed quietly. "Don't separate yourself from your heart by trying to listen to it as something outside yourself. Love your heart first. Then it will guide you and be the source of your strength and will. Then, truly, your life will be guided by Allah."

Though Daria didn't call God by the name of Allah, she respected Gateefa's preference and knew the woman was giving her good advice. Still, Daria didn't understand.

"When you laugh," Gateefa explained, "let it be your heart that laughs. When you cry, it is because your heart is filled with sorrow and for no other reason. When you want to do something, be somewhere, or have something, let the desire be that of your own heart and nothing else. That is how you be yourself, be your heart, and be the daughter of Allah."

"How do you know what your heart wants?" Daria asked. She turned on her side to face her friend, who was now lying in bed.

"What does your body want to do right now, my dear?"

Daria thought a moment. "Sleep," she said, and then quickly added, "I also want to talk."

"Your mind wants to talk," Gateefa said. "Your body has

been honest with you. The body is the heart's best friend and confidant." Gateefa turned onto her back and looked up at the ceiling. "Now, tell me, what answer are you looking to find from an old woman that you cannot find within yourself?"

"I want to learn to listen to my heart."

Gateefa smiled broadly. "You have made the request," she said. "Allah has heard. It is in his hands. Sleep well my dear. *Tesbahhee ahlah khayr* [good night]."

"*Wentee minahl el-khayr* [good night]." Daria replied.

Was that it? Was that all Gateefa would say? Daria wanted to prod her for more wisdom. Yet the woman clearly trusted God in a way that Daria had never experienced before. Was it enough to voice a desire with complete honesty? Is that how you communicated with the Divine?

Gateefa reached for the lantern and turned it off. The tent was now completely dark.

Sleep didn't come easily for Daria. Her thoughts were too busy to let her body relax. Wanting to reconnect with her heart was task enough—she also had a capstone in her possession. What was she to do with that? Daria hadn't a clue. And sharing it with her colleagues at Yale now felt like a bad idea.

She thought about what Gateefa had said. Was there a link between loving your heart and loving yourself? The concept of self-love had always seemed to Daria like an excuse to inflate one's vanity and ego. Gateefa had explained it in a way she now could understand: love your heart, then it will talk to you.

She practiced sending love to the center of her being. She felt relaxed but there was something more. How could she put her feelings into words? The sheik had suggested she voice what she knew. She knew she felt loved.

That was it!

Whenever she tried to love her heart, she instead felt love *coming from* her heart. The more love she gave, the more she got. In fact, she found she couldn't stand apart from her heart and love it as something outside herself. It wouldn't work.

This proved to her two things. One, that her heart was a

source of love. And second, that her heart was indeed herself. Wasn't that what Gateefa had said?

Daria then wondered how loving yourself, or your heart, would lead to inner guidance. Wait, what was she thinking? She didn't believe in inner guidance. Or did she? Suddenly the concept didn't seem so foreign or strange. Had she really let go of her attitudes about it? Mikta had told her that the beliefs people held most fervently were the beliefs they were most ready to let go. Had Daria just proved him right? Yet gone also was a stress that she didn't even know she'd been carrying. It was the stress of holding so tightly to those beliefs. Without them, she felt more herself than ever before.

Now her body was so tired it began to tug upon her mind, begging it to slow down. Soon she drifted into welcome sleep. A moment later, she began to dream of Mikta. She was sitting with him inside his tent as they had been earlier that day.

"I want to show you something," Mikta said, "regarding your father's death."

45.

"What about my father's death?" Daria asked Mikta suspiciously. Her dream experience seemed so real she didn't even think to doubt it, or to resist the fact she was actually dreaming.

The dream vision then changed and she saw her house the way it looked on her twelfth birthday. Mikta held her hand while they walked through the front door and tiptoed through the clutter strewn on the floor. They headed down the hallway toward the French doors that opened to her father's ominously quiet office.

Daria knew what to expect. After all, she'd been here twenty-five years ago. When she saw her father's lifeless body on the floor, all her unresolved emotion flooded forward. She buried her face in Mikta's shoulder. He wrapped his arm around her. He felt strong, and in the dream, he looked decades younger.

"I don't want to see this again." Daria sobbed.

Mikta waved his hand, and time moved backward a few hours. Now Daria and Mikta watched her father speaking to his visitors about the Key to the Capstone they insisted that he had. First they spoke civilly, and then they began shouting.

Daria and Mikta watched Ian move away from his desk and toward the center of the room, trying to lure the visitors from the open window behind the desk where they would undoubtedly see Daria in the backyard. Then one of them thought he caught on.

"So what's in your desk that you don't want us to see?"

"Look through my desk all you want," Ian said.

Then the dreaming Daria could hear what her father was thinking, as if he had spoken aloud. "Daria! Hide behind the tree!" The message was telepathic, and Daria didn't remember hearing it at the time. Although she did remember how comforting it felt to be near the oak tree, she didn't hide behind it.

The dreaming Daria watched the men move toward her father's desk. One started opening drawers while another moved toward the window. "I don't suppose you've hidden the key out there?" he said.

"If I had something as important as you claim, why would I leave it out in the weather?" Ian said.

His comment didn't stop the man, who appeared to be the one in charge. He continued walking toward the window. If he got close enough, he surely would see Daria. Suddenly, Ian lunged at him. They fought only briefly as it didn't take long for the other three men to restrain him.

"So, what's in the window you don't want us to see?" the leader asked. He began studying the wooden framework for loose boards.

Ian struggled again, even as one intruder pressed a gun, fitted with a silencer, into his chest and pulled the trigger.

"No!" the dreaming Daria exclaimed. But she couldn't change events that had already unfolded. Moments later, Ian was dead.

"Idiot," the leader said. "Now take this place apart," he ordered. "If the Key to the Capstone is here, we are going to find it."

Daria looked over at Mikta, "Why?" she sobbed. "Why did my father attack that man? Why didn't he play it cool, like he usually did, and negotiate himself out of the situation? Why?"

"Watch what happens," Mikta said.

They saw a replay of the moment when Ian's body dropped to the floor. At the same time as it fell, another image of Ian—a brighter, sparkling, and somewhat transparent form of him—gracefully stood up. Then like an apparition it rushed outside the house, flying directly through the walls, with a determination Daria didn't expect.

"He's still alive?" Daria exclaimed.

"Soul never dies."

"He's going to heaven?" She didn't think he would be so eager.

"Not yet," Mikta said. "Look."

The dream scene changed again, and Daria and Mikta now stood in the backyard. A frightened girl cowered beside a large oak, grasping the pendant that her father had just given her for her birthday. She was in full view of the window in Ian's office.

Just then, the ethereal form of Ian wafted through the air and landed in front of his frightened daughter. He stood between her and the house.

The dreaming Daria saw the intruders at the window and tried to call out a warning to the young image of herself standing beside the tree.

"That isn't necessary," Mikta said.

Ian's radiant body, unseen by his murderers, created a shield that made his daughter invisible.

Suddenly Daria realized the truth. "He died to protect me," she said. Saving her had been more important to him than his own life. But how could he have been so sure that if he died he could save her? They had often talked about the possibility of life after death and of a person's spiritual essence moving from one lifetime to the next. She was never convinced it was true. Come to think of it, her father never pushed his ideas on her. He just talked about them.

Nevertheless, she was alive because of him, and it made her feel warm inside and deeply grateful. These feelings melted away the anger and bitterness that had gripped her for so long. She felt lifted, and lighter.

It was time to live the life that her father had given her.

"I'm ready," Daria said.

Mikta nodded. "Your heart has opened. Now you'll be able to hear it."

Mikta started to sing a simple mantra that he repeated melodiously. It sounded like HUUU. The chant calmed Daria, and her sleep grew deeper, dreamless, and healing.

46.

Sunday, September 14th.

Daria awoke at dawn to the sounds of the villagers busy with their morning chores. She was alone in the tent except for the memories of her dream, which seemed real enough to have a distinct presence of their own. Somehow she felt more whole than ever before, as if something missing had been returned. Yet it had been only a dream—hadn't it?

Neatly folded beside her, Daria found her shorts and the t-shirt she was wearing when she arrived. The clothes had been washed and a tear in the shirt mended. She dressed and then ate the bread and drank the goat's milk that Gateefa had also set beside her bed.

Gateefa soon came in with men's clothes for her to wear over her own: a brown gallabiya and jubbe, and a man's kufiyya cloth and an agal rope. They would help Daria blend in with the camel herders who awaited her outside. Gateefa helped Daria put on the clothing, and then they left the tent. Five Bedouins, each carrying a rifle, stood amidst a crowd of onlookers. She spotted Gateefa, who smiled and nodded her head. Then the sheik arrived to bid Daria farewell.

Daria and her escorts mounted their camels. Daria scanned the crowd for Mikta but didn't see him. She wanted to thank him too. One conversation with him had reacquainted her with her heart; one dream had opened it. She felt different about herself, and her outlook had been renewed.

Their camel train moved slowly but steadily the rest of the morning over mostly sandy terrain. Hours later, the land became rockier. This made travel easier, because the camels' feet didn't sink into the sand. The group passed tall rocky outcroppings that had the most unusual shapes. Daria thought they must be made of especially hard rock to withstand eons of blowing sand.

Daria's thoughts moved forward. Somewhere along the way she would meet a man named Muhammad. He would help her leave Egypt and return to the States. She thought about what she should tell her boss, Albert Winslow, about her absence. How much could she tell him? Then she realized that if Winslow had told her grandmother that Daria hadn't met her students on time, Sarah would be fraught with worry. Daria couldn't wait to contact Sarah to let her know she was fine, and also ask for news about the hurricane.

Suddenly, from behind a rocky outcropping ahead, gunfire whizzed into their company. The herders screamed something in Bedouin. The camels scattered, hers among them. Daria clung desperately to her saddle while kicking her camel's sides, urging it on. Daria had no idea where to lead the camel — she just encouraged it to run. It knew the terrain better than she and hopefully, it also knew which way to go.

Holding onto the saddle wasn't easy. She crouched as low as she possibly could on the animal's back, although she realized sitting atop a camel made you as obvious as a bull's-eye, but it was all she could do.

Suddenly the camel lurched sideways, and Daria fell.

The ground came hard and fast. Her shoulder hit first, and for the privilege it was rewarded with shooting pain. Her camel kept running. Daria labored to a kneeling position and noticed she had landed near some large rocks. They would provide the perfect hideout, if only she could reach them in time. The uphill walk was agonizing, as each step sent waves of pain through her chest and down her arm. Finally she reached the boulders and collapsed in their shade. She removed the kufiyya cloth from her head, bunched it up and rested her head on it like a pillow.

Her respite was interrupted by more gunshots. This time the sound came from the other side of the rocks. Curious, Daria climbed a few more yards and found a place to peek between two large boulders. Not far below her, she could see several soldiers with jeeps and SUVs riding circles around her escorts and firing into the melee. Two of the Bedouin had fallen and were apparently dead. The other three had their hands up.

These men had been protecting her, and now they faced death. Daria felt sick by what she saw and retreated to huddle against the rocks.

Another gunshot.

Then another.

Daria peeked again through the rocks to confirm her fears.

A third gunshot.

Daria sat back. Overwhelmed with horror and pain, her body began to shake and breathing became difficult. She reached for the velvet pouch and emptied its contents into her palm. She wanted the vial of bergamot oil, but the capstone's sphere came out too. She held the sphere in her hand, then opened the vial and inhaled. It barely relaxed her. She returned the vial to its pouch and absent mindedly kept the sphere wrapped in her palm. Then she pressed her hand against her chest, trying to contain the pain.

Meanwhile, the sphere had begun to heal her. It registered the disrupted vibrations of Daria's broken body and designed a mirror-image harmonic. As long as she held the sphere in her hand, it would send this harmonic into her cells to cancel out the vibrations of the damaged tissue. The sphere would then restore the cells with vitalizing energy. The healing would take some time, and the pain made Daria drowsy. As she drifted into unconsciousness, the sphere countered every wave of pain that radiated from Daria's broken collarbone and dislocated shoulder. She awoke thirty minutes later, pain free, and oblivious to the sphere's gift.

"Perhaps I wasn't hurt so badly after all," she thought to herself. She didn't have time to think any more about it. The soldiers might still be looking for her. She had to escape. After returning the sphere to its pouch, she peeked through the rocks and scanned the valley below. She noticed an unmanned SUV.

Carefully Daria crept around the rocks, running from one to the next to keep from being seen. Finally, the SUV was only thirty feet away. She checked the area thoroughly for guards and saw one on the opposite side of the same pile of rocks she had used for cover. Gratefully, she hadn't sneezed or made any other sound. Otherwise, they would have found her.

Now, if only the guard kept looking away she would be fine.

Daria took a deep breath and ran. She reached the vehicle and hid behind it. She peered around it to check the location of the guard. He wasn't there. Good news and bad news, Daria thought, for that also meant she didn't know where he was. She crept to the driver's-side door, and then carefully and quickly opened it, and crawled inside. She groped the floor underneath the seat for the keys.

In the next moment, a hand reached over the back seat and pressed itself against her mouth while another hand grabbed her shoulder and threw her down on the seat. Daria looked up. She could clearly see her assailant's face, and she stared into his eyes like the Bedouin women had looked into hers. She also sank her teeth into the fingers that kept her from screaming.

47.

With his chin resting in his hands, Tom sat on the lone chair outside Greer's office. He'd practiced what he wanted to say, but nothing sounded right. Finally Greer called him in.

"What is it," the colonel grumbled, fumbling through paperwork, not even looking up at him.

"Sir," Tom began. "We have a problem."

"We have a lot of problems, Seymour."

"We have a really big one, Sir." How was he going to get through to the colonel? Finally he said, "I think you need to come down to the pyramid." The invitation startled Tom the moment the words tumbled from his mouth. Why hadn't he thought of that before? Let Greer see for himself what the pyramid had just shown him.

"There's nothing you can say down the hole that you can't say here, Seymour." Greer still hadn't looked up.

Tom gathered his nerve.

"I found a way inside the pyramid," he began. "I found the control room and a computer viewscreen. It still works, Sir, like a television screen. And it showed me images of something happening right now at the bottom of the Atlantic."

Greer finally looked at him.

"The world is in grave danger, Sir. I think you need to come see for yourself."

"And the nature of this danger, Seymour?"

"It's a power source—a large bright sphere, about three feet wide. It's sending beams around the earth, and some are directed at our pyramid. Other beams have spawned a Category 5 hurricane, which is now moving over the Atlantic Ocean toward the East Coast. Worse storms and earthquakes will follow. They'll wipe out modern geography unless we do something."

"And you learned about this from the pyramid, you say?" Greer looked at him distrustfully.

General Taylor had told Greer about the power source and its beams during their last conversation. This was top-secret intelligence. Had Seymour overheard them and then gone wacko? Yet he was sure Tom wasn't present when Taylor had called, and Tom offered a detail the general had withheld—that the power source was in the shape of a sphere.

"Sir, the pyramid knows everything," Tom tried to explain. Then he thought of something the viewscreen showed him that might make Greer more agreeable. "The Yankees beat the Tampa Rays yesterday, and also earlier today in both games of a doubleheader. They're leading the Red Sox by four and now have the best record in the majors: ninety-two wins, only fifty-six losses."

"That so?"

Tom nodded.

Less than an hour ago, Lieutenant Manning had given him the good news that the Yankees were indeed ahead and had repeated those same numbers. Greer would enjoy seeing the Yankees win the World Series again. He wondered what else the pyramid knew. His expression turned from impatience to interest.

"Sir, the storms will only stop if the sphere gets a signal returned. And the pyramid can do it."

"Send the signal," Greer said. "On my order."

"I would like to, Sir, but we need the top of the pyramid to do it, and as you know, it's missing. You see, the pyramid's capstone is the mechanism that collects and focuses the pyramid's energies and then directs them to a chosen target."

"Any target?" Greer asked. Maybe the pyramid could also be

used as a weapon.

"Yes, I believe so, Sir."

"Well then, where's the capstone?"

"I don't know, Sir, but the writing on the pyramid's flat top can tell us."

"I'll have Davison e-mail your photographs to the Pentagon," Greer said. "Our guys in intelligence will figure it out."

"Excuse me, Sir." Tom pulled out the pencil rubbings he had made of the writing. "Look at this detail. There's tons of it. We need an expert in ancient languages. We also may need the pyramid's control room to provide certain details for a correct translation. The job has got to be done here. And since time is of the essence, this expert has got to be able to read archaic symbols."

Greer changed his mind and admitted he agreed with Tom. But before Greer contacted General Taylor to send such an expert, he wanted to inspect the control room himself. The pyramid might prove very useful to the United States military.

"Seymour," Greer said. He picked up Tom's rubbings and studied them. "Do you know anyone who can read this?"

"Yes Sir, I believe I do."

48.

"Hey, lady," whispered the man whose middle finger was bleeding from Daria's bite. He spoke thickly accented English. "I here to he'p you." His self-control had been remarkable. Anybody else would have called out in pain. "I he'p you go Mersa Matruh."

Daria finally let go, "Are you Muhammad?"

The man nodded.

"I'm so sorry," Daria whispered. "Are you okay?"

"Yez, lady. We need go."

Daria scooted over to the passenger seat, while Muhammad climbed into the driver's seat.

"Keep head down, lady," he said.

Muhammad took the car key from behind the visor, started the engine, and turned the car around. He headed slowly for the road, trying to appear as though he was part of the search. They'd counted six Bedouin and found only five. Daria, of course, had escaped.

The leader of the search party, indignant that someone had taken a vehicle without permission, began yelling for them to stop. Muhammad floored the gas pedal, and the soldiers opened fire.

Four jeeps pursued them. Since Muhammad and Daria were first in line, they enjoyed fresh air. Those behind them choked in clouds of dust. The pursuers also fired an incessant rain of bullets.

"You can shoot dis?" Muhammad asked Daria, as he pulled out a gun.

Daria grabbed the gun and climbed into the back.

"Lower the window," she shouted. Using the back seat for protection, she began to fire. Under her grandfather's tutelage she'd become pretty good with a pistol, but that was years ago.

One of her shots hit a jeep's radiator, and the vehicle soon veered from the chase. Three left, and they were closing in and still pumping bullets. It would be only a matter of time before their SUV was disabled.

"Drive faster!" Daria yelled.

Muhammad had been swerving left and right to avoid being hit. When he increased his speed, he swerved less. This strategy worked, as the gunfire gradually diminished, and their pursuers were lost in billows of dust. Minutes later the SUV reached the asphalt road that lead from Siwa Oasis to Mersa Matruh. It usually took about three hours to reach the coast. Muhammad would try to make it in half that time.

When they entered the outskirts of the city, they met their welcome. A jeep with a mounted machine gun emerged from a side street.

"Dammit they had a cell phone!" Daria yelled. Or, more likely, a citizens' band radio. She just hoped the gunfire would subside when they got closer to the city.

It didn't. Pedestrians and a motley variety of cars, pack animals, bicycles, and push carts flew to the side as the two vehicles came storming through. The gunfire also attracted local police, and Daria counted at least two squad cars joining their pursuit. Daria held her fire and slumped in her seat. Shooting at officers was not her idea of fun. Her trip to Egypt was *not* turning out as she had planned.

"Uh oh," Muhammad said, and then began to recite an Arabic prayer so fast it sounded like gibberish. They were approaching a railroad crossing, and an oncoming train would be there before they could cross. Muhammad slowed down the car.

"Turn left!" Daria shouted.

Daria directed him off the asphalt, onto a strip of desert alongside the train tracks. By the look of the flattened grasses, other vehicles had driven there, but it certainly wasn't a road. The dust they kicked up wasn't as heavy as before, and the cars behind them continued their close pursuit.

"We won't stay living," Muhammad said matter-of-factly. They both knew that soon their pursuers would reach them. The chase would end or the road would end. Either way, so would their lives.

The train was now moving beside them.

"I have an idea," Daria said, inspired. It was dangerous, but she knew it would work.

"Drive closer to the tracks," she told Muhammad. "I'll hold the wheel while you jump the train. Then I'll tie the gallabiya to the wheel to keep the car going straight and jump after you."

"You crazy!" Muhammad yelled at her. He didn't think her plan would work but was impressed by her bravery. "Is okay you jump now. I follow."

Since Muhammad was already at the wheel, his plan made better sense. Daria removed the gallabiya that she still wore over her clothes and gave it to Muhammad.

Muhammad took the car farther up the slope that bordered the tracks. Daria unrolled the passenger side window.

"We will have to do this quickly," she yelled over the din of the moving train. Muhammad nodded. He got the SUV as close to the train as he could. Despite the steep slope, the vehicle hugged the ground. Clinging to the roof rack, Daria climbed out the window. She crouched low with her feet on the car door.

"Closer!" she called out.

"*Khally balak*" [be careful]! He shouted back.

Then she reached for a handrail on the train and jumped.

49.

As Daria leaped onto the moving train, she banged her knees and strained her shoulder. She held fast to the handrail and pulled herself up a few of the steps that led into the train. Then she turned to help Muhammad make his jump. To her horror, he turned the vehicle away, and began driving down a side street into an adjoining neighborhood.

"Ensh Allah," Daria whispered.

She climbed to the other side of the train and before she allowed herself a second thought, jumped off. She knew her assailants had seen her board the train and would soon catch up with her. This was her only hope of escape, and her decision had come spontaneously, without thought and without concern for consequence. Her heart-inspired body simply knew what to do.

She hit the sloping ground and rolled at least a dozen times before the momentum petered out. Finally, she laid face down, her body caked with dust and blood. The train chugged into the distance, gaining speed.

Seconds later, Daria was swarmed by children. They were dressed in loose-fitting garments made of un-dyed fabric that was torn and dirty. The children spoke quickly, a mixture of Arabic, French, and local street talk. Daria caught most of the words, but she didn't need to. Their faces spoke volumes. They were in awe of her: a white woman, falling out of nowhere into their toyless, dusty world.

The children helped her to her feet. They led her down a street lined with cardboard shacks, entered one whose floor was covered with pieces of tattered rugs, and made her sit down on an old crate. An older girl wiped the dust from Daria's face and the dabbed the blood from her cuts. Daria was in pain, though she managed a smile. The boys watched by the doorway, chattering about who she might be and from where she might have come. One boy offered her a half round of pita bread. It would be inconsiderate and ungrateful of their hospitality to refuse the bread, no matter how poor she knew they were. The children squealed with delight when she took her first bite.

Daria knew she was still in great danger. It was only a matter of time before her pursuers discovered she wasn't on the train. She hoped Muhammad would be all right, though she feared he had already met his death.

Her priority now was to reach the ferry to Piraeus. For that, she needed the children's help. What if they turned her in?

What would her father do if he were here?

"*Awlad*" [children], she said in Arabic. "I want to tell you a story of ancient Egypt. It is my gift to you in return for your hospitality."

The children's eyes grew wide. They had seen white tourists from overseas before, but none had ever spoken their language. Eagerly they crowded around her, the littlest ones vying to be in her lap.

"A very long time ago, when pharaohs ruled the land, there was a pharaoh's daughter named Jameelah, which, in ancient

Egyptian means 'beautiful and good.' Jameelah was indeed beautiful. She had big brown eyes, like yours," Daria touched the eyebrows of one girl. "And very long black hair, like yours," she stroked the long hair of another girl.

"Jameelah was an only child and had nobody to play with. She was lonely because her parents were too busy ruling Egypt to spend time with her. So one day, she sneaked out of their palace in Alexandria to find other children to play with. Down the streets she walked, and soon she heard the sounds of the market place. Curious, she went there and found a group of Bedouin herders selling camels. The Bedouin children invited Jameelah to play. And so Jameelah and the children ran up and down the rows of kiosks, played hide and seek amongst the baskets, and danced for the vendors in exchange for pieces of bread and fruit. At sunset, Jameelah went home with them on a camel train. Their destination was Mersa Matruh."

"That's here!" called out several members of Daria's now-captive audience. Enchanted by the story, the younger ones snuggled closer to Daria.

"Yes, that's right," Daria continued. "When the Bedouins were ready to return to the desert, Jameelah stayed behind because she had overheard someone say that Princess Jameelah had been kidnapped and taken to Greece. Her parents had sailed there to find her, because they missed her so much. Jameelah was surprised at the news because she didn't think they cared. Terribly sad, Jameelah sat down and wept.

"Her friends comforted her. They agreed to help her find a ferryboat that would take her to Greece so she could find her parents. In return, Jameelah gave each of them a gold coin.

"Are you Jameelah?" asked a little boy who had been swept up in the story.

"No," Daria laughed. "But I do have people who want to kidnap me. And I do need to get to a ferryboat to Piraeus. Can you help me?"

"We can. We can." The children called out.

"Good." Daria reached for her travel pouch. "Usually reward

is given *after* the good deed is done. Once you take me to the ferry, I may not have time. So I will thank you now and entrust in you the responsibility of fulfilling the deed. Ensh Allah."

"Ensh Allah," they said almost in unison.

Daria's waist wallet was thick with coins and small bills for baksheesh. She gave coins to the youngest children, and bills to the older ones.

The oldest boy announced he would take Daria to the ferry. The children vocalized their agreement. He chose four boys to come with him and sent four others to scout ahead. He ordered the rest of the children to stay behind.

"We must hurry," he said to Daria.

Daria knelt down to hug the children, in twos and threes, since none would allow just one to hug her at a time. "I will remember you," she promised.

"Hurry, Ma'am," said the oldest boy. "We must leave now."

The children followed them to the end of the street. Daria waved good-bye. Then she followed her escorts, who began to walk briskly down one street, then another, turning this way and that, avoiding the main streets and certain side streets, and often turning in what seemed to be the wrong direction, but she trusted them—she had no choice. And they seemed to know exactly where they were going.

Soon they reached the dock. It was crowded with people, dogs, livestock, and cargo boxes. And it reeked with the smell of fish, sewage, oil, perfume, and spoiled milk. The boys walked behind her and beside her, pressing her gently forward or left or right as necessary. Finally they stopped beside a large ferry, whose gaping mouth was still accepting the last cars and trucks.

The oldest boy spoke to someone and then turned to Daria. "This ship leaves for Piraeus in thirty minutes."

Perfect timing. The ferry would sail most of the night, arriving in Greece just in time for Daria to buy some clothes and soon after catch her plane to New York.

Daria bought her ticket and then gave the boy a generous wad of bills. She made him promise to use it to take care of the children. She told him that they were his family, he was in charge, and he was responsible for them. He nodded his agreement and straightened as he shook her hand, as adult like as he could.

Daria gave one more hug to each of her other escorts and boarded the ferry.

50.

Tomas, Greer, Davison and two armed soldiers rode down the elevator and into the hole. They walked barefoot along the side of the pyramid and through the door Tom had found. Everyone put his boots back on when they entered the ancient monument. Their helmet lamps lit their way.

"The lights will come on momentarily," Tom assured them. He wasn't ready to share the secret with these men, so he began to hum nonchalantly while he sang the HU mantra in his thoughts. He hoped this would work, and it did.

When they reached the control room, Tom offered Greer a chair and sat down next to him. The pyramid's viewscreen was radiating a blue glow.

Tom didn't think it was a good idea to let Greer know the viewscreen was thought-driven. Word commands would work just as well.

"Hello, pyramid," Tom said aloud. "How's the weather?"

The viewscreen showed a picture of the brisk breezes rearranging piles of snow around the Jamesway station.

"What about weather in Kauai?" Tom asked.

The screen responded with a view of the beautiful Hanalei Bay, complete with sunbathers in bikinis and surfers enjoying the unusually rough waves. Even the Pacific Ocean was affected by the activity of the anomalous sphere on the floor of the Atlantic.

"Show me the hurricane," Greer said.

The viewscreen hesitated. In his thoughts, Tom assured the pyramid it was okay. The screen then revealed a satellite view of the monster hurricane heading straight for the East Coast.

"Show me the President of the United States," Greer tested.

The viewscreen complied. It showed the President outside the White House giving a news conference.

"Show me Osama bin Laden," Greer said. The viewscreen showed bin Laden sitting at a table with a dozen men in a plainly decorated dining room. He was talking on the phone.

"I wonder what the bastard's saying," Greer mused.

To everyone's disbelief, the viewscreen revealed its ability to relay sound. Bin Laden's conversation was heard loud and clear.

"Does anybody here understand him?" Davison asked.

Bin Laden looked up and looked around, as though he'd heard something strange. He ordered one of his guards to go outside and look around, and then returned to his conversation.

"Show me General Robert Taylor," Greer ordered.

In seconds, they saw Taylor sitting at his desk in the Pentagon doing paperwork. "Hello, General," Greer said.

Taylor pressed a button on his phone. "Yes?"

"Turn it off, Bob," Greer said with a laugh. "I'm not talking through the intercom."

Taylor stood up and walked to the other side of his desk.

"Who is this?" he demanded. "Is this some sort of joke?"

"General, it's Brett Greer."

"What the ...?" Taylor swallowed hard. "Colonel Greer?"

"Yes. By the way, how do I sound?"

"Very clear," Taylor replied carefully. "Where are you?"

"At the bottom of a hole in the middle of frozen hell," he chuckled. "I'm in the control room of a goddamn pyramid."

Taylor wiped his forehead with a handkerchief and returned to his desk. Tomas Seymour had been right. There was indeed something important located at his coordinates.

"Greer, what's going on?" Taylor demanded.

"We found a pyramid. A big one. And a powerful one. Sir, with this baby, the U.S. military will be able to take control of every square inch of the goddamn planet."

"Colonel, are you feeling okay?"

The colonel's eyes were glazed with greed. "Sir, all we need is the damn capstone. Then we can stop the beams being sent by that sphere, send our own energy beams around the world, comb every foxhole in Afghanistan, find bin Laden, tap the telephone conversations of every suspected terrorist we know, and who knows what the hell else."

"How did you know the beams were being sent by a sphere?" Taylor asked. It had been a top-secret detail he had withheld from Greer.

"The pyramid showed us."

"What kind of technology ..." Taylor began.

"Who cares what the technology is," Greer said. "It works!"

"Greer, I command you to dynamite the shaft and bury that pyramid now," Taylor ordered. Once again, the power of Atlantis had fallen into the wrong hands. And how quickly!

"Can't, Sir. Sorry, Sir," Greer replied, defying a direct order for the first time in his career. "We need to find the capstone and stop the hurricane. Greer out." Then he said, "Viewscreen off."

The screen went blank.

"Seymour," Greer ordered, "I want you to find out as much as you can about this pyramid. I want a complete list of everything it can do."

"Yes Sir," Tom said. Then he added, "Excuse me, Sir. Do you still want me to proceed with another melt?"

"Negative. We have more important things to do now."

Part Three –
The Atlantean Pyramid

Connecticut, Andrews AFB, Hawaii,
New Zealand, Antarctica

September 15th – 18th

51.

Monday, September 15ᵗʰ.

The day after Daria caught the ferry to Greece, she was on her way home. Delta Airlines flight 133 left at noon, Athens time, for New York City. The flight would take a northerly route to avoid Hurricane Ingrid and last about eleven hours. Her scheduled arrival time in John F. Kennedy airport was 3:45 P.M., Eastern Daylight Time.

Daria had a window seat and found a semi-comfortable position leaning against the side of the plane. During the flight, she found it difficult to relax, even though she'd had little sleep on the ferry. Her body ached from her fall off the train and her mind kept wandering to the events of the past few days. It had been a miracle that the Bedouins had found her in the desert; otherwise she'd surely be dead. She wondered if Omar and Akbar had survived and felt a twinge of regret, for even if they had, she'd never see Omar again. She thought about Gateefa, who had cared for her like a mother; the camel-herders, who had been shot while escorting her; and Muhammad, who also may have lost his life. She reflected on the children of Mersa Matruh who had come to her rescue. What if someone had spotted her with them? Were their lives in danger? She wished them safety.

Her thoughts turned to the Shemsu Hor prophecy. How quickly it had been fulfilled—on her very first trip to Egypt since she had received the Key to the Capstone on her twelfth birthday. Now the capstone was in her possession too. Finding it had either been a coincidence or a miracle.

She felt the shapes of the capstone pieces inside the pouch around her neck and decided to take them out and practice putting them together.

The puzzle drove her to frustration. She wished she'd asked Mikta how to put it together. She got out the sphere to examine it too. To her amazement, the sphere and capstone pieces became magnetized in each other's presence and within a minute Daria rebuilt the capstone. Daria held it between her fingers and studied its shiny surface. She wondered what power it really had, if any.

But power it did have. Programs downloaded into the pyramid's memory banks thousands of years ago were awakening on cue. It was time for Atlantis to be reborn. With the capstone intact, and without the protection of Mikta's presence, the Great Pyramid of Atlantis was able to use thought waves to reach the one who held the capstone, and it began to call Daria back to itself. It was also time for her to complete her destiny as ruler of the Atlantean Empire.

Daria's thoughts were swept into an ancient web. Her pyramid-driven thoughts, which seemed intimately her own, took shape with little resistance. Through a growing headache, Daria wondered if she could use the capstone's power for good. What if she could eliminate world hunger, disease, and poverty? The idea filled her with hope and enthusiasm, especially as she thought of the children of Mersa Matruh and the happiness she could bring them. She fantasized about all the good she could accomplish in the world if she had the power to make it happen.

Suddenly, the plane bounced in a pocket of low pressure. The aircraft leveled only briefly, but then the turbulence continued. The pilot instructed passengers to take their seats and buckle their seatbelts. Daria put the capstone, with sphere inside, back into one of her pouches. Never before had she flown in a plane that heaved and tossed so badly. A few of the passengers began screaming with each sudden shift in altitude.

Meanwhile, Daria felt the capstone heating up inside its pouch. She removed the capstone and, using the key, took it apart.

The turbulence stopped, and the capstone cooled down.

Curious, Daria put the capstone back together again. More

turbulence. She took it apart. All was calm. Clearly the intact capstone affected the weather surrounding their airplane.

The pilot apologized for the bumpy ride and advised everyone to stay buckled in until he was sure they were clear of the unstable air.

Daria told herself the turbulence had been a coincidence. But she decided to test the capstone once again. This time, she rebuilt the capstone without the sphere. Nothing happened. She let the capstone pieces fall apart in her hands, and then she put them together with the sphere inside. Almost immediately the plane began to pitch. She took the capstone apart. The ride quieted.

So the capstone did cause the turbulence! How could she harness this power? She would have to learn all the capstone's secrets if she was to use it to make any positive impact on the world. Maybe her heart could help her.

Yet when she turned to her heart, the idea about changing the world sounded foolish. She was no leader and had no desire to be. But the idea tempted her, and she had to keep reminding herself how wrong it felt.

Daria practiced loving her heart and reveled in the love she felt coming from it. This relaxed her. The headache subsided and she finally drifted into sleep.

She dreamed she was inside Mikta's tent, sitting across from him on a pile of rugs.

"I almost died," she told him in the dream. "Yet I lived. Why? Why me?" It didn't seem fair that she had survived when others hadn't. "What does life want from me? Where's it leading me?"

"Be careful where life leads you," Mikta said.

In the dream, Daria looked up at him. Would life take her down a different path than her heart would?

"Life will lead you along well-worn pathways," Mikta explained. "Life will repeat itself from one lifetime to the next, and your destiny can get tied to the past. On the other hand, if you think with your heart, then you have a choice to step into the freedom of a new future. Only your heart can set you free."

"How do you think with your heart?" Daria asked.

"Thinking with your heart begins by distinguishing its whispers from those of your mind," Mikta said.

"I'm not sure how to do that."

"To listen to your heart means to pay attention to your Self. To respond to your truest, deepest desires — and not those impressed upon you by others. Or even those you may have impressed upon yourself long ago. Listening to your heart is natural and effortless. It isn't something you work to do. The more you allow yourself to hear, and the more truthful and honest you are with yourself, the more successful you will be.

"The next step is to think with your heart. This means allowing your heart to use your mind's analytical talents, without letting the mind take control. When you're not sure the best course of action, think with your heart. Explore the options available. In your thoughts and imagination, take a few steps down the path of a potential decision. Meanwhile, constantly monitor your inner peace, ever watchful for sensations of tightness in your chest or stomach that might suggest your heart is beginning to close. If you get these feelings, immediately turn your attention to your heart, and the sensation should ease. Try again with another potential course of action and then another, until you find one that inspires you and opens your heart with an expanded sense of freedom."

"How do I know I'm thinking with my heart and not my mind?" Daria asked.

"The mind's thought process is purely analytical. The mind cannot intuit, create, or feel anything. Only the heart can. However, the mind can process the heart's input and help to implement its choices. And always look out for the mind's unruly thoughts, which are usually based on fear, greed, anger, or jealousy. If an action, idea, choice, or even something you say seems wrong or negative, it cannot be coming from your heart.

"Your mind can also throw phony 'guidance' into your path. Do not listen to these thoughts unless your heart concurs with them. If your mind takes hold, your heart will continue to warn you only for as long as you keep trying to listen."

"It isn't easy," Daria lamented.

"Divide any challenge you face into the smallest steps possible. Identify one step at a time, and take each one using your highest and best guidance. Keep your heart, your mind, and your ears open, and commit to fulfilling every step the best you can."

"My next step is to get home," Daria said.

"And to protect your capstone."

Daria was still feeling remorse for the deaths of her protectors and for missing her opportunity at Saqqara.

"This capstone is wrecking my life," she complained.

"Or it is giving it to you," Mikta replied.

Mikta waved his hand gracefully from side to side, and the dream ended.

When Daria later awoke, she wasn't sure what to make of her dream. Weren't dreams simply electrical signals sent from the brain that conjured random images? That's what she believed. Except this dream, like the one the night before, seemed logical and sensible and had a definite message for her. This dream seemed like an outpouring of her deepest concerns, yet each was answered in a clear and direct way. Could some dreams be real and others not?

As her plane approached New York City, the ride again became bumpy. Daria wondered: if the capstone caused turbulence when the ride was otherwise calm, could it also calm a turbulent one? She considered putting it together to find out. On the other hand, what if the capstone caused an even greater disturbance and the plane crashed? Daria decided to take the risk, but checked the feeling in her heart first. It motivated her to act. She removed the sphere and the capstone pieces from their separate pouches and put them together.

The turbulence did indeed stop, and the plane landed smoothly and safely at John F. Kennedy Airport.

52.

A fter landing at Kennedy Airport, it took Daria hours to go through customs. Security was tighter in New York than overseas. Although the sphere and the key passed through uneventfully, the capstone pieces set off the alarm. The guards were suspicious of them. Daria finally put them together — without the sphere — to convince them they were simply a brain-teaser puzzle. The delay made her miss her flight to New Haven airport, so she had to wait for another.

She called her grandmother at her first opportunity.

Sarah was relieved to hear she was safe but overcome with emotion. Sarah'd had a strong sense that Daria would be okay, but wanted to find out what exactly happened. "You weren't kidnapped, were you," she said.

"Of course not," Daria replied. "Where did you get that idea?"

Sarah told her about the call from Faoud Fayed announcing Daria's abduction.

"I met a man named Omar Fayed," Daria said. She wondered if he and Faoud Fayed were related. "He tried to protect me."

"From whom?"

"I think I was mistaken for someone else," Daria said, trying to make light of her ordeal. "We got lost in the desert. Look, Grandma, I'll explain later. I need you to contact Winslow to let him know I'm all right."

Sarah agreed to call Daria's boss to give him the good news and to ask him to pass the word along to Daria's students. Then she made Daria promise to call her the next day.

While waiting for her flight, Daria went to the newsstand to buy a newspaper. She paid with a ten dollar bill and received a handful of one dollar bills in change. As she was arranging them into her wallet, she noticed the picture on the back of them. It was a pyramid with a separated capstone that contained an eye.

Daria looked at the bills more carefully. The Eye of Horus was depicted inside the capstone on the one dollar bills! She inspected each dollar to make sure they were the same.

Someone else knew about the sphere inside the capstone, she realized.

Omar had told her the Shemsu Hor liked to make truth available to all, but even then only the initiated could see it. Daria chuckled to herself. She'd been handling dollar bills all her life and never noticed the capstone until now. Her initiation must have been a personal awakening, as certainly she hadn't undergone any ceremony. Every truth you accept gives you the strength to accept more, she thought. What would come next?

53.

It was 10:00 P.M. and raining when a travel-weary Daria parked her car behind the old Victorian. It felt good to be home. The motion-sensor floodlights came on as she ran through the rain and up the back steps to her apartment. The temperature was unseasonably warm and wet. She unlocked the door, hurried to turn on the lights, and went straight to her computer to search for information about the capstone and sphere she had seen on the one dollar bill.

She found a U.S. government website and learned that the illustration of the pyramid with its detached apex and the eye inside it was the reverse side of the Great Seal of the United States of America. The obverse side depicted a shield with the American bald eagle, as printed on the front face of the dollar bill.

On Independence Day, 1776, a committee was created to design a seal for the new American nation. Benjamin Franklin, John Adams, and Thomas Jefferson eventually hired an artist to help them. They consulted with Pierre Du Simitiere who suggested using the eye in a radiant triangle, along with several other symbols. The decision to print the Great Seal on the dollar bill was made in 1935 by President Franklin Roosevelt.

At another site Daria learned that in 1934, Henry Agard Wallace brought the reverse of the Great Seal to the attention of President Roosevelt. According to Wallace, Roosevelt was struck by the all-seeing eye—a Masonic representation of the Grand Architect of the Universe. She googled 'Grand Architect of the Universe' and found it simply referred to whatever God an individual believed in. That seemed appropriate enough for a country that espoused religious freedom. She then discovered a quote online from Wallace's book, *Statesmanship and Religion*. Wallace wrote, "It will take a more definite recognition of the Grand Architect of the Universe before the apex stone is finally fitted into place and this nation in the full strength of its power is in position to assume leadership among the nations in inaugurating 'the New Order of the Ages.'"

Something about this quote gave Daria a strange feeling, like that of a strong déjà vu. Except this felt more like a premonition of something about to happen rather than something that already did. It sounded like Wallace was predicting that someone, likely an American, would return the apex stone, or capstone, to its proper place.

She recalled what her father had told her about Mikta's prediction, "Whoever bears the key shall find the capstone, and then the capstone will lead the key-bearer to its original home. It is destiny. There can be no other outcome." She bore the key; she had found the capstone, but why fit it back into its place? There was no way in the world she was returning to the Egyptian desert to try to find that pyramid again. Wallace must be talking about some other capstone, she decided.

Daria shut off the computer, grabbed a snack, turned on the

television, and sat at her dining room table. She worked on the jigsaw puzzle while listening to the Weather Channel.

A newscaster stood before a satellite map of the Atlantic Ocean. "For the last seven days Hurricane Ingrid has been fluctuating between a Category 4 and 5 storm. It continues to blow 150 m.p.h. winds. Ingrid is an impressive example of a hurricane, with a perfectly round eye. This eye is fifty miles wide, which is impressively large."

A video clip followed of weather expert Jim Singer standing by the Nags Head Pier in North Carolina earlier that day. So far, all was quiet he said, but residents were shoring up their homes and preparing to evacuate the coastline as Ingrid had the potential to be the worst hurricane in history. The exact location of Ingrid's landfall was yet unknown.

Back in the Weather Center, the newscaster continued. "Ingrid has recently started a gradual turn to the northwest, and it looks increasingly likely that the hurricane will strike somewhere between North Carolina and New England by Friday. The National Weather Service has alerted millions of residents in the area to keep a close eye on the progress of Ingrid and warns that evacuations may become necessary."

Daria turned off the television and finally checked her answering machine. There was one message that her grandmother had left just an hour ago.

"Hello Daria. I called Winslow and told him you were back. He said to tell you he has been worried sick and that you should never disappear like that again. He also said the U.S. government has called the department several times asking for you. Apparently they have some consulting work for you. They say it's urgent. Oh, and Daria, it's good to have you home."

It was too late to call Winslow and the government could also wait until tomorrow. Daria filled the tub and got in to relax. Her thoughts turned to her students. Considering the university's investment in their assignment at Saqqara, she assumed her students had continued without her; they were certainly capable. And the Egyptian archeologist who was to be their official guide had no reason to cancel the trip. She was certain Winslow had already informed them about her safe arrival home.

Her students weren't scheduled to come back until next week. What if she spent the next few days in Vermont? More than anything, Daria felt she needed a vacation. Her girlfriend, Carol, had loaned Daria the key to her log cabin there. It was a comfortable home in a peaceful location. She fantasized about an early blizzard, getting snowed in, and reading a pile of books by the fireplace.

Daria then wondered about the assignment the government had for her. Probably they wanted her to appear as an expert witness at some congressional hearing, or else wanted her to translate some dusty old documents. She'd done both these tasks before. She slid beneath the bubbles. This was *her* time. In fact, maybe she should pretend she never got the government's message, sneak away to Vermont, and let someone else do the consulting job.

54.

Tuesday, September 16th.

Daria slept late the next morning. After breakfast she went to the front window to let in some fresh air. How refreshing the humidity was compared to the dry desert. She'd earned a new appreciation for clouds too.

A car stopped and parked across the street. Daria noticed two men wearing business suits get out. They looked familiar. Could they be the same two men who tried to accost her at the Sphinx pavilion? Omar said they were Renegades and wanted her key. The men crossed the street and walked toward the front door of her house. Daria confirmed their identity when one of them looked up at her window just as she threw herself backward. Had he seen her?

Quickly, she strapped on her yet-unpacked waist-wallet. The entrance to her apartment was in back of the house, and the men were headed to the front. She had about two minutes before the homeowners would direct them to her door. This was just enough time to run downstairs, get in her car, and take the tenant's driveway out to the side street.

She made it.

Daria's hands and legs shook as she drove away. Her inner peace and the safety of her home ground had been violated. These men didn't belong in her world but came from some nightmare she had just fled.

Pulling herself together, she got on Interstate 95, and drove east over the Q-bridge, then got off at the exit to her grandmother's house. It was then a ten-minute drive on a narrow, winding road through forested neighborhoods. Finally she reached the quaint town of Stony Creek and followed the shoreline road.

Daria drove up the driveway of her grandmother's house and parked beside the front porch. Sarah met her at the door.

"I'm so glad you're okay," Sarah said. She was teary-eyed as she hugged her granddaughter.

Daria embraced the thin woman whose greatest strength had always come from her conviction that nobody could defeat or outsmart her. Daria thought her grandmother worried about her way too much, but she admired her intelligence and cleverness. Sarah was the youngest of seven children, and her siblings, all boys, had been killed in military service. Born into a family of entrepreneurs, Sarah had started a business designing puzzles. By age thirty, her company was international. Nowadays, puzzle design was simply a hobby.

"Where's Martha?" Daria asked. Her grandmother rarely answered the door herself. Martha was in charge of the household and took good care of Sarah and David.

"She won't come anywhere near the coast," Sarah explained. "She's afraid of the hurricane."

"And you're not?"

"Of course not."

Daria took off her shoes and walked into the living room, which was located in the back of the house. They had eliminated the ceiling between the first and second floors and replaced the walls with windows. The view of the Long Island Sound and the nearby Thimble Islands was stunning.

Daria sank into the couch. This was the home she had lived in all her teen years and it felt like a sanctuary.

"Did you get my message?" Sarah asked.

"About the consulting job?"

"Winslow said they called five times."

"Geez, you'd think I was the only language expert on the East Coast."

Then they heard a hard knock at the door, followed by the doorbell.

Daria sat up quickly. Was it the Renegades?

Sarah answered the door.

Daria wondered if she should run and hide but realized that would be futile. So she picked up the phone lying on the coffee table and prepared to dial 911, just in case.

In walked two uniformed men.

"Dr. McHenry?"

Daria sighed with relief and put down the phone.

"Good afternoon, Ma'am," the officer said, extending his hand to shake hers. "My name is Captain Clark and this is Lieutenant Martinez. We're from the United States Air Force, and we have orders to summon you immediately to Washington for official duty." He spoke with a pleasant Southern accent.

"You have good timing," Sarah chimed in. "Daria just arrived."

"Yes, how can I help you?"

"We need you in Washington immediately, Dr. McHenry. We

were hoping you could come with us now."

Daria hesitated. The men offered both protection and escape. She would go to Washington, D.C., fulfill her civilian duties to her country, and if she had time, sneak away to Carol's cabin. Whoever was after her should eventually give up.

"I would be glad to," Daria replied. "Please, have a seat. I'll get my things." She turned on the television to keep her guests occupied. She then ran upstairs to her old bedroom, where she stored her less favorite clothes, as her apartment was short on closet space.

"Daria?" her grandmother called.

Sarah followed Daria upstairs. She wanted to talk about what had happened in Egypt.

"Tell Winslow I'll be in Washington."

"What about your students?"

"They won't be back until next week," Daria said.

Sarah lingered in the room. She knew Daria wanted privacy, but she wasn't ready to let her granddaughter go again so quickly. It hadn't been easy to deal with Daria's kidnapping, or supposed kidnapping. Besides, Daria had promised her an explanation and Sarah wanted to hear it. She could tell Daria was hiding something.

"I think I'll change before I leave," Daria said.

Sarah finally got the message and left the room.

As Daria packed her duffle bag, she glanced at the clock. It was almost 11:00 A.M. She then remembered that Mikta had told her to protect her capstone, albeit in a dream, but a dream that had been as real as life. Daria took the lamp off her nightstand and then moved the nightstand aside. She pulled up a floorboard to reveal the hiding place her grandfather had made for her years ago. It was empty now, but it once had housed her diary and other personal treasures. Daria removed the leather pouch that contained the pieces of capstone and put them into the hiding place. If the Renegades ever caught her, they would have to keep her alive to get them.

Suddenly, as she was about to replace the floorboard, she had second thought. She was unaware that the Antarctic pyramid, in contact with her via the capstone, could feel its connection to her wane. Through telepathy, it rekindled her thoughts about the capstone's powers.

Maybe I should bring the capstone? Daria pondered. If nothing else, it would promise a smooth flight to Washington if they encountered turbulence. Having a sense of control over the weather felt empowering. Maybe the capstone could protect her in other ways too. After all, she'd had it when the Bedouins had miraculously found her in the desert. She certainly would be dead otherwise. And Mikta had seemed far more interested in the capstone than in her key. He had even warned her to take care of the capstone. Somehow, the capstone was tied to her destiny. It felt irresponsible to leave it behind. She decided to take it, just in case.

As Daria lifted the pouch out of the hiding place she was overwhelmed by a feeling of wrongness to remove it. Taking the capstone just didn't feel right.

She hesitated, overcome by indecision.

The pyramid's powers were strongly insistent. It wanted its capstone. The idea of being able to help the children of Mersa Matruh crossed her mind. Then she was infused with a sense of power. It rushed through her body and made her feel strong, bigger than life, able to conquer any fear and beat any challenge. The feeling was intoxicating.

Yet the feeling in her heart was strong too. The conflict within her made her stomach feel queasy

Then she remembered the hassle at the airport security checkpoint and didn't want to risk another when she entered a government building. Leaving the capstone behind seemed like the sensible thing to do. This time, Daria's heart had spoken through her memory of the delay in customs. Feeling pressed for time, she quickly put the pouch that held the capstone pieces inside the hiding place and returned the nightstand and lamp to their original positions. As if to compromise, she kept the sphere. The key, of course, remained around her neck.

Daria felt better immediately and knew she had made the right decision. She changed her clothes and then rummaged through the hall closet for some toiletries.

"I'm ready," she said, bounding down the stairs. She hid her anxiety about being followed by the Renegades by turning it into a veneer of enthusiasm.

Sarah sensed it. "Daria, we need to talk," she said.

"When I get back," Daria promised, and hugged her grand-mother before following the officers outside to the limo that awaited them.

"Good day, Ma'am," each officer said to Sarah, while tipping his hat.

"Today and forever," Sarah said.

55.

The officers took Daria to the back entrance of Tweed New Haven Airport where the private planes were kept. To get there, they had to drive through neighborhoods that didn't seem as though they could possibly harbor an airport. After turning down a long driveway, however, they arrived at a small parking lot lined with office buildings and hangars. They parked the car at Gate 20, and walked through the gate toward the largest jet on the tarmac.

Daria hadn't seen a plane like this before. Its wings looked proportionally longer than those of commercial jets and its wing-tips were bent upward ninety degrees. Two jet engines were located on the fuselage, near the tail. Most impressive were the six oversize black circular windows, plus a row of smaller windows above them.

Clark saw her eyeing the jet. "She's a C-37. The military's

version of the corporate Gulfstream V. She's a *nice* aircraft. She can cruise faster and higher than commercial aircraft, and can go farther without refueling."

Daria climbed the steps into the plane, as Clark babbled on about its specs. Everything inside was first class. The six leather seats up front were armchairs that reclined and swiveled. Two leather sofas, facing each other, were located in a separate room in the back. The walls of the aircraft were covered in a soft taupe fabric, and the taupe carpet was plush and well padded. Daria chose a seat in the second row and put her pocketbook on the mahogany table in front of her. The window beside her was twice the size of any airplane window. Next to the window, a small personal television set with a DVD player protruded from the wall. Daria fastened her seatbelt and pulled up the foot-rest. Clark and Martinez took seats behind her.

The plane took off at two o'clock in the afternoon.

Daria turned to her escorts. "By the way, what's the hurry?" she asked. The cabin was conversation quiet. You barely could hear the hum of the engines.

"You'll be briefed later," was all they would say. Earlier, during their drive to the airport, Daria's attempts at small talk had been thwarted with one-word answers. It looked like a conversation wasn't going to happen on the plane either. So she rested her head against the seat-back and looked out the window.

About an hour later, the pilot spoke on the intercom.

"Good afternoon. We will be landing at Andrews Air Force Base, home of Air Force One, in approximately five minutes."

After a smooth landing, they taxied from the runway onto the expansive tarmac ramp that bordered the terminal. A black wrought iron fence with formal red brick fence posts separated the ramp from the terminal. An entrance designed to impress visiting dignitaries, Daria thought.

A black minivan met Daria and the two officers at the plane and transported them through the base, past huge airplane hangars to a large two-story brick building. They drove up the circular drive and stopped in front. The sign above its entrance read,

"United States Air Force 89th Airlift Wing."

In the building foyer Daria stopped to read a large plaque mounted on the wall. It outlined the purpose of the 89th: "Provide special air mission support for the President and other dignitaries. Maintain readiness and ensure quality support for global reach."

Daria again wondered what they wanted her for.

They hurried her through a metal detector, which was similar to that of any airport. Then they led her down one hallway, up an elevator, and down another hallway. They stopped at a small office, where someone inspected her driver's license and gave her a visitor's pass. She was then taken to a waiting room and invited to sit until called. None of the magazines on the coffee table interested her, so she turned on the small television set in the corner.

The Weather Channel was showing a large satellite map of the Atlantic, covered with swirling clouds. The newscaster explained how Hurricane Ingrid was now heading directly toward New England.

"As of 11:00 A.M. today, the sustained winds of Hurricane Ingrid jumped to a staggering 180 m.p.h. This makes it the first Category 6 storm in history. Mandatory evacuations have already begun as this storm promises catastrophic devastation along the New England coast." It was expected to reach landfall Thursday afternoon.

Then it struck her, did the newscaster say the hurricane began to get stronger at 11:00 A.M.? Wasn't that the time when she finally decided to leave the capstone behind? She knew the intact capstone with the sphere inside it aggravated weather, but now the two were separated and the capstone was in pieces. Did her decision to leave the capstone, or to separate it from its sphere, cause the increase in the hurricane's wind speed? The coincidence seemed improbable.

Daria's thoughts were interrupted when a young officer invited her into the next room. He introduced her to Colonel Greer and then left the room, closing the doors behind him.

Greer was sitting behind his desk wearing a well-decorated

uniform.

"Come in, Dr. McHenry," Greer said. "Make yourself comfortable." He was trying to be polite, but his tone still sounded as though he was giving an order. The grueling two-day flight from Antarctica had put cramps in his shoulders and aggravated his sciatica. Compounding his sour mood, Dr. Daria McHenry wasn't waiting for him when he returned. He had come home to find his house flooded from a broken water pipe, his wife gone—good riddance—and a pile of paperwork that would take weeks to get through.

McHenry was prettier than he expected. Younger too. Seymour had assured him that she was the best historical language authority in the United States. They had shown the symbols to military experts, who had no clue what they were. Greer hoped he wasn't wasting his time with her. At least she wasn't blonde, he thought, and chuckled at his own joke.

Daria sat in one of the two chairs in front of Greer's large desk. An American flag and the blue U.S. Air Force flag hung in one corner. The paneled wall was adorned with a few photos of Greer and his buddies, plus autographed pictures of baseball teams as well as individual players.

Greer opened a briefcase and shuffled some papers.

"You're a professor of foreign language?" he finally said.

"Yale University."

"Are you good?"

Daria ignored the innuendo. "I know language," she said. "I have a particular interest in ancient written language and can read a few that aren't used anymore, such as Latin, Amdo, Ancient Egyptian, and Sanskrit. I can identify almost every modern written language and can say at least a few words in many of them. I am fluent in twenty."

Unimpressed, Greer pulled out some photos from a briefcase and slid them over the desk toward Daria.

"Can you tell me what this says?" he asked.

Greer had tried to be clever. Since he knew nothing about the ancient writing, he didn't want a civilian who might be able to read it to find out too much. So each photo showed only isolated symbols from the pyramid's flat top. Everything surrounded these symbols had been digitally eliminated.

Daria studied each photo carefully.

"You aren't giving me much," she said. "The symbols are definitely very old. They look like one of the few languages that don't fit the genealogical classification of languages, which organizes hundreds of ancient and modern languages into a family tree of sorts. I'd say this was an ancient version of Aymaran, which comes from Chile, although some of the symbols remind me of Paucartambo, an old language of Peru. They could indeed be part of a written script. Alone, they're hard to decipher."

Greer frowned.

"Where did you find it?" Daria asked, wondering at the coincidence of seeing what looked like Aymaran symbols both here and on her capstone.

"That shouldn't matter."

"It would help me decide what language it is."

"Just tell me what you know, based on what you see."

"I can tell you these photographs depict a recent copy of something ancient. Look at the edges of the engraving; they aren't worn by time." Daria leaned forward in her seat, holding a photo for Greer to see.

"We know that," Greer said. "What else can you tell me?"

Daria tried to explain. "It's like … you're giving me individual letters, and asking me to read the paragraph they belong to."

"Look again."

Daria complied. She tried arranging the photos in various ways as if trying to piece together a puzzle. Greer was obviously not an agreeable person, and Daria found it impossible to relax enough to drift into the trance that would allow her to read the writing.

After a few minutes she said, "I'm sorry, I don't think I can help you. Are you sure you don't have better or more complete photos?" She was ready to leave. Vermont was waiting.

Greer shuffled through his briefcase once again and produced a photo of the circle that lay in the center of the capstone base—the one that Tom had thought was a map.

Daria recognized it immediately and feigned a cough to hide her recognition. It looked exactly like the circle on the base of her little capstone!

"Excuse me," she said. "Something I ate on the way over here." And she cleared her throat a second time.

Greer grunted an acknowledgement.

"Let me take a look at this," she said, refocusing on the picture. The photo gave no hint of the object's size, but the grain suggested it was much larger than her capstone. Mikta had referred to the circle's contents. Now what did he say? She should look at a globe when she got home? That she was too accustomed to seeing earth from the viewpoint of North America? If this was a map of the earth, then certainly it wasn't a view she was familiar with.

Then it hit her. This was the planet as seen from the south with Antarctica at its center. Sure! All the continents were there, albeit rather squished and distorted around the edges of the map, and they surrounded Antarctica almost entirely. The only difference between this photo and her capstone was that the symbols in the hub were missing. She looked closer. Something there had been blurred too.

"Did you find this with the other writing?" she asked.

"Do you see a correlation?"

"Possibly." Now Daria had a problem. She sensed he was testing her. If she gave him enough information, she might be shown more. If she claimed no knowledge at all, she would undoubtedly be sent home. She wanted to know more.

"Let's assume all these photos came from the same place," she looked Greer in the eye. When it came to languages, *she* was the expert and she wanted him to know it.

"I suggest that the symbols are Aymaran, from the Lake Titicaca region of the Chilean Andes. The structure of this language is so rigid, logical, and unambiguous that mathematicians have suggested the language didn't evolve but was constructed from scratch."

Then she remembered one of her father's pet theories. He believed the Atlanteans had constructed Aymaran to communicate with the many people around the globe that they had conquered.

She explained, "In 1984, a Bolivian mathematician used Aymaran as an intermediate language to simultaneously translate English into several other languages. In 1984," she added, "not even our most advanced computers could do that."

Greer didn't look impressed.

Daria tried again, "Aymaran is so logical it can be written in algebraic shorthand that computers can understand."

"Algebraic."

"Yes. And if these symbols are associated with this map, they may be coordinates, or nautical readings."

"Go on." Now they were getting somewhere, Greer thought. He wanted to know exactly what else she knew. If these were coordinates, he needed them as soon as possible.

"To read them, I need to see them in the context in which they were found," she told him. "I'm getting nowhere trying to piece these individual photos together."

Greer said nothing.

"Let me explain it this way," Daria continued. She ripped a blank piece of paper from her notepad, tore it into four pieces, and wrote something on each. Then she placed one in front of Greer. On it was the word *miss*.

She put a second piece of paper beside the first one. On it were the letters *ing*.

"Together, these two words spell *missing*," she said.

Then she replaced the second paper with one that said *tress*, to spell *mistress*.

"I'm losing patience, McHenry."

She replaced the third paper with another one that had *ile*, to spell *missile*.

"Now, tell me, Colonel Greer, are we dealing with missing

pieces, mistresses, or missiles?"

Greer knit his eyebrows.

Daria could tell her point had gotten through.

"Wait here," he said and left the room.

"Captain Clark," he called. The captain had been chatting with Matthews. "Did this woman have anything to eat on her way over here?"

"Nothing to eat, Sir," he replied. "Only a bottle of Perrier on the plane."

Greer grunted and turned to Matthews. "Alert the pilot and ground crew. We will be leaving in one hour. And have a set of cold weather gear waiting for Dr. McHenry in Christchurch. Clark, prepare the woman for departure."

Then Greer walked down the hall to the officers' quarters, where he took handful of aspirin and began collecting his gear for another grueling flight.

56.

Daria waited impatiently in Greer's office. He didn't sound happy with the scant information she provided. She knew he was holding back details that ultimately would have helped him. After all, she thought, if you take the trouble to bring in an expert it's foolish to withhold information. You only hurt yourself. Well fine. She didn't care much for Greer anyway. She assumed she would be sent back to New Haven, in which case she would go directly to Carol's cabin in Vermont. Then again, if the Renegades trailed her there, it would be weeks before anyone found her dead body. The thought made her shudder.

The door opened. It was Captain Clark. "Come with me please, Ma'am," he said.

Daria followed him down the hall.

"Do you understand that you have agreed to consult for the United States government?" he asked, while they walked.

"Yes," Daria said. Apparently she had gotten the job.

"That you do so voluntarily and that your expenses will be taken care of, but that we offer no additional compensation?"

"Yes."

"And are you willing to take an oath of loyalty to the United States of America: that anything you might see, hear, or experience will be shared with no one under pain of death?"

"Yes," Daria replied suspiciously. Clark led her into an office and took a Bible from the drawer. "Place your right hand on the Bible and repeat after me. I, Daria McHenry," Captain Clark began.

"I, Daria McHenry."

"Do solemnly swear to keep all knowledge of events, people, locations, or any other information or experience that I might be privy to during this assignment, under supreme secrecy, for the rest of my life, so help me God."

Daria repeated the promise.

Clark put away the Bible and got out a thick form. "Now that we have covered your moral obligation to secrecy, this spells out your legal obligation as well as the ramification of any breach to this agreement, no matter how small. Do you understand that sharing any knowledge or information—no matter how remotely related to this assignment—even admitting your association to this assignment, however remote, is an act of treason?"

"I understand," she replied, feeling daunted by the formality. Whatever the job was, it must be extremely sensitive. No wonder Greer had shown her only pieces of the photographs.

"And do you understand the penalty for treason?"

"Permanent incarceration?"

"Or death."

Daria took a deep breath.

"Read this and sign here," Clark handed her the form. "Press hard, Ma'am, there must be a dozen carbons."

Daria looked up at him. He gave half a smile. So he wasn't completely humorless after all. Daria felt better about the ordeal.

"Now what?" she asked.

"You have a long trip ahead of you, Ma'am. Lieutenant Breck needs to measure you for your gear."

"Where are we going?"

"That's classified, Ma'am."

"Well, it won't be when I get there," she mumbled.

Clark pretended not to hear. He led her down another hallway, then down the elevator to another office. He asked her to wait there for a Lieutenant Breck. Then he tipped his hat and left.

Daria waited about thirty minutes and was getting hungry.

Finally, Breck arrived and gave Daria the once-over.

"Follow me," she said

Breck led her to the woman's room. "I need to take some measurements. I'll need you to remove your outer garments."

"Measurements?"

Breck didn't explain. She put down her clipboard and retrieved a measuring tape from a nearby locker.

"Measurements," Breck repeated, holding up the tape.

Daria undressed except for her underwear, and Breck then measured the circumference of Daria's head, neck, bust, waist and hips, plus the length of her back, arms, inseam, as well as her foot length and circumference. She recorded the measurements on her clipboard.

"You may get dressed," she said. "Your gear will be waiting for you at your destination."

"May I ask where that might be?" Daria asked.

"No."

Daria didn't understand why Breck was so cold. Maybe she needed a few Midol. Then again, maybe she was using her stony façade to protect her vulnerability. If she listened to her heart, she wouldn't need to do that Daria thought. The heart gave you an inner strength that allowed you to be yourself, in any environment, without the need to wear a social mask.

How did one listen to the heart? As a child Daria had heard its whispers. She hoped she would remember how to do it. The thought that she might have ever acted anything like Breck felt repulsive and made her feel ashamed.

Breck led her to the building's entrance where Captain Clark then escorted Daria to the minivan which took them back to the C-37. Daria reboarded. A flight attendant offered Daria something to drink and some snacks while they awaited takeoff, after which she promised to serve a hot meal.

Half an hour later, Greer stepped onto the plane. He nodded briefly at Daria, as he walked past her to the couches at the rear.

Another officer followed him in. "Good day," he said to her, as he tipped his hat and smiled politely before joining Greer. They were the only other passengers on the plane.

Soon afterward the plane took off.

"How long is the flight?" Daria asked the attendant when she arrived with the hot meal.

"A little over seven hours," she replied.

So, they were headed to South America after all, Daria thought. She had been right about the Aymaran.

A few hours later, Daria began to nap. The heavy weight of her body dropped away, as she slipped somewhere above it. This was odd, she thought. Her body was asleep, yet she was wide awake. She wasn't frightened because it seemed so natural. Besides, she was curious about the light she saw in the distance and moved toward it.

A moment later she was standing in her father's office. She saw a little girl about six years old, sitting on her father's lap. His arms were wrapped around her and as he nodded his head, his cheek gently stroked her soft brown hair.

"Did I ever tell you the story of how the pyramid builders got their power?" Ian McHenry asked the little girl.

Daria watched the scene from her past replay itself in her dream.

The young Daria giggled. She had heard the story a thousand

times. "No, Daddy," she said.

Ian held her close. "Once upon a time, in the ocean west of Africa, fishermen found a woman floating on some driftwood. Her name was Sileen, and she had survived a shipwreck. The fishermen brought her home, where their wives and daughters nursed her to health. While she was healing—and this may be complete coincidence—the rain poured kindly on their crops, their sick were healed, and the old people felt much younger. The Africans were sure the woman was good luck. So a few of them offered to help her. She was intent on finding the big river that flowed north."

"The Nile!" the young Daria exclaimed.

"Yes, Honeycakes."

Ian continued, "They sailed up the coast of Africa, then east into the Mediterranean Sea. One day, they did reach the Nile and met other people who knew Sileen. Among them was Prince Hapu, who was overjoyed to see her.

"'Hapu, my Beloved, I have the capstone,' Sileen told him.

"She took it out of the pouch that she wore around her neck and showed it to him.

"'What about its big brother?' Hapu asked.

"The Great Pyramid of Atlantis had two sources of power," Ian explained to his daughter, "a big one and a little one. The big one empowered the pyramid itself so that it could serve civilization, and the little one empowered the individual members of the royal family. Egypt would need both to have the great wealth and technology that had blessed Atlantis.

"Sileen felt sorry for losing the big power center in a storm and was hoping they could build a pyramid without it. They could, but the small capstone didn't have nearly as much power as the larger one did.

"And that, my Honeycakes, is how ancient Egypt became an extraordinary civilization that lasted thousands of years. And that is also why Egypt never became the worldwide empire that Atlantis had once been."

"What happened to Hapu and Sileen?" the six-year-old

asked.

"They lived happily ever after."

"And had lots of children," the young Daria added.

"Who did as they were told," her father said, as he lifted her gently off his lap, kissed her goodnight, and sent her to bed.

When Daria awoke sometime later, the dream was still fresh and she smiled at the recollection of this favorite story. This was a good dream, Daria thought, and she replayed it in her mind. Although the dream could have been her brain churning up memories, she reasoned, what sweet memories they were.

What was odd about this dream was that even though her father was dead, he felt close. Maybe it was because her heart was a little more open now. It felt healing to be able to think of her father. Before, thoughts of him brought up pain. Now the pain was gone, thanks to Mikta. She could think of her father and smile.

Daria checked her watch. It was just after midnight. Two hours to go.

Wait a minute.

The sun was still up, though it was low on the horizon. She looked outside. They were flying over water. There was ocean as far as the eye could see.

The flight attendant served Daria another meal. While she ate, she tried to figure out where the plane was taking her.

57.

The pilot turned on the intercom. "In five minutes, we will be arriving at Hickam Air Force Base. Please prepare for landing."

Wasn't Hickam near Honolulu? Daria'd never been there before, and smiled at her good fortune.

The sun had just set but the lights of the city were already sparkling and defined the shape of the shoreline. Daria didn't realize how big Honolulu was or how many tall buildings it had. She saw the sprawling communities that crept into the foothills, and the looming mountains beyond them. The pilot circled Pearl Harbor, and then turned to land at Hickam.

When the door to the plane opened, a stiff breeze filled the plane with ocean scents. It was seventy degrees and balmy outside. This is Heaven, Daria thought. She deplaned and breathed in deeply. Who cared what her assignment would be. She hoped they would keep her there indefinitely.

"Excuse me, Dr. McHenry?" The voice came from behind her. Daria turned. It was the officer who had accompanied Greer on the flight. "I'm Major Davison," he said cheerfully. "Colonel Greer's Executive Officer." His eyes twinkled.

"Pleased to meet you," Daria replied.

"Ma'am, I'm supposed to escort you to the Royal Alaka'i Hotel, the on-base lodging where you can get some rest—if you can." Davison's tone was lighthearted and jolly, his accent a thick Virginian. "It's only about a block away. Care to walk?"

"Sure." Daria's legs were stiff from the plane ride, and she appreciated the exercise. Davison was a likable fellow, Daria thought. Too bad he got stuck with Greer.

"Now for the bad news," Davison said.

"Bad news? We're in Hawaii." Daria replied with a spring in her step.

"We will be refueling and need you back on board at 23:30 hundred hours. That's 11:30 P.M.," he added, converting to civilian time for Daria's convenience.

Daria checked her watch.

"That's in three hours."

"We have a long way to go yet, Ma'am."

The Royal Alaka'i was a two-story white building surrounded by palm trees and large tropical plants. Daria noticed a snack stand in the open-air foyer and wandered toward it.

"Need some dinero?" Davison asked and tried to hand her some change.

Daria looked at him questioningly.

"Compliments of the United States government," Davison said and again offered her the money.

Of course. Daria remembered her room and board would be provided. Daria took the change.

"Want anything?" she asked.

"Nah. I'm fine. I'm dreaming of breakfast."

"Breakfast?"

"Back home," Davison replied wistfully, "French toast, eggs, bacon, coffee, grits, and fresh cinnamon buns." He had fond memories of his wife's baking.

"Sounds delicious," Daria said.

Davison laughed. "Yeah. And after tomorrow morning, nothing we'll be seeing."

"Why?"

"You don't want to know. Stack up on those chocolate bars, though. They're good for trading."

"Trading what?"

"Oh, privacy mostly. Or to be first in line for a shower so you get a warm one. That itself is worth at least a few bars." He didn't tell her the warm water was cool at best and lasted only a minute before turning ice cold.

Daria was certain he was teasing. She bought a half-dozen candy bars, while Davison checked in at the front desk.

"Here's your room key," Davison said. "Don't worry about falling asleep. I'll wake you with a phone call."

"Thanks," Daria said. She stopped in her room only long enough to freshen up. There would be no sightseeing on this trip. And sunbathing was completely out. But this was Hawaii. She just had to do *something*.

Daria left her room and went up to the clerk at the front desk. "Excuse me," she said. "Is the beach nearby?"

"Aloha, Ma'am," said the clerk, a large young Hawaiian who was dressed in a bright pink and orange floral shirt. Daria noticed he was wearing a large Egyptian ankh on a gold chain around his neck.

The clerk glanced at her necklaces too, paused a moment in disbelief, and quickly refocused on answering her question. "The Hickam Harbor is a long walk away, ya. About five miles. The Sea Breeze Beach there is way nice, ya."

The clerk spoke with a Hawaiian accent, and Daria was curious about the interesting way he ended his sentences. "Anything interesting that's closer?" she asked.

"Oh ya," he said. "Check out the Freedom Tower. Go out the hotel, turn right, and follow 9th Street. It's at the end of a long grassy mall. You can't miss it, ya."

"What's the Freedom Tower?"

"It's an old water tower, but the Japanese thought it was a shrine, ya, so they didn't destroy it in the attack."

"The attack?"

"In 1941."

"Oh, right."

"And check out the eight concrete eagles at the top of the tower. They're way cool, ya. They weigh about two thousand pounds each, ya."

"Thanks," Daria said and turned to leave.

"*Mahalo*" [thank you and blessings], the clerk called out and reached for the telephone.

Daria stepped out of the hotel into the fresh, salty, humid night air. Every so often she caught the scent of flowers. Hibiscus and plumeria grew everywhere, and she spotted a banana tree in someone's yard. This was another world—and so different than both the desert and Connecticut! She saw the well-lit Freedom Tower and headed toward it along tree-lined streets.

Suddenly her heart, which had been feeling so light and happy to be in this beautiful place, got heavier. She knew it wasn't a heart attack or indigestion. It was like a foreboding, and it was growing by the moment.

Something was wrong. But what? She was half a world away from the Renegades. She looked up and down the street. She was alone. What was her heart trying to tell her? She decided to test it. She would send her heart love by being grateful for its warning. The more you loved yourself, she was beginning to believe, the clearer your guidance would be. Wasn't that how it worked?

"I love myself, I love my heart," she whispered.

Feeling pressure on her back, she looked over her shoulder and in the darkness of the night noticed the silhouettes of three young men about fifty feet behind her and moving toward her. She was alone but for them, and froze with fear. Love is stronger than fear, she shouted to herself. But how was love going to save her now? Maybe the men are just out for a walk, Daria reasoned. I shouldn't fear them. So bravely she turned and headed straight toward them. Caught off guard by her conviction, the men stopped and looked at each other.

The moment they took their eyes off her, Daria leapt sideways into the bushes. This was no conscious decision. Her body had heard her heart's command long before her mind could pick it up and process it. As a result, when the men turned back in her direction, it looked as though she had disappeared. Daria took the opportunity to sneak around the building whose property had provided her cover. She emerged on the street and looking back saw the men, who were now mere shadows in the distance.

She hurried to the hotel and returned to her room.

Daria sat on the bed, her heart pounding. "What was that all about?" she said aloud. She took some deep breaths to calm the anxiety that came as an aftermath. She buried her head in her hands, weaving her fingers through her hair, and then closed her eyes and relived the experience in her imagination. Had her heart given her any warning not to go outside? No, it had not interfered with her free will. But it had certainly saved her from what could have been a very unpleasant experience. Most importantly, she had remembered to listen to her heart. Its guidance didn't come in a way she might have expected. On the other hand, had she known she was going to dive into the bushes she might have talked herself out of it. Maybe it was best that the heart and body excluded the mind from their communication.

Daria turned on the television. Weather reporters predicted Hurricane Ingrid would reach landfall in two days. Daria considered calling her grandmother, but decided against it. Sarah would undoubtedly ask where she was, and Daria wouldn't know how to answer.

Just before 11:00 P.M., Davison called as promised. Daria washed up and met him in the hallway. She casually kept her eye out for the Hawaiian clerk as they left the building, but didn't see him.

"Our next flight is also a little over seven hours," Davison said.

"We're going home now," Daria teased. "Thanks for the vacation."

"Yes, Ma'am. Hope you enjoyed the ride." He winked at her. "Actually, we'll be there in thirty-one hours," Davison added.

"*Thirty-one?*" Daria repeated. Was he joking now or before? Daria couldn't tell by his boyish grin.

"We're crossing the International Date Line," he explained. "Add twenty-four hours to the seven-hour flight time, and you get a total of thirty-one hours. Then, of course, you have to subtract two hours for passing time zones."

Where on earth were they going? Daria boarded the plane

and took her seat. She wished Davison sat close enough to talk, but he was busy in the back of the plane with Greer.

58.

Thursday, September 18th (New Zealand time).

Daria, Greer, and Davison landed at Christchurch International Airport a little after five o'clock in the morning, on Thursday. Because they'd crossed the International Date Line, she missed an entire Wednesday.

The flight attendant gave her a parka before landing and reminded Daria that the seasons in the Southern Hemisphere were opposite those in the north. Here it was early spring and still very cold. As they disembarked, a chilling wind whipped the passengers as they clung to the railing of the airplane's stairway. An airport jeep took them to a large, modern building near the airport terminal. Its white block construction was accented by two rows of large black windows that wrapped around the building. A sign on the front read, 'Antarctic Center.'

Greer spoke briefly with Davison, and then disappeared down a hallway.

Davison and Daria went to the cafeteria. When they finished eating, Davison said, "Now for some real fun."

They walked down a hallway and into a busy warehouse. Rows and rows of racks stuffed with red clothing were lined up like 18th Century soldiers on a battlefield. Boxes were piled here, there, and everywhere. Over a hundred people were bustling about.

"This is the supply warehouse for the U.S., New Zealand, and Italian Antarctic programs," Davison said. "It services over three thousand scientists and support personnel each summer."

"I didn't realize so many people worked in Antarctica," Daria said.

"The U.S. has three stations," Davison said. "McMurdo is the largest and houses about eight hundred people, then there's Palmer, and Siple. Of course, there's also the multi-national South Pole Station.

"The people here are the first of the 'mainbody' which is when the majority of passengers and cargo are flown in, usually in September. Remember, that's when the Antarctic spring begins. Most people return home in May or June, before winter starts."

Daria saw a sign, 'USAP Clothing Distribution Center.'

"USAP?" she asked.

"United States Antarctic Program," Davison said. "If anyone asks, tell them you're a language expert here to help an international team of researchers communicate with each other."

"So that's what I'm doing."

"You'll be flying to McMurdo Station with many of the folks you see here. Then you'll be taken to a remote location."

"Is that what's really happening?" Daria asked.

Davison nodded.

"Wow, I'm going to *Antarctica*!"

"Yes," Davison said.

"But the military isn't allowed on Antarctica," Daria protested.

"The National Science Foundation, which funds and manages the USAP, is supported by the U.S. Air Force, the New York Air National Guard, and the U.S. Coast Guard," Davison explained.

"I had no idea."

"Useless trivia," Davison said. He searched through a pile of orange duffle bags and picked out three with Daria's name on them. "These are yours," he said, handing her the bags. "There's the ladies' changing area," he said, pointing. "Make sure everything fits. And gear up; the next leg of our journey will be very cold."

"What about my own duffle bag?"

"Your clothing won't be suitable for the Antarctic weather," Davison said. "We'll return it to you later. You have everything you need in these bags." Then he added, "I too have to get changed. I'll meet you back here."

Daria went into the dressing room and opened the USAP duffle bags. They were indeed well packed. She found a heavy red parka with the USAP insignia, bibbed overpants with suspenders, polar-fleece pants and jacket, two pairs of flannel-lined blue jeans, two heavy flannel shirts, two turtle-neck sweaters, two pairs of thermal underwear, two heavy cotton sports bras, four sets of wool socks, five kinds of mittens and gloves, a balaclava, neck gaiter, knit hat, work boots, and snow boots.

She also found sunglasses, a water bottle, and a bag of toiletries. Daria tried on the clothing, as other women there were also doing, and then put on an outfit of cold-weather gear. Out of curiosity she rummaged through the toiletry bag and found, among the usual items, a five-inch long plastic tube that was flattened at one end. The thing looked like a wide spoon with a tubular handle.

"What's this?" she asked aloud to herself, holding up the item and trying to decide its use.

One of the women looked at Daria and smiled.

"That's a pee funnel," she said.

"A what?"

"A pee funnel," the woman said again. "It allows us to pee without having to drop our pants and freeze our butts off. You simply unzip, stand like a man does, and insert the flat end against your body. Then, presto."

Daria laughed. "I've never seen anything like it. Does it work?"

"You get used to it," the woman said. "I'm Leah. You headed to McMurdo?"

"Yeah, but just for a short while," Daria said. She didn't want to start a conversation. How would she explain where she was going if she didn't know? "I'm Daria. It was nice to meet you, and thanks for the info. You'll have to excuse me. I have to go meet someone." She wanted a graceful exit.

Daria met Davison as planned. He led her to a large airplane hangar crowded with people standing in line. They took their place at the end.

"What are we waiting for?" Daria asked.

Davison nodded to three dogs. They were sniffing every bag and person for illegal substances. When their job was done, everyone went through a security checkpoint, before going onto the tarmac. A bulky, four-motor propeller plane, the LC-130, squatted on the runway waiting for them. It was fitted with wheels as well as skis for landing on ice.

As they boarded the plane, a woman handed everyone a bagged lunch and a packet of yellow earplugs.

"These are motion sickness pills," she told Daria.

Daria looked at her with astonishment. The pills were huge!

"Gotcha!" the woman said, and chuckled. It was a joke tried on anyone who looked like a first-timer. They were really ear plugs.

Daria grinned and entered the plane, following the passengers ahead of her. The seats were made of red cargo netting and were attached to the plane's fuselage. Passengers sat facing each other. Duffle bags and personal gear were stuffed between each seat as well as on the floor between passengers. The back of the plane was packed with cargo that was chained to the deck. Each side of the plane had only three small windows, and these were partially obstructed by life vests. Luckily, Daria found a seat near a window, so she could periodically turn around and look outside.

Whereas Daria's first two flights had been luxurious, she now felt like a piece of freight. This time Davison sat next to her, but conversation would prove impossible because the plane's engines were too noisy.

"How long is the flight?" she asked before they took off.

"Could be anywhere from six to nine hours, depending on the weather," Davison replied.

Another long flight, Daria sighed, and this one promised to be very uncomfortable. She wriggled in her seat, unsuccessfully looking for a position that gave her lower back some support. Daria's physical discomfort brought to mind another source of uneasiness.

"Is Colonel Greer coming with us?"

"He's probably sitting in the cockpit, schmoozing with the pilot," Davison said.

Daria couldn't understand why she felt so uncomfortable around Greer. He may have been stern and gruff, but she had no reason to hold that against him. Maybe her heart was telling her something about him, she thought.

Davison rummaged through his bag and pulled out a small guidebook on Antarctica. He handed it to her.

"Reading material," he said. "In case you get lost out there." He winked.

Daria groaned and rolled her eyes.

After takeoff, the passengers were told they could move around the plane as they pleased. At this announcement, USAP veterans quickly unbuckled their seatbelts and raced to the back of the plane. Flat surfaces large enough to lie down on were available first-come-first-serve and were snapped up quickly.

The ride was loud, bumpy, and nauseating. At times, Daria wished her ear plugs really were motion sickness pills. After four hours, someone came out of the cockpit and shouted to everyone that they had reached the point of no return. They were halfway between New Zealand and McMurdo. At this time, the weather at McMurdo was clear. If it suddenly turned bad, like it could do, they would not have enough fuel to make it back to Christchurch.

The news made Daria nervous, but everyone else responded by whooping and clapping.

On several occasions, Daria looked out the window and saw only blankets of clouds below and blue sky above. On another attempt, the sky had cleared, and she saw sharp black peaks of rock jutting from a vast white plain of glacial ice. On one side of the mountains the low-lying sun cast long, deep shadows, which made the ice appear blue-gray.

At about three o'clock in the afternoon they landed on one of McMurdo's two airstrips, a hard-ice runway they called the Pegasus. The plane's door opened, a stairway unfolded from the plane, and everyone filed out.

It was cold.

The cloudless sky was a deep blue — deeper than anything Daria had ever seen, even in high altitudes.

"Look at that!" someone called out, pointing to the sun.

Everyone looked.

"It's a sun pillar," explained someone else.

The sun, which hung just above the horizon, didn't appear like a round circle. Instead, it looked like a column of yellow light rising up from the earth.

"It's a phenomenon caused by ice crystals suspended in air," explained a man with glasses and a beard who sounded like he knew what he was talking about. Daria remembered she was among scientists.

"The ice crystals can also produce halos, arcs, and spots around the sun as well as icebows, which are like rainbows, except the prism effect takes place on the ice itself." Then his tone became nostalgic. "Sometimes the air fills with frost crystals and the whole sky turns pink. The pink reflects on the ground too. It can last for hours and sometimes days. It's like living in a pink world." Then his tone got techy again. "Be careful not to look at the sun directly," he warned. "It can damage your eyes."

Daria squinted a few moments more at the trick of nature and then spied a red jeep approaching. In the distance it looked big. Up close, it was huge. This jeep-on-steroids had wheels taller than Daria and the floor of its chassis must have been fourteen feet high. It had been specially designed to handle deep snow and any terrain in any weather, and was large enough to carry everyone. Several passengers dawdled a few moments before boarding, as they drank in their new surroundings.

Davison called to Daria, "We're going over there," he called out and pointed to a helicopter.

Davison and Daria loaded their duffle bags into the helicopter and then returned to the plane for several more crates of supplies. Then they climbed into the back seats of the heli. The pilot turned around to greet Daria by tipping his hat. Greer was sitting next to him and ignored her.

After a three hour flight, they reached the remote Antarctic station. Daria debarked with the others. The air was so cold it stung her eyes and nose, but Daria was too excited about this new adventure to complain. Once the helicopter engines revved down, the only other sound was the droning of the generators that provided both heat and light. With no moon, it was pitch black everywhere except for some floodlights that illuminated large canvas tents with rounded rooftops, and one other floodlight that lit a roped-off field with some strange looking equipment. Daria noticed someone working there, and started toward him.

59.

"Dr. McHenry." Davison said. "You need to come this way." Seeing her hesitate, he added, "You'll get the tour later."

He picked up Daria's largest duffle bag, and she took the other two. They walked toward a tent that had over a dozen antennae and a few small satellite dishes sticking up from its roof.

"These buildings are called Jamesways," Davison told her. "They're portable and leftover from the Korean War, but they've been recently updated with Nanoprotect insulation. This Jamesway houses Colonel Greer, me, and three other officers. You'll be staying here too. The one over there is the dorm."

"What's that?" Daria asked, pointing to a one-person, A-shaped tent.

Davison grinned. "That's the poop house."

"The *what*?"

"Seeing is believing, Ma'am," Davison replied. "The red flag up means it's occupied."

Daria followed Davison inside the Jamesway. The anteroom was the Jamesway's only defense against incoming cold air. Parkas and snow pants were neatly hung in a row on one side. Boots were lined up on the other, along with a row of M-16 machine guns. The guns startled her. Who were they meant for? There was nobody around for miles. Antarctica didn't even have polar bears. Daria removed her boots and set them down beside the others. Then she hung her ski pants and parka on an empty hook.

"Set your duffle bags here," Davison said. "I'll have someone bring them in for you."

They entered a smaller room packed with computers, radar, seismic recorders, and scads of other equipment. Two men, wearing fatigues and headsets, sat amidst the technology. Upon seeing Major Davison they put down their headsets and stood to salute him.

"At ease," Davison said.

"Dr. Daria McHenry," Davison announced. "This is Lieutenant Eichert and Lieutenant Manning."

"How do you do, Ma'am," both men said, extending their hands to shake hers.

"Who gets to ask her the million dollar question?" Manning asked.

"You do it," Eichert said.

"Ok. Dr. McHenry, what do fast, frazil, pack, pan, brash, blink, growler, grease, cirque, crevasse, firn, floe, nip, nunatak, pancake, bergy, and sastrugi have in common?"

Daria hadn't a clue. She recognized the words 'pan' and 'pancake,' and 'sastrugi' sounded like sausages. She was about to say they had something to do with food when Davison interrupted.

"Ok, that's enough," Davison was more tired than his personality would ever allow himself to reveal, but his patience was wearing thin. "I need to show Dr. McHenry to her room. Manning, please get her bags."

Davison nodded to the door on their left and said it led to the kitchen, storage area, generator room and furnace, which melted ice for fresh water. Straight ahead were Greer's office and their all-purpose room. The hallway to the right, where they were headed, housed the officers' and the guest quarters.

It was a narrow hallway with narrow doors on either side. Along the ceiling ran an aluminum heating duct, with side vents that poured heat into each room. Light fixtures, which consisted of uncovered light bulbs, were strung along the hallway and above each room.

Davison led her to a room on the right. Inside, the wall opposite the door was made of canvas and covered with shiny black Nanoprotect. The wall was windowless and a cot was set up against it. To the right of the bed stood a nightstand with a clock and a lamp. To the right of that, a desk with shelves. The shelves held a bottle of water, paper cups, a bath towel, paper towels, and a flashlight. The plywood wall adjacent to the door supported several hooks to hang clothes.

Manning came in and placed the duffle bags on the floor beside her bed. He tipped his hat to her then left.

"So what's the answer to the million dollar question?" Daria asked Davison.

"Oh," Davison replied, chuckling. "They're names for the different kinds of snow in Antarctica." He added, "there's a sink and a shower at the end of the hall. Get yourself settled; I'll bring you a sandwich."

When he returned with the food, he also brought more bottled water and a large box. "The box is from Mr. Seymour," Davison said. "You'll probably meet him tomorrow. By the way, you also have a meeting with Colonel Greer at 08:00 hundred." Then he added, "And you're lucky Greer didn't schedule it any sooner. You should be able to catch a few hours of sleep. I'll knock on your door at seven, so you have time to get ready."

Daria looked at her watch. It was 6:30 P.M. New Zealand time.

"What time is it here?" she asked.

"By camp agreement we keep time with Washington, D.C.," he replied. "It's now 2:30 A.M. Eastern Daylight Time. So it's Thursday again — not Friday, as it is in New Zealand."

After Davison left, Daria eyed the box that he'd brought and opened it. It contained a humidifier. A humidifier? Who was Mr. Seymour and why did he give her a humidifier?

Daria would soon learn that Antarctica was the most arid continent on earth. Despite the snow on the ground, half the continent got less snowfall than the Sahara got rainfall, and the air was just as dry. The Jamesway's diesel fuel heaters stole what little moisture remained in the air, leading to nosebleeds and horribly dry eyes and throats. Humidifiers were treasured, and some people were unable to sleep without them.

As she unpacked the humidifier she accidentally bumped into the bedside lamp. As it fell, Daria tried to catch it before it hit the floor but couldn't. The bulb shattered and one piece sliced her finger.

"Ouch!" She put the cut to her mouth.

Glass was everywhere. She got up to ask Davison for a broom.

Her door was locked.

That was strange, she thought. She tried the door again. It was indeed locked. Daria fought a wave of anger. She didn't enjoy being locked behind any door.

Daria turned and looked around the windowless room. "Don't panic," she said to herself. "You'll look like a fool if the door had been locked by accident." After all, there was no place she could go.

She found a wastebasket in the corner and carefully picked up the larger pieces of glass. Then she checked her finger again. It was still bleeding. She wrapped a paper towel around it and finished eating her lunch — or dinner — or whatever meal this was supposed to be. Only two days ago she had flown in from Athens

… or was it three days … or had it all been just a dream? Daria had never felt so jet-lagged or disoriented.

She lay down on the bed to try to ease her anxiety, but her mind wouldn't rest. Why would they lock her door? She couldn't run away. Were they hiding something from her? That didn't make sense. Obviously they wanted to show her something — why else go through so much trouble to get her here? And for how long were they going to keep her? She hoped long enough for the Renegades to forget about her.

Daria began playing with her pendants. She opened the velvet pouch and took out the sphere. Holding it between her fingers, she began talking to it, silently, in her thoughts. "Are you worth all this trouble? Maybe I should just give you and your silly little capstone to the Horus people."

Then she noticed her injured finger didn't hurt anymore and opened the towel that surrounded it. The cut was completely healed. Daria examined all her fingers on both hands and could find no wound or painful spot anywhere. Maybe the cut was so thin she couldn't see it, except when it bled.

Daria looked again at the sphere. Could it have healing properties? She recalled the fall from the camel and how badly her shoulder and chest had hurt. She had held the sphere back then too.

Daria searched her memory for anything her father might have told her about the capstone or its contents. It felt as though she was brushing aside centuries-worth of cobwebs in her mind. She was grateful the memories no longer felt so painful and attributed the healing to her experiences with Mikta. Spontaneously, she touched the sphere to her forehead. Suddenly, she remembered another one of her father's stories. It played through her mind like a movie, feeding her imagination with vivid images.

"Once upon a time," she heard her father's voice narrate the story, "when Egypt was a great kingdom and the pyramids had been serving the people for centuries, a pharaoh's daughter fell in love with a captain of the palace guard. Their love grew strong and deep, and they were soon to be married. Then invaders from the south swept into their country.

"The captain was among the first to defend his kingdom. Bravely he led his men into battle but caught three arrows in his chest. Medics brought him quickly to a tent to try to save his life. With all his waning strength, he called for the princess. She came secretly, since her kingdom was about to be overthrown and she was sure to be captured.

"When she saw him, she kissed his face and hands, and smiled.

"'My love,' said the captain, 'you are brave not to cry. You are stronger than you think.'

"'I do not cry because I know you're going to live,' said the princess.

"The captain didn't reply. He knew his wounds were mortal. His princess was denying the truth to save her heart from breaking.

"The princess then opened a pouch she carried around her neck and removed a small capstone from it. The captain recognized it immediately.

"'You have taken the capstone from the Great Pyramid of Giza!' he gasped. 'Are you out of your mind?'

"'Our country is falling,' the princess replied. 'I cannot risk that our enemies will take our power.' Then she opened the capstone and removed a beautiful sphere hidden inside. The sphere greeted the air with a flash of light. The princess took the sphere in her fingers and held it over her beloved's body. Then she placed it in his palm and closed his fingers around it.

"'Now you will live,' she said. Then she replaced the capstone in its pouch. Before she could put it back around her neck, a flurry of soldiers began storming the tents, looking for her.

"'I must go!' she cried, leaving the capstone and its sphere behind.

"'No!' shouted the captain, reaching for her in vain.

"The princess took one last look at him and ran."

Daria took a deep breath as the memory of this story filtered through her mind. How she loved her father's stories. Sitting on his lap, listening to him, feeling his cheek rub gently against her hair. These were such sweet memories.

Daria thought again about the tale. So her father had known about the sphere and the capstone, and that the sphere had the power to heal. But *how* did he know? Did all his stories come from Mikta? How did Mikta know them? How many of these stories had Omar also heard? Her mind exploded with possibilities.

Then Daria wondered what else the sphere could do. She got up, filled a cup with water, and dropped in the sphere. She swirled the cup, but nothing happened. So she removed the sphere and moved it toward her open palm and then away from it, trying to sense any magnetic properties it might have. She didn't feel anything. She reached up and held it near the light bulb hanging from the ceiling. The sphere grew warm and soon a beam of light shone through the sphere, creating a circle of light on the canvas wall. Moments later, it looked as though images were forming inside the circle. The circle had miraculously become transparent, and Daria could see outside. She saw the roped-off field and the man who was still out there. She watched him enter what looked like a small room and then watched the room disappear beneath the surface of the ice.

They're mining! Daria's thoughts began to buzz and her emotions got the better of her. Mining in Antarctica was prohibited by international treaty. Not to mention the environmental hazard it posed. So why did they need her? To intercept foreign radio messages and alert Greer when other nations began to suspect this travesty? She had signed an oath of secrecy. Would she have to keep such an oath if her own country was breaking international law? Davison must be involved, but he seemed too nice a guy. She had to find out what was going on.

Daria moved the sphere away from the light bulb. The window in the canvas was gone, as though it never had been there. She tried the door once more. The sphere, which she was holding in her other hand, pulsed with light. She was sure it did. She looked closely at it. Nothing about the sphere appeared different.

She tried the door handle once more. This time the door opened. Daria took the miracle in stride—the sphere was probably full of surprises.

Daria returned it to her velvet pouch.

Then she crept down the hallway.

60.

Daria tiptoed past the two men sitting at the computers. They were facing away from her and wearing headphones, so they didn't notice her. She stepped into the anteroom, donned her ski pants, boots, and parka, and went outside. Nobody was around. Daria braced herself against the cold and headed for the roped-off area. There she found the enormous hole.

"They *are* mining!" she said aloud.

Inside the elevator's housing she found a lever she assumed would call the elevator back to the surface. It was a long wait, and Daria controlled her impatience and kept herself warm by jumping up and down. She was amazed at the effort the military had put into this endeavor. Had all the equipment been flown in? Probably by the same cargo plane that had brought her to McMurdo. But why would the U.S. government break an international treaty? What ore could be worth it?

She looked around, wondering what they had done with all the snow that had once filled the hole. She saw no sign of snow piles or cranes or dump trucks to account for the huge volume of snow that had been removed. Furthermore, the hole was perfectly square, and its walls appeared perfectly smooth. Could it be a natural occurrence? Maybe they were investigating a fluke of nature, and they weren't mining at all.

Finally the elevator arrived, and Daria stepped inside. She didn't know what to expect at the bottom of the hole, but was anxious to find out. The descent was another long wait. The icy cliffs reflected the elevator's floodlights above and below and kept the shaft illuminated with an eerie blue. Soon the shaft grew less cold and the temperature was only about thirty degrees Fahrenheit. Daria removed her ski pants but kept the parka.

Near the bottom of the hole the elevator began to slow. She looked down and couldn't believe what her eyes were telling her. Even her mind couldn't form a thought. The miracle of having found her capstone seemed trivial compared with what she now saw. She leaned against the elevator wall for support, as her knees had grown suddenly weak. Below her, the hole was entirely filled with the top of a gigantic pyramid. Each of the pyramid's silvery surfaces reflected the elevator's floodlights at a different angle, making the capless pyramid look absolutely otherworldly.

When the elevator stopped, Daria traversed the scaffolding that led to a ladder, which she descended to the crevice between the ice wall and the pyramid. Then, filled with wonder, she climbed the second ladder that leaned against the pyramid and which led to the pyramid's flat top. She crawled to the center of its flat surface.

Daria immediately recognized the inscriptions she found there. "So this was what Greer wanted me to interpret," she said aloud. She picked out the symbols he already had shown her and used her fingers to outline some of the other ones. They did indeed look like an old form of Aymaran writing. She also noticed the similarities between the symbols on her own tiny capstone and wished she had it with her to compare.

Then she laughed to herself when she recalled how she had tried to convince Greer that the writing he had shown her must have come from South America. "Since we both know that Antarctica has no native population," she had proclaimed, "we know this writing couldn't possibly come from there." And because the edges of the script were not worn by time, it must be "a recent copy of something ancient." She had wanted to sound certain to impress Greer. Instead she had been completely wrong.

Daria was so fascinated by the ancient writing she neglected to look for the man she had followed down. In fact, she had forgotten all about him. Of course, Tom had gone to work inside the control room. When the pyramid's viewscreen showed him that he had company, he went outside to greet her. Daria was too engrossed in the inscriptions to see him.

He now stood barefoot on the far side of the pyramid, studying her, and waiting for her to see him.

"Hello," he finally said.

Caught by surprise, Daria jumped backward. Her heart skipped a beat, and a wave of adrenaline flushed through her body. Her hand raced to clutch her pendants.

"You scared me half to death!" she scolded him.

"I'm sorry. I truly am. I've been standing here five minutes, and you didn't notice me. I didn't know what else to do."

"Five minutes?" Daria said apologetically. She could usually tell when she wasn't alone. "I'm sorry. I must have been deep in thought."

"Down here, there's a lot to think about," Tom replied.

"Yeah, like, this continent wasn't always covered in ice."

"So much for the theory of ice ages."

"And people once lived here — in Antarctica!" Daria added.

"So much for the textbook view of human origins ... unless the builders weren't human," Tom teased.

"Ugh. Don't give me the creeps."

"Sorry." Tom said. He braced himself for the moment she would recognize him. He sat sidesaddle on the top of the pyramid, dangling his feet over the edge. He was wearing blue jeans and a red and gray flannel shirt with its sleeves rolled up, revealing a white long-sleeved thermal undershirt beneath. He turned to Daria and extended his hand.

Daria leaned over and shook it. "I'm Daria McHenry."

So, she was using her maiden name again. He wondered

what had happened to her husband, Giorgio Chavez.

"I know you," he said.

"You do?"

"I'm the one who convinced Colonel Greer to bring you here. You're probably the only one alive who can read these old inscriptions."

Daria looked closely at his face, trying to see beyond the beard. "Tom? Tomas Seymour? Is that you?"

He nodded.

Daria instinctively moved backward and stopped, realizing that a graceful exit was impossible. What should she do or say? It had been years since she had left him without even saying good-bye. They hadn't seen each other or spoken since.

Tom sensed her uneasiness and wrestled with a good dose of his own. He recalled how deeply he'd been hurt—especially when she married someone else so soon after their breakup. Hadn't Tom been good enough for her? Admittedly, he'd been busy working on ice-melt technology throughout their relationship. After Daria left, he redoubled his efforts to keep his mind off his broken heart.

Daria let a tone of bitterness escape into her voice. "So all the time in the lab finally paid off," she said, looking around and assuming the science behind the hole and the pyramid's discovery had been his. She'd wished Tom had paid more attention to her. She had longed for his devotion. She wondered how many days or weeks it had been before he even noticed she was gone.

"I'm sorry," Tom said gently. He could have listed a hundred specific things he could apologize for, but chose to keep it simple.

Daria hadn't expected an apology. It eased the hurt she'd unknowingly been holding onto.

"I'm sorry too," she said. She really meant it. It was something she had wanted to resolve for so long. Since she'd never heard from him, she thought it best to forget him and try to move on with her life.

"So, what do you think of the pyramid?" he asked.

"Awesome," Daria said, relieved that he had changed the

subject. "How did you find it?"

"What did Greer tell you?"

"Nothing. I sneaked out and came down on my own."

Tom laughed. "Good for you!" So her curiosity and audacity hadn't changed. "You'll catch hell for it, you know."

"Only if he finds out," she paused. "It helps to be a civilian."

"With talents the colonel needs."

"So what's so important about reading the top of this pyramid?" Daria asked, nodding toward the ancient writing. "I assume that's why I'm here."

"There's more." Tom doubted she would believe him if he told her. "May I show you?"

"Sure."

"Then take off your boots and socks," Tom suggested. "You'll need bare feet to walk down."

Daria sat down and removed her footwear. Then she swung her legs over the edge of the pyramid. She was about to step onto the pyramid's steep slope when Tom naturally held out his hand.

To his amazement, Daria accepted his help. Years ago she would had insisted on doing everything by herself.

Daria stepped carefully onto the pyramid's side. When she got her balance, Tom let go of her hand. A few steps down, she stopped and turned to her old friend.

"Tom, how did you dig this shaft?"

"We used ice-melting equipment."

"You *melted* all this ice?"

"Turned it into vapor actually."

Daria continued walking down the pyramid's side. "How did you know where to melt, or rather, vaporize?"

"Believe it or not, the geographic coordinates for this location were given to me in," Tom caught himself, but then decided to finish the sentence anyway, "in visions and dreams."

Daria paused. "I've been wondering about dreams lately," she finally said.

Tom didn't respond. Years ago even mentioning the word

dream caused an argument between them.

"What about inner guidance?" he asked. They'd argued about that too.

"What about it?"

"Do you still think it's bunk?"

"Do you still swear by it?"

"We're here, aren't we?"

Daria couldn't deny that. Of the fourteen million square miles of ice that covered Antarctica in winter, the probability of melting a hole precisely over a buried pyramid was about nil.

Tom led her to what seemed like a random spot on the pyramid's side. He pushed a small rectangular block in the side of the pyramid and its door opened.

61.

"Holy Shepseskaf!" Daria exclaimed, as she peeked inside the pyramid. She stepped into the dark corridor. "Is there a light in here?" she asked. At the sound of her voice the hallway lit up.

"Did you do that?" Daria asked.

"It responds to sound," Tom explained. "Here, watch this."

Tom swore. The lights went out. "HUUU," he sang briefly.

The lights went on.

"Damn!" Daria exclaimed in amazement.

The lights went out.

"It doesn't like swearing," Tom said.

"No, I mean that word you used." Mikta had sung it to her in a dream. It had been peaceful and healing.

"You mean, HU?"

The lights turned on.

"Yes."

"I learned it from a friend," Tom replied. "It's a great word. It's got a million uses."

"Besides turning lights on in pyramids?"

Tom laughed again. "Yeah, besides that."

After all the fantastic things Daria had experienced recently, she realized she shouldn't be surprised Tom also knew about HU.

Daria followed him down the corridor and up the stairs. Tom opened the door to the first room and invited her to enter.

"What are these?" she said as she scanned the shelves of tubes.

"Maps."

"*Maps?*" This was too good to be true. She reached for a tube and Tom showed her how to work the light table. The map she had chosen was a nautical map, but they couldn't tell what part of the ocean it charted.

"There's more, Daria," Tom said, as he returned the map to the shelf.

Daria followed him up the spiral stairs to the next floor. Tom didn't stop but continued upward when Daria spied the dead-end hallway.

"Is there a room down there too?

"It's empty," Tom said and continued up the steps. "C'mon, I want to show you what's up here."

Daria walked down the hall anyway, found the small block in the wall, pressed it, and the door opened.

Tom walked back down the steps. "The room's empty," he repeated.

"I want to see it."

She stepped inside the room. It was bare but decorated. A row of symbols lined the upper edge of the walls like a wallpaper border. The entire floor was inlaid with circles, each about two feet wide. The walls themselves were as shiny as glass. "Hmm," Daria said to herself, taking it all in.

Tom watched her. Ever since they'd met at a lecture at the Massachusetts Institute of Technology in his hometown of Boston, she'd been the woman of his dreams. Now she was standing merely three feet away from him. What a fool he'd been to take her for granted. He wished for a second chance.

"You should see what's upstairs," he said.

Daria followed him up the steps. When she reached the top, she stood speechless in front of the control room's console and the glowing blue viewscreen. It was too much to take in all at once, and it made her feel light-headed.

She reached for one of the chairs to sit down.

It rolled sideways on unseen wheels. "Whoa," she said, stabilizing herself. "These chairs look like the ones in Egyptian artwork that the pharaohs sit in. I had no idea they might have been covered in fabric," she said, stroking the chair's surface. "Not to mention being mounted on rollers. Egyptians back then supposedly hadn't yet invented the wheel."

The blue screen began to pulse. Lights on the console flickered.

"This hasn't happened before," Tom said.

"What hasn't?"

Unprompted, the viewscreen revealed its pyramid, with capstone intact, shining in the sunlight.

Tom thought it must have been something Daria was thinking that triggered the viewscreen's response.

"Let me show you something," he said, and demonstrated how the pyramid's viewscreen responded to thought commands by giving her a tour of Kauai, a view of the earth from miles above, and a glimpse of the Jamesway station.

Daria was impressed. "Can I try?"

"Go for it." Tom kept his own thoughts quiet.

Curious how up-to-date the pyramid's viewscreen could be, Daria thought about her room in the Jamesway tent. A picture of it came up on the viewscreen. It included the broken pieces of the light bulb still on the floor.

"Amazing."

"Ask it a question," Tom suggested.

Daria recognized this as an opportunity of a lifetime and a million questions came to mind. Which one should she pick? What would her father have asked?

"How big are you compared to the Great Pyramid of Giza?"

The viewscreen showed a picture of its pyramid on the left hand side of the screen, and on the right, a picture of Khufu's Great Pyramid. They were identical. Even their tops were both missing.

"That doesn't surprise me," Tom said. "The measurements of the Great Pyramid are intimately connected with earth's dimensions."

"So I've heard," Daria said, recalling her conversation with Omar at the Sphinx Pavilion.

Tom continued, "If the Great Pyramid utilized earth's energy, I'll bet this pyramid did too."

"Okay," Daria challenged, "how was the Great Pyramid built?"

The viewscreen gave a slide show of ancient Egyptian art, apparently in no random order.

"I asked that question too," Tom said. "And I got the same answer. It's showing us technology that may be hard to believe, but its existence has been visible to Egyptologists all along."

"What do you mean?"

Tom explained. "Egyptian art and science are interconnected. Except for statues, which exist in three dimensions, the people who are depicted in all other Egyptian art are shown in two dimensions. Their heads are always shown in profile; their shoulders always square. I think the viewscreen is trying to tell us the pyramid builders had control of both the two- and three-dimensional worlds. Perhaps they could transmute things from one dimension to the other and back."

"A two-dimensional block would be easy to refine into precise measurements," Daria said.

"And much easier to carry," Tom added. "Unfortunately, I haven't been able to ask the right questions to find out how they removed the space between the atoms to reduce the blocks to two dimensions."

Daria touched her pendant. It was two-dimensional. Was the Key to the Capstone essential for building the pyramids using dimensional technology? Was that another reason why pyramid building ground to a halt — when the key was lost?

The viewscreen responded to her thoughts by showing a picture of her key. Tom recognized it immediately.

"That's the pendant your father gave you," he said.

On the screen, the complex shape of the key transformed into a simpler shape. An Egyptian ankh.

"Amazing," Daria said. Then she thought to herself: The key had been staring everyone in the face for centuries. Nobody knew it could actually unlock something like a capstone or manipulate dimensions.

Again, reading her thoughts, the viewscreen showed a series of bas-relief wall carvings, this time of Egyptian gods. All of them held the ankh in one hand and a long staff, called an 'uas' in the other. At the base of the staff was a cup that obviously held a small sphere. This must have been one way the powers of the Eye of Horus were accessed, Daria thought.

Then Daria decided to test the pyramid's viewscreen by projecting memories of her father. The viewscreen erupted with bright white light.

"What are you thinking?" Tom asked.

"About my dad."

Her thoughts wandered to his final expedition at Giza.

To her amazement, the viewscreen showed a diagram of the underground architecture beneath the Giza plateau. It was a subterranean city! Her father's tunnel was only a fraction of what he could have found had he dug only a little deeper. Daria felt remorseful for judging him and believing his inner guidance had failed him so miserably.

Then another question occurred to her. "Has the Great Pyramid of Giza ever burned?"

"You mean, caught on fire?" Tom asked quizzically. "The pyramids are made of stone; stone doesn't burn."

The viewscreen proved him wrong. Against a black night, billows of flame arose from the pyramid, which looked like a torch of biblical proportions. Everything nearby burned to a crisp, but the fire abruptly ended.

"Diamond," Tom mused.

The viewscreen went blank for a moment and then showed a line drawing of a geometric form, a four-sided tetrahedron, just like a pyramid. Seconds later, a mirror image of the form appeared, so that it looked like a second pyramid was attached to the base of the first one. This created an eight-sided octahedron.

"That's one of the forms of carbon crystal," Tom explained. "Carbon comprises diamond."

The viewscreen displayed more and more octahedrons, which fit against each other to form what looked like a perfect patchwork quilt. This layer was then superimposed against the side of a pyramid.

"The pyramids were covered with a thin layer of diamond?" Daria asked.

"Diamonds may be the hardest substance on earth," Tom said, "but they do have weaknesses. They're brittle if struck in a precise way and they burn at a high enough temperature."

"But fire didn't turn the pyramids' surfaces black," Daria protested. "The viewscreen didn't show any ashes."

"Burning pure diamond turns it to carbon dioxide instantly," Tom said. Much like his ice crystals had sublimated into hydrogen and oxygen. "It simply would ignite and then disappear."

Daria was dumbstruck. Had her dream of the burning pyramids been real too? She remembered telling the dream to her father, how he'd listened without disbelief or judgment. He believed in dreams. Grandma Sarah had taught him how to understand them, yet she never discussed them with Daria except for that one time in Egypt. Daria suddenly felt as though she had missed out on something invaluable. Yet after her father's death, she wanted nothing to do with dreams and had done her best not to remember them. How odd that her mind had somehow associated the topic with her father and talking about it evoked the pain of losing him. She decided to ask her grandmother to teach her more about dreams when she got home.

Thoughts of her grandmother prompted the viewscreen to reveal Sarah's house.

Tom recognized it from when he and Daria were dating.

The screen zoomed in on the front porch, where Sarah stood at the door talking to ... the two Renegades!

"My grandmother's in trouble!" Daria said standing up. Her reaction made the viewscreen go blank.

"Who are those guys?"

"People you *don't* want to know," Daria replied. She hoped they were just inquiring about her whereabouts and would leave Sarah alone.

Daria noted the cause-effect relationship between her fear and the blank viewscreen and tried to calm herself. She thought about her capstone, hidden safely under the floorboards of her bedroom.

Suddenly the viewscreen came alive again. It again showed its pyramid glorious and shining brightly in the sunlight, with capstone intact.

Daria caught the link between her thoughts about the capstone and the viewscreen's image. Was her capstone somehow associated with this pyramid?

"What are you thinking now?" Tom asked.

"I'm just worried."

"About your grandmother?"

"That's only half of it."

"Is there anything I can ..."

"Tom," Daria interrupted.

"Yes?"

"Where are we? I mean, where are we really?"

Tom knew better than to answer directly. The possible truth could sound too absurd.

"Where do you think?"

Daria hesitated. "Is this Atlantis?"

62.

The two Egyptian men, whom Daria had seen at the Sphinx pavilion and who had followed her to Connecticut, stood on the front porch of Sarah's house, soaking wet despite their umbrellas.

Sarah answered the door.

"Good day, Madam, my name is Hakim Ahmed and this is my associate Alec Masud."

"What can I do for you, gentlemen?" Sarah replied. She was polite but was distracted by the workmen who were boarding up her windows and moving her precious antiques to the second floor. She was preparing to evacuate before Hurricane Ingrid hit.

"Our boss, Faoud Fayed, wants to know if you could spare a few moments of your time." Hakim glanced over his shoulder, and Sarah looked up and saw a black stretch limousine parked on her driveway.

"Yes," Sarah replied curtly. She did indeed have a few words to say to Mr. Fayed. After being incorrect about Daria's abduction, she was surprised he had the nerve to come all the way to Connecticut to speak to her in person. She wanted to slap the man for causing her so much worry.

Moments later Fayed was at her doorway. He removed his hat and bowed to her, "My pleasure to meet you in person, Mrs. McHenry," he said.

"Uh, huh," Sarah replied, and folded her arms. "By the way, Daria wasn't kidnapped."

"Not against her will."

"She wasn't abducted, willingly or otherwise."

Fayed reached for his wallet and presented Sarah with an

official-looking badge with Fayed's picture. The writing was in Arabic.

"I'm with the Egyptian Secret Service," Fayed lied. "I have reliable evidence that suggests your granddaughter may have unwittingly gotten involved with terrorists. We believe they gave her something to take out of Egypt. Something small but of tremendous value. We suspect it is their way of bringing money into the United States to fund an attack on your country."

Sarah moved backward to lean against the stairway railing. "You're making a grave accusation."

"I accuse Daria of nothing," Fayed assured her. "I believe she has innocently accepted something from someone who gained her trust but who has used her for his own antisocial motives."

"I see," Sarah said, still unconvinced.

"Until we find that object, your granddaughter is in great danger. It is essential that I speak with her immediately."

"That's impossible," Sarah said. "She's been called to Washington D.C."

Fayed was effectively silent, prompting Sarah to say more.

"They often require her linguistic expertise. I really have no way to contact her."

"This object that the terrorists gave her," Fayed said, "Do you think she might have taken it with her? It is essential that we find it before it falls into the wrong hands."

Sarah recalled her granddaughter's strange behavior when she'd come to visit. There was no doubt in Sarah's mind that Daria was hiding something.

"And you say Daria might be involved with terrorists without her knowledge?"

"Yes," Fayed said. "We are certain of it."

Sarah began to worry. Her granddaughter had always been an outgoing person who made friends easily. Sarah also felt Daria was naïve when it came to choosing friends. She would trust them until they hurt her.

Sarah recalled how Daria had run upstairs when the officers came for her.

"I assure you, Mrs. McHenry, any information you give us could save your granddaughter's life, if not the lives of thousands of people."

"Wait here, please," Sarah instructed, and she went upstairs to Daria's room.

Fayed gave Sarah a head start and then followed her.

"Excuse me, Mr. Fayed," Sarah said as she entered Daria's old bedroom. "I asked you to wait downstairs."

Fayed shrugged. "Just thought you might need some help, Madam."

Sarah scowled but asked him to move the nightstand beside Daria's old bed and then lift the loosened floorboard.

Daria's secret compartment was revealed. Inside was one of Daria's pouches. Sarah picked it up. "This is hers," Sarah said and sat down on the bed. She emptied the contents of the pouch into the palm of her hand. Nine shiny angular pieces of something fell out.

Sarah smiled with pride. She wondered if Daria had had anything to do with the puzzle's intricate design.

Fayed didn't understand Sarah's reaction. He was disappointed that the pouch did not contain the Key to the Capstone.

"May I?" he asked.

Sarah dropped the pieces into his hands.

He sat down beside her on the bed and tried to put the pieces together, unsuccessfully.

"My turn," Sarah said. She'd been studying each piece as Fayed toyed with it. "Quite ingenious," she said quietly. Then she put the capstone together in her third attempt.

"A tiny pyramid," Sarah announced.

"A capstone!" Fayed whispered in disbelief. His agents told him that Daria had been lost in the desert for a few days. Could she have found the capstone then? Could this really be it?

"May I?" Fayed asked again.

Sarah handed it to Fayed, and it fell apart.

Sarah took it back and reassembled it. "It has been designed to fall apart," Sarah said. "Unless it contains one other piece."

Fayed gently took the capstone from Sarah. Carefully he released his hold just enough that the capstone pieces began to separate. He peeked through the opening between the pieces, and saw an empty space in the center. The other piece Sarah was referring to must have been hidden inside, Fayed surmised.

"Is this capstone the item you're looking for?" Sarah asked.

"Yes."

"What's it worth?"

Fayed's eyes gleamed. "It is priceless." He gripped the capstone and held it against his chest and closed his eyes, waiting for a surge of power that he knew must soon pour into him.

He felt nothing.

He held the capstone against his forehead and looked into his third eye, fully expecting to see a vision.

Again, nothing happened.

"Mr. Fayed?" Sarah said.

Fayed realized his actions looked unusual and changed the subject. "The terrorists are looking for this. When they find its contents missing, they will assume your granddaughter has it."

"Maybe Daria obtained the pieces unassembled," Sarah offered. "Perhaps she was unable to fit them together."

"Perhaps, but only Daria can tell us. Until we know for sure, her life is in great danger—and so is yours, as long as you have the capstone in your possession."

Sarah took the capstone from Fayed, let it fall apart, and returned the pieces to the pouch. "Then we will make sure they do not find it," she said. "Meanwhile, I'm sure Daria is safe in Washington. I will contact you as soon as I hear from her."

Sarah returned the pouch to the hiding place. "And I'm sure you'll agree it is best kept hidden, where Daria put it," she said. "No one will find it here."

Fayed had no choice but to agree. He felt it wise to remain in Sarah's good graces, and now that he knew where the capstone was hidden, he could have it removed any time he wished.

63.

"Atlantis."

Daria could hardly believe her ears — but she'd said it herself. The pyramid Tom had unearthed couldn't belong to anything else.

"But in *Antarctica*?"

"The only written description we have of Atlantis comes from Plato," Tom said. "This location matches his description."

"How?"

"Plato described Atlantis as a large island continent, high above sea level, and mountainous. Of all continents, Antarctica has the highest overall elevation and some of the most rugged mountains. More specifically, he also told us that the island of Atlantis was the way to other islands, and from these you might pass to the whole of the opposite continent which surrounded the true ocean. He also said that this ocean is a real sea, and the surrounding land may be most truly called a boundless continent."

"Sounds confusing."

"Only if you place Atlantis in the Atlantic Ocean. If you read Plato's description with a global perspective and from the viewpoint of Atlantis being in Antarctica, it makes perfect sense."

"How?"

"Traveling from Europe, which was Plato's homeland, Antarctica is on the way to other islands — those found throughout the Pacific, such as Indonesia, New Zealand, and Australia. From these islands Plato says you might pass to the opposite continent. This would be Asia. But he also says the opposite continent surrounds the true ocean. One ocean does surround Antarctica. It's comprised of the Atlantic, Pacific, and Indian Oceans. The boundless continent that Plato says surrounds this real sea is all the other continents put together. If you look at a world map with Antarctica in the middle, all the other continents appear connected, as though they're one, and they appear to surround the one world ocean."

Tom took a breath. "Clearly, Plato is describing the position of Antarctica."

"You're overlooking something," Daria said.

"What?"

"Ice. Antarctica is buried in it."

"Not twelve thousand years ago," Tom replied. "When Atlantis was thriving, most of Antarctica was ice free. This pyramid was once in a temperate zone, twenty-five hundred miles north of here."

"I thought continents moved slowly over millions of years."

"They do," Tom explained. "The theory of plate tectonics explains continents slowly drifting against each other along fault lines like those along the California coast. There's another theory called Earth Crust Displacement. Crustal displacement occurs when the earth's crust slips over its mantle while remaining basically in one piece. Actually, some scientists believe the shift occurs within the mantle rather than the crust. So, we should more accurately call it a mantle shift.

"But anyway, it happens about every forty thousand years, resulting in instant deep freezes in certain areas. There's evidence of it around the world. Each time the shift occurs, the poles are located over different land masses. Old icecaps melt and new ones form. Polar regions that were once consumed in an ice age become habitable, while temperate land becomes too cold to support life. It explains why, for example, when the pole was over the Hudson Bay, ice covered most of Canada and North America, while Russia, Europe, Siberia, and Alaska were warmer than they are today. The land bridge that then connected Siberia and Alaska was much wider, making human migration to the Americas a more logical possibility."

"So the pole shifted closer to Antarctica," Daria said.

"Rather, Antarctica, or Atlantis, shifted closer to the pole," Tom replied.

"I've read that Eastern, or Greater Antarctica is covered with ice that's twice the depth of that in Lesser Antarctica, where we are now."

Tom explained, "That's because twelve thousand years ago the eastern half of the continent was already covered with glaciers. It was already near the pole and had a head start for accumulating ice. You've got to remember, Antarctica is huge—it's about the size of the United States and Western Europe combined."

"But where'd all the ice come from? I've read that inland, Antarctica gets as much snowfall as the Sahara—about four inches a year," Daria said.

"Remember the stories of the Atlantean deluge? The shifting crust caused enormous tidal waves. I used to believe the floodwaters that wiped out this city froze, although I can't find any evidence of that near the top of the pyramid. There's only one other way to explain the extraordinary amounts of snowfall that could accumulate thousands of feet deep."

Tom explained, "You probably know that precipitation, whether rain or snow, requires evaporation, and evaporation requires heat. After the shift occurred, a massive amount of warm ocean was displaced into cold latitudes. Until that warm ocean cooled, evaporation must have been intense. It must have snowed like the dickens for years. Each layer of snow compressed previous ones until it compacted into ice. I think that's where most of Antarctica's ice came from. Over time, as the ocean temperature cooled, evaporation waned until we got the scant precipitation we do today."

"Wait," Daria said, as another objection occurred to her. "Archeologists think they've found Atlantis everywhere from the Bahamas to Crete."

Tom agreed with her. "Atlantis itself was located here, but its empire included cities and ports throughout Europe and the Americas."

"So everyone who believes they've found Atlantis in one corner of the world or another is right."

Tom nodded. "Atlantis didn't rule the world, however. In fact Plato mentions a war between Atlantis and the Athenians of Eastern Europe, which was won by the Athenians. But Atlantis was a worldwide maritime civilization that promoted global trade and cultural sharing. There's a huge amount of evidence for this. For example, ancient Japanese pottery that's identical to potshards found in Ecuador. Ancient statues of similar age and design unearthed in both China and Peru. Huge statues of African men found in Mexico. Symbols in stones from the Canary Islands that are nearly identical to those found on the shores of Lake Superior. There are striking similarities between the Aztec calendar and the Hindu lunar zodiac. Mummification of the dead was practiced in Egypt and Mexico and their royalty wore similar headdresses. Serpent gods are found everywhere from India to South and Central America. Not to mention tales of a devastating flood in the folklore of peoples in every culture on the planet."

Daria had never heard of this before.

Tom continued, "Ignatius Donnelly, who wrote *Atlantis: The Antediluvian World* can give you a lot more examples. This one in particular might interest you. He suggested that the Phoenician and Mayan alphabets were derived from an Atlantis alphabet."

"How did he come to that conclusion?" Daria asked.

"The characters of these alphabets each represent a single sound. This was unique among alphabets when these alphabets were in use."

"In other words they were phonetic alphabets?"

"That's what I've read."

"Mayan has only recently been deciphered," Daria said. "It consists of logograms, which represent whole words, syllabograms, which represent syllables, and glyphs representing the names of places and gods. I'm sorry, it wasn't phonetic. But it is pictorial, like Egyptian hieroglyphs, and I wouldn't be surprised if there were links between them."

Tom felt taken aback by evidence that seemed to refute Donnelly's claim.

"It's okay," Daria said, observing his reaction. "Nothing I say contradicts what you say. It just adds to the universal tapestry of knowledge." She omitted telling him it was the way of the Horus brotherhood to share what they knew.

Tom was completely surprised by Daria's response. He wondered what else had changed about her since he'd known her.

Daria added, "Contradiction should open the door to further inquiry. Not close minds or alienate people."

Tom wished his peers thought so. He would love to get beyond the petty bickering, agree to disagree, and then work together and pool resources to find the real truth.

"What about the Phoenician language?" Tom asked.

"Donnelly may have been right about Phoenician," Daria said. "Most scholars will tell you that European alphabets, including Hebrew, Samaritan, Syriac, Arabic, Greek, and Roman were derived from Phoenician, and that Phoenician can be traced to the Egyptians. Most people believe Egyptian hieroglyphics to be pictograms. However, 1822, a Frenchman, Jean-Francois Champollion, discovered that most hieroglyphs were largely phonetic, although they are also pictorial."

"Does anybody know where the hieroglyphs came from?" Tom asked.

"No," Daria said. "The ancient Egyptians called their script *mdju netjer,* or 'words of the gods.' The patron deity of writing and scribes was Thoth, the ibis-headed god, who was one of the original gods of Egypt."

Daria suddenly remembered her conversation with Omar. Thoth was one of the original rulers of Egypt, the Zep Tepi, or the first ones. Each of the Zep Tepi brought something unique to the Egyptian civilization. Thoth brought writing. Had he been one of the lords of Atlantis, marooned in Egypt during the great flood?"

"Perhaps the Atlanteans were the fathers of the hieroglyphs," Tom said.

Daria looked up at him, roused from her thoughts.

Tom added, "Just because Donnelly was wrong about the

Mayan language being phonetic, doesn't make him wrong about his underlying premise — that American and European languages may have roots in the same source."

Daria searched her brain for similarities between Mayan and any European language.

"Guess what?" she said.

"Fascinate me."

"The Greek symbol for the letter 'k' means 'the palm of the hand.' And the Mayan 'keh' is represented by a hand. Come to think of it, the next letter in the Greek alphabet is lambda; the next Mayan symbol is 'lamat' or 'lambat.' The next letter in Greek is 'mu' which means 'water.' In Mayan, the next symbol is 'mulu' which is associated with the shark god and corresponds to the Aztec day of water.

"And get this: 'Atl' means water. It comes from Mayan and Nahuatl languages of Central America. So how did Plato know to call 'Atlantis' by that name?"

They were silent a few moments, digesting what each other had said.

"You need to know something else," Tom said.

64.

As Tom and Daria sat in the pyramid's control room, Tom asked the pyramid's viewscreen to show Daria the anomalous sphere beneath the Atlantic Ocean.

Daria eyed the underwater sphere with the broken submarine. She'd seen this before. Somewhere.

Then it hit her. "I dreamed this," she said quietly.

She wondered if she was dreaming now. Her surroundings seemed surreal, but why would she dream of Tom? Was her relationship with him something else she needed to resolve?

"You what?" Tom exclaimed.

"It was more like a nightmare. I woke up when the submarine exploded."

Tom took her admission in stride. He then told her about the beams the sphere was sending to the pyramid and the return beam that could stop the sphere. As he spoke, the viewscreen provided illustrations.

"Why is the sphere sending the beams?" Daria asked.

"Have you heard any of the myths about Atlantis rising again out of the ocean?" Tom replied.

"The return of Atlantis? I thought that was a metaphor for a spiritual renaissance of sorts."

"Well, it's happening *now*."

"Now?"

"Look at that hurricane," Tom said, nodding toward the viewscreen, which was now showing the weather over the Atlantic.

"What about it?"

"The anomalous sphere is causing it. And look, there's another tropical depression already forming near the Cape Verde Islands, where the anomalous sphere is located." He paused. "Watch this," he said.

At Tom's mental request, the viewscreen's images moved quickly forward through time.

"See how storm follows storm? The sphere will cause increasingly dangerous earthquakes and volcanic eruptions. Soon, the sphere's intensity will get strong enough to displace the earth's crust once more. Again the poles will change their locations. Antarctica will no longer be at the South Pole." The viewscreen showed the pyramid free of ice and the city of Atlantis revealed.

Daria felt a thick silence grow between them. "You're telling me that if we *don't* send back a signal, we face another earth crust displacement?"

Tom nodded.

"What happens if we do send a signal?"

The viewscreen showed the sphere quieting and the storms ending.

Tom turned his seat to face Daria. "We must stop the storms."

As he spoke, Daria saw the viewscreen from the corner of her eye. Even after the sphere was stopped and the storms quieted, the ice around the pyramid melted anyway.

"Look," she said, pointing.

"What?" Tom asked and turned back to the viewscreen.

But it had gone blank.

Daria doubted what she'd seen. "Oh, nothing," she replied, but she thought it curious. "So how do we stop the sphere?" she asked.

"We need the capstone to send the return signal back to the sphere. We are hoping you can help us."

Daria blushed. Had the viewscreen told them about the capstone she'd found?

"How did you know?" she asked quietly.

"The capstone's whereabouts is written on the top of this pyramid. If you can figure it out, then we can …"

"Wait," Daria interrupted. "So you don't yet know where the capstone is?"

"No. That's why we brought you here. To help us read the inscriptions. To help us find it."

Daria sighed with relief. So they didn't know about her capstone. Just as well. She wasn't ready to share it before she learned more about it, like what powers it might have, and what she was meant to do with it.

Suddenly Daria felt a pressure in her head. It reminded her of the headache she'd had in the airplane on her trip back to New York.

The pyramid, acting on programs inputted thousands of years ago, was again trying to communicate with the key-bearer. It wanted to regain the control it once had as the power source for the entire planet. Daria hadn't practiced inner guidance enough to discriminate the difference between her own thoughts and those from outside herself, so the pyramid's thought programs seemed like her own.

"Why do you want to stop the sphere?" Daria blurted.

Tom looked at her.

"Just because you think we can?" she continued. "Maybe it isn't wise to interfere with the earth's natural evolution. Why not let destiny take its course?"

"To prevent worldwide destruction for one," Tom said, not sure what Daria had in mind.

"If Atlantis is revealed," Daria argued, "we'd have access to its wealth and technology. We could have worldwide prosperity and abundance. War, hunger, and disease could be things of the past. Maybe our modern civilization with its atom bombs and air pollution and disregard for rainforests and Mother Nature has proved incompetent. Maybe the sphere is trying to save us from ourselves."

"If this is destiny," Tom replied, "and if we let it take its course, then millions of people will die. Cities will be demolished and coastlines completely rearranged. If Antarctica is no longer at the pole, then another country will be. Meanwhile, populations will be displaced. Modern technology will be wiped out. Humankind will become primitive all over again."

Daria nodded her head, but her thoughts told her to disagree. "What if Atlantean technology came to the rescue? What if this pyramid could help us help people rebuild new and much better lives than ever before?"

Tom argued, "I'd like to believe our destiny is to prevent death and destruction if we can. After all, the pyramid has been calling me for years. Now we've found it. Is the timing coincidence? I think not. I think the pyramid is inherently good and wants good for all. I think it wants to help us stop the sphere. I think that's what we're meant to do."

Daria didn't want to mention her own series of coincidences. Maybe the pyramid had been calling to her too? Daria remembered the image she'd just seen of the ice melting regardless of what they did. What choices did they really have? She'd found a capstone and ended up inside an Atlantean pyramid that happened to need one. What were the odds of that? Would an Egyptian capstone work on an Atlantean pyramid? Was it too small for the job? If not, then why did she leave her capstone behind? If this pyramid were calling her—if it really needed her capstone— she knew her heart would have urged her to take it with her.

Had she made a mistake?

She wished her inner guidance spoke more loudly and precisely. She recalled Mikta's advice about unraveling one's destiny. Identify one step at a time, he had said, and take each one using your best guidance. Daria focused on her heart. The pyramid again lost its clutches upon her mind.

The next step became obvious. She needed to read the pyramid's inscriptions and find the pyramid's original capstone. Maybe she would also find the confirmations of destiny that Mikta had spoken of. Then she would know for sure that her tiny capstone could play a part in solving the trouble caused by the anomalous sphere.

"I have a meeting with Greer at eleven o'clock this morning," she said. "He's either going to bring me down here to decipher the pyramid's top, or he'll show me some photographs that are hopefully more accurate than the ones I've already seen."

"Greer thinks he can use the beams that would stop the sphere to gain military supremacy over the world," Tom said.

Daria sighed. Why was everything always so complicated?

"If the pyramid is inherently good, as you say, then maybe it won't let Greer take control," she said. "So there are pros and cons no matter what we do. But we have to read those inscriptions and find this pyramid's capstone." Then she added, "And we have to believe in destiny. I concede, there may be more than one possible destiny unfolding. If we're meant to stop this thing, then we'll be given the knowledge and insight to do it. If we aren't, then life will provide us with other choices, though we won't know what those choices are until we reach them."

"Daria?"

She nodded. "I know. I've come a long way in the last few years." She meant the last few days, but why tell Tom. Then she added, "Who knows, it all might be bunk anyway."

They laughed.

Daria then wondered if anyone had discovered she was missing. The viewscreen complied and showed a picture of the surface. Nobody was outside looking for her.

"You better get back before Greer finds you're gone," Tom said.

Daria stood up to leave, but lingered in the doorway. It felt comfortable to be with Tom. Their relationship had always been easy and hassle-free—when they were together. When they weren't, it seemed as though Tom forgot about her. 'Out of sight out of mind,' she used to complain. She searched her heart for any feelings she might still have for him and to her surprise, they were there.

She wanted to say something that might spark a conversation about their relationship. "It's hard to believe we're actually here. It feels like something from the past."

"Do you believe in reincarnation?" Tom asked.

She'd meant the past of this lifetime, not previous ones. "I'm not sure what I believe anymore," Daria replied. Obviously, and as usual, Tom was clueless. But her meaning hadn't been exactly clear, either. As usual, she'd said the first thing that came to mind.

"Are you coming up too?" she asked.

"No. Greer expects me to learn as much as I can about the pyramid, but these other controls don't seem to work anymore. I wish I could find out more about the capstone."

"Can the viewscreen do anything else besides respond to your thoughts?" Daria asked.

"What do you mean?"

"Has it initiated any communication?"

Good question, Tom thought. He'd have to pay attention to that. "Learning to decide which thoughts are yours and which are imparted by an outside source isn't something we learn in school."

"I wonder if the Atlantean children were taught such things."

Tom didn't reply. He was too struck by the thought that the pyramid might have been trying to communicate with him telepathically, and that his own stubborn thinking might have been getting in the way. From now on, instead of him doing all the talking and asking, he would listen for a change. Open himself more. Be as perceptive as possible.

"See you later," she whispered. Daria could tell he was deep in thought and wouldn't reply.

As she left the control room she thought about Greer, and a sense of urgency came over her. She hurried out and rode the elevator up. When she reached the top, she sent the elevator back down for Tom to use later.

Daria tip-toed into the Jamesway, hung up her gear, and crept past the two men who were dozing in their chairs by their computers. Then she walked down the hall and slipped into her room.

She was careful to relock the door.

65.

Daria was exhausted and would need every minute of sleep she could get. Yet she wanted to stay awake and think about her foray into the ice shaft. She flopped down on her bed and thought about Tom, the pyramid, the anomalous sphere, her little capstone, and what the pyramid's inscriptions might say.

It was unsettling to have previously dreamt about the anomalous sphere and the hurricane it caused—not to mention the broken submarine and all who must have died inside. It was also unusual for her to be thinking about her dad and remembering his stories. Visiting Egypt had somehow opened a door, rather broken a dam, and now she was flooded with thoughts of her past. Stranger still were the recent events in her life. She'd found a pyramid buried in the sand and removed its capstone. Then she found another pyramid that needed one. It all seemed surreal.

Truth can be stranger than fiction, she reminded herself. She took a deep breath to relax her mind and drifted into the peaceful darkness behind her closed eyes.

"Daria, come here, Honeycakes!" It was her father's voice, and it sounded clear and distinct.

In her mind's eye she saw her house as it looked when she was a young child. Her father's voice was coming from his office. In the dream, Daria hurried to him.

When she saw him sitting in his chair beside the fireplace, she stopped. His hair was gray, his skin wrinkled, and his clothes hung loosely on his thin frame. He had aged, but his smile was as bright as ever. This time, there was no younger Daria in the room. Ian was looking at the dreaming Daria as though she were right there with him.

Ian stood up and stepped toward her with open arms.

"My darling, my Daria," he said. He held her close in a warm embrace.

Daria reveled in the sensation of his hug, which felt real. Interestingly, her father wasn't leaning over to hug her, as he did when she was a child; he stood tall.

He stepped back to admire her while holding her hands in his. "You've grown into a fine, beautiful woman," he said. They smiled at each other.

This dream really was real! If only Daria had a moment's notice, she would have prepared a list of questions to ask her father. Now she could think of not one. Just being with him felt healing and wonderful and fulfilling beyond belief.

"Come here," Ian said. "Sit down."

Daria sat down and scooted the chair next to his. She leaned forward so she could continue holding his hand.

"Mikta tells me you found the little capstone."

"Yes, Dad, I did."

"Do you remember how the pyramidion that once supported it came to fall beneath the waves?"

Daria nodded as the memory of her father's fairy tale came to mind. The empress-elect, Sileen, had moved Atlantis's power source out of the evil ones' reach. She had flown on the pyramid's pyramidion, using its magnetic propulsion system, to Captain Rohn's ship. Then in a powerful storm, a bolt of lightning split the pyramidion apart, the ship sank, and the pieces of pyramid and the sphere inside it drifted to the ocean floor.

But that was just a story!

Ian said, "The magnetic forces that once moved the pyramidion and its sphere to the ship can also reassemble the pieces of the pyramidion. These forces can then move the intact pyramidion, with its sphere inside, back to the pyramid. But the pyramid needs your capstone to do that."

"My capstone?"

"Yes, Honeyca-, uhm, er, Daria."

"That's okay, Dad," she said squeezing his hand. "I'll always be your Honeycakes."

"And I will always love you," he said.

The dream image began to blur, even as Daria struggled to keep it alive.

"Dad!" she called out. "Daddy, I love you too." She hoped he'd heard her. The vision receded, and she fell into a deep sleep.

Part Four –
Power Unleashed

Antarctica, Connecticut, Egypt

September 18th

66.

Thursday, September 18ᵗʰ (New York time).

At precisely 7:00 A.M., a persistent hammering noise began to rouse Daria from sleep. At first, it seemed miles away, then gradually it grew closer until it sounded as though the door would break down, at which point, Daria finally woke up.

"Dr. McHenry, are you okay?" Davison kept repeating.

Daria forced herself up and opened the door, which she found unlocked.

"Good morning, Ma'am," Davison said. "It's Thursday again, Washington time," he added, trying to cheer her up. He felt sorry he'd awakened her. Daria looked bedraggled, and her eyes were puffy.

"I brought you some breakfast."

Daria took the plate of oatmeal, toast, and sausages. She was most interested in the coffee.

"Remember, Greer wants to see you at eight," Davison said.

"Then I'll need a pot of this stuff," Daria said, holding up her cup.

"It will be waiting for you, Ma'am," Davison replied and left.

Daria ate the oatmeal, took a few more sips of coffee, and then took a few steps down the hall to the bathroom, which consisted of a sink and shower. The door didn't have a lock and she felt too cold to shower, so she settled on washing just her face and hands. The ice-water from the faucet worked better than the coffee for waking her up. She looked around for the latrine and remembered she would have to go outside.

She walked back down the hall to the Jamesway anteroom,

exchanged "good mornings" with the two lieutenants on duty, and looked out the window to make sure the red flag on the poop-house was down. It was, so she put on her boots and parka and headed into the unknown. The A-framed tent had a canvas door, which she unzipped and stepped through. Inside, she found a bucket framed with a toilet seat. A second bucket, tightly lidded, stood beside it with a pile of plastic bags and a roll of toilet paper on top. Apparently, when the bag inside the toilet became offensive enough, you would tie it closed, add it to the other filled bags inside the lidded bucket and then put a new bag in its place. Daria decided that that would be a job for someone else.

Daria returned to her room and fished through her duffle bag for clean clothes and changed. Then she ate the cold sausages and finished her cold coffee. At a few minutes before 8:00 A.M., Davison returned. He led her down the hall and into a room on the right.

"This is our mess hall, meeting room, recreation room, and room for whatever-else-we-can-think-of," Davison said. On the table in the middle of the room sat the promised pot of coffee on a portable burner. A tray with napkins and a few packaged pastries lay beside it.

"Thank you," Daria said. She was ready to get to work.

A few seconds later, Greer walked in.

"Good morning," he said flatly.

"Good morning, Sir," Daria replied.

He put some papers on the table. They consisted of a complete set of photographs of the pyramid's flat top, plus the set of rubbings that Tom had done. Daria recognized immediately where they had come from.

"We want you to translate this for us," Greer said. "If you need resources, we can connect you to the Internet for brief periods of time."

Daria looked at him questioningly.

"Security," Greer replied. Internet access required satellite communication links that could reveal their presence.

Daria decided to work with the photos, which seemed more accurate. She'd start by assembling them into a patchwork that resembled as closely as possible, the pyramid's flat top. "I could use some scissors and tape," she said.

"Davison?" Greer said.

"Yes, Sir." Davison left and soon returned with the supplies.

"Excuse me, Sir," Daria asked Greer. "If you don't mind my asking. Why take me to this remote location to translate these? Why couldn't I have worked on them in Washington?" She was curious about how much he would tell her.

"You will be given information as you need to know it. The entire set of inscriptions is here."

"Nothing in these photos is erased or altered?"

"It's all here." He paused as though considering what he wanted to say next. "Dr. McHenry, I had second thoughts about asking you on this assignment," Greer said. "But trusted sources convinced me you're the finest expert in archaic language in America. I hope you will find this assignment interesting to say the least. However, time is of the essence. The security of our country depends upon your ability to translate this, and I expect a preliminary report in an hour."

"You'll have it," Daria replied, as he left the room. His pep talk was unexpected but reassuring and admittedly stimulating. She wasn't sure how much she'd include in her first report. She could just as easily put him on a need-to-know status too, but she wouldn't tell him that. Tough men like Greer needed to believe they were in control.

The notebook and pencils arrived, and Daria got to work. Slowly she turned the photos, viewing them from all angles. She arranged them and taped them together. Eventually a patchwork of photographs that depicted the entire three-foot diameter circle of writing lay on the table. Daria looked down at it, her chin casually resting in her hand, strands of her hair stubbornly falling over her face.

The meaning of several Aymaran symbols was immediately apparent, but she'd have to decipher the rest. She felt herself falling into the familiar trance that allowed her to know the meaning of any written language. Clearly there were references to oceans, voyages, distant lands, foreign peoples, and mystical happenings. There were phrases that alluded to things that happened 'beyond the sky,' and long strings of mathematical calculations.

There also was a description of the pyramid having 'fingers' in every atom of the earth's land, sea, and atmosphere.

So that was how the pyramid's viewscreen could show images of anything happening anywhere on the planet! Daria's realization interrupted her trance, but that was okay, it was part of the process.

Her attention moved to the middle of the photographs. The map there certainly looked like the one on her capstone. A modern map would confirm her theory.

"Davison?" she called, as she opened the meeting room door. Colonel Greer was standing nearby.

"Excuse me, Sir. Do we have any maps here?"

This was exactly the kind of question Greer wanted to hear. If Daria wanted a map, maybe she had a clue to a location.

"What kind of map?" he asked.

"A world map, with Antarctica in the center."

"I'll see that you get one."

"Thank you. I'll also need to know which way is north."

"North?"

"On the engravings. I need to know the orientation of the object that was engraved. I'm assuming it's immovable, otherwise you would've brought it to me."

Greer nodded. "Davison!"

"Yes, Sir?"

"Get Seymour up here."

"Yes, Sir."

"Anything else?" Greer asked Daria before leaving her alone once again.

"No. Thank you." Daria closed the door behind him.

Then she blushed with embarrassment. *Which way is north?* She admonished herself for asking such a stupid question. What moved her to say it? From there, just about every direction was north, though they weren't exactly on the Pole.

Silly as her comment may have been, they were going to bring up Tom. She smiled to herself. It had felt comfortable and natural to be with him, as if she'd known him for years. Well, she had. Yet something was different. Had he changed? Certainly *she* felt different. Her inner turmoil had evaporated. Gone was her grief about losing her father, and gone were her attitudes about dreams and inner guidance, which she now realized had narrowed her viewpoint about life in general. Somewhere between her adventures in Egypt and this moment, she had begun to realize what it meant to think with her heart. It was all about being honest with yourself. The more honest she could be, the clearer her heart would communicate its wisdom and the easier it was to discern true guidance from the voices of the mind. It also was essential to trust that her heart knew what was best and that whatever decision it prompted was for the good of all, including herself.

Daria wanted to give Tom some new information when he got there, so she brought her attention back to her task. As she often did when deciphering text, she imagined herself the scribe and asked herself some questions. To find the answers, she'd let herself fall into a trance-like state and simply knew them.

She asked herself: Were these engravings made when the pyramid was built? If so, the writer would have been excited. His peoples had constructed a monument to be proud of, but Daria didn't pick up those kinds of feelings. She sensed that the writing came long afterward.

In her thoughts she said, "The pyramidion and power center of my civilization has been removed. I am asked to write something in its place. Who am I to have such an honor? Or, if this is graffiti, such guile?"

No, wrong direction, Daria told herself. The writing is too perfect, too purposeful to be graffiti.

Who am I writing this for? My people? No. In the downfall of a civilization, people have little regard for their old monuments. Their primary concern is survival. Besides, writing on a flat surface that faces upward is no billboard. This writing was meant for future viewers. Or air travelers. Daria couldn't overlook that possibility. But that couldn't be true either. The writing was far too small to be read from the air. Unless it was lit? Yet the elevator's floodlights had lit up the pyramid, and she didn't notice the writing until she had gotten close enough to read it.

What would I want to say to someone in the future? Daria mused. Indications of my civilization's power and might? No, the pyramid itself would suggest that. How to avoid a similar catastrophe? In that case, were the inscriptions warnings? Except that Daria didn't detect a fearful writer.

Were these instructions for replacing the pyramidion? Then the writing must have been done after the pyramidion was removed. Otherwise, why put instructions underneath such a heavy, usually immovable object?

The writer must have known his work would one day be read. But by whom? Daria felt herself drifting deeper into her trance. For whom were these symbols written?

For the one who found them and could read them.

She could read them.

Was this writing for me? Daria snapped back to wakefulness. Could these symbols contain the confirmations of destiny that Mikta had spoken of? If this were true, what would an ancient engraver want to say to her?

Suddenly, she knew. She passed her gaze over the symbols, drinking in the story they told.

Then Davison brought in a large rolled up map.

Tom followed him in.

67.

"Dr. McHenry," said Davison. "I'd like you to meet Mr. Tomas Seymour. He's the one who took these photographs."

Tom extended his hand, "Pleased to meet you."

Daria shook his hand, amused by their charade.

"Please, call me Daria."

"Mr. Seymour has been sworn to secrecy," Davison explained. Then added, "So please don't ask him any questions he's not allowed to answer."

"And how will I know which ones those might be?" Daria asked.

Davison laughed.

"Don't worry," Daria added. "I'll behave."

"I'm sure you will," Davison said and winked at her before he left the room. He knew Tom would probably tell her more than Greer would want him to, but Greer hadn't shown her the pyramid. He was withholding vital information. After all, the future of the world depended on her finding the top of the pyramid and putting an end to the anomalous sphere's mischief. Davison wanted it stopped as soon as possible. He missed his wife and son, who lived on the coast of Virginia. His concern for their well-being weighed heavily on him—especially since they were threatened by an oncoming hurricane. Davison used optimism and humor to fend off his worry.

"Tom!" Daria exclaimed as soon as Davison left. "Look at this." She pointed to the symbols surrounding the map. "You won't believe what this says," she said.

"Try me." Tom was eager to hear.

"I'm going to paraphrase," Daria said. "The sentence structure isn't anything like that of English. And remember, this was written over twelve thousand years ago."

"Go on."

"Apparently, before the great deluge, when the earth's climate began to change, hurricanes became more devastating, earthquakes more prevalent, and miles of coastlines were demolished by killer waves. Many of Atlantis's top scientists recognized the planet was simply passing through a cycle. The extreme weather was the earth's effort to try to re-balance its energies to regain stability. Yet millions of lives around the world were at risk. To save them as well as the continent of Atlantis from destruction, scientists of all fields banded together to devise a solution. Archeologists, astronomers, geologists, engineers, even physicians, artists, and musicians were invited to help. No one's input was denied and everyone's research was available to all.

"Their solution was to place giant pyramidal structures, similar to their own great pyramid, at critical locations around the globe. These structures would help the earth modulate its excess or deficient energies and correct its imbalances, and in doing so, supply the local communities with something useful like electricity. So the Atlanteans began to build pyramids from South America to China, Egypt to India, and North America to Japan. Each region personified its pyramid with the artistry of the local culture—as long as certain criteria were met. The Giza pyramid was unique in that it was a replica of the Atlantean pyramid. As its measurements incorporate information about earth, the other two pyramids of Giza incorporate information about earth's sister planets.

"About two hundred years later, the construction was nearly complete. The last and most critical part of the plan was to move the power generator from this pyramid—the one you just unburied—to a certain pyramid of Giza, where the geography was found to be the most stable on the planet. Yet the earth had quieted by then. The storms had abated and the seasons resumed their familiar character. People doubted the pyramids had anything to do with the planet's newfound quiet. The government of

Atlantis now had no reason to move its power generator or its capital city."

Meanwhile, Davison had been eavesdropping in the adjoining room and recording their conversation. He was dumbfounded. It was history he'd never heard before. Moreover, how did McHenry know about their pyramid? Davison was too interested in what she was saying to leave and get Greer. Besides, he wasn't sure he liked what Greer had in mind for the pyramid. And he completely disagreed with Greer's ideas about using it to dominate the world.

Daria continued, "Tom, you'll really like what it says over here." She pointed to another area of inscriptions.

"I'm listening," Tom urged her on.

"The earth is rare among planets, because it produces magnetic energy," Daria continued, "This energy is responsible for life and is a special commodity. Over time, this energy amasses in certain areas, leaving other areas deficient and vulnerable to radiation from the sun and outer space. This energy tends to collect under bodies of water. Its presence, however, makes the planet unstable, and the planet shifts in an effort to release this energy or to redistribute it throughout its crust.

"Some of the shifts are local. Others, which happen in cycles of long time periods, affect the entire planet. These worldwide shifts, though destructive in the short term, release the excess magnetic energy and prevent the greater destruction caused by excess radiation. Ultimately, the shifts give life on our planet a chance to renew. But they don't happen without warning."

Daria paused. "That was an introduction of sorts. A more personal message from the writer comes next."

"Are you sure it says the earth's excess energy is a 'commodity?'" Tom asked excitedly.

Daria studied the symbols again. "Yes, I'd say that word comes closest to the writer's original intent. Why?"

"Some people say UFOs are mining our planet's resources. I've read many accounts of people who've seen UFOs diving beneath bodies of water. Maybe they're collecting our planet's excess magnetic energy?"

"Tom ..."

"After all," Tom continued, animated with his enthusiasm for the topic, "if you compare earth to other planets, look at the life we possess. We have oceans of water and a complete atmosphere. Maybe the aliens are taking our excess magnetic energy not only to provide life energy for their relatively barren homelands but to prevent our planet from shifting too. It's a win-win situation — until we learn to harness this energy, maybe even collect it ourselves, and then trade it to them."

"Tom." Daria said in a louder voice this time. "You've gotta be kidding me."

"Sorry," Tom said. Obviously, although Daria had opened her mind to subjects like dreams and inner guidance — even Atlantis — some topics were still best avoided.

By now, Davison had heard enough. Apparently, the pyramid they'd unearthed had something to do with Atlantis, and now they were suggesting that UFOs might be involved? If this was indeed Atlantis, Greer would want to melt more ice to steal its riches. Davison rewound the tape recorder he'd been using to record Daria and Tom's conversation and erased what he'd recorded so far. He had to act quickly as the colonel was expected to return any minute. Davison opened the recorder and pulled out a wire. He'd tell Greer the recorder was un-operable, due to technical failure.

Daria looked back at the writing and began to decipher more of it aloud. "When our people first learned of the relationship between the magnetic buildup and an inevitable shift, they ignored the data or distorted it to prevent global panic. But enough of us believed in the data and devoted our lives to researching how to stabilize our planet's energies artificially without a planetary catastrophe. We learned that our Pyramid drew upon the earth's excess magnetic energy to serve our society. We realized all we needed to do was to build enough pyramids around the planet at certain key locations. Eventually, when this network of pyramids was finally built, it used the excess energy in positive ways that contributed to the societies that grew up around them."

Daria was amazed by what she was reading. Didn't her father tell her a similar story? No doubt Mikta had told it to him, but where did Mikta hear it? And how did it get here?

Tom thought Daria's silence might mean she was finished. "The key locations you mentioned have been mapped," Tom said. "They're situated either at regular distances from the Giza pyramids or from old pole coordinates."

"So they were geographically significant before the earth's crust shifted," Daria said.

"Yes."

"There's more," Daria continued. "With the pyramids releasing the excess magnetic energy in positive ways, the earth had no need to release it with destructive crustal shifts. Civilizations around the globe were free to thrive and prosper without the threat of being wiped out ever again.

"With the earth again quiet, no one believed the pyramids had helped the planet. The pyramid builders were labeled charlatans.

"It then gives a prediction for the future," Daria said. "Inevitably, the protocols for releasing the planet's excess magnetic energy and using it constructively will end up in the hands of naïve priests, who will convert the protocols into empty pomp and phrase. The essential pyramids and the communities that surround them will decay and eventually be lost to history. Excess earth energy will build up once more. The crust again will shift."

Daria looked over at Tom. "It sounds as though the pyramids were at least temporarily effective."

"If so, that sheds light on a major discrepancy," Tom said.

"About what?"

"Astronomer-archeologists have discovered that the Giza pyramids are in perfect alignment to the stars of Orion's belt only in 10,500 B.C. All other evidence points to the final deluge, or crustal shift, occurring in 9,600 B.C. So some historians believe the pyramids were built at 10,500 B.C. while others believe the date was

9,600 B.C., and the two groups can't come to terms about their differences of opinion. Of course modern Egyptologists believe the pyramids were built in 2,500 B.C., and they think any older date is ludicrous."

Daria chimed in, "So the original pyramid network was built at the earlier date, and it delayed the crustal shift for about nine hundred years." Then she realized a correlation between the date of 9,600 B.C. and another event in history—when the pyramidion's power center was transferred. In her father's stories, Sileen had tried to move the power center from Atlantis to Egypt around 9,600 B.C.

"Help me find Egypt on this map," she said.

"Egypt?"

"I'm wondering if our pyramid has any connection with the pyramids of Egypt. Some legends say that the Egyptian pyramids were built by refugees from Atlantis," she said, again recalling her father's stories.

Tom and Daria opened the world map that showed Antarctica in the center.

"Plato was right," Daria mused. "It does indeed look like there's one worldwide continent that surrounds one ocean that surrounds Antarctica."

She then pulled out the patchwork of photographs she'd made of the pyramid's top. They compared the two maps. The one in the center of the inscriptions was smaller but similar. They decided to put the modern map aside and use the photographs of the ancient one.

Tom put his finger on a location on the northern end of the squished-looking African continent.

"Egypt is about here," he said.

"Now show me our location in Antarctica."

Tom touched a point on the photographs that indicated their approximate position at coordinates 81°52'05" South; 111°18'10" West.

"Do you think the top of this pyramid might be somewhere in Egypt?" Tom asked.

"If this is where the Atlantis power center was located," Daria said, putting her finger on the map where Tom had indicated. "And the top of the pyramid—rather its pyramidion—was taken to Egypt, it likely was brought by ship over the South Atlantic." Her finger traced a possible course. "Then, before it reached the Mediterranean, the ship got caught in a storm about here, which is where the pyramid's viewscreen had illustrated the location of the anomalous sphere. So it fits the picture."

"What picture?" Tom felt completely lost.

Daria blushed. That the anomalous sphere had anything to do with the pyramid was a fact that only she would know. She explained, "Some people believe that just before the flood that destroyed Atlantis, the Atlanteans' power center was taken to Egypt, to start civilization anew. But the generator never made it because it was lost at sea. That's why the Egyptian civilization was never as powerful or widespread as the Atlantean one. Legend also says this generator was a sphere and was kept inside the pyramidion. The anomalous sphere belongs to this pyramid."

"Are you sure?"

"Positive."

"Then we're sunk," Tom said, not intending the pun. He looked down in despair. "If the capstone is under the Atlantic ..." his voice sounded lifeless. "There's nothing we can do. You saw for yourself what the pyramid's viewscreen predicted," he said. "Worldwide chaos if that sphere is not stopped. Half our population might perish. According to the viewscreen, the hurricane will hit New England this afternoon."

"We're not out of options yet," Daria reassured him. She studied the writing. She needed to find the confirmations of destiny that Mikta had spoken of and decided to look for the glyphs of woman and capstone that Mikta had taught her. If she could find references to her presence in Antarctica, then perhaps her little capstone's powers would suffice.

Tom, of course, had no idea what Daria was looking for.

Daria drew a line on the map between their location in Antarctica to the approximate location of the Great Pyramid of Giza.

Then she extended the line outward through rows of surrounding inscriptions. Almost immediately she found the pair of glyphs Mikta had taught her for *woman* and *key*.

"Holy Shepseskaf, son of Menkaure!" Daria exclaimed.

"What'd you find?"

"See these symbols?" she said. "See if you can find them anywhere else."

They carefully combed the writing in the photographs.

"Here's a pair of them," Tom said. "What do they mean?"

Daria drew a line between the glyphs that Tom had found and their Antarctic coordinates. An extension of the line passed through a part of the map that represented the northeast coast of the United States.

A wave of goose bumps passed over Daria's body. Is the woman really me? She still wasn't convinced. She needed to find a third set of symbols to confirm her presence in Antarctica. When it came to inner guidance and numbers, her father had often mentioned the number three as being significant.

"There should be one more set," Daria said.

Tom still hadn't a clue why these particular symbols were important, but he trusted Daria would explain things in time.

They scanned and rescanned the writing in the photographs without luck. On one hand Daria felt deeply discouraged. It meant that her capstone would be unable to stop the storms. On the other, she felt relieved to know that there were no confirmations of her destiny belonging in Antarctica.

Just then, Tom saw them. Inside the map of Antarctica, within a collection of glyphs was a small pair of Daria's symbols.

"I found them," he said.

Daria looked at the symbols depicting woman and key, so obviously placed, right in the center of the map.

Suddenly Daria knew what she had to do. No matter the consequences, it was time to retrieve her capstone.

But her thoughts were not confined to her own mind. The pyramid was capable of reading thought waves, and when it picked up ones about the capstone, its programming immediately awoke. The pyramid wanted its top back and needed Daria to make it happen—and now she was willing. It was her destiny to rule and the pyramid would do all in its power to ensure her success. It began to send her waves of energy, making her feel strong physically as well as emotionally and mentally. The pyramid also telepathically sent her details of just how to accomplish her mission. Daria began to feel unusually brave and self-confident. She would need these feelings to succeed.

"I know where the capstone is," she said. "We have to get back to the pyramid at once."

Daria quickly rolled up the patchwork of photographs, tucked them under her arm and opened the door.

Greer, who had overheard her last comment, stood in their way.

68.

"Excuse me," Daria said as she tried to walk past Greer and the four soldiers with him. "I have work to do." She liked the feeling of heightened self-confidence, artificial though it was. It made her feel much larger and taller, and in a way, invincible.

Greer stood his ground.

"Sit down," he commanded. "Both of you." Then he motioned for his men to make sure they complied. The soldiers seated Tom behind Daria so he could see her but she couldn't see him.

Daria resisted sitting down. A soldier grabbed her shoulders and forced her onto the chair.

Greer loomed over Daria and looked down at her. "Where is it?" he growled.

"Where is what?" she replied. Daria still felt strong and was undaunted.

He grabbed her chin. "Don't toy with me, bitch," he said in her face.

"Leave her alone!" Tom said.

Greer ignored him. "Dr. McHenry, I know you can tell me where the capstone is. You can either give me the information … or I can get it from you." He unsheathed his knife and placed the edge beneath her breast.

Daria winced.

Greer laughed evilly.

Tom tried to stand up to protect her, but the guards pushed him down.

"Tie him up," Greer ordered.

"No!" Daria commanded, but her will couldn't match Greer's. A wave of fear began to erode her false, pyramid-fed self-confidence.

"Tie them both up."

Following orders, the guards secured both Tom's and Daria's hands and legs to their chairs.

"I will ask you one more time," Greer said. "Where is the capstone?"

Daria kept silent. Anger now mixed with her fear. She could feel her face getting hot. She wanted to tell Greer what a stupid fool he was. Didn't he see how blind his lust for power had made him? Maybe that was why her heart had told her to leave her capstone behind. Greer might have already gotten hold of it.

Greer slapped her face.

"Leave her alone!" Tom shouted.

Greer's face twisted as he nodded to his men. "Bloody him up."

"No!" Daria yelled.

The guards took turns punching Tom's face and body.

"Stop it!" Daria screamed.

Tom had never suffered such pain. It felt like bombs going off inside him, one explosion after another, each more painful than the last. The anticipation of each forthcoming punch was almost as bad as the blow itself. He never knew where the pain would come next, though he couldn't protect himself if he tried. Never before had he felt so helpless and at the mercy of forces he couldn't control. He endured only by putting all his attention on one thing: controlling his emotions. He didn't want Daria to hear him cry.

"Stop hurting him! Stop it," Daria pleaded.

Greer turned again to Daria. "They won't stop until you tell me where the capstone is," he said. Greer stood with his arms folded, wearing a twisted grin while he watched the beating.

"Don't tell them!" Tom blurted between blows. Despite the pain, he'd rather die. Better to let the earth changes continue. Natural disaster could never be as bad as the havoc Greer could inflict with the pyramid's capstone intact.

Tom's body was starting to get numb. He was going into shock and felt like he would pass out, but the next blow would always wake him up again. He began to groan.

Daria's heart ached with compassion for Tom, yet her mind kept feeding her reasons to keep her mouth shut. She also understood why Tom was willing to die then and there. Greer would be a ruthless ruler, and with the pyramid at his control, he would bring the world to its knees.

Finally, she decided she wouldn't let a friend be tortured when there was something she could do to end it.

"Okay!" she yelled. "Make them stop. I'll tell you."

By now Tom was unable to object.

Greer glared at her and gave the order. The beating ceased.

"We have to go to the pyramid," Daria said. "That's where we were headed when you stopped us."

Greer slapped her again. "Where's the capstone?"

Daria was dazed by Greer's heavy hand and needed a few moments to recover. The right side of her face, where he had slapped her twice now, was red and blood oozed from her skin. It would be a nasty bruise. Her words came out slurred.

"The anomalous sphere was once inside the top of the pyramid," she said, resisting tears that flowed anyway. "It's now at the bottom of the Atlantic."

Greer began fuming. This wasn't the news he wanted to hear. He felt like taking out his anger on Daria and raised his fist.

"We can retrieve it," Daria added quickly. She had suddenly remembered her dream from the night before and hoped it was true. It had to be. Certainly her other dreams had been. At least her statement would buy them some time. "The same way it got there," she said, "we can get it back — or the pyramid can."

Greer's expression now looked hopeful.

"We have to get down to the pyramid. And I need Tom's help — he knows more about the control room than anyone." It was the only thing she could think of that would assure Tom's company down the hole. Otherwise they would surely leave him there.

"Untie them," Greer ordered.

Daria stood up quickly and ran toward Tom. She gasped when she saw him. His face was smeared with blood that dripped from cuts on his cheeks and temples, and his entire face was swollen and discolored. She draped his arm around her shoulder, helped him stand up, and supported him at his waist as they proceeded to the station's foyer. There, Greer allowed them to put on their parkas, hats, and gloves. As Daria helped Tom put on his parka, she positioned him so he stood between herself and Greer.

As quickly as she could, she took the sphere from her pouch and put it in Tom's hand. She wrapped his fingers around it and inserted his fist into a large mitten.

"Don't lose it," she whispered, imploring him to keep hold of the sphere.

"What did you say?" Greer wanted to know.

"I told him not to lose it," Daria said aloud. She'd carefully chosen a phrase with two meanings, now implying that she wanted him awake and focused. "He's feeling faint. We need him down there." She put a mitten on his other hand and secured the parka's hood to his head. Then they went outside.

For Tom, it was a long walk to the elevator. Thankfully, the cold was numbing. He hadn't seen what Daria had given him, but it felt round and made his hand feel hot. It wasn't until they were descending into the hole that he began to appreciate the sphere's rejuvenating effects. First, its warmth spread throughout his body. Then energy poured through him, into him and out of him, coming and going as if his body was a sponge held up to hoses of running water spouting in all directions. Soon, Tom began to feel healed and renewed. When the elevator stopped, he was able to walk out on his own.

Greer noticed. "See. The beating wasn't so bad, you damn wimp." Then he kicked him.

The soldiers who accompanied them on the elevator sensed something strange about Tom and exchanged glances. The men knew the extent of their damage, but could see a difference in Tom.

Tom could have sprinted down the pyramid, but to keep the soldiers' curiosity at bay he instead limped, hunched over, and groaned to fake pain. Daria knew what he was doing and continued to give him the support he should have needed.

Meanwhile, Daria pondered what had happened: at a critical moment, she had remembered her dream from the night before. In that dream, her father had come to her. He had given her information she would need that very day—information to save Tom's life and maybe her own.

For Daria, this dream was proof enough of life after death. Somewhere her father still existed and was able to communicate with her in her dreams. Not only did he still remember her, but he also told her that he loved her. Could someone still love you after they died?

How refreshing it was to feel her father's love again! All these years, Daria believed his love had died with him. The belief had made her heart ache with a vacancy that defied description; now that emptiness was filled. Her father still existed and he still loved her. The thought made her feel strong, but it was a sincere, genuine, inner strength.

Furthermore, he was again protecting her. Had he always been watching over her? How many dream experiences with him had she deprived herself of because she refused to believe in dreams or remember them?

How interesting that she had remembered the dream at the perfect time. Did her heart help her recall it? Had it prompted her to tell Greer about it just like it had urged her body to leap into the bushes back in Hawaii?

Daria wondered if her father had asked for guidance before his death. Since then, she had renounced inner guidance because she believed it had betrayed her father by not saving him. Maybe inner guidance had been with him all along. Maybe it had been with her too.

Daria concluded that inner guidance couldn't be calculated or anticipated. Nor could you always identify how it would make itself known. Listening didn't guarantee you would evade an unpleasant future, but it could soften and ease the inevitable. Inner guidance was like air, everywhere and always there. One could not live happily without such inner wisdom working in your life. It emerged from the heart. Yet its true source lay beyond the heart and surpassed comprehension.

When the group reached the pyramid door, Tom pressed the rectangular block that had opened it before. This time, nothing happened. He pressed it several times.

Still, nothing.

That was strange, Tom thought. Then he wondered if the pyramid could read his thoughts even though he wasn't inside the control room. After spending the past few days there, certainly the pyramid had learned his mental patterns. And weren't such patterns unlimited by distance? If so, it also knew what Greer had done to Tom and how Greer was planning to use the pyramid. Was locking its door its way of defending itself?

No wonder the door stayed shut.

"Thank you pyramid," Tom said mentally, hoping the pyramid could hear.

Once again, Tom pressed upon the block. He even gave a loud dramatic command, "Pyramid Open!" Nothing happened, just as he expected.

"Let me try," Daria offered, not realizing why the door was locked. Still nothing. She tried to quell the fear growing in her. Why wasn't the pyramid responding? Was it broken?

Now what were they going to do!

"What's going on?" Greer bellowed. His voice echoed against the walls of the ice shaft.

"It isn't opening, Sir," said Tom in a forced whisper, faking pain again. The cuts on his face had already healed, but the blood had caked upon his skin, so he still looked dreadful.

Greer's face twisted again and he erupted with profanity.

Suddenly an earthquake began to rumble. Chunks of ice and snow broke free from the ice shaft's walls and crashed upon them. Two of the guards lost their grip and slid halfway down the pyramid before their bare feet regained their hold on the pyramid's sides. Tom held tightly to Daria with one arm wrapped around her waist. He gripped the pyramid with his other hand. Bare skin was the best magnet against its smooth, shiny surface.

While Tom held her, Daria pressed her unhurt cheek against the pyramid. It was like pressing your ear against someone's chest to hear their heartbeat. Daria heard a humming sound, which relaxed her despite the terrorizing quake. She felt secure against the pyramid's side, not only because of Tom's arm. It seemed as though the pyramid was also embracing her in a hammock of magnetic support. She was grateful and let her body relax. Already she, like Tom, had begun to develop a kinship with the artificial intelligence that ran the pyramid's viewscreen. It felt like an old friend.

The quake lasted a few seconds, though it seemed like an hour. Greer was obviously disturbed. Being buried alive with an ancient pyramid wasn't on his agenda. He ordered his men out of the hole. Davison was to stay behind with Tom and Daria and alert him when the door opened.

"But, Sir!" Davison called out, feeling betrayed. He'd

worked — or rather slaved — for Greer for four long years. Why couldn't the colonel have ordered someone else to stay?

"Kill them, if necessary," Greer added.

Davison couldn't believe his ears. Something strange had happened to his boss. Greer was known for his rough edges, but Davison had never seen him act so cruelly.

The colonel's last order was to Tom and Daria. They were to find another way into the pyramid and retrieve the capstone or die there trying.

Davison wondered if he'd have to die with them.

69.

As soon as Greer and his men left, Tom tried to open the pyramid's door once again. It still didn't work.

"Maybe you're pushing the wrong block," Davison suggested and began wandering down the pyramid's side looking for another similar one.

"Could he be right?" Daria asked.

"No. This is it, I'm sure," Tom replied. When Davison was out of earshot he whispered, "Don't worry, I think the pyramid has purposefully locked the door."

Daria hoped so.

Tom looked up at the receding elevator lights. "We'll try again in another minute." Then he removed his mitten and opened his palm, "What's this?"

Daria took the sphere from him and pressed it against the bruised side of her face. But she was more concerned for her friend. "How are you feeling?" she asked Tom.

"Fine. In fact, perfectly fine."

Even the swelling around Tom's eyes had gone. There wasn't an ounce of pain in his body. "What is that?" he asked again.

"I'll tell you later," she whispered. "First, we need to get inside the pyramid."

Daria's face felt better, so she returned the sphere to its pouch around her neck. She then tried the door again. This time it opened.

"Hey, you got it to work!" Davison called. He made his way back to them and noticed that Tom was standing straight. "Are you okay?" he asked.

"Yes."

"But you got beat up bad. I saw it."

"This pyramid is healing," Tom replied.

Davison pushed up his sleeves to inspect the rashes on his forearms. "Gee, maybe this will clear up too," he said hopefully.

Tom and Daria entered the pyramid. As Davison pulled down his sleeves, he overheard Tom say something that turned on the lights. Davison followed Tom and Daria to the control room. Daria stood before the control panel and looked squarely into the viewscreen.

"Hello, pyramid," she said aloud for Davison's sake. Then she thought about the capstone she'd found in Egypt. Would it be able to stop the anomalous sphere?

The viewscreen responded with a picture of a fully formed pyramid, capstone and all, standing before a golden sunrise. The pyramid's shadow was enormous. Then the viewscreen panned out far and fast until it showed the Atlantic Ocean quiet once again. An image then appeared of the control room and the console. Daria and Tom looked down and saw a one-inch square depression in the console light up. Daria knew her capstone would fit there perfectly.

"It'll work," Daria said aloud.

"What will?" Tom asked as he picked off the caked blood from his face and neck.

The idea that then came to Daria's mind seemed far-fetched and downright impossible and she yearned to doubt it. But her heart urged her to trust it.

The viewscreen displayed her grandmother's house. Waves had engulfed the home and the front porch was under six inches of water.

"Whose house is that?" Davison asked.

"It's her grandparents' house," Tom said. "In Connecticut."

"I'm sorry," Davison said, regretting the destruction.

Then the view of Sarah's house began to flash repeatedly.

"Tom, put your boots back on. Hurry!" Daria exclaimed. They were both still barefoot from climbing down the pyramid's side. "Come on!" She hurried past Davison and raced down the stairs. Tom followed her into the empty room. Its lights were also flashing.

"I don't believe this," Tom said, sensing what would happen next.

"What's going on?" Davison called out, following them downstairs.

"We've got to get the capstone," Daria replied and positioned herself inside one of the circles on the floor. "Stand inside a circle," she said to Tom.

The lights flashed faster and faster.

Suddenly Tom's and Daria's bodies disappeared.

Davison stood there, stunned.

70.

Tom and Daria watched the walls of the room inside the pyramid transform into the scene of her grandmother's house. Their bodies tingled momentarily as their physical atoms repositioned themselves in time and space.

Suddenly Tom and Daria were hit with pouring rain.

Davison, who had returned to the control room, saw them on the viewscreen. What would he tell Greer? Tom and Daria had used the pyramid's powers to transport themselves to Daria's grandparents' house — in Connecticut!

"We made it!" Daria screamed and began to run through the now knee-deep water for the shelter of Sarah's front porch.

"Yeah, but how do we get back!" Tom called out.

Daria punched a few numbers on the keypad of the security system, which, thankfully, was still working. She opened the front door and sloshed through the water-filled entry way. Tom followed her upstairs and into her bedroom.

Daria moved the nightstand, lifted the floorboard, and opened the secret compartment.

It was empty!

Shocked, Daria sat down heavily on the floor and leaned against her bed. A dazed and defeated look spread across her face.

"It's gone."

"What's gone?" Tom sat down beside her.

"You won't believe me."

"I unburied a pyramid in Antarctica," Tom replied. "We just transported ourselves across the planet in two seconds flat. Try me."

"The capstone that I found in Egypt is missing. I put it here before I left for Antarctica."

"You found a capstone in Egypt?"

"I assure you, it's no ordinary capstone. I even presented the idea to Pharaoh, and he seemed to confirm that it would work."

"Pharaoh?"

"It's the name my dad gave the Atlantean pyramid in his stories."

"Your father knew about the pyramid?"

"Not really. I mean, well, maybe. When I was little, he told me fairy tales about the Great Pyramid of Atlantis and its power generators."

"This is no fairy tale, Daria."

"Tom, the sphere I found inside the capstone healed you. That should be proof enough that I'm telling the truth."

"You found that sphere inside the capstone?" Tom asked.

She nodded.

"And the pyramidion also had a sphere," Tom said. "It's on the ocean floor. Do you think you have its apex?"

"Maybe," Daria replied, her eyes staring into the distance. "Somehow it survived." The memories of her father's stories about the capstone's journey from Atlantis to Egypt ran through her mind. Sileen and Rohn, the ship's captain, and the Egyptian princess and her beloved captain of the guard—they were just story characters, weren't they?

"I'm sorry I doubted you," Tom said.

"That's okay," Daria said. The line between fairy tales, dreams, and reality had blurred. She'd either have to doubt it all—in which case she'd be paralyzed—or trust everything without judgment until something proved untrustworthy. To do that, she'd have to listen to her heart, look for coincidences, and pay attention to her instinctive gut feelings. She'd also keep an eye out for inconsistencies.

One inconsistency was that the all-knowing pyramid didn't know—or didn't tell her—that the capstone was missing from Sarah's home. Moreover, it had repeatedly showed itself free of ice, with both its pyramidion and capstone intact. Obviously, the pyramid wanted their help to get its top back. Would the storms then continue no matter what they did? Were the earth-changes inevitable?

Daria rested her forehead in her hands and fought the strands of wet hair that kept falling in her face. "I can't believe it isn't here," she said, wondering who else might have known about the hiding place. Didn't her grandfather say it was their little secret?

"Who could have taken it?" Tom asked.

Grandma Sarah was the only person who might have known. She was probably riding out the storm at a friend's house.

Then they heard a roaring sound, as a large wave rolled in. It almost reached the second floor before receding. The house began to creak and moan.

"We've got to get out of here," Tom said.

Tom and Daria ran down the stairs and through the water that was up to their hips. Holding hands to help each other stay balanced in the waves, they waded across the street, beyond the reach of the flood waters. Their parkas were soaked with rain. They removed them, wrung them out as best they could, and slung them over their arms.

"We need a car," Daria said, looking around the neighborhood. They walked around the corner and headed uphill.

Moments later, a red BMW 745i sped up the street behind them and screeched to a stop. It was Sarah. She lowered the passenger side window.

"What are you doing here?" Sarah called out. "The neighborhood is under mandatory evacuation."

Daria climbed into the front seat, and Tom sat in the back.

"What are *you* doing here?" Daria replied.

Sarah was reluctant to tell her. "I was just going to check the house," she said. She had done a hero's job of getting past the guards who were keeping people out of her neighborhood. After leaving with a carload of valuables to store inland, Sarah had intended to return for another load—and to retrieve Daria's pouch with the pieces of the little pyramid inside. But the water had risen faster and sooner than everyone expected. Sarah had found her street road-blocked.

"I'm sorry, Grandma, but the house will need a lot of repair after this," Daria said.

"You were there?"

"Yes."

"Inside? Upstairs?"

"Yes, what's the matter, Grandma?"

"Your grandfather told me about your hiding place."

"Did you take my pouch?" Daria said hopefully.

"It wasn't there?"

"No," Daria replied.

"Damn," Sarah said and hit the steering wheel. "I knew I shouldn't have let him upstairs."

"Who?"

Sarah looked in the rear view mirror and saw her backseat passenger.

"Tomas?" She glanced back again. "¿Cómo estás?"

"Muy bien gracias. It's nice to see you again, Mrs. McHenry."

"What have you two been up to?" Sarah asked, eying their wet red parkas and snow boots.

"It's a long story," Daria said. "Do you know where my pouch is?"

Sarah looked again in her rearview mirror, and this time she saw a car behind them. It wasn't Fayed's limo. Maybe it was just another evacuee. Feeling suspicious, Sarah drove as fast as she could through the back streets of Stony Creek and up the hill toward Branford.

"A man named Faoud Fayed came to visit me," Sarah replied. "He said some terrorists gave you something to bring home from Egypt that was very valuable, and until you handed it over to the proper authorities you were in great danger."

It was so untrue Daria didn't know what to say.

Sarah continued, "On a long shot, we looked in your hiding

place."

"We?" Daria exclaimed.

"He was a very determined fellow. Followed me right up the stairs. We found the pouch with the puzzle pieces."

"Did you put them together?"

"Took me three tries," Sarah said. "We could tell something was once hidden inside the tiny pyramid, and Fayed thinks you have it. He thinks it's precious and important, and I'll wager it was he who stole your pouch." She added, "I'm sorry I looked in your hiding place, but I was worried about you. You acted so strangely before you left for Washington, I knew something wasn't right."

They traveled inland to higher ground, and reached Francis Walsh Intermediate School. The Red Cross had converted the school into a shelter for hurricane victims. A few National Guardsmen stood at a makeshift gate. One of them waved to Sarah and let them inside. Sarah parked the car.

"It's okay, Grandma," Daria said, hugging her. "I'm not involved with any terrorists."

"I know that," Sarah said. She was having her own lessons in discerning truth.

Then Daria, Tom, and Sarah got out of the car and rushed through the pouring rain into the building. They stepped over the outstretched legs and sleeping bodies of storm victims who lined the hallways. Left homeless by the rising waters, they'd found refuge at the school and had been given food and blankets. Some slept, others talked in whispers. Even the children were quiet. In the classrooms, large groups of people huddled before television sets, their eyes glued to the Weather Channel, hoping good news would come soon.

Daria, Tom, and Sarah found the school cafeteria and sat down with some hot soup.

Then Daria looked up and gasped.

71.

It was Omar!

Tom watched Daria get up and jog across the cafeteria to a man who was smiling at her. Their embrace was brief but eager.

Tom sighed. What a fool he'd been to think Daria's friendliness and openness might mean she could be interested in him again. After all, he noticed she was still wearing the wooden leaf pendant he'd given her, and that gave him hope. He lamented the fact he never phoned her after she'd left him years ago. He needed to take a walk.

"I thought I'd lost you," Omar said.

"I got rescued and then flew home." Daria made light of her escape. "What about you?"

"We found our camels and headed back to Cairo. It took us several days. If it wasn't for the camels, we would've died."

"Then we were both lucky," Daria said. "How'd you get here?"

"I was following my father. I was worried about you. I wanted to make sure you were safe."

Daria searched his eyes, and her heart, to discern his true intention and also her feelings.

"You mean you wanted to make sure my key is okay."

"Not only that." Omar stroked a loose strand of hair away from her face.

Daria's heart did not respond to his touch. It confirmed for her that they were, and only would be, just friends. Although he might want a relationship, her heart told her that his greatest interest was in her key and the capstone.

"Let's find some privacy. I need to talk to you," Omar said.

Daria scanned the room looking for Tom but didn't see him. She followed Omar to the nearest exit, which led to a paved area with basketball nets. Several teenagers were taking advantage of a lull in the rain to shoot hoops, despite the puddles.

They found a spot off to the side where they could talk without being overheard.

"My father is looking for you," Omar said.

"Why?"

"He's a Renegade leader and thinks you've found the capstone. He wouldn't hesitate to kill you for it."

Daria reflected for a moment. "Was your father a Renegade leader twenty-five years ago?"

Omar knew what she was asking. "I'm sorry."

So Faoud Fayed had been responsible for her father's death. Another missing piece from Daria's past was now found. She took a moment to absorb it.

"Omar," Daria said. "I did find the capstone."

"Where?" Omar gasped with surprise. "Will you show it to me, please?"

Daria shook her head.

"Why?"

"I don't have it anymore."

"My father thinks you have it."

"Omar, your father stole it."

"Impossible. I've followed his men here. They're looking for you."

"That's because there was something inside the capstone they want."

"And you have it?"

"Yes."

"I knew it!" Omar exclaimed. "It's the power source isn't it?"

Daria nodded. Fayed would still need the key too — if he ever reassembled the capstone and sphere — but she didn't mention that.

"Daria, give me the power source, please. Then nobody will

bother you anymore, and you can get back to life as usual. You'll be safe. No one will hurt you."

"No," she said, with a certainty that surprised her. "I may not know much about the capstone, but I'm sure my destiny with it is not over yet."

Daria's last dream of her father came to mind. Maybe with the little sphere alone they could still retrieve the big sphere from beneath the waves. That would stop the storms. Maybe they already had all they needed. She wished she'd asked the pyramid about her little sphere's capabilities before they'd left. No matter. Take one step at a time, she reminded herself, and make the best choice in each moment.

"If you want to protect me," she told Omar, "and help me fulfill my destiny, then I need a plane. Something that can fly me a long, long way."

Daria's conviction inspired Omar. Apparently, if she was willing to leave without the capstone, then it was worthless without its contents.

"I can help you," he said. "The plane I flew in on. It's a Shemsu Hor plane. As we speak it's preparing to leave for Washington, D.C. — to find you actually. Since I found you here, I can have them reroute it. It can take us anywhere you'd like." He explained where the plane was located.

The boys on the playground saw them talking and began to whistle. In fun, one boy threw Omar the basketball. He caught it, dribbled, and tried to make a basket. He missed, then looked back at Daria and shrugged. The boys tossed him the ball for another try.

Meanwhile, Tom was walking on the other side of the school. In the parking lot he saw a crowded minivan, driven by one of the men they'd seen at Sarah's porch on the viewscreen. Daria had seemed very concerned about them. The minivan stopped and everyone got out. The men proceeded to walk in various directions, as though they were looking for someone. Tom noticed they were carrying automatic rifles under long, dark raincoats. He ran back through the school to try to warn Daria.

A few minutes later, Omar saw Hakim peer around the corner of the building with a rifle raised. Quickly, Omar threw the basketball in the gunman's direction, hoping to buy a few seconds by distracting him. Then Omar ran in front of Daria to protect her.

Hakim fired anyway.

Omar caught a bullet in his chest.

Daria screamed.

Hakim retreated.

Omar fell to the ground and Daria leapt to his side. "Omar!" she cried as she knelt beside him. Then she shouted, "Someone! Call an ambulance!" She turned back to her friend and stroked his forehead.

Omar looked up at her and whispered a question about the capstone's contents.

"It's the Eye of Horus," Daria said in his ear.

Omar smiled. Then his body relaxed a final time.

Daria reached for her pouch to retrieve the sphere, but it was too late. Omar was dead.

"Hurry! We need an ambulance!" Daria shouted once again. She looked up in the direction from which the bullet had come but was unable to see past the growing crowd of onlookers.

Then someone broke through the crowd and fell to his knees beside Omar. He was wearing a white linen suit but didn't seem to mind getting his pants wet and muddy.

"My son!" he cried, and cradled Omar's head in his arms.

"He took a bullet for me," Daria told him, her throat was so tight she could barely speak. "He saved my life." She and Omar had spent so little time together, yet all he wanted to do was protect her. His death shook her, and opened a wound of loneliness she didn't realize was within her.

Then she realized the man who knelt opposite her must be Omar's father, Faoud Fayed—the cold-hearted man who had killed her father. Fayed had also stolen her capstone pieces and would kill her for its contents. These thoughts sobered her. She watched him. This dangerous man was now crying like a baby over the son whose death he ultimately was responsible for. Had the capstone pieces softened his heart?

Suddenly Daria had an idea.

"If only I had the capstone!" she said just loud enough for Fayed to hear. She covered her face with her hands and pretended to cry. "Then we could bring him back," she sobbed loudly and tried to sound convincing. "When used together, the capstone and its key have healing properties. We could use them to bring Omar back!"

So the capstone needed the key, Fayed thought. That must be why he felt nothing when he had held it. Though grieving, he was mindful enough to realize that this was his chance to learn how Daria used the key to activate the capstone. Then, at his next opportunity, he would acquire both key and capstone for his own. He reached inside his jacket pocket for the pouch. Without a word, he handed it to Daria.

"Bring him back," he pleaded.

Daria took the pouch with the capstone pieces inside. Her ploy worked.

Tom had seen the shooting and ran to Daria. He had stood behind her and watched her interaction with Fayed. When he saw her receive her old pouch, he grabbed her arm and pulled her away from the crowd.

Tom knew his reaction was born of jealousy and he began to feel guilty. Could Daria really bring the man back to life? If so, was disallowing her to do that a crime? Yet Daria hurried ahead to the school and didn't look back. She seemed unconcerned. In the cafeteria, Tom had watched her embrace this man who had just taken a bullet intended for her. Tom felt confused.

"Tom, have you seen Grandma Sarah?" Daria asked.

"No."

"I'd rather not leave without telling her. But we may have to." Daria put the pouch that contained the capstone pieces back around her neck, and began jogging down the hall.

"Where're we going?" Tom asked.

"The airport," Daria replied. "Omar has a plane there waiting for us. It can take us back to Antarctica."

"Omar? You mean the guy who was shot?"

"Yes."

Tom's thoughts were racing. Who was Omar? Daria had treated him as though he was a lot more than just a friend. He had saved her life too, no less. Was Daria in love with him?

Tom and Daria reached the school doors and hesitated. These were not the doors that they had originally entered.

Where was Grandma's car parked? Daria wondered.

Tom had other concerns, too: where were the armed men and what was Fayed going to do to get the capstone back?

72.

"What the hell!" Greer said when Davison told him how Daria and Tom had disappeared from the pyramid and reappeared in Connecticut on the viewscreen.

"Sir, a transport room is no less science fiction than finding a pyramid underneath 4,950 feet of ice in the middle of Antarctica," Davison argued.

Greer grumbled a string of profanities while he thought about what to do. Daria McHenry had tricked him. She'd told him the pyramid's top could be found on the floor of the Atlantic Ocean and that she needed the pyramid to retrieve it. Yet she had told Davison she was going to get the capstone—and went to Connecticut. McHenry lived in Connecticut. Maybe she had found something there, or else she was hiding something. Either way, *he* needed that capstone. Finally, Greer gave his orders, "I want every man down the hole right now, fully armed! Now! Leave no one behind!"

"Yes Sir!" Davison said, quickly saluting. He left Greer's office to assemble the men. As many soldiers as could fit into the elevator crammed inside and a few sat on top. When they reached the bottom of the hole, they sent the elevator back up for Greer, Davison, and the rest of the soldiers. None of the men had any idea why they would need to be fully armed, but they were excited to find out.

When everyone was assembled at the bottom of the hole, Greer ordered the men to follow him to the pyramid door. Davison had left it open on his way out. They stepped inside. It was pitch black.

"Turn on the damn lights, Davison," Greer ordered.

Now what had Tom said? Davison tried to remember. Something like, "Whoooo?" He said it aloud but with a tight throat. He couldn't ignore the gut sense that he was doing something wrong, taking part in something he couldn't stop, flung into a play that wouldn't end until it was over. Against his conscience he was a key player with no way out even if he wanted one. It might mean his death. How he missed his family!

Apparently, the pyramid was satisfied with Davison's rendition of the sacred word, HU, and the lights went on.

They reached the control room and Davison addressed the pyramid's viewscreen. "We need to find Dr. McHenry and Mr. Seymour," he said aloud.

The viewscreen showed the Frances Walsh School. The image began to flash.

Thank you, pyramid, Davison thought, relieved that the viewscreen was cooperating.

"Sir!" called one of the men, who was standing downstairs. "The floor of this here room just lit up."

"Is it flashing?" asked Davison.

"Yes, Sir."

"Colonel," Davison said. "I think that means it's ready to transport, Sir."

Greer ordered two men to stand inside circles.

"Now what?" one of them asked, but time would answer his question, for in the next instant, they both vanished.

"Look at the viewscreen, Sir," Davison said. Sure enough, the two men were suddenly on the screen, standing in front of the school, wearing bewildered expressions on their faces.

"I'm going next," Greer said to Davison. "Keep beaming the men over in groups of three and four. You go with the final group."

"Yes, Sir."

Greer went downstairs and stood inside circles with two others. In the next moment, they too were visible on the viewscreen. Greer briefly looked around for a return doorway. It was a detail they'd have to save for later. Their first business was to find McHenry and Seymour.

Davison ordered the rest of the men into the transport room, and then he himself was ready to go. He paused. Should he ask the pyramid to beam him home instead, to his wife and kids? He had such a bad feeling about following Greer, and he felt, in this one moment, he could make a different choice.

Davison hesitated and his window of opportunity closed. Unbidden, the viewscreen gave him a bird's-eye view of the school. Davison could see Daria and Tom standing in a doorway. Around the corner to the left was a man with an AK-47 talking with someone sitting in an old minivan. Six armed men were waiting nearby. Davison watched Daria and Tom head straight toward them.

"Daria! Turn around!" Davison warned.

On the viewscreen he saw Daria look over her shoulder, trying to find the source of his voice.

"It's me, Davison!" he yelled at her. "Run the other way!"

Daria and Tom made an about-face and started to run. Davison could see they were now headed toward even greater danger—Greer himself.

Davison had to do something. He tried calling to Greer to lure his attention the other way. The men had heard, but Greer had not. Davison would have to deliver the call in person.

73.

Davison arrived in the schoolyard just in time to turn Greer's attention away from Tom and Daria, who reached Sarah's BMW unseen.

"You drive," Daria said. "I want to check the capstone."

They got in the car. "Grandma hides an extra key in the ashtray," she told Tom. He found it, started the car, and drove out of the parking lot.

"Over here!" Davison called to Colonel Greer from the opposite end of the parking lot. Greer and his men ran toward him.

Just then, Hakim and the other Renegades rounded the corner behind Davison. They saw the oncoming soldiers and began shooting at them. Davison was caught in the middle and caught a fatal shot.

The colonel's men returned a rain of fire that struck down two Renegades. Greer ran to them. One was dead. The other could barely speak. Greer grabbed him by the collar.

"Where is it?" Greer demanded. "Where's the capstone?"

"She … bears … the key…," the man whispered, as he fought to stay awake.

"What key?" Greer demanded.

"The Navu …" the man said hoarsely, "ba … la." His eyes closed and his head fell backward.

"She bears the Navubala?" Greer repeated. "What the …" Greer was about to spout a string of profanities but was interrupted.

"Sir!" said one of Greer's men. "Seymour and the girl are getting away." He pointed to a red BMW that was speeding from the parking lot.

"Follow them!" Greer ordered. He ran to a nearby National

Guard jeep, pulled the driver out and got in. His men comman-
deered other vehicles and followed, leaving Faoud Fayed, Hakim,
and the Renegades behind.

Meanwhile, Sarah had been watching the commotion. She
saw Tom and Daria escape in her BMW and a band of soldiers in
red parkas chase after them. She also had seen how Daria had
obtained the capstone from Fayed and how, once the capstone
was out of his hands, Fayed's expression quickly changed. A face
once wrinkled with grief now looked cold and determined.

Fayed saw Sarah, walked up to her, and grabbed her arm.

"You know the roads?" he demanded. He needed someone to
guide him and his men.

"Yes," Sarah replied, freeing her arm and straightening her
posture. She would be a willing accomplice. To protect her
granddaughter, she'd feign alliance with Fayed, and then she'd
find a way to outsmart him.

74.

"Which way?" Tom asked Daria, as they drove away
from the school. Daria led him down the streets of
East Haven toward the Tweed New Haven airport.

"It isn't far," she said. "But we need to hurry. The pilot
doesn't know we're coming."

Daria removed the pouch from her neck and emptied the
pieces of capstone in her lap. She was relieved that all of them
were still there. Then she assembled them without the sphere.
Holding the capstone together with her fingers, she showed it to
Tom.

From the corner of his eye, Tom recognized the capstone's
color.

"Is that electrum?" he asked.

"Yes. I think so."

Then his brain registered its shape. "It's a pyramid."

"A capstone," Daria corrected him.

"Where did you find it?"

"I told you. I found it in Egypt, by accident, in the sand. It's worth an awful lot to an awful lot of people."

"But it's so small."

Daria got out the sphere and moved it near the capstone. The sphere glowed in the same odd way the anomalous sphere had done on the pyramid's viewscreen. Then she reassembled the capstone with the sphere inside. She put it in the palm of Tom's outstretched hand. They both looked at it while Tom glanced back and forth between it and the road. For many long seconds nothing happened.

Then thunder clapped. Its timing was like something from a B movie, and both of them laughed. Then a bolt of lightning hit a nearby tree, splitting it in two. It wasn't funny anymore. Street lights began flickering on and off. Streams of blue electricity danced across the electrical wires. Tom looked at Daria with amazement.

The capstone was getting stronger, Daria realized.

"Convinced?" she asked.

"Take that thing apart," Tom said and sped the car forward. Daria put the sphere and the capstone pieces away.

They drove through the maze of residential streets to the back of the airport. Tom made a right turn into the airport's rear entrance. At the end of the road, a green chain-link fence, strung with barbed wire, separated them from the tarmac. All the gates were locked.

"There's the plane!" Daria said, pointing to an old Egyptair jetliner alone on the runway, revving its engines for departure.

"Hold on," Tom said. He floored the gas pedal and drove the car through the gate, breaking the lock. In the process, the gate came off its hinges and stuck to the car's front end. Tom stopped the car, put it quickly into reverse to dislodge the gate from the hood, and then raced around the fallen gate and onto the tarmac.

By this time, the plane had started down the runway. Tom sped alongside it, testing the Beamer's engine. When he got in front of the plane, he slowed down. The jetliner stopped.

An angry pilot opened the cockpit door. He yelled down at them in a mixture of English and Arabic. Daria leapt out of the car and ran toward him. In Arabic she called up to him, "We're friends of Omar Fayed! From the Shemsu Hor! He said you could help us. It's very urgent!"

The captain looked uncomfortable. Nobody mentioned the name 'Shemsu Hor' aloud. Members had other, secret ways to identify themselves, but she obviously knew Omar. He ordered that the stairs be lowered and waved for Daria and Tom to come aboard.

"Are you the captain?" Daria asked in English, after she and Tom stepped onto the plane.

"I am."

Daria introduced herself. "Omar sent me," she added. "He said you'd take us anywhere. We need to leave *now*." In case it might help to convince him, Daria held up the Key to the Capstone.

The captain's eyes widened, as Daria expected.

"Where is Omar?"

Daria spoke quietly, "He's dead."

The captain looked shocked and pained by the news. He leaned against the cockpit door.

"How?"

"Shot." And then, as if to give some reason for his untimely death—some purpose for the terrible loss—she explained, "He was saving my life."

The captain took a long, deep breath. Then he straightened up. "Omar was dear to me," he said. "I will take you wherever you need to go."

"We need to go south. Just get us as far south as you can."

"And then some," Tom added, realizing the jet could get them only partway to their destination.

"Who is he?"

"A friend," Daria replied. "We must hurry."

"Go sit," the captain said and then spoke in quick Arabic to the other passengers, who were all armed. He explained they were no longer headed for Washington to find the key-bearer, as she had just found them. Also, she needed their help, and they would do whatever they could for her. The passengers clapped for Daria as she entered the cabin and took a window seat. Tom sat beside her.

The plane taxied back to the beginning of the runway, turned, and again revved its engines and began takeoff.

Daria took a deep breath, trying to relax. Then something outside the window caught her eye. A National Guard jeep was speeding alongside them.

"Is that Greer?" Daria asked.

Tom leaned over her and looked out the window. He couldn't help but catch her scent and it distracted him for a moment. "They followed us," he said.

They heard gunfire.

"Why's he shooting the plane?" Daria asked. "Greer needs it as much as we do."

"Maybe he just wants to get on board."

"Damn stupid way to do that," Daria replied. "What does he expect? That these guys will actually slow down?" She unfastened her seatbelt, stepped quickly over Tom, and ran for the cockpit. "Captain!" she yelled. "We can't stop the plane!"

"Sit down!" he yelled back. The engines grew louder and the plane began to move faster.

Despite the gunfire, the captain kept the plane moving. Daria tripped on her way back to her seat and fell to the floor. Tom recognized the wisdom of being on the floor, below the line of shooting bullets, and lay down beside her.

Just then a bullet hit one of the tires and made the plane lurch to the left. It began to skid sideways.

"Stay down!" Tom said and covered Daria's head with his arms.

75.

The Shemsu Hor's jetliner spun out of control for what seemed a long time before it reached the end of the runway. Finally, one wheel got caught in the mud and the plane flipped over. A wing tore off, leaving a gaping tear in the fuselage. Tom and Daria toppled onto the ceiling of the plane, which was now the floor. Everyone else, protected by their seatbelts, quickly righted themselves, grabbed an assortment of weapons, and positioned themselves near the wide-open hull to return the gunfire that was pelting the plane.

Tom had bumped his head hard and struggled against the blackness that threatened unconsciousness. He touched the pain and felt a stream of warm blood. Using his fingers, he applied pressure to his wound.

"Daria," he whispered.

No answer.

"Daria!"

Still no response. Tom looked around for help. The captain and co-pilot stepped over Tom and Daria to join their comrades.

"I will help you once we secure our position," the captain said.

Tom checked Daria's pulse but could not feel it. She was hardly breathing if at all. He had no idea where she was hurt but could find no blood anywhere on her body. Her injuries must be internal.

Why not use the sphere?

Tom removed it from its pouch around Daria's neck and tried putting it in her hand, but she was unable to hold it as he had once done. To Tom's amazement, the sphere seemed to have a mind and power of its own as it began to guide his hand to certain areas of her body. There, it would circle a few times before moving to another area. Tom continued the treatment for several minutes amidst the sound of gunfire. Finally, Daria opened her eyes, gasped for breath, and coughed a few times. She saw immediately what Tom had been doing and sat up. She also saw his hand covered with blood.

"Tom, you're bleeding!" Miraculously, Daria was fully awake.

"It's not bad," he assured her.

"Use the sphere to heal yourself."

"We don't have time," Tom said. "Look!" A fire had started in the back of the plane, and it was spreading.

Daria grabbed the sphere from his hand. As if self-propelled, the sphere guided her hand up Tom's arm to the back of his head. The wound closed, and the bleeding stopped.

That was fast, Daria thought.

"I'm better now," Tom said.

"Good, let's get out of here," Daria said, putting the sphere away.

They reached an emergency exit across from the tear in the fuselage where Omar's friends were defending themselves from Greer's gunfire. A few of the men and women were down, but Daria had no time to help them. Tom lifted the latch, but the door was stuck.

"Let's try another door," he said.

"No," Daria replied. The only other escape route was now engulfed in flames. She took out the sphere and held it against the latch. The sphere pulsed with light and the door tore open as if blown out by dynamite. Daria quickly returned the sphere to its pouch, and she and Tom ran out of the plane, across the lawn at the end of the runway and through a forest of marsh reeds.

From the road in front of the airport, Sarah, Fayed, and the Renegades could see the entire runway. They witnessed the airplane's crash. They saw Greer open fire upon its occupants and spotted Tom and Daria as they escaped.

"Where are they heading?" Fayed asked.

"I know the area," Sarah said. "Let's go!"

76.

Tom and Daria soon reached a chain-link fence that marked the border of airport property. It was too risky to climb over, as they might be seen, but they found an area where the soil had been washed away underneath, giving them enough space to belly crawl through. Afterward they were caked with mud.

They reached a ditch that was half-filled with water and slippery, but they followed it.

"This should lead us to the coast," Daria said.

"And then to Antarctica?" Tom muttered. They were both aware of their ultimate destination, but neither knew how they would get there.

Then things got worse. The closer they got to the coast, the more water filled the ditch until it became a stream and then a river. Tom and Daria clung to reeds on the side of the ditch for as long as possible, but eventually they had to swim. Daria shuddered with cold but was glad the water washed the mud off their clothes.

The river became choppy as it approached the Long Island Sound, and it became nearly impossible to swim. Luckily, Tom and Daria saw a small dock on the right bank. Several small boats tied to it were bouncing dangerously in the waves. They had to approach carefully. They reached the ladder at the end of the dock and climbed out of the water. A sign identified the small nearby building as The Little Red Marina. Tom and Daria decided to take shelter there while they decided what to do next.

They knocked at the door. The marina was empty and locked. Daria held out the sphere to open the door, and they went inside. It was a one-room building with a few curtained windows, a table, benches, lockers, and piles of nets and fisherman's gear.

"Now what?" Daria asked.

"I don't know," Tom replied. "We'll think of something."

Again Daria felt defeated. But how many times had life taken her to a dead end, only to reveal an opportunity where none had appeared to exist? It would take a miracle to get back to Antarctica. They had to be patient, watchful, and aware—then an answer would come. She was sure of it.

Tom and Daria's first priority was to get dry and warm. Scrounging for clothing, Daria used the sphere to open some lockers. At last she found something suitable. The bathroom was too small to change in, so they decided to face away from each other while they got dressed.

"I wish we had figured out how to get back to the pyramid before we used the transport room," Tom said. It was stupid not to plan ahead, he thought. What if they had accidentally beamed off the planet or into some uninhabited jungle? Tom sighed. They were lucky they had gotten this far. For that, he thanked the pyramid.

Suddenly, he got an idea. "Let's put the capstone together," he said, and turned around.

Daria had just finished dressing and was zipping up a jacket.

"It would cause a tidal wave," she half joked.

"No, seriously. What if we held the capstone and imagined ourselves back in the control room?" Tom suggested. "We know the pyramid responds to thought. Thought isn't tied to space, so it shouldn't matter where the thought originates. With the capstone as a power generator, maybe it can amplify our thoughts enough that we can beam ourselves back."

Daria agreed to try his plan.

They stood facing each other. Daria put the capstone together and held it in her palm. Tom's hands supported hers. They closed their eyes and imagined being inside the pyramid's control room.

As soon as Tom put his attention on the control room he felt a renewed connection to the pyramid. He only wished his senses were more acute and refined so he could pick up any instructions the pyramid might give him. He trusted they would come. After all, the pyramid had been communicating with him most of his life. It had given him its coordinates and then taught him how to melt ice to uncover it. He looked forward to what other technology it would share.

After a few minutes of holding the capstone, nothing seemed to happen. No thunder. No electrical problems. All they heard was the beating of the wind and rain against the small building.

"Sense anything?" Tom asked.

"Nothing," Daria said. She had briefly envisioned the control room. Then she focused on loving her heart, feeling gratitude, and listening. Doing this, she knew, would prompt her inner guidance. So far she felt nothing. No nudges or urges, no inspirations or ideas, and no tightness or warnings of impending danger.

"This place doesn't feel right," Tom said. He wondered if the idea was his own. "We're not far from the coast," he added. "I think we should go there."

"There's a lighthouse on the point just west of here," Daria said. "We could try to make contact there."

Tom agreed.

They kept the capstone intact, hoping it would somehow guide them. They agreed to take it apart as soon as it started playing games with the weather or the electrical lines. They hiked up the hill toward the lighthouse, pressing their bodies against the wind. Their clothes were again soaking wet.

While they walked, surges of energy began pulsing through Tom's body. He'd never felt anything like it before. At first, he thought he was only shivering from the chilly dampness. Then he blamed it on his emotions. He tried to ignore them, but they kept growing. Where was his usual calm-and-centered self?

Finally he couldn't contain himself anymore.

"Who was that fellow at the school?" he asked. His voice was shaking.

"A friend," Daria replied. "Omar Fayed."

"A friend?"

Daria looked over at Tom, "You're jealous!"

It looked like Tom was blushing, which made Daria feel endearing toward him. Actually, he was raging with anger.

"Don't worry," she assured him. "He was just a friend."

"*Just* a friend?"

"He saved my life twice. Once in Giza when a gang of hoodlums were after me. And then," she paused, "again today." She grew silent. It was the ultimate gift to give up one's life for another. She felt profoundly grateful. She knew a lot of emotions normally would accompany such an experience. There just wasn't time to feel them right now. Later, she promised herself.

"Did you sleep with him?"

"Tomas Seymour! That's none of your business!"

"I want to know if you slept with him."

Daria stopped walking and looked at Tom. "No, I did not."

Oddly, her answer made him even angrier, as though he didn't believe her.

Never had Daria seen him like this. Then she realized the capstone might be affecting his emotions, even though she was the one holding it. Daria slipped the key into the tiny pyramid and took it apart. She put the sphere and capstone pieces back in their pouches.

Tom swaggered and almost fell. He looked dazed and felt embarrassed. "Did I just say what I thought I did?" he asked, as he regained his footing.

Daria nodded.

"I am so sorry," he said.

"It's okay," Daria said. "The capstone was influencing you. Come on, let's go."

They continued to the top of the hill.

It was windier at the lighthouse, and the rain drops stung

their faces. To the south, the gray waters of the Long Island Sound were covered in whitecaps. Looking west, they barely could see the homes and factories that lined the New Haven harbor. To the north, the peninsula on which the lighthouse was located was forested.

Now what? Daria asked herself. She again recalled Mikta's advice: divide your destiny into steps and achieve them one at a time, using your best guidance in each moment.

Their next step was a big one—to find a way back to Antarctica.

77.

Tom and Daria stood downwind of the lighthouse so that it sheltered them from the brunt of the wind and rain. This put them between the lighthouse and the forest.

"Let's try to reconnect with the pyramid's control room again," Tom suggested.

Daria agreed and put the sphere and the capstone back together. "But if either of us feels anything strange," she said, "we take the capstone apart right away, okay?"

"Okay."

Once again, she and Tom faced each other with Daria holding the capstone in her outstretched palms and Tom's hands beneath hers. They closed their eyes.

What do we do now? Daria asked in her thoughts, directing her question deep inside herself. It was the first formal request of her heart she had made since childhood. Now all she had to do was listen to its reply, right? She wished it would speak in words, simple and direct. But then the mind, whose forte was words, might twist and confuse them, she realized. So she tried to keep her mind quiet as she listened carefully within. Once centered, she would try to think and make decisions from her heart, as Mikta had taught her.

Tom, on the other hand, immediately felt a connection to the pyramid. It was stronger this time. He could almost see the control room in his mind's eye.

What do we do, Oh Pyramid Pharaoh? Tom said with his thoughts. Although Tom couldn't feel it, the pyramid had begun to build a mental connection between itself and him.

Meanwhile, the pyramid was also trying to make a link with Daria, but her attention was on her heart, and beyond the pyramid's reach.

"Can I try holding the capstone?" Tom asked.

Immediately, Daria sensed this wasn't a good idea. After all, it was *her* capstone. Besides, it was her destiny that was intimately tied to it.

"I just want to see if it can help us connect with the pyramid," Tom said. "Since I've been working in the control room, maybe it would be more tuned in to me."

But something about the idea felt wrong. Daria wished she hadn't stopped practicing inner guidance all these years. Then she might have the skills to weed out those parts of the plan that didn't feel right. The part about contacting the pyramid seemed right, because they'd need its help to get back to Antarctica. Maybe it was just the part about giving Tom the capstone. He was an old friend, and now they were partners of sorts. She had to trust him, didn't she? Finally, she convinced herself it wouldn't do any harm to let Tom have the capstone for awhile. She could ask for it back whenever she wanted.

She handed him the capstone.

Now Tom held the apex that had once crowned both the Great Pyramids of Atlantis and of Giza in his outstretched palm. Tom and Daria faced each other; again they closed their eyes. Tom gave his full attention to the control room. Daria focused on her heart. Tom imagined looking at the pyramid's viewscreen and asked how they could return.

Daria felt heat radiating from Tom's body, and she opened her eyes.

"Tomas!" she whispered. Lines of blue energy were zipping up and down Tom's arms, legs, and body. They emanated from the capstone and then returned to it. The blue crackling lines of energy formed a visible aura around him. Something about his face had changed too.

"Can I hold the capstone now?" she asked, trying to control a feeling of dread.

"No," Tom responded quickly. "I need to maintain the link with the pyramid that I have established."

Daria was taken aback by his firmness. This wasn't the quiet, introverted scientist she had known years before. Nor was it the more confident and expressive Tom she had met again at the pyramid, and who had so boldly gunned the BMW through the locked airport gate. Obviously, since Tom had begun holding the capstone, some sort of power was growing in him, and it didn't feel positive.

Daria wished she had thought with her heart and not let him have the capstone, but Tom had seemed so sure of himself. And maybe he was right—they did need to get back to the pyramid to stop the earth changes. On the other hand, didn't the viewscreen show her the pyramid would be free of ice anyway? She couldn't help but suspect that the pyramid would have its way, with or without them.

"Don't be afraid," Tom said. "The earth changes happening now are meant to happen now."

"How do you know this?"

"The pyramid's viewscreen is telling me. Eleven thousand, six hundred years ago, the Atlanteans unleashed negative powers so great that the earth's crust shifted. If this had not occurred, then the Atlantean civilization would have lived out its natural course. Instead, it was drastically cut short. The cycle of its civilization was supposed to end about now. So the earth changes happening now are inevitable. They're going to push Lesser Antarctica into a temperate zone. The ice will melt and, ironically, the capital of Atlantis will again be revealed."

Daria wasn't satisfied with this prediction. After all, she could use the powers of the capstone to stop the geologic shifts and the worldwide catastrophe that would ensue. The problem was how to get back to Antarctica.

"What should we do?" Daria asked aloud, not necessarily to Tom. He answered anyway.

"I'm not sure yet. I keep asking the pyramid for guidance, but I'm not certain what I'm getting."

"You don't ask a pyramid for guidance," Daria scolded him.

"Since when do you know anything about getting guidance?"

"Since when do you need to put something between yourself and your knowing?" Daria replied defiantly. "The only link we need is the one with our heart."

Tom had fallen into the oldest trap in the book: dependence on a false master. Somehow, she had to snap him out of it.

"Your heart isn't going to protect you from this hurricane," Tom pointed out.

Daria was undaunted. "Don't you see? You're asking a pyramid what to do, when you should be looking to a higher source."

"Since when did you become the expert?"

Daria didn't want to argue. The entire time they'd dated, she never discussed her childhood. He never knew her father had ingrained in her the skills of listening.

She remembered how Mikta had spoken calmly when she had been angry. She hoped the same technique would help Tom too. "The capstone is increasing your personal powers," she said, keeping the rhythm of her voice slow and quiet. "Look to your heart for answers. Then give your orders to the pyramid. It's a machine—a tool—nothing more."

"You want to get back to Antarctica, don't you?" Tom said.

That was the goal, wasn't it? It was no coincidence she had found the capstone when she did—and she must have found it for a purpose. Wasn't that purpose to stop the anomalous sphere? To do that, she needed to get back to the pyramid.

But her heart seemed to be saying nothing. It felt calm and peaceful, despite her wracked nerves. Did this mean their plan to return to the pyramid was the right decision? She was beginning to have second thoughts.

Then Tom became sarcastic. "It's your destiny, *Key-bearer*."

Daria was stunned. How did he know that term? She'd never mentioned it before. His aura was becoming so strong it was now palpable.

Identify one step at a time, and take each one using your highest and best guidance, she reminded herself. Keep your heart and your ears open. Choose the best course in each moment.

Then Tom called out. "Daria! Look! A portal is opening."

A portal? Of course! Daria thought. How else could they beam back?

Daria looked in the direction Tom was pointing. Indeed, something odd was happening to the air inside a large rectangular space in front of the lighthouse. Inside the rectangle, the lighthouse wall looked like a water color painting that had gotten wet. The air inside the rectangle was also becoming brighter. Daria was amazed. Maybe she really was going to make it back to Antarctica after all! She would use her capstone to stop the sphere … and then what? Hope to God that Tom wasn't going to become a tyrant like Greer? Daria could already see the glaze of power clouding his eyes.

Suddenly, they were interrupted by a gunshot that hit the lighthouse and sent chips of its white-washed brick flying. Colonel Greer was announcing his return. He had seen Tom and Daria escape from the burning aircraft. When it had finally exploded, Greer employed tracking skills and the jeep's GPS to locate them.

78.

M en in red USAP parkas now surrounded Tom and Daria.
        "Where's the capstone?" Colonel Greer demanded.
        Tom and Daria said nothing, but Tom closed his fingers around the capstone and lowered his arm to appear as though he was standing casually beside Daria.

Greer whispered something to the men. They raised their guns and pointed them at Tom and Daria.

Daria gasped. Could the capstone protect them from bullets?

"I'm going to ask you one more time," Greer snarled. "Where's the capstone?"

Tom and Daria looked at each other. Through their eyes they communicated their mutual intent. They'd rather die than reveal the capstone. They'd dismantle it so that if they were shot, Greer wouldn't know what they were holding.

Daria reached for the key but didn't have enough time to use it.

Greer couldn't handle their silence.

"Last chance," he called out.

He waited only a few seconds, whispered something to his men, and then shouted: "Fire!"

The men lowered their guns and riddled the ground around Tom and Daria with bullets.

Daria screamed and huddled against Tom, who wrapped her in his arms.

The shooting stopped. Greer grabbed Daria's arm, pulling her away from Tom. He pointed his pistol at her head and reached around her throat with his forearm. Daria started to gag, and struggled in vain to free herself from Greer's iron like grip.

"Seymour! Where's the capstone?"

Tom suspected that Greer wouldn't hesitate to kill Daria. After all, Tom was supposedly the pyramid expert. Greer probably assumed Daria had told Tom as much as she knew. So Daria's life was expendable. Tom gave his full attention to the pyramid and its viewscreen, begging for help.

Then a movement behind the lighthouse caught Tom's attention, and he looked up.

Greer looked too. So did his men, but they were helpless. The event of the next moment happened too quickly.

From his hiding place behind the lighthouse, one of the Renegades jumped out and shot Greer in the head. Greer's men scattered into the trees for cover and began trading gunfire with the other Renegades, who wanted revenge for the loss of their comrades' lives in the schoolyard.

Sarah, Fayed, Hakim, and the Renegades had followed Tom and Daria. They'd spotted the soldiers, also in pursuit, and decided to hold back and wait for the right moment to attack. When the soldiers entered the forest, Fayed remained in the car, while Sarah led Hakim and the Renegades to the lighthouse. She wished they'd gotten there sooner—before Daria was traumatized by the man who'd been holding a gun to her head and choking her.

Sarah ran to her granddaughter to comfort her. On her way, a stray bullet pierced Sarah's chest and she doubled over and fell.

"Grandma!" Daria cried. She helped Sarah lie down. Kneeling, Daria pressed her hand against Sarah's bleeding wound.

"Tom!" Daria called out, "I need the sphere."

Hakim appeared at Sarah's side. "Are you okay, Mrs. McHenry?" he asked. He knelt down beside her, across from Daria, and held Sarah's hand.

"You?" Daria exclaimed to Hakim and resisted an urge to run away. She was both afraid of him and dumbfounded that he seemed to care about her grandmother.

"Do you know this man?" Daria asked her grandmother.

Sarah nodded.

Daria looked at Hakim, "You tried to kill me in the school-yard."

"No, Ma'am," Hakim insisted. "I was under orders to shoot at Omar to frighten him. I never aimed at you, Dr. McHenry. And I never meant to kill him. That was an accident."

"Weren't you following me in Giza too?"

"Omar's father told us to keep an eye on Omar. When we saw him talking to you, we wanted to find out who you were. His father would have wanted to know," Hakim said in his defense. "Then you ran away. Only later did we find out that you were the one we were to meet at the airport the following day."

"Then why did so many of you chase me around Giza?"

"There was only the two of us," Hakim replied. "Myself and Alec."

"But there were ..." Daria's voice trailed off. "Are you sure?" she stammered.

"We weren't following you," Hakim said. "We were follow-ing Omar. He was the one trying to catch you. I think some of his men were trying to catch you too."

Daria wondered how could she have so badly mistaken what had happened.

Suddenly Sarah gasped for breath. "Help me," she groaned. Sarah was fighting to stay awake, yet Daria could see the life slowly draining from her face.

In the next instant, Greer's men started shooting in their di-rection. Daria protected Sarah's body with her own. Hakim suc-cessfully diverted their fire by running behind the lighthouse and around the other side.

"Tom!" Daria called, "Grandma's dying. I need the sphere. Now!"

"We can't take apart the capstone now," Tom said. "The portal is almost complete. Look!"

The portal now looked like an arched doorway. A clear vision of the pyramid's control room phased in and out.

"We made the portal once, we can make it again," Daria in-sisted. "Tomas, give me the capstone. I need the sphere."

Tom stared at her. He couldn't move.

Daria turned back to Sarah. She gently laid Sarah's own hand over the bleeding wound.

"Today and forever," she said.

Then she got up, wiped the blood off her hand against her jeans and approached Tom. She looked into his eyes, past the glaze that was hypnotizing him, past his present personality and the imprints of all his lifetimes, and directly into his heart. It would be the only way she could reach him.

"Tom," she said softly. "I love you." It was the first time she'd ever said those words to him. Ever. It also was the first time she realized how true they were. She could feel the love she had for him. It was an ageless love. "And I know you love me," she continued. "You love me. Remember? You love me."

Yes, Tom loved her. From deep inside him the memory of how much he loved her emerged. The memory was strong and capable of piercing the thickest clouds of delusion. He remembered how long he had loved her. He would do anything for her. But giving her the capstone meant they might lose their chance to return to the pyramid. On the other hand, as Daria suggested, they could always reconstruct the portal. His mind's brief objection to Daria's request was overcome instantly when he remembered again how he felt.

He extended his hand, which held the capstone.

"I love you too," he said.

His eyes were clearer now, and once he gave her the capstone the blue lines of energy that had been zipping around his body diminished, though they didn't completely disappear.

Daria quickly took apart the capstone and used the sphere to fix her grandmother's wounds. A minute later, Sarah looked up at Daria and smiled brightly.

"Thank you," Sarah said quietly. "Nothing hurts anymore." She took a deep breath. Then her eyelids grew heavy. "I think I need to sleep," she said peacefully. "Give my love to your Grandpa David." She sighed and added, "Today and forever." Then she closed her eyes for the last time.

"Grandma Sarah!" Daria's eyes filled with tears as she shook her grandmother's shoulders in a vain attempt to revive her. The weight of Daria's grief pressed against her heart and gripped her stomach. She could hardly breathe. "Oh God, not another death," she moaned.

"She's gone, Daria," Tom said. He knelt behind Daria and put his arm around her. "It's her time. Let her go." His words were gentle.

Daria didn't want to stop crying, but the ongoing gunfire in the forest reminded her that right now, once again, she had to stuff her feelings and focus elsewhere.

"Daria, we have work to do," Tom said quietly.

Daria nodded and they stood up. "Let me hold the capstone this time," she asked. "Please?"

This time Tom agreed. The love he had for Daria, which had emerged from deep inside his heart, loosened the pyramid's hold on him. Now he didn't think it mattered who held the capstone.

"Let's focus on the control room," he said.

"Okay."

Daria reassembled the capstone and held it in her outstretched hands.

79.

Tom and Daria closed their eyes. Daria tried to think about the control room, but her attention kept drifting to what would happen next. They would enter the portal and return to the pyramid in Antarctica. She would insert her capstone into the control panel and send a beacon to the anomalous sphere. The beacon would create a magnetic pathway that would retrieve the sphere and the pieces of its pyramidion that lay strewn on the ocean floor. The pyramidion would be reconstructed, magnetically drawn home, and the Great Pyramid of Atlantis would be whole once again. The storms would stop, the ice that surrounded the pyramid would melt, and Daria and Tom would be in control of a powerful pyramid.

Or someone else would be.

On the other hand, if they dismantled the capstone and stayed in Connecticut, the anomalous sphere would soon change the face of the planet. The earth's crust would shift and Lesser Antarctica would enter a temperate climate zone.

In either case, the land surrounding the Atlantean pyramid would become ice free.

Daria thought about all the good she could do with the pyramid's power at her control. She could end war and hunger, and teach everyone about their heart and how to listen to its guidance. With the pyramid's help, she could catapult science, medicine, and technology to new heights. Maybe this was the 'new order of the ages' that Henry Agard Wallace had predicted? Moreover, the pyramid could answer all the questions she'd ever dreamed of asking about ancient Egypt. It could take her anywhere she wanted to go. She could explore every ancient culture and every language and script. Fill in the holes of history, and bring peace to the world.

That was her ultimate destiny. Wasn't it?

Then, within a split second, a memory of one more of her father's stories flashed through her mind. It was the sequel to the one about the Egyptian princess who was in love with the captain of the guard. After her palace was attacked and her captain wounded, the princess had given him the capstone and sphere of the Great Pyramid of Giza to heal his injuries. The princess had run into the night to save herself from being captured, but her efforts were in vain. Although the invading soldiers never knew her true identity, they arrested her and sold her into slavery. Somewhere amidst the pyramids of Giza the chain around her neck that held the Key to the Capstone had broken. The key had fallen into the sand.

Meanwhile, the captain survived and fled to Western Egypt. He organized thousands of war refugees and with their help established a city. It was far enough away that nobody bothered them. Back then, the water table in that area of the desert was higher and the land was fully capable of supporting the population. They eventually constructed a pyramid using the capstone that the princess had left with him. The captain hoped the pyramid would give him the power to locate his beloved princess. Every night he used the capstone's power to call her to come to him, but she never could.

The final phrase of the story stood out in Daria's mind. "She never could ..." Then an inner voice, which seemed to come from deep within her, provided the ending of that sentence: "until centuries later."

Centuries later it was Daria's own father who found the princess's lost key. It was Daria herself who finally answered the captain's call and found his pyramid. She then removed from this pyramid the very same capstone that the princess had taken from the Great Pyramid of Giza during the war.

Had Daria been that princess in a past life? Had she also been Sileen? How many times before had she taken capstones from pyramids? Would returning the capstone to the Atlantean pyramid fulfill an ancient destiny? And then what? Assume the rulership that was originally meant for Sileen? Were these thoughts preposterous? Where did they come from? Daria didn't think she even believed in reincarnation. Yet it all seemed so real.

She was Sileen, and it was her destiny to rule the Atlantean empire. That was where life was leading her. So maybe that was her ultimate destiny.

Daria looked at Tom, and wondered about the parts he might have played in her past. Had he been Captain Rohn or the captain of the guard? If so, it explained why she and Tom had been unable to maintain a relationship in this lifetime, since they'd also been unable to in their past lives together. Once again, the present repeated the past. Daria felt her love growing for Tom and wanted to carve a new path for their relationship too.

Daria's thoughts returned to Sileen and the Egyptian princess. These women were rulers who had the power of intact pyramids at their control. Still, their lives were challenged by forces that seemed as powerfully dark as the pyramid was supposedly powerfully good. In fact, these women had had to remove the capstone to thwart the dark forces. Now Daria was about to replace one. Did a civilization need a pyramid to prosper? A pyramid was supposed to stabilize the earth's energies, to channel excessive buildups of magnetic energy out of the earth's crust. To convert it into a power source to enhance the lives of those who lived nearby.

Yet the Atlantean pyramid also had a power source that could be used in other ways, and power drew evil like trash attracted flies. Prosperity, on the other hand, was a product of virtue, with each individual member of society acting within the highest standard set forth by his or her heart. Virtue didn't require high technology — or pyramids.

In that case, Daria thought, maybe it would be better to stay in Connecticut. But whether she stayed or returned to Antarctica, the viewscreen had shown her that the ice around the pyramid would melt. The earth's ocean levels would inevitably rise and millions would perish.

Daria found herself at the most significant crossroads of her life, perhaps of her many lifetimes. She wondered if, ultimately, her decision would make any difference at all. Both choices had equally unpleasant consequences.

Daria thought of Mikta. If ever she needed his counsel, it was now. He'd warned her about fulfilling old destinies. Didn't he say they kept you trapped in a loop? Time after time, life after life, you would be faced with the same decisions. If you repeated a decision you would once again fulfill your destiny, but you also stayed in the loop.

How did you carve a new path for yourself?

By thinking with your heart.

What was her heart urging her to do? She wasn't sure. Life was setting up all the conditions she needed to repeat the past.

Mikta had warned her about this. "Life," Mikta had said, "would lead you along well-worn pathways. Only your heart can set you free."

And she and her heart were one.

All at once Daria knew what her heart wanted. More than anything she wanted to be free of the strings that tied her to the past. She wanted to enjoy life on her own terms, based on who she was here and now, in this moment, in this lifetime.

She reminded herself that the pyramid and its viewscreen were only machines that responded to the operator's thoughts. As key-bearer and Keeper of the Capstone, Daria was now that operator. To fulfill her heart's plan, she realized she needed her father's help. The viewscreen had always responded to her thoughts by displaying them. She hoped the portal could do more than that—maybe it could manifest them.

Daria recalled her father and how much love they had shared—and, miraculously, still did. She felt waves of gratitude for the good times they'd had together, the things he had taught her, and the legacy of all his wonderful stories.

She directed her thoughts to the viewscreen and imagined her father standing in the portal. Then, just as she suspected would happen, the viewscreen responded. She saw her father inside the portal, an old man, smiling, and waving at her. She hadn't imagined him waving, so she knew the apparition was real.

"Let's do this together," she called out to Tom.

Tom thought he understood. It was time to step through the portal and go back to the pyramid in Antarctica.

With a quick movement, Daria instead closed her fingers around the capstone, drew back her arm, and tossed the capstone into the portal.

"Daria!" Tom screamed with dread.

In the portal, Ian caught the capstone.

"What have you done?" Tom said loudly. "Your dad's dead. The capstone will be lost forever!"

But Daria knew how alive her father really was—only in

another dimension. The capstone wasn't lost, it was simply relocated. Most importantly, she knew in her heart that her father would know what to do with the capstone. It would be safe, and so would be the earth and all its population. The storms would die down, and the Atlantean pyramid would remain buried under nearly a mile of snow.

Ian blew a kiss to his daughter.

"I love you, Dad!" Daria called out, waving her hand to him.

"I love you, too, Honeycakes."

Ian held the capstone in his open palm. Powerful beams of light began to radiate from it in all directions.

In an explosion of light, the portal closed.

The blue streams of energy that had kept Tom hypnotized disappeared without the capstone to replenish them. His anger also faded, but it was replaced with remorse. Tom fell to his knees and held his head in his hands. Along with the capstone, his entire life's work had been tossed into oblivion. He would never again see the Atlantean pyramid or communicate with its viewscreen.

At least he had Daria back.

They heard the sirens of approaching police cars. The few remaining soldiers and Renegades scattered.

Daria knelt down next to Tom and put her arm around him.

Tom looked up, "Daria, are you okay?" he asked.

She smiled, gently grabbed his beard with both hands, and put a kiss on his lips. Her heart had never felt so light before.

"We're free," she said. "We're finally free."

Rays of sunlight began streaming through the clouds and the winds calmed. Weather experts would proclaim it was the effect of a high pressure zone moving rapidly in from the west that abruptly broke apart the hurricane's circular movement and pushed its remains out to sea.

80.

Meanwhile, the Great Pyramid of Atlantis registered the loss of its capstone. So did the pyramid's power center, which was the anomalous sphere hidden beneath the Atlantic Ocean. The sphere would be unable to fulfill its programming to return the earth to its Atlantean geography—at least for now. It immediately canceled all the forces it was using to feed the hurricane, and sent the Atlantean pyramid one last, very strong beam of energy.

The beam shook the pyramid. The walls of the ice shaft collapsed, drawing the ISLAPS, the Jamesway station, the helicopter, all the equipment, and tons of surrounding snow into the hole. A freak storm followed. It dumped more snow on the region than it had seen in decades, and its winds smoothed the snow over the site like a baker frosting a cake.

Days later when the weather cleared, the U.S. Air Force flew a reconnaissance mission over the area. Many countries involved with the Antarctic Treaty had reported suspicious electromagnetic beams being sent there. Among them: England, France, Australia, South Africa, and even the United States. Officials wanted to know who or what might be receiving the strange beams. They gave any possible receivers the code name *snowmen*.

"Woodchuck," the pilot said, addressing his co-pilot, "do you see anything down there?" They were circling the area for the third time.

Co-pilot Captain Charles 'Woodchuck' Hunt responded. "No, Sir. Nothing but snow."

"Are you sure we have the right coordinates?"

Hunt double-checked the map, his global positioning system, and the orders they had received.

"Yes, Sir," he replied. "81°52'05" South; 11°18'10" West. We're where we're supposed to be."

"Roger that," the pilot replied. He then radioed the aircraft carrier they had flown out of, "Motherbird, this is Recon One."

"Recon One, this is Motherbird. Go ahead," came a voice though mild static.

"Roger, Motherbird. Recon One has completed the search of the designated area and reports negative snowmen. Repeat. No snowmen. How copy?"

"Motherbird copies all. Return to roost."

"Recon One copies. We're RTB [returning to base]."

81.

Somewhere in the Sahara Desert, the moment Daria had thrown the capstone into the portal, Mikta stumbled. The boy walking beside him caught the sage's arm.

"Are you okay, Sidi Mikta?" the boy asked. He was about eight years old and was orphaned with Mikta's tribe after his French-Moroccan parents had been killed in a raid.

"I am. Thank you, Zaq," Mikta replied. Then he gazed up into the clear blue sky, as though looking for something.

"What is it?" the boy asked.

"A great change has occurred in the course of the Earth's future," Mikta replied. Apparently, Daria's mission had been successful.

"Is the change good or bad?"

"It will be good, for now," Mikta said. "The people of Earth have been saved from imminent catastrophe." He paused, "but whatever caused the change also created a rift."

"A rift?"

"Yes. Something has torn the fabric between this world and the next." Mikta thought of Daria's capstone. Only something as powerful as the capstone could have caused such a tear. He wondered how it happened. Apparently, Daria made a decision that had not been prophesied by the most gifted of seers. It must have been original and creative. Mikta smiled to himself. Her choice must have originated in her heart.

"What does this mean?" Zaq's question interrupted Mikta's thoughts.

Mikta sobered. "It means great challenges lie ahead."

"What kind of challenges?"

"The rift will strain the laws that keep the physical universe separate from other worlds. Vibrations that do not belong here may now be funneled through the tear. The effects will occur globally as well as in the life of every individual. Extremes will become wider, opposites more pronounced, and cycles more severe. Consequences will come more quickly.

"On one hand, some of the incoming vibrations will be good ones, and will help people find healing and upliftment. However, negative vibrations can also come through. Our planet's natural defenses may weaken. Disease may become more widespread. It will be harder for individuals to find stillness, become centered within themselves, and think with their heart."

"Then we'll have to fix the rift," Zaq announced.

"Indeed."

Zaq looked up at the sky with wide eyes.

Mikta watched as the wheels of the boy's imagination spun with dreams of how he might actually accomplish such a task.

THE END

Gratitude

When the story of *The Capstone Decision* was given to me, I was told it would change my life. I had no idea what it would take to manifest the story, and because it was originally revealed through visionary images, it began as a screenplay. When that format didn't allow me to fully express the conflicts within Daria's heart, I realized I'd be writing a novel. Little did I know the research required and the number of rewrites in store. I'd written non-fiction before, but novel writing is an art of itself.

I am deeply grateful to Bob Silverstein who told me my original character portrayals needed help (to say it mildly). He then suffered through two more rewrites, each time giving me essential advice that helped me take the writing to higher levels. Thank you, Susan Hanniford Crowley, Linnie York, and Mindy Canter, who each edited and critiqued the book and gave me ideas for leading it through more metamorphoses.

Thank you Rand Flem-Ath, co-author of *When the Sky Fell* and *The Atlantis Blueprint*. Your research on Atlantis in Antarctica has been tremendously inspiring and is echoed in this book. Thank you, Terry Cermola, for exploring the greater Yale-New Haven area with me while scouting for scene locations. Thank you to all the wonderful people I met on a research expedition to Tenerife, Morocco, and Egypt in 1995. You were generous in so many ways. Thank you, Lt. Col. Paul Bedesem USAF, for answering so many questions; and Maj. M. Brian Bedesem USAF, for additional input and for routinely asking me when the book would be done, which helped to keep my enthusiasm alive.

I am very grateful for the help with technical details that I received from: John Miller LTJG USNR Ret., M. Steven Williams, Dennis O'Brien, Kitty Ansaldi APRN, Dan Smiley MD, Martial Arts Grand Master Frank Corbo, Aaron Katz, Glenn Andrew, Pat Hopkins, and Sameh for help with the Arabic. Thank you my dear friends, Blanche and Everard Hughes, for reading the story and encouraging me to continue working on it.

And thank you to my husband, Bob, for your love, patience, and support even as I worked on this book into the wee hours of the night.

What Does the Key to the Capstone Look Like?

I began writing *The Capstone Decision* in 1995, and by 2004 I had a good idea what the key to the capstone looked like. Also about that time, I felt it prudent to start sketching ideas for the sequel to make sure *The Capstone Decision's* plot was headed in the right direction. One of the alternative/new science topics I wanted to include in the sequel was crop circles.

In June of 2004, on a trip to Maine, I began collecting books on the topic. Sometime in July, I began researching crop circles on the Internet. To my absolute surprise, a circle had appeared in England the night of June 19-20th, 2004, that looked more like the key than the image I had envisioned!

Clearly it was Daria's key, manifested in whatever mystical way crop circles appear.

Visit
www.isabellemorton.com
to view an aerial photograph
of the crop circle that illustrates
the Key to the Capstone.

P.S. I'd be happy to speak to your book club. Please contact me at isa@isabellemorton.com to schedule an appointment.